MEET THE PASSIONATE MEN AND WOMEN IN THIS EXTRAORDINARY NOVEL OF INTRICATE HUMAN DRAMA AND SEARING MEDICAL SUSPENSE!

Myrl Caton—A dead man worth a fortune in insurance money if he was murdered—and not a cent if he committed suicide. **Pat Caton**—She was eager to inherit his business, his money—and his partner. **Kirby Moody**—He liked his women easy, and his money easy—and Pat was both. **Angela Gaito**—She couldn't say no to Myrl Caton—until that last night. **Vincent Irafino**—Trigger-happy and temperamental, he may have been the last man to see Myrl alive—and the first to see him dead. **Jerry Leatherman**—A crack medical pathologist assigned to determine the cause of Myrl's death. As this cool, quiet professional readies his scalpel for the first deft cuts into the heart of a mystery, human emotions blaze out of control!

As real as the glint of a cold steel scalpel, as powerful as the passions it contains, **AUTOPSY** is a gripping picture of a medical sleuth at work in a jungle of twisted hopes and destinies . . . *AN ELECTRIFYING SAGA OF OUR TIME!*

AUTOPSY

JOHN R. FEEGEL

AVON
PUBLISHERS OF BARD, CAMELOT, DISCUS, EQUINOX AND FLARE BOOKS

AUTOPSY is an original publication of Avon Books. This work
has never before appeared in any form.

AVON BOOKS
A Division of
The Hearst Corporation
959 Eighth Avenue
New York, New York 10019

Copyright © 1975 by John R. Feegel.
Published by arrangement with the author.
Library of Congress Catalog Card Number: 75-772.

ISBN: 0-380-00269-8

First Avon Printing, March, 1975.

AVON TRADEMARK REG. U.S. PAT. OFF. AND
FOREIGN COUNTRIES, REGISTERED TRADEMARK—
MARCA REGISTRADA, HECHO EN CHICAGO, U.S.A.

Printed in the U.S.A.

For my mother and father

1

Myrl Caton eased his white Cadillac into the angled parking space in front of the office of the Brownstone Motel. The sign claimed that it was one of Connecticut's finest. He had made the lonely trip from Ruskin, Florida, in nine days, calling on his contracted tomato wholesalers in as many states. Not that it had been all business. He had found time in Atlanta to see Lillie and the two-year-old boy she claimed was his. Kid or not, she made a night in Atlanta worth the extra three hundred miles off his route.

He felt under the seat for his .45 automatic to reassure himself that he hadn't left it in Newark the night before. Caton never carried the gun with him when he checked into a motel, but went out to get it after dark. Once, in North Carolina, when he got drunk with a jewelry salesman from Washington, he let go several shots into the motel-room wall, just for the hell of it. The jewelry salesman jumped right through the window screen to get out of the room. The motel manager had made a hell of a fuss about the shooting, but forgot the whole thing when

Caton gave him a hundred dollars to patch up the holes in the wall.

Caton grabbed his suitcase and an armload of clothes from the back seat—he wasn't much for packing between motels—and entered the motel office through a swinging glass door that emitted a gasp of air when it closed itself. The air-conditioned office felt cold after the July heat of the Connecticut Valley.

The man behind the desk smiled at Caton.

"Hot," Clyde Peabody announced in a crisp New England twang.

"Bet your ass it is," Caton drawled as he put his suitcase and clothes in a pile in front of the desk.

"Planning to spend the night?" the motel manager asked cheerfully.

Caton stared at him with practiced impatience, then picked up the desk pen and shook it toward the rug as if to remove a clogging drop of ink.

Peabody's smile froze. "Ballpoint," he offered softly.

Caton was busy writing M-Y-R-L C-A-T-O-N in a large, childlike scrawl, his tongue protruding from the corner of his mouth.

Clyde Peabody rotated the office blotter and inspected the name.

"Yessir, Mr. Caton—we're happy to have you at the Brownstone. All the way from Florida!"

"I want a big bucket of ice and six Cokes right away," Caton ordered.

"Yessir," Peabody said. "I'll check you into number 15. It's quiet over there."

"I don't care if it's noisy or quiet. All I need is a room and a hot bath."

Peabody scurried around the room, completing the checking-in chores.

"Here's your key and the bucket for your ice. You'll find the machine in the utility room at the end of your wing."

Caton flipped the key into the paper ice bucket and returned to his car. Number 15 was the next-to-the-last room in the row across from the motel office, its door partly obscured by a medium-sized maple that stood in the gravel driveway.

Caton parked the Cadillac in front of his door. Inside, he saw that the room was nothing more than standard— no luxury here. It had a few special features. The plaster around the top of the tub leaked sand into the shower, giving the user an odd sensation of being at the beach; the ceiling over the bed was cracked and seemed about to drop on Caton, who had dumped his armload of crumpled clothes on an overstuffed chair near the window and flopped on the bed with a sigh. He pried off one shoe with his other foot and let it drop to the floor with a thump. The second shoe resisted a similar removal, and he sat up to pick at the knotted shoelace. His intensive effort, punctuated by selected profanity, was interrupted by a knock at the door.

"Who is it?"

"I brought your Cokes," Peabody called. He held three Cokes on a small tray when Caton opened the door. "That's all there were cold," Peabody added as he marched into the room and placed the bottles on the dresser.

When Peabody left, Caton brought out a bottle of bourbon from his suitcase and poured a drink. He added half a Coke and tried to enjoy the drink without ice. Then he put the ice bucket under his arm, unlocked the door, and clumped down the walkway toward the utility room wearing his one shoe.

His ice bucket filled, Caton returned, repaired his drink, and took a long pull. The drink gave him increased strength and the stubborn shoe came off easily, knots and all. He flopped on the bed again and began to thumb through the yellow pages. He found the name of Vincent Irafino under "Wholesale vegetables." He dialed the number and Peabody interrupted on the line.

"Give me the number, Mr. Caton, and I'll be happy to connect you."

Caton carefully recited the number and listened as the phone went through a series of clicks.

"Connecticut Valley Produce," a gruff voice said.

"Get me Vincent," Caton said in an equally unpleasant tone. "Tell him Myrl Caton from Florida."

"Hold the line." In the receiver, Caton could hear the sounds of a vegetable-wholesale business. The shouts, the banging of crates, and the rumble of forklift trucks were the same in every state.

A sudden and impatient voice spoke into the phone. "Irafino," the voice said.

"Vincent," Caton said in a relatively friendly tone, "this is Myrl Caton."

"The tomato queen," Irafino said with a chuckle.

"Best god-damned winter tomatoes in the country, you wop bastard."

"When did you get into town?" Irafino asked in a fading Italian accent. In Irafino's group, real business was argued in Italian before being legally contracted in typed English.

"Just now," Caton said. "I'm at the Brownstone."

"Hey—I suppose you want to talk to Angela," Irafino asked.

"Is she still working there?" Caton joked. He pictured the dark-haired secretary who had said goodbye to him on a foggy New England morning.

"Sure, Myrl," Irafino assured him. "You know how good she is."

"At what?" Caton quipped. "I'll give her a call later. I got to get a little sleep. You know, long trip and that kind of crap. But right now, I need to get an idea about your order for the winter."

"All you think of is them rotten tomatoes," Irafino chided. "Let's go somewheres for a drink."

"Come on over to this firetrap and I'll pour you some homegrown bourbon. It's a damn sight better than that Dago red you got in your office."

Vincent thought quickly and then accepted. "I'll be there in twenty or thirty minutes. What room?"

"Number 15." Caton squinted at the key to make sure.

Caton hung up the phone and pushed the pile of wrinkled clothes from the chair to the floor. He sat heavily in the chair and put his feet on the bedside table. He made another bourbon and Coke, but dozed off before he could finish it.

2

The sixteenth floor of The Bank of Tampa occupied by Chatam, Kellogg, Hurst, Mitchell and Rodriguez, Attorneys, had been decorated by one of the better self-appointed guardians of tasteful decor. His finished product was an acceptable turn-of-the-century motif with heavy, gilded frames, oil lamps, and red velvet walls. The law firm, a stately fixture in the local Bar Association, had existed long enough that most of the downtown attorneys had, early in their careers, been junior members of the firm. The original partners still surviving had achieved the seniority required to forget the days when they arranged tax settlements for Ybor City whorehouses and defended bootleggers against the charge of bribing a policeman. In those days, the firm occupied a ground-floor storefront room near City Hall and its members could often be seen smoking hand-rolled cigars on East Broadway near the Spanish Labor Clubs. Now the prestigious corporate, tax, and probate firm listed Ruscaton Tomato Growers, Inc., among its clients.

The managing partner of Ruscaton, Kirby Morris, Jr., and the wife of his hustling partner, Pat Caton, were in the law firm's office. Morris's grandfather had begun the family agriculture venture with summer squash and oranges in Plant City. Kirby Sr. followed with a few thousand acres of cooperative strawberry farmers who somehow, one by one, saw the advantages of selling out their individual holdings. Kirby Jr. was away at Florida State when Continental Cyanamid decided that the phosphates under the ground were worth far more than the dirt on top could yield in strawberries or oranges. With the proceeds of this sudden sale, young Kirby dropped out of college and plunged into the truck-farming business in Ruskin. After a few years of speculation, Kirby Jr. found that a smaller but steadier profit could be made year after year in tomatoes. In Ruskin, tomato know-how meant Myrl Caton. With Caton's knowledge and Morris's new-found capital, a partnership was born. Some said that from that day forward, Kirby never left the front office except to go to the golf course. And it was fairly common knowledge among the members at the Palma Ceia Golf and Country Club that Kirby was willing to help only in the cultivation and management of Caton's wife, Pat. The theory under which this unveiled affair flourished was that if Myrl was kept busy enough with the business, he would not miss this one particular tomato who had caught his eye when he was twenty-three and poor.

Pat Caton, looking slimmer and younger than her thirty-seven years, sat in a leather chair in front of the massive mahogany desk of G. Markham Hurst. She was dressed for the June weather in a well-tailored light blue suit which quietly advertised itself as expensive.

"Mr. Morris," Hurst said with a measured patience, "This policy and its terms amount to well over half a million dollars. I'd hoped that you would give me a little more of your attention so that I can feel assured that both you and Mrs. Caton understand fully."

Kirby looked up at G. Markham Hurst with a slightly sheepish expression. He had merely scanned the confusing legal terms in which G. Markham Hurst and/or associates had drawn the insurance contracts for Ruscaton Tomatoes and its executive employees.

"I'm sure that your firm has seen to every last detail," said Kirby apologetically.

"We hope we have," said Hurst, folding his hands across the slim folder of typed and printed papers. He carefully adjusted the blue-and-silver cuff link in his left sleeve. After undergraduate school at Emory, Hurst had been sent to Duke University for law, following in the family tradition. In later years, the local law firms had preferred to hire young graduates from the University of Florida or Stetson on the rationale that they needed sharp Florida lawyers in the office rather than old family contacts.

"The way I understand it, Mr. Hurst, if either Myrl or I dies, the business will get $100,000 to help us recuperate from the loss," said Kirby.

"Yes, and if one of you is killed in an accident, there are additional benefits up to $500,000 to be divided between Mrs. Caton and the corporation in the event of Mr. Caton's death, or between your estate and the corporation in the event of your sudden passing," Hurst intoned impassively.

"OK, then I think we understand the policy more or less," said Kirby impatiently. He reached into his inside jacket pocket for a pen and uncapped it.

"As you both know," said Mr. Hurst, "Mr. Caton insisted on signing this contract in blank and refused to read any of its contents."

"Myrl leaves that type of problem to me," said Morris. "If his wife and his partner can't look out after his interests, who will?"

Pat Caton moved restlessly in her chair.

"I'd prefer," she said in a soft Southern accent, "to go somewhere for a tall cool drink than sit around here and listen to you two fuss with all of this insurance nonsense." She turned to face Kirby Morris intently and then smiled broadly at the unabashed G. Markham Hurst.

"Don't look at me," Hurst said chuckling. "The medical crowd over at One Davis Boulevard won't let me have anything stronger than instant breakfast." The medical crowd at the once prestigious One Davis was composed of some of Tampa's best internists and cardiologists. Their practice came mainly from the downtown law firms and old-time offices which were equally entrenched in the traditional financial sections of the city. To run across town to the new medical school would have meant another competitive world of young doctors.

"I think I can oblige you, Pat," Kirby said solicitously. He put his hand on her shoulder and squeezed her firmly enough to be understood, but delicately enough to avoid the undue attention of G. Markham.

"Can't we finish up this stuff real soon, Mr. Hurst?" Pat asked in her sweet-child tone.

Hurst slowly closed the manila file and made a brief note on the front.

"The details are all quite in order, and I'll be in touch with the company today," Hurst said. He turned to Kirby and admonished, with mock seriousness, "Stay alive until they accept this contract officially, or someone will have a hell of a legal battle on his hands."

"What time am I insured?"

"About three o'clock, I would imagine." All that remained to be done was to take the signed policies down several floors to the regional offices of the insurance group.

"I will personally guide your every step to the bar at the Palma Ceia," said Pat as she took Kirby's arm and led him toward the door.

"The steps you should worry about are Myrl's," G. Markham said ponderously.

Pat turned and smiled at the old lawyer. "Mr. Hurst, I stopped being concerned about Myrl's steps years ago," she said. "When he's ready, he's going to go, but until he is, he'll be out hustling tomatoes."

Kirby pushed Pat playfully through the open door.

Pat Caton's blue Cadillac convertible sniffed the downtown air with disdain, and headed instinctively toward the country-club parking lot.

17

3

Caton woke to the sound of giggling outside his motel door and recognized that he had been asleep in the chair.

"Myrl, you're a no-good son of a bitch," Irafino shouted as he threw his arms happily around the Ruskin tomato king. Caton looked at Angela Gaito standing in the doorway. The sun behind her gave her hair a Hollywood-like radiance that made her suddenly as young as Caton's memories of her.

"Angela," he said softly, oblivious to the arm-waving Irafino.

Angela moved silently into the room and put her arms carefully around Caton's neck. She looked briefly into his eyes and then kissed him on the mouth.

Irafino went to the dresser to make himself a drink.

"No ice, for Christ's sake," Irafino said as he fumbled in the ice bucket. He picked up the ice bucket and walked quickly out the door toward the utility room.

Angela broke from the kiss and moved quickly toward the dresser and began to fuss with her hair. Caton moved behind her and looked at the two of them in the mirror.

"It's not going to be that way this time, Myrl," she warned.

"Angela, you look good enough to bite," Caton said. She turned to face him and dabbed a Kleenex at the bright red lipstick smeared on his mouth. He put his arms around her waist and planted a big hand on each buttock. He drew her closer so that they were in hard contact from the belly to the knees. Angela felt his growing passion and attempted to push away.

"Please don't, Myrl," she said struggling. "Vincent will be back any minute."

"How 'bout later at your place?"

"I'll call you," she said, freeing herself again. Caton moved to the dresser and poured bourbon in two glasses.

"You sure make a mess," she commented, looking around the room.

"Hell, I ain't even been here yet," said Caton. "Give me a week and it'll look like a real shithouse."

"You staying a week?" Angela asked.

"Unless you make it more interesting," he said with a leer.

"I told you, it won't be that way this time, Myrl," she said firmly.

"Got someone else?" Caton asked.

Angela looked at her hands folded in her lap.

"Who is it?" asked Caton with more insistence. "Vincent?"

As if announced, Irafino entered the room and put the ice bucket on the dresser. He scooped a handful of the tiny ice squares into each drink and grinned broadly at Caton.

"That the same Cadillac you had last year?" he asked. He moved to the doorway and looked out at the car as he sipped his drink.

"Same wreck," said Caton.

"I hope you left that damn gun in Florida," said Vincent.

"Rather go out without my jockstrap," said Caton.

"Shit, last year he almost got us arrested for shooting

19

up a bunch of cantaloupes on the loading dock," Irafino reminded Angela.

"And you couldn't hit your own ass with that .45," said Caton.

"It sounded like a war or something," said Angela. "I thought the Mafia was shooting up the market." She laughed and bounced from the bed to put her hand in the bend of Caton's arm.

Irafino suddenly pushed open the door with his foot and scrambled to the car. He opened the driver's door and reached quickly under the seat. The sunlight glinted off the shiny blue of the pistol in his hand. He waved it playfully in the general direction of the room.

"That son of a bitch is loaded," warned Caton without flinching. Angela ducked behind the door and giggled into her drink.

"So am I," Irafino said. He pulled the trigger, and the automatic emitted a roar that sounded like midsummer thunder in Tampa. A bullet hit the steps in front of Myrl Caton and tore out a large fragment of wood and cement. Irafino looked astonished and handed the pistol to Caton.

Back in more sober hands, the pistol looked less menacing. Caton released the hammer and slid the safety into place. He released the clip and inspected the six shots which remained. The clip snapped into place with an authoritative click and Caton put the gun back in the car without speaking.

"You could have killed us both," Angela shouted from behind the door.

"He wouldn't shoot you, Angela," Caton reassured her as he closed the car door. "He'd sure 'nuff have to find himself another broad and he's too lazy to sort out half a town of big-assed Dagos."

"Caton," Irafino growled, "You're a redneck with a big mouth. Somebody needs to close it for you."

"It won't be any cheap wop from Connecticut," Caton said. "It'll take a man."

"Dirt-farming rebel bastard."

"Look, Irafino, I am sick of you and your piss-ant orders for my tomatoes," Caton said through his teeth. "And I am sure 'nuff sick to death of your Eye-talian stink, too."

Vincent Irafino's hand was brought quickly around by an arm toughened by throwing cases of vegetables. It crunched against Myrl Caton's puffy cheek, and the Ruskin tomato king crashed across the hood of his car. Irafino leaped on the slightly stunned Caton and rammed a knee into Angela Gaito's fond memories.

The sharp internal pain doubled Caton onto the gravel of the driveway. Instinctively, he butted his head into Irafino's soft belly, and heard him emit a loud groan as he was driven backward, stumbling and falling across the driveway into a canvas folding chair on the lawn. Caton ran after him in a crouch still dictated by the pain in his own groin. He crashed heavily on Irafino and rammed the base of his hand in a sudden, vicious thrust against the Italian's nose and upper lip.

Angela came from the motel room screaming for them to stop. She jumped onto Caton's back and bit him on his right ear. Caton threw her off with a massive movement of his right arm, but the same action allowed Irafino to roll away and run toward his car. Irafino spit blood into his hand and looked at it with rising panic.

"You can stick your tomatoes up your ass, Caton," he shouted as he fumbled for his handkerchief. "From now on, I'm buying from Texas."

Caton sat alone on the lawn and grinned at the scene around him. Irafino was sputtering a bloody mess on his own car door and Angela hid behind the white Cadillac. Caton's laughter began as a deep chuckle and then could be heard all over the motel. As Irafino and Angela drove off, throwing gravel around the driveway, Caton reentered room 15 and shut the door. He looked at his cheek in the bathroom mirror and ran a searching tongue around his mouth. There were no new spaces.

The phone rang. Caton held the receiver in one hand as he pressed a cold wet washcloth to his bruised cheek.

"What's going on down there?" asked an obviously annoyed Clyde Peabody.

"Nothing," drawled Caton. "Just some crazy Eye-talians bent on smashing up the area, but they've gone." Caton reached across the dresser and took a long pull on his bourbon.

"I don't abide shooting in this motel," Peabody proclaimed.

"There won't be any more shooting," Caton promised. "Those bastards won't be back, and they took the gun."

"I'd hate to have to call the police," the clerk warned.

"I'll bet you would," Caton chuckled. "Give me a long distance call and I promise you there will be no more noise from over here. Get me Tampa. Area code 813, 685-8511. I'll talk to anyone who answers."

"Tampa, Florida?" the motel manager asked with his Connecticut Valley twang.

"Yeah. Yeah," Caton said impatiently.

"I've never been south of New Haven, myself," Peabody said apologetically.

The phone rang in Ruskin, and Caton automatically counted the number of times it rang again before it was answered.

"Ruscaton," a female voice said with a rural Southern accent.

"Who the hell is this?" Caton barked.

"This is Mary Nell," the tiny voice explained.

"This is Myrl Caton. Get me Morris."

"I'm sorry, Mr. Morris is out," the tiny voice trembled.

"Out? Out where?" thundered Caton.

"Him and your wife—I mean Mrs. Caton—just left for the country club, they said. Almost everybody's gone now, 'cept me, and I'm fixing to."

"You tell them I called and that I said they can park their asses at the club all year for all I care." Caton paused and took another deliberate pull on the bourbon bottle. "And Mary Nell . . ."

"Yes, sir?"

"Tell them I'm having a ball in Middlebrook, Connecticut. Tell them I'm up to my ass in dancing girls and they're sending in pink champagne every hour by a topless waitress who wants to chase me around the bed just for fun. You got that?"

"I think so, sir," said the tiny voice.

"And you tell Morris that for all I care, he can take that Pat and stuff her full of fine Ruskin vine-ripened tomatoes and stick her out front like a neon sign." He slammed the phone onto its cradle so hard that it gave a little ring as if to register official disapproval. Caton crashed his big frame onto the bed.

He knew he had lost another order and had wasted the trip.

"Miserable bastards, all of 'em," he said quietly as he rolled over to face the wall.

4

It was mid-afternoon when Ruby Green's patience ran out. When Caton had not answered her knock, she had left his room until last. But now her day was ending and she was not about to go home leaving a room undone.

She had been at the Brownstone Motel for as long as there had been one. The things she had found left in motel rooms, the messes she was expected to clean up, would comprise an endless foreign film. Fetuses in toilets, contraceptives distended by slowly dripping faucets, bloody beds, slashed sheets, graffiti in feces, shower stalls filled with vomit and beer cans, had all become common enough that she had stopped reporting such findings to the management or mentioning them at home to her own family. Her family, previously rapt with fascination, now yawned and turned their attentions to the TV.

She would tolerate a "do not disturb" sign on a door all day if the car in front had the stigmata of a recent wedding on its sides. But when the register showed only one man booked into room 15, Ruby's tolerance ran thin by noon.

She knocked loudly on the still-closed door. She waited

in the afternoon sun and listened for a response. None came.

"Mr. Caton?" she called several times. She had looked up the name to assure herself that he was alone.

Ruby moved her mobile cleaning cart to one side, crossed the driveway, and entered the motel office. "Mr. Peabody," she began, "there don't seem to be nobody in number 15 and I'm going to use my passkey to change the linen."

Clyde Peabody continued to sort the papers on his desk. He did not look up as he commented dryly, "The man's got his right to be left alone."

The comment did not satisfy the compulsive Ruby Green. She did not recognize any man's rights to unclean sheets. "What about soap and toilet paper?" she inquired professionally. "What if he's sick in there and just wishin' that someone would come and find him?" Ruby stood in front of her employer's desk, hands on her bulky hips, eyes bulging out of her sweating black face.

"He's not sick, Ruby, because he would have called me on the phone and asked for help."

"You mean if he could," she persisted.

Clyde Peabody prided himself on being slow to act, tenacious in his conclusions, and indifferent to those situations which provoked others to near-panic. He had tried to turn Ruby several times before. But like a charging elephant, her course once set was immutable. It was easier to give in to her and get it over with. He plugged a cord into a switchboard hole marked 15 and flipped a switch. "I'll ring his phone and offer him a clean towel."

The telephone in Caton's room rang several times. "Maybe he's in the bathroom," offered Peabody.

"He ain't," said Ruby. "I just came out of 16 and I listened through the inside door. There wasn't no noise in 15." She pouted her lips and frowned impatiently.

"All right, Ruby, I'll go with you and we'll look. But if Mr. Caton doesn't want clean sheets, you are going to stay out. Understand?"

Ruby nodded and followed Peabody out of the office

and across the courtyard to 15. Caton's car was still parked in front of the motel door. Peabody knocked politely and waited quietly. Ruby brought her mobile cleaning cart into range so that she would be ready to pounce on the bathroom if allowed in. The polite knock was followed by equally unsuccessful but insistent thumps. These were followed by uncharacteristic smashes and one series of doorknob rattles.

"I'll use the passkey," Ruby offered eagerly. She unlocked the door and opened it against the night chain.

"Mr. Caton," Peabody called through the few inches which the chain allowed the door to open. He called twice more but no response greeted him. Peabody put his thin face to the opening and looked in. The room was darkened by drapes drawn across the only window. It had a musty stale-air odor. The bed could be partly seen from the door, and on it lay Myrl Caton, fully dressed.

"I can see him," Peabody said. "He's on the bed and he's got his clothes on."

"Is he breathing?"

"Can't say," said Peabody. "I can only see his right foot and his arm. His arm is hanging down from the bed. Oh my God!" he exclaimed.

"What do you see?" said Ruby, eagerly pushing up to the door and attempting to look through the narrow space.

"There's blood on the carpet and there's a gun on the floor."

"I knew it was trouble," moaned Ruby, "just knew it was trouble."

"Go back and call the police. I'm going to push the chain off and get in there."

"You better wait for the police," Ruby advised, but Peabody was already exerting force against the chain to test it.

"He might need help," said Peabody.

Ruby shook her head knowingly. "The only help he's going to need is an undertaker," she said. "I'll go get the police." She trotted toward the motel office with her bulk bouncing under her dress.

Peabody put his shoulder against the door and gave a sudden push that pulled the chain mount from the wall. He stumbled two steps into the room and stared at Myrl Caton.

"Sweet Mother of God," he said. Myrl Caton's body was sprawled across the bed. He was on his back and his eyes stared blindly at the ceiling. His mouth was partly opened and his shirt was bloody in front. The right arm hung limply from the bed and the other was almost behind the left ear. There was blood across the bed and on the floor beneath the right hand. About two and a half feet from the bed, a .45 Colt automatic lay, its muzzle still pointing towards the lifeless Caton. Peabody stepped carefully to the edge of the bed and felt for a pulse in the dangling right wrist. The hand was cold and Peabody pulled away in revulsion. He walked quickly from the room and closed the door. He held the two fingers that had touched the dead body in front of him. Peabody walked quickly to the motel office and immediately washed his hands.

"Did you get them?" he asked Ruby. She was still on the telephone and nodded affirmatively.

"That's right, the Brownstone," she said on the phone. Peabody quickly took the receiver from his chief maid.

"This is Clyde Peabody. There's a man that's been shot here at the motel." He paused. "Yes, dead." He listened briefly to further instructions from the police and nodded as he did. Without further comment, he put the phone on its cradle and advised Ruby not to touch anything or to return to the motel room until the police arrived. Ruby assured him that she wanted nothing whatever to do with the room or the body.

In about ten minutes, two police cars turned into the driveway and parked in front of the motel office. The nasal crackling of the police radio filled the air in the courtyard.

"Units ten and eighteen at signal seven, Brownstone

Motel," the driver of the second police car said into his microphone. He waited for the reply which came almost immediately: "Roger, eighteen. Stand by for Lt. Casper."

"Ten-four," the officer said in a monotone and hung the microphone on its hook. His wide leather gun belt crackled as he got out of the car, clipboard in hand.

Clyde Peabody came out of the motel with a somewhat inappropriate calmness and walked over to the nearest police car. A blue Ford without police insignia squealed into the motel driveway and stopped in front of him. The back door opened and a red-faced, middle-aged man in a wrinkled brown suit climbed out. He turned to the motel manager.

"Lt. Casper," he announced, thrusting his big hand forward for Peabody to shake. Peabody pumped the hand firmly and slowly as he studied the face of the police lieutenant.

"We met once before, Lieutenant. At the appreciation luncheon for Chief Fowler when he retired last year."

The lieutenant looked at Peabody with a small squint as if to see him more precisely. "Yeah, I remember," he said automatically. If he didn't actually remember Peabody, he certainly knew the manager by reputation and through his official knowledge of the motel. The police department was well informed about the clientele of the Brownstone.

"You had a little trouble?" Casper inquired as he mopped his brow with a wrinkled ball of a handkerchief.

"Lieutenant, I've got a dead man in room 15," said Peabody carefully.

"Shot?"

"Guess so. There's a gun on the floor and blood all over."

"Which one's 15?" Casper looked up and down the row of motel rooms next to the office.

"It's across the court," said Peabody, pointing toward the room behind the maple tree. Casper started in the direction of the room with the two patrolmen, his driver and Peabody in pursuit. Ruby chose to stay in the motel office.

Casper stopped to look first at the window and the ledge beneath it. "Window's OK," he said to one of the uniformed officers, who dutifully made a note on his clipboard. Peabody opened the motel door with his passkey and Casper grabbed him by the elbow. "You opened this door before, so that much is OK, but after we go in, I don't want you to touch nothing."

Peabody nodded in agreement and stood back to let Lt. Casper enter. The lieutenant glanced at the body and then looked carefully at the door casing.

"Who busted the chain slot off the wall?" he asked.

"I did when I saw the body through the crack," Peabody said.

"You touch anything else?"

"Just his hand to see if he was alive."

"How long ago was this?" asked the lieutenant, looking at his watch.

"About ten minutes ago, I guess," said Peabody.

Casper went carefully to the bedside and felt for a pulse. In the center of the bloody shirt there was a ragged round hole about the size of Casper's fingertips. Casper poked at the wound and then lifted the shirt to inspect the chest. The hairy chest was bloody and there was another round hole in the skin over the heart.

"Tell 'em to get the photographer and the coroner over here," Casper barked to one of the officers. Casper looked quickly at the pile of dirty laundry next to the chair and the empty bourbon bottle on the bedside table. "Who was this bird?" he asked Peabody.

"Name's Myrl Caton—from Ruskin, Florida," said Peabody in a matter-of-fact tone.

"Better notify his family," said Casper.

"He gave a Florida number when he checked in."

"Probably a phony name and number," Casper said cynically.

"Don't think so," said Peabody. "This guy didn't strike me as being a phony registrant."

Casper moved slowly around the room looking into wastebaskets and behind furniture. "Anything been taken out of this room since you found the body?" he asked.

"Everything was just as you see it," Peabody said.

Casper nodded slowly and ushered Peabody out of the room. They stood on the narrow sidewalk outside the room, and Casper lit a cigarette. "Soon as the doc gets here and makes him officially dead, I think we can get rid of the body for you," he said.

"I'd appreciate that, Lieutenant," Peabody said. "This kind of thing doesn't help the motel business."

"When did you see this guy Caton last, Mr. Peabody?" Casper asked.

"Well," said Peabody slowly and deliberately, "when I checked him in. Then I handled some calls for him. He called someone in Florida, but he hasn't made any other long-distance calls. Made a couple of local ones, though."

"To who? You remember?"

"One was to Connecticut Valley Produce. Used to buy acorn squash out there myself."

Casper looked at his watch and counted the hours by pointing at each numeral with a broad finger. "Well," Casper said in a bored tone, "I don't think this one will be much trouble. Looks open and shut to me."

Peabody nodded in agreement. A police van pulled into the driveway and a middle-aged man proceeded to unpack photographic equipment.

"What have you got, Lieutenant?" the police technician asked.

"Looks like a suicide, Marvin. Just shoot the body and the room from a couple of angles," the lieutenant ordered pleasantly.

"Anything to dust?" the technician asked.

"Naw," Casper said. "Oh, there might be a few prints around, but what's it going to prove? Just make a set of prints off the dead guy—for the file."

The technician moved his camera, lights, and several black suitcases inside the room. The room began to flash like a tiny lightning storm as the police photographer methodically recorded the scene on film. He appeared at the door after a few minutes and called to the lieutenant. "You want that gun dusted or anything?"

Casper pursed his lips. "Hell, let's not get involved with that gun, Marvin. Just uncock the bastard and put it on the dresser. Automatics scare me."

The coroner arrived and was brought to room 15 by one of the uniformed officers. He nodded silently to the lieutenant and mumbled some garbled greeting to Peabody. Dr. Fortunelli was in his late sixties and had a general practice. He didn't enjoy these police calls, but a few years previously, Chief Fowler had asked him to serve as coroner. Because they were personal friends, Dr. Fortunelli had agreed. Now, with Chief Fowler retired, each call became a little more of a burden, and ideas about resigning the position came to his mind more frequently. Without further conversation, he went into the room and looked at the dead body. He lifted one of Caton's eyelids.

"You want us to roll him over or anything, Doc?" the lieutenant asked.

The doctor shook his head. "He's not going to get any deader." He turned abruptly and walked out of the room. "I'll send you a copy of the death certificate," he called to Casper. "Call my office later and give me his name and stuff."

"OK, Doc," shouted the lieutenant, "and thanks for coming right over." The doctor nodded and got into his car. "He's a funny duck," Casper explained to Peabody. "We can't get him to do a goddamned thing, but at least he signs the death certificates. I guess he used to be pretty active in his practice until his wife caught him plugging his nurse on the examining table."

Peabody maintained his placid expression and refused to raise his eyebrows over the lieutenant's rehash of a ten-year-ago minor scandal.

"Can I use your phone, Mr. Peabody?" the lieutenant asked.

"Ayah," said Peabody and let the policeman herd him toward his own office.

"Just a couple of formalities, and then we'll let the undertaker clear that room for you," the lieutenant promised. He dialed the police headquarters and asked for the homicide division. "Harry, I'm going to clear the signal seven at the Brownstone as a suicide," he explained to the desk man in homicide. "I got pictures and the doc has seen the body." He nodded to agree with some comments on the phone and hung up.

"What was that vegetable company that this bird called yesterday?" he asked Peabody.

"Connecticut Valley Produce," said Peabody. "It's there on Caton's card." He produced a phone log from the mail slot marked room 15, and handed it to the police lieutenant. Casper made a note of the calls on his pocket pad. He dialed the first set of numbers.

"Connecticut Valley Produce?" he asked the girl who answered, despite the fact that that was exactly what she had said. "Do you know a man named Myrl Caton over there?" The office girl said she did not, but Casper persisted.

"Well, let me talk to your boss."

"Mr. Irafino?" she asked.

"Whoever he is, honey," said Casper with mock exasperation. There were several clicks and a male voice answered.

"Yeah—what?"

"Mr. Irafino?"

"Yeah."

"This is Lt. Casper with the Police Department."

"I paid the ticket," Irafino said quickly. In the Italian section of town, the green Lincoln could be left next to a fire hydrant without any trouble. But further downtown, Irafino frequently got a two-dollar ticket.

"Do you know a guy named Caton?"

"Caton?" Irafino asked cautiously.

"Myrl Caton."

Scenes of their fight and thoughts of a charge of assault and battery flashed through Irafino's brain.

"Shit," Irafino said, "he went and made a stink about the fight, didn't he?"

"He's dead," said Casper without emotion.

The phone became almost silent as Irafino softly whispered, "Jesus Christ."

"I'd like to ask you a few questions," said Casper.

Irafino felt his heart pounding as his mouth became foul-tasting and dry. Somewhere in the back of his throat he ached slightly and his hands began to sweat. "OK, so I hit him, but not that hard," he said.

"When was that, Mr. Irafino?" asked Casper.

"Yesterday—right after he got in town. I went over there for a drink and he got tough. We had a scrap and I got the hell out. That's all, Lieutenant, honest."

"He's been shot, but it looks like he done it to himself," explained Casper.

"Balls!" said Irafino. "I knew him for years and he wouldn't do that."

Casper checked the suicide evidence for a moment. Gun in the room, body in bed still dressed, gunshot wound in chest, door locked from inside, chain on the latch.

"It's definitely a suicide," said Casper with authority. "Do you know how we can reach his family or somebody in Florida?"

"He owns a tomato-packing plant in Ruskin, Florida—that's near Tampa." Irafino gave Casper the number from his flip-up pad. "Ask for a guy named Morris. Kirby Morris."

"That's K-I-R-B-Y?" asked Casper.

"I guess so," said Irafino. "I never met him. I did all my business with Caton." He paused briefly. "Suicide, eh? I'll be a son of a bitch. Where is he now?"

"Still in the motel room. Do you know if he would have any preference as to funeral parlors? I mean is he Jewish or something?" Casper asked.

"Shit, he wasn't nothing," said Irafino. "Look, if you want, I'll call his wife for you, Lieutenant. I met her once at a convention."

Casper thought over the offer and agreed. "OK, but somebody down there has got to give us permission to send that body out for embalming and make arrangements for shipment. Get us a telegram, will you?"

"Can I call you at the motel, or where?" asked Irafino.

"I'll be at police headquarters writing up this report. Ask for homicide."

"Was it that .45?" asked Irafino.

Casper closed on the question like a trap. "What do you know about any .45?" he asked.

"Hell, everybody knew about it. He used to carry it in the car and shoot road signs when he got drunk."

Casper mechanically recorded the comment in his notebook. "We've got the gun. Call me, Mr. Irafino," the lieutenant said.

"Just as soon as I call Florida," he promised. He put the phone down and pushed his desk intercom lever. "Tell Angela to come in," he said softly.

5

Tampa and St. Pete faded below them as the Eastern
jet climbed gracefully. Kirby Morris and Pat Caton held
hands in the first-class section as the stewardess put two
fresh drinks before them. Pat stared ahead without speaking. She wore a black suit but no veil. She dabbed at her
eyes with a small handkerchief from time to time, although there was no real evidence of tears.

"I told Irafino to meet us at the airport and drive us to
Middlebrook," Kirby explained.

"I don't think I ever met this Irafino, did I?" asked
Pat.

"He was at that blast we all went to in Freeport two
years ago when the Florida Truck Farmers Association
had some of those northern buyers down for the weekend.
But you probably didn't meet him."

"That was a real mess," remembered Pat. "You'd think
those guys were leaving for overseas the way they went after the booze and the broads."

"Well you know how those guys are when they get
going."

Pat lifted her drink and drained the glass. Kirby mo-

35

tioned to the stewardess for a refill. "I'm sure glad there's booze on this plane," she said. "I don't think I could stand flying without it."

"Hell, you couldn't stand walking without it," chided Kirby. Pat pulled her hand away and turned slightly to face the window. Kirby chuckled into his drink and looked at his watch. The jet was scheduled to stop in Atlanta and then fly direct to Bradley Field in Windsor Locks, Connecticut.

Atlanta passed by in a blur of airport activity, and the hitch to New York was quickened by dinner at thirty thousand feet.

"That looks like some big city," she said, pointing out the window with her fork. Kirby leaned over to get a better look and smelled the perfume on the side of her neck. For years her perfume had been heavy and sweet, but with the help of the owner at Sally's Beauty Shop in Orangeburrow, she had lately toned it down to a fainter, more haunting scent.

There was a change in the sound of the engines when the plane dipped into the approach pattern for Bradley Field. Pat gripped Kirby's hand when the wheels let down, and held on even harder when the pilot reversed the engines on the runway.

The plane came to a stop in front of the terminal and the stewardess announced in a Southern drawl, "Ladies and gentlemen, welcome to Hartford, Connecticut."

Kirby ignored the airline arrival patter and stood up, bumping against the overhead luggage rack. Behind the boarding area stood Vincent Irafino, smoking a small, twisted, black, dangerous-looking Parodi cigar.

"Mr. Irafino?" Kirby inquired in a soft Southern accent.

Vincent smiled and nodded as he shook Kirby's hand, then stared somewhat awkwardly at Pat Caton. She held out a gloved hand and Irafino shook it slowly and gently. "I'm awfully sorry about your husband, Mrs. Caton. We was real good friends."

"My husband has spoken about you," Pat lied.

"We're sure going to miss him," said Irafino, shaking his head as if to indicate a deeply tragic loss.

"We appreciate the help you've given us by contacting all those people up here for us," said Kirby.

"You'll like the funeral home, I think," said Irafino. "We buried my mother from there." He led Pat toward the baggage area. The rough grip on her arm gave Pat the uneasy feeling that Caton had returned.

Irafino wheeled his green Lincoln effortlessly toward Middlebrook. After an hour along the seaport towns which dotted the Connecticut River, Irafino made a turn onto a quiet street and announced, "The Brownstone." Kirby studied the place with interest as Irafino pulled up in front of the motel office. The three of them went in.

"Is Peabody around?" asked Irafino abruptly.

"No, sir, he's not on duty this evening," said the clerk. He looked curiously at the well-dressed woman who had presented herself without embarrassment in the company of two men. The Brownstone was not opposed to parties, but usually the girl stayed in the car until her customers checked in.

"This is Mrs. Caton and Mr. Morris," said Irafino. "Mr. Peabody wanted to be called when they arrived." The clerk leaped to his feet and began to fumble with room keys.

"Yes, sir," he stuttered, "Mr. Peabody said to put Mrs. Caton in 36 and Mr. Morris in 37. He already registered you folks, so you can go right over." He ran from behind the desk and pushed open the door for Pat Caton.

"If there is anything we can do for you, Mrs. Caton," he offered, "anything at all."

The clerk unlocked the 36 side of the adjoining door to room 37 and then went around to open that room. He reappeared through the adjoining door and said, "You can lock these double doors from each side, but I thought you'd like them open for a while."

"How about some ice and a couple of glasses?" said Kirby.

"The glasses are in each bathroom," the clerk said officiously. "I'll get you some ice." He took the bucket and went out.

"Like I told you in the car," said Irafino, "we got Hitchcock's Funeral Home to handle the body. I don't think you have to call them tonight, but maybe you better give them a ring in the morning."

Pat stared at the empty bed and shook her head slowly. "I just don't get it," she said. "Why would Myrl come all the way up here to a dump like this just to shoot himself?"

Morris opened his suitcase and took out a bottle of J&B. "I suppose he always stayed in places like this," he said.

"But not Kirby Morris, eh?" Pat asked with a tone of contempt. "You take the fifty-dollar-a-day suite when you're on the road. But poor Myrl could rot in fleatraps while he sold those crummy tomatoes."

Kirby opened the scotch and poured two drinks. He offered the bottle to Irafino, but the Italian looked at his watch and mumbled some excuses about having to get up early in the morning. Scotch tasted like iodine to him. Kirby handed Pat her drink and tossed his own down with a shudder.

Irafino opened the door in response to a small knock and took the ice bucket from the clerk. He put the ice on the dresser and held out his hand to Morris. "See you tomorrow," he said pleasantly.

"Mr. Irafino," said Kirby, "we sure thank you for the ride and all you did."

Pat nodded vigorously and offered her hand to be shook. "I'm happy that Myrl had such good friends way up here in Connecticut," she said.

Irafino left the room thinking of what Pat's reaction would have been to Angela.

Kirby put ice in both drinks and began to unbuckle his pants. "You think I ought to muss up both beds so that the maid won't get the wrong idea?"

"I don't give a shit what they think now," Pat said as her dress slipped silently to the floor.

6

The body of Myrl Caton lay outstretched on the porcelain embalming table at the Hitchcock Funeral Home. It was nine o'clock, and the evening crew of attendants assumed the heavier parts of the preparation. The finer points of cosmetology would be left to Merton Hitchcock II, who would apply the traditional Hitchcock rules about facial expressions and hairstyles. When Merton II prepared a face, the lips were set in a nonsmiling horizontal slit which was exactly as wide as the nose was long. He was unconcerned by those who pointed out that some people do not possess such uniform features. At Hitchcock's the deceased received a Hitchcock face.

With little difficulty, the attendants cut off Myrl Caton's bloody garments. They dropped the clothes into a grocery-sized paper bag and pushed it into the corner of the preparation room. Later, one of them would stuff the bag of clothing into the incinerator and personally supervise its destruction. Everything at Hitchcock's boasted personal supervision. The body was washed with an antiseptic-smelling soap. At the same time, the face was lathered with Noxzema shave cream—which promised not to pull or burn—and carefully shaved. After the shave, the head was lathered with a lanolin-base shampoo, and the hair washed as carefully as in a beauty parlor. The shampoo was rinsed with a small hose which ran up the table from a combination faucet nozzle and suction apparatus. The suction would come later.

Deftly, the attendant clipped away a few patches of hair above the ears and from the back of the neck. No real haircut was intended or permitted, but since Merton II shared the family conviction that everyone wanted to remember a friend who had "passed on" in the best possible light, little things like a trim which the dear one had overlooked in life were thoughtfully supplied.

When the shirt was removed, both attendants inspected the bullet wound in the chest. The younger attendant let out a low whistle.

"Look at that hole!" he exclaimed. "It must have been a cannon."

The older attendant belittled the wound left by the bullet after it had crashed through Caton's chest. "Shit, once we had a guy who blew his head clean off with a shotgun."

His partner looked astonished.

"Put both muzzles in his mouth and blew his brain across the room. We found a big hunk of it in a chair and the rest stuck to the ceiling." As he described this to his partner, he attached a long sharp trochar to the suction hose, rammed it through Caton's abdomen, and explored in several directions. Intermittently, the water from the suction attachment at the sink gushed blood, bile, stomach contents, and feces. "At least we can put this guy's bullet hole to good use," he said. He pushed his swordlike suction trochar through the entrance wound in Caton's chest and sucked the blood from his heart and lungs with long probing stabs. After he was satisfied that he had extracted all the unwanted fluids from the body cavities, he began the bath, using a hospital-smelling liquid soap which was claimed would kill "all diseases."

The embalmer made a careful incision—as careful as

most surgeons'—on the front of the thigh in an area called the femoral triangle and found a large artery and vein lying beneath the skin. He opened both and with the aid of an aneurysm hook inserted small, curved artery tubes into the vessels. He prepared his artery solutions by putting six bottles of pink-colored liquid into the tank of his ancient Porti-Boy embalming machine and adding water to the six-gallon mark. He set the pressure gauge to nine pounds and hooked the hose to the silver tube sticking upward from the artery like a tiny erection. The little erect tube looked somehow obscene next to the limp organ of the big tomato grower. The embalmer inserted another, longer tube with an internal slide into the opened vein to let Caton bleed freely. The embalmer threw his switch. With a mechanical heart action, the machine pumped embalming fluid in and spurted jets of blood onto Caton's thigh and down the drain. Whenever the bleeding slowed, the slide in the tube received a few pumps, and, as if coaxed from hiding in the darkness of the circulatory system, a troublesome clot would appear at the opening and ooze onto Caton's skin.

The pumping machine pushed the pink embalming fluid into the body and was shut off. The tubes were removed from the blood vessels and each vessel was tied with a short length of ordinary string.

The embalmer put two bottles of stronger Royal Bond Cavity Fluid into the machine and inserted the pointed trochar into the bullet wound. He pumped half of the stronger-smelling fluid into the chest, and the rest of the fluid into the abdomen. Into the abdominal wound that he had made, and the chest wound that he hadn't, he screwed short plastic plugs. Caton's body had become pinker as the eosin in the arterial fluid found its way into the skin capillaries. "Fleshtone," the arterial fluid bottle had read.

The door to the preparation room opened and Merton Hitchcock II entered. The younger embalmer put out his cigarette in the same sink that had accepted Caton's blood. Merton II didn't approve of smoking in the presence of a dead body.

"He finished?" Merton asked as he felt the face and legs for firmness.

"Yes, sir," said the embalmer. "We shot six bottles in him. Is he hard enough for the ride?"

Caton was to be shipped to Tampa for the funeral services, so Merton II had only to perform the embalming and preparation necessary for transportation across the state lines. He was to be flown in the baggage compartment of an Eastern jet, dressed only in undershorts and wrapped lightly in a white sheet.

"He's hard enough—but a little too pink," Hitchcock said, caressing the face to judge the closeness of the shave. Small plastic caps with tiny protruding hooks had been placed on Myrl's eyeballs to hold the lids closed, and his jaws had been wired together by the embalmer, giving him a set jaw that was not out of character. Merton Hitchcock II took a small steel machinist's ruler from his inside jacket pocket and measured the length of the nose. He quickly molded the lips into a firm, emotionless, perfectly horizontal line exactly as wide as the nose was long.

It was nine-thirty the next morning when the intercom crackled and a voice said somberly, "Mrs. Caton is here, Mr. Hitchcock." Hitchcock gave no reply and the speaker clicked off. Merton II examined himself carefully and critically in the mirror. He combed his hair, now sufficiently gray at the temples that he no longer felt the need to add this touch of maturity. He wore a dark—but not black—coat modest in its styling. His trousers were wider than those in style. His shirt was plain, white, and starched. A dark tie with a faint silver diagonal was neatly tied in a medium knot. His black shoes were carefully polished, and three points of a white handkerchief peaked from his breast pocket. The lower half of the handkerchief was cardboard, but always out of sight.

Merton II entered his early-American office. A grandfather's clock ticked in the corner. His associate, looking like a carbon copy, slowly and gently presented Mrs. Caton. Pat was wearing yesterday's black outfit; it was beginning to show a few wrinkles across her trim behind.

"Mrs. Caton," Merton II began in a low-register, evenly paced voice, "you have our every sympathy." He paused, still holding Pat's gloved hand in both of his own. "At these times, one needs the comfort of knowing that every detail has been taken care of by one thoughtful enough to have due regard for your grief."

Pat gazed into his eyes like a helpless doe.

Merton continued, slowly, carefully, with a stream of saccharine verbiage calculated to ease the widow into a mood receptive to purchasing the best casket he had to offer.

Pat withdrew her hand from Hitchcock's gentle grip and dabbed the corner of her eye with her tiny handkerchief. Hitchcock's associate immediately thrust a small paper cup of water into the director's hand. Hitchcock gave the water to Pat with the assurance that it would make her feel so very much better.

Kirby Morris had stood silently behind Pat's chair, but now felt restless enough to move along the office wall inspecting each diploma with mock interest.

Skillfully, Merton moved Pat to a chair near the big mahogany desk and began to suggest that he be allowed to select something "suitable" in a medium price range. He paused to let the ugly concept of money sink into Mrs. Caton's grief-dulled mind.

"The airline will accept passage from Hartford to Tampa without any personal involvement of your part, Mrs. Caton." The airline wanted $27.50 per hundred pounds including body, casket, and canvas pouch. It didn't really care whether it was 215 pounds of cold Caton or of maraschino cherries; freight was freight. The "no personal involvement" was useful in keeping the widow out of the way when the forklift truck packed the box in the belly of the plane. (Once an airline had dropped a casket on the runway and was happy that the policy of "no family witnesses" had paid off. With a quick phone call and a fast ride to the shipping mortician, another casket had been substituted, courtesy of the airline. The widow, carefully booked on an earlier flight, was not burdened with any announcement concerning the accident.)

"We suggest that you allow us to finalize the preparation and give you the peace of mind of knowing that your late husband is comfortable during his trip home," Merton gushed.

Pat stifled a slight gag in her throat.

"Alternatively, you can have your local director perform the final preparations and we will provide only those things necessary for shipment. This would, of course, be somewhat less expensive." Merton II took the empty paper cup from Pat. She wished it had been Scotch.

"How much?" she said dryly.

"Perhaps you would care to view our selection of fine caskets," Merton II said. He gently took Pat's arm, raising her from the chair, and led her through another office door, opened by the associate on the cue, "How much?"

The associate moved over to begin idle conversation with Kirby. The preferred arrangement was to get the widow alone in the casket display and to exclude male advisors. Invariably, the widow's companion was along to see that she didn't get screwed. Merton's job was to see that she did—gently.

The room lights were soft, and somewhere far away an organ played nothing recognizable. Nearest the door were the cheaper caskets. The customer never buys the first item shown. Along both sides of the room yawned metal caskets in various subdued colors. At the end of the room, like a high altar, gleamed a copper casket with a white silk interior.

"This one is 20-gauge steel and is hermetically sealed to keep out moisture and air, madam," Merton intoned. His hand caressed the closed lower half. The sealing, of course, also kept the mold, the juices of decomposition, and the stink in, but emphasis was placed on the protective aspects. Merton II waited for an opening into which to slip the price. It came without delay.

"Is it expensive?" Pat asked as she felt the soft fabric of the pillowed interior.

"Let's see," Merton II said, looking for the price card inside. He could have given the price of each box from memory, calculated the tax, accurately estimated the weight and air-freight charges to any major city in the U.S., and recited the finance charges offered by the Connecticut Bank and Trust for two years, thirty-six months, or longer, depending on down payment.

"This one runs $1125 with services and full use of our facilities," he said blankly. He was not apologetic about the price, since it was chickenfeed next to the $3,400 solid copper one at the end of the room. After she decided on one, Merton II could move in with the "extras."

They walked along the display with Merton II giving the relative merits of each box. A casket made of aluminum was touted as lighter for the pallbearers and corrosion-proof. It was $1500. Another box bore a guarantee that after it had been carefully and skillfully made by workmen in the old tradition, there had been a final test by vacuum; it came with a thirty-year insurance policy (up to a $3,000 limit) to back up the guarantee against rusting through, corrosion, vacuum leak, water seepage, or hinges breaking; all one had to do to make a claim was to be suspicious and worried enough to dig up and inspect the casket inside and out.

Pat selected a baked-finish 20-gauge metal casket with adjustable mattress (Myrl always tossed and turned so), sealed top, heavy-duty hinges (that would only have to work once), and silver-colored handles (he was a large man, Mrs. Caton). She balked at an optional memorial record tube to be artfully attached at the foot of the casket to provide a list of the mourners who attended the services.

They returned to Hitchcock's office, where Merton II was ecstatic to see Pat take out her checkbook. The associate moved Kirby gently into the casket room where he would give a modified tour of all the boxes, pausing at each just long enough to point out a few highlights but no accurate prices. The one that had been selected would be described in terms just a little less glowing than those he would use to praise Mrs. Caton's good taste, foresight and, above all, prudent but appropriate economy.

Merton was able to sell Pat on the idea of a $50 suit from a funeral-supply drygoods house for $125—including white shirt, tie, and socks, of course. All of Myrl's clothes were too rumpled even for a casket.

At Hitchcock's suggestion, Pat wrote a check for $2,400 as "a retainer" and signed a note ("a mere formality") for whatever "incidental" fees might arise after her departure. Hitchcock quickly placed the check out of sight in the desk drawer, and began the lead-out patter. He assured the widow that his firm stood ready day or night to be of service to her.

She took Kirby's arm and headed for the big Cadillac provided by the ever-thoughtful Merton Hitchcock II.

"Oh, and Mr. Hitchcock," chirped extra-Southern Pat Caton, "I do hope you will get rid of all those awful clothes."

"We'll see to it immediately," promised the silken director. The bloody clothes had already been burned in the roaring incinerator in the back room of the mortuary.

He opened the rear door of the Cadillac and let Pat in. She carefully exposed much more thigh than necessary as she entered the car. Kirby saw it but didn't notice, while Merton Hitchcock II felt an unnerving twitch in his pants.

"Have we got time to do it before the plane goes?" she giggled at Kirby as the Cadillac left the funeral-home driveway. Kirby shot a quick glance at the Hitchcock driver, who refused to demonstrate that he had fully understood her.

7

The police headquarters in Middlebrook, Connecticut, had been constructed of brownstone blocks quarried across the river in Chatam around 1904. Since then, the large wooden immobile windows had been replaced with aluminum immobile windows. The front steps led to a massive door which opened onto the second floor.

Homicide occupied the third floor along with robbery.

Casper sat at a cluttered desk in a large room shared with several other homicide detectives and investigators. He was writing his report of the suicide at the Brownstone Motel in a cheap spiral notebook. Some of the newer men, armed with academic training in police science from junior college, used words that seemed to Casper to be deliberately obscure. Casper had been on the police force for twenty-three years, including two years out for the service. He had become a cop shortly after his graduation from Middlebrook High School, and had advanced through the years to lieutenant's rank in the homicide division. In two years more, he would retire, take the small pension offered by the city, move to Fort Lauderdale, and get some kind of a job in the sunshine. He had a couple of contacts in Lauderdale—retired cops from Connecticut.

On the scratch sheet of his notebook, Casper had diagramed the names of Myrl Caton, Pat Caton (wife), Kirby Morris (business associate), Vincent Irafino (local contact). The name of Clyde Peabody had a line through it. On his desk lay Caton's .45, tagged with an evidence label. He casually studied the photographs of Brownstone Motel and room 15. The gun was still on the floor in one picture, and bloody spots were easily identified in another. Several other views of the room and the body on the bed were included in the set, including a shot of the door to the adjoining room.

Casper dialed the identification section. "Marvin," he said when the ID technician answered, "did you check that door leading from the suicide's bedroom to the next room?"

"No, sir," said the tech. "I didn't check the lock and I didn't dust for prints. I figured you had checked it. Why? Got a problem with it?"

"Naw," the lieutenant said. "It's just my menopause itching."

"Any chance of us making a murder out of this case, Lieutenant?"

"Not a chance. It's an open-and-shut suicide and that's the way she stays," he announced. "By the way, call the doc and give him the name and address on this bird, will you, Marvin? And make sure the time on his death certificate and our record time correspond."

"Ten-four," the technician said.

Casper put the phone down and stared at the photograph showing the adjoining door. He tapped his pencil on the phone as he studied the picture. The phone gave a quick intercom ring, almost as if it were responding to the tapping.

"Lt. Casper," he said dryly.

"Ah, Lt. Casper? This is Clyde Peabody ... over at the Brownstone Motel?"

"Yes, Mr. Peabody. What can I do for you?" A small frown appeared on Casper's brow.

"Oh, it's probably nothing, but I just happened to think. You know that room next to number 15?"

"The adjoining room, Mr. Peabody?"

"Ayah. I just remembered that Mr. Caton rented that room the night before we found his body." He paused briefly, as if to give Casper sufficient time to savor his message. "You think that means anything, Lieutenant?"

"Oh, it might," Casper said casually. "Who did he rent it for?"

"Well, let's see," Peabody said as he opened the motel register to the proper page. "Here it is. That's room 16. We rented that one to a Mrs. Jones."

"At what time?" Casper sounded interested.

"About seven o'clock in the evening, it says here. My night desk clerk was on duty."

"Any address on the Jones woman?"

"Yes, sir," Peabody announced dutifully. "4205 West Main Street, Sacramento, California. But it's kind of funny, if you ask me."

"Why is it funny?" Casper asked patiently.

"Because my night clerk . . ." he paused and started over. "Can I trust you on this one, Lieutenant? I mean, we don't want no more trouble over here. Had enough of that already."

"Try me," Casper reassured him without promising anything.

"My night boy went over there later to bring some Cokes and when he pushed his cart across the sidewalk in front of 16 he bumped her car and dented the fender a little. He called my house to tell me about it. I chewed him out and all that, but night clerks is hard to get and even harder to keep. You know what I mean?"

"Yeah, Peabody, I know what you mean. Go on, go on." Casper's impatience began to appear.

"Well, I got to worrying about it, and so I rode over to the motel to take a look at the dent for myself. We're insured, you know, but I just hate to report them ten-buck fender benders and get my rates pushed up."

"Go on, Mr. Peabody," Casper urged.

"Well, Lieutenant, the car was parked right in front of number 16 just like the night boy said it was, and I saw that he had made a little dent in the right front fender. Nothing much, you understand, just a crease. But I figured there might be trouble if she spotted it, so I checked the registration plates. Just in case I had to find her later."

"And?"

"And the car was registered in Connecticut. It had a Middlebrook dealer's sticker on the back too."

"What kind of a car was it?" Casper asked.

"Pinto. It was a new Pinto, too. Blue, I think, but it was getting dark. That's when I figured the California address was a phony. But you know, lots of local people give us out-of-town addresses when they want to stay here."

"I'll bet they do," Casper said quickly. "Do you remember the number on that Pinto?"

"Yup," Peabody said in his Yankee twang. "It was A-N-G-E," Peabody spelled slowly and carefully. In Connecticut, it was not unusual for a registration plate to carry a combination of capital letters without numbers. Every now and then, some character would request an obscene four-letter tag, but the MVD would just throw those applications out.

"When did she check out?" Casper asked.

"Oh, she was gone before the maid came by the next morning. But the maid didn't report nothing unusual about the room. Leastwise, she didn't say nothing about it to me."

"Do you recall whether the door that leads from room 16 into room 15 was locked, Mr. Peabody?" The pencil snapped in Casper's hand as he waited for the motel manager's reply.

"Locked? Locked when?"

"Locked when your maid was cleaning the room."

"Can't rightly say."

"Was it locked when this Mrs. Jones took it?"

" 'Spect so. We always rent them adjoining rooms out with the door between them locked. Besides, Lieutenant, room 15 was already rented to Mr. Caton."

"Yes, Mr. Peabody. Thank you. I know that." Casper held the mouthpiece of the phone to his shirt and stole ten seconds of silent thought. "I'll call you back later. I want to check out the tag you gave me. By the way—have Mrs. Caton and that Kirby Morris checked out yet?"

"Not yet, but they're getting ready to. They've already come over to the office and wanted to pay for the two rooms," Peabody explained. "But I didn't take nothing from them. In view of the circumstances. And besides ... they only used one room."

"OK, thanks," Casper said hurriedly. He put the receiver on its cradle and made another note on his pad: Morris and Mrs. Caton—one room.

He pushed his desk set intercom button and waited for a response.

"MVD," a female voice said officially.

"Get me a make on Connecticut, A-Able, N-Norman, G-George, E-Edward. This year. Pinto. Color: blue. This is Casper in Homicide. Call me right back."

"Roger," the woman said. The intercom shut off and Casper picked up Caton's .45. He pulled back the slide and completed the cocking mechanism by depressing the safety. He aimed at the ancient clock on the wall and squeezed the trigger. The hammer snapped onto the firing pin with a loud click and Casper jerked the muzzle upward to simulate a recoil.

The intercom emitted static and a dull tone to indicate an incoming call.

"Casper. Homicide," he said, still enjoying the link between those names despite his years of experience.

"Sir," the female voice said in a practiced monotone. "A-Able, N-Norman, G-George, E-Edward, Pinto, Color: blue. Registered to Angela Gaito, Miss. Race: caucasian; age 43; height: 5 feet 4 inches; eyes; brown; address of record: 2036 West Colazzi Street, apartment 2, Middlebrook. No previous convictions. No points against the tag."

"Thank you, sweetheart," Casper said. He released the intercom and clicked to an outside line. His fingers dialed the numbers with the ease that habit creates. He continued his pencil tattoo on the desktop as the phone rang and rang. No one answered. There was a small metallic buzz as another incoming intercom line competed for his attention. Casper abandoned his call to Angela Gaito.

"Yes?" he said, depressing the blinking intercom button.

"Lieutenant, this is Marvin again. You remember that empty .45 cartridge we found in the Caton room?"

"Yeah. What about it?" Casper squinted at the blank wall across from his desk and made a mental promise to hang something there.

"How many times have you seen a shell land exactly on its base and stand up like that?"

Casper was silent in thought. Then he said, "Could happen, I guess."

"Yeah, but Lieutenant—this shell was standing on its end right there on the frame of the bed between the mattress and the headboard."

"So?"

"So nothing, I guess," Marvin said. "But you know, it's kind of bothered me. And so I spent most of last night's TV movie flipping an empty .45 shell onto the floor just to see if it would land standing on its base."

"And did it?" Casper asked.

"Not once, Lieutenant."

"But you don't deny that it could happen, do you, Marvin?" Casper snapped. "Or are you saying it was a plant?"

"Oh, hell—I don't know why it would be, Lieutenant. It was just a wild-assed idea I had." Marvin had a shy personality that was better suited to the protected environment of the police lab than to activities involving the public. Chief Fowler had described him as a pipe-smoker who putters around the evidence lab at a careful pace, slow enough to madden the most patient detectives. But his careful puttering had on one occasion settled the question of whether an automobile involved in a hit-and-run had been using its high or low beams. Marvin had proved it by a meticulous reconstruction of the headlight fragments and a microscopic examination of the filaments. On another case, he was able to match the dents in the hood of an automobile with the body impact which would have been produced when the pedestrian arched backward and smashed onto the car. In that case, two small hairs were pulled out of the cracks in the paint and matched to the dead girl's hair. His relationship with Lt. Casper had ripened into a cordial one when he found out that Casper's bark was impotent and when Casper realized that Marvin produced only when loved.

"Why don't we test-fire that .45 to see if it throws the empty shell in a direction which would match the headboard and the body position?" Marvin suggested.

"You want to lay on the bed and shoot yourself at the same angle?" asked Casper.

"I think I can reproduce that angle accurately without going to that extreme," Marvin said quite seriously.

Casper thought over the idea for a while and then rejected it. "Marvin," he said slowly, "we've got a suicide. The gun's still on the floor and the body is right there on the bed. Let's leave well enough alone."

"Ten-four."

8

Pat Caton and Kirby Morris relaxed in room 36 of the Brownstone Motel. The plane for Tampa did not leave for several hours.

She stretched out on top of the motel bed and wore only a black brassiere and red panties. Her black suit, still serving as the proper symbol of her grief, hung on the bathroom door, wrinkled from the miles she had wrung from it during the past two days. She smoked a green Benson and Hedges and watched the smoke climb toward the motel ceiling. Around her neck she wore a single strand of cultured pearls.

Kirby sat in a lounge chair covered with slightly adhering, easily overheated plastic, and read the *TV Guide* out of habit.

"Kirby," Pat drawled lazily.

"Um," he said distantly.

"Do you suppose they've sent Myrl on to Tampa already?"

"Either have or they will shortly. They said that the body will be home and waiting for us at Spottswood's when we get there tonight." For many years, Spottswood's

54

Funeral Home had been the only such establishment in Orangeburrow, Florida. Up to about 1956, there really hadn't been much of an Orangeburrow to service. But now, the building boom had made this former crossroads into an affluent suburb and brought competition. Spottswood's still remained the best known of the three funeral homes, and Spottswood himself actively participated in the business and in the community. His ambulances were seen at every high-school football game.

"Do you think Spottswood will show him?" asked Pat.

"I don't see any reason why not," said Kirby without hesitation. "He wasn't shot in the head, and if this local clown, Hitchcock, hasn't screwed up the embalming, you should be able to have the casket opened for view."

"Just wondered," said Pat. She continued to stare at the ceiling and picked absently at her navel. Kirby returned to his *TV Guide* and studied the late-movie schedule for the following Thursday in New Haven. The telephone rang, jarring both of them back to reality.

"Hello?" said Pat, answering the bedside phone with minimal movement.

"Mrs. Caton?"

"Yes."

"This is Lt. Casper. I wonder if I could trouble you and Mr. Kirby with a few more questions about your husband's death."

"Lord, you asked me everything I know as it is," she pleaded. She looked up from the phone and silently mouthed the name "CASPER" in a bigger-than-life lip movement which would be easily read by Kirby.

"Well, there are a couple of loose ends that I want to clear up," Casper said. "It won't delay your departure for Tampa. I checked your flight time."

"Oh, all right," she said. "Do you want Mr. Morris too?"

"Very much so, Mrs. Caton," the lieutenant said. "I'm over here in the motel office. Would you want to come over here or can I come over there?"

"Well, give me time to straighten my hair and then

you can come on over here. We've got these two big adjoining rooms and we can talk in private." She sat up on the side of the bed and reached for her pantyhose.

"I'll be over in ten minutes, if that's all right with you," said Lt. Casper.

"Ten minutes will be fine," said Pat. She put the phone down and rushed to the mirror in the bathroom. "Get the lead out of your fat ass, Kirby honey, John Law is on the way over to ask some more damn fool questions." She finished with her pantyhose and shoes and began to pull her dress on.

"You think you ought to call G. Markham Hurst?" asked Kirby.

"I ain't got nothing to hide from that police lieutenant," declared Pat. "How 'bout you, Mister Morris?"

"It wouldn't do any harm to let Hurst know what's going on. He knows Myrl's dead, but I don't think he'd like us shooting off our mouths to the local cops without his having had time to get the insurance settled," Kirby said.

"But if you call him now, Peabody will just hand over the phone to the cop. And if you go out to call, they'll wonder why you didn't place it through the motel switchboard."

"I guess we'd better sit tight and see what the lieutenant is after," Kirby said thoughtfully. Pat Caton combed a few snarls out of her hair and repaired her eye shadow. She was startled by the knock on the door.

Without a word, Kirby unlatched the door and opened it. In front of him stood Lt. Casper and Clyde Peabody. He motioned them in.

Kirby made appropriate motions toward the available beds and chairs as Peabody cannibalized the furniture from the adjoining room to provide seats.

"Mrs. Caton," Casper began, "I don't want to cause you any further discomfort or delay. And I don't think there is any need to make a lot of trouble for anyone else." He paused to capture each person's attention. "But all of you in this room had some connection with the unfortunate death of Mr. Caton." Unconsciously, each of the three turned to look briefly at the others. Kirby felt like a character in a Charlie Chan movie.

"Mrs. Caton, I have just had a long talk with Mr. Irafino and Miss Gaito. They told me some things that I think you should know about. Now if you'd rather hear these things from me in private, we can go into the next room." He pointed toward the adjoining door.

"Tell me what you have to say," she said. "I've got a plane to catch." She looked at her watch impatiently.

Casper shifted in his chair but accepted Pat Caton's impatience without comment. "As you know, Mrs. Caton, your husband did business up here with Vincent Irafino."

"Myrl did business with a lot of guys."

"But did you know that Mr. Irafino and your husband had a fight?" Casper placed his tongue in his cheek testily.

Pat looked quickly at Kirby Morris and then at Clyde Peabody. "A fight? About what?"

"Mrs. Caton," Casper began again, "I don't want to keep you from that plane, but—"

"Yeah. Yeah. But what did they fight about?" Pat's impatience was showing badly.

"Well, there were some remarks passed, I'm told," Casper explained.

"Remarks? What remarks? You mean Myrl said something to this Irafino?" Kirby asked.

"You know Myrl," Pat said softly.

Peabody raised his eyebrows but found himself reluctant to agree or disagree.

"Seems like your husband found a certain woman from the vegetable company attractive," Casper supplied.

"Who? What woman?" Pat asked quickly.

"Angela Gaito," Casper said.

"Oh," Pat said in a small voice. She was no longer capable of surprise or genuine outrage when she found out about another one of Caton's girls on the road.

"We also have reason to believe that Miss Gaito was over here the night that Mr. Caton died," Casper said.

"Here? At the motel?" Morris asked.

"What the hell does all that mean?" Pat asked. She was becoming more excited. "This Gator woman have something to do with Myrl's death?"

Casper held up his hand like a traffic cop to slow her down. "Now, I didn't say anything like that, Mrs. Caton."

"What about Irafino?" Kirby Morris asked. "Is he clean?"

"Far as we can tell at this time he is. Actually, I don't think either Miss Gaito or Mr. Irafino were directly involved in Mr. Caton's death. I'm working the case as an open-and-shut suicide, and I don't expect to get any additional information to change my mind."

Clyde Peabody found himself nodding in agreement with Lt. Casper, but he was not sure why. "We heard a shot," Peabody volunteered.

Casper gave Peabody an angry glance. He preferred to guide the conversation himself.

"A shot?" Pat Caton asked.

"Not the shot that killed him, Mrs. Caton," Casper explained. "Sometime the afternoon he arrived, Mr. Caton and Mr. Irafino were fooling with his gun."

"Fighting over the gun, I heard," Peabody added. He took another scowl from Casper.

"That damned .45, I'll bet," Morris said philosophically.

"There were some words exchanged and I guess a punch or two was thrown before one of them fired a shot that ended up harmlessly in the step out front of the room," Casper said. "I don't think that either of them intended to shoot anyone."

"You mean he had that woman over in his room?" Pat asked.

"They had adjoining rooms," Peabody said stiffly.

"But Angela—er, that is, Miss Gaito—claims that she slept in her own room," Casper added quickly. "She says that Mr. Caton got quite drunk."

Pat nodded slowly. "He could sure do that all right."

"But what about the next morning?" Morris asked. "Did she say that Myrl was OK?"

"She says she knocked on his half of the adjoining door, but that she didn't get any answer," Casper offered.

"You buy that?" Morris asked him.

Casper gave a small shrug. "So far it checks out OK. She says that Mr. Caton had been in a depressed mood the night before and that he was really drunk when she left him in his room. I guess she wasn't surprised that he didn't get up the next day to say goodbye to her."

"You think he was dead in there when she left?" Pat asked.

"Probably," Casper said. "At least that's what I get from the coroner. You know, rigor mortis and all that."

Pat, Kirby, and Peabody nodded in unison as if they really knew about rigor mortis and all that.

"What time did she leave?" Peabody asked.

"About six, she says," Casper supplied. "You have any reason to doubt that?"

Peabody shrugged. "Nope. Sounds OK to me."

"But wouldn't she hear the shot if Myrl killed himself that night in the very next room?" Morris asked.

"You'd think so," Casper agreed. "But she says she sleeps like a rock. Especially when she's been drinking."

"But a .45?" Morris persisted.

Casper shrugged again. "Who knows? Maybe the gun was smothered in a pillow. Maybe she does sleep like a rock. But answer me something else." He turned toward Pat Caton. "Don't you stand to gain a large amount of money from your husband's death? You know, the insurance."

"What insurance?" Morris snapped.

"I don't know," Casper admitted. "I'm just guessing that a guy with a big tomato business carries a pile of insurance. No?"

Pat nodded in agreement. "He had a couple of policies. But they weren't all made out to me. Some of them went to the business and to Kirby here."

"For business purposes," Kirby added quickly.

"Sure," Casper said dryly. He made a cryptic note on his pad and snapped it closed. "I'll be in touch with both of you if anything else comes up. Better not miss that plane."

"Thank you," Pat said. She began to scan the room again for unpacked items. "But so far, you think it was suicide?"

"Doesn't look like much else, Mrs. Caton," Casper said confidently.

"Right!" Kirby Morris said enthusiastically. "And I think you have done a real fine job, Lieutenant. No sense wasting any more time on the case, is there?" He stood up and took Pat by the arm. "Now if y'all will excuse us?"

Casper held out his hand and took Pat's. "If there is anything I can do—"

"Thank you, Lieutenant," she said. "You have been very kind to both of us." She allowed him to shake her limp hand gently and resumed her widow's expression.

"Mr. Morris," Casper said in a stern tone. He shook Morris's hand firmly.

"Thank you, Lieutenant. And thank you, Mr. Peabody," Morris said, doing the rounds. "You've been more than considerate."

Peabody basked briefly in the compliment. "Always try to be of help," he announced. "Hope you stay with us at the Brownstone the next time you're in Connecticut." Peabody opened the door for Casper and followed him out of the room.

"Do you think that cop really buys the suicide?" Pat asked. "What did he come over here for, anyway? After all, what did he think we could tell him?"

"Cops are cops."

Pat snapped her suitcase shut. "I hope you're right, Kirby. This insurance policy ain't no bet at the dog track."

9

Two squeals and a small puff of smoke from the tires announced that Eastern had touched down on time in Tampa. Kirby Morris stood up and put on his jacket. Pat was still asleep in the window seat. He shook her arm and she squinted at him. She looked out the window and was pleased to see the familiar sight of her home airport.

Kirby's car was in the airport lot and roared into service at the first twist of his key. Pat had never appreciated the effect of sitting down inside the low-slung Porsche, and silently wished for her own Cadillac. Kirby moved the car across the parking lot and paid at the gate. He turned onto I-75 and rapidly accelerated through all available gears.

Pat surveyed the downtown skyline as the sun went down behind her. In the crown of one of the tall bank buildings lay the Downtown Club with its restaurant and bar. Pat wondered whether G. Markham Hurst was up there. It was like wondering whether the Pope was in the Vatican.

The car passed the downtown exits and sped eastward toward Orangeburrow. Kirby allowed an acceptable squeal to escape from the tires as he skidded all four wheels to his exit. He guided the machine along the narrower county roads and the familiar turn into the driveway of the Catons' home. The house was new, two-story, and pseudo-Spanish. There were archways and wrought-iron gates at each entrance. The windows were rounded at the top and Myrl had had red Spanish tiles put on the roof. The overall effect was not unpleasant. It was not sufficiently Spanish to be a showpiece, and yet it showed enough imagination to look more expensive than the sixty-two thousand he had paid for it.

Pat struggled out of the Porsche. Kirby lifted her suitcase from the narrow rear-seat space and brought it to the front door. Pat found her key, the door opened with difficulty and a rush of cool, air-conditioned air hit them pleasantly.

Pat flipped off both shoes and padded to the phone on the bar. She opened the phone-side number folder by depressing "S," and dialed quickly. She struggled to light a cigarette before he answered, but at Spottswood's, the phone was not allowed to ring more than twice. This time it was Spottswood himself.

"Spottswood Funeral Home," he said in an evenly paced voice. Pat wondered whether all funeral directors were coached to speak in the same tone.

"This is Mrs. Caton," she returned in a thinly veiled mime of his somber voice.

"Hello, Mrs. Caton," he said pleasantly. "How was your flight from Connecticut?"

"As good as could be expected under the circumstances," she said. "How did Myrl's flight make out?" Spottswood was quite familiar with Pat Caton's kind of humor. Spottswood's drugstore psychology reasoned that her remarks would come not out of disrespect, but from an attempt to lessen her anxiety over an unfamiliar situation.

"Mr. Caton arrived safely and is resting in the front viewing room at this very moment," Spottswood assured her.

"Do we have to do anything tonight?" she asked the funeral director.

"Only if you would care to view the remains privately," he mewed. "There are no services planned until tomorrow."

"Services? What services?" shouted Pat. She whirled around, phone in hand, to face Kirby. Kirby nodded slowly and quietly.

"After talking to Mr. Morris yesterday," Spottswood went on, "I engaged the services of the Reverend Billie Alford of our local Friends of the Redeemer Chapel."

Myrl Caton had never been much for attending church. As a child, he had gone to the local Baptist church with his mother and sister a few times, but he had not been to church since leaving their mother's home. Even when Pat had asked that their wedding be held in the little Episcopal church in her hometown, Myrl had flatly refused. Hypocrisy was not among his failings.

"The Reverend Billie who?" asked Pat incredulously.

"Alford. The Reverend Billie Alford," said Spottswood. "His flock meets Wednesdays in a little chapel in Tampa. They claim to be almost nondenominational, although they hold to the central Christian theme, more or less."

"But he didn't even know my husband, did he?" asked Pat. Her eyes and facial expression searched Kirby, who had extricated himself from this situation temporarily by setting a glass on the bar and starting a drink.

"I supplied Reverend Billie with a sufficient number of selected facts about Mr. Caton. He will be able to insert them into a short comment reflecting the loss to us all," intoned Spottswood.

"We'll be down in the morning to see what kind of a job you've done, Spotty. You keep everything nice and quiet down there tonight, you hear?" She laughed and put down the phone. Kirby handed her a Scotch.

"Did you call G. Markham?" she asked him.

"Why should I do that before we got back?"

"What the hell, you called old Spottswood and hired

some preacher, didn't you?" She lit a cigarette and took in half of her drink.

"I called Spottswood to make the arrangements for some sort of a transfer from that fairy undertaker up in Connecticut to Orangeburrow. The Connecticut place wouldn't complete the shipment until I gave them at least the phone number of Spottswood's Funeral Home. As a matter of fact, it was Hitchcock's assistant who called Spottswood while you were picking out the casket." He paused in his explanation to study Pat's face and was satisfied that she was accepting his story. "Spottswood asked for the name of the family preacher, and I told him to find somebody local who wouldn't make too big a fuss about the whole burial. For all Myrl would care, you could have asked for Fulton Sheen."

Pat giggled and stared into her drink. "Do you think G. Markham is home yet?" she asked.

"Don't you think calling him will make you sound a little anxious about the money?" asked Kirby.

Pat thought about that for a few moments and then nodded slowly. "But I still want to know what the hell is up," she said defensively. She opened the telephone file to the appropriate letter and found Hurst's home number. After dialing, she handed the phone to Kirby Morris and sat back grinning devilishly. The phone buzzed distantly in Kirby's ear, but in the quiet home of G. Markham Hurst, it gave off a polite chime. The Hurst residence was located on a choice waterfront lot on the west side of Davis Island. The area had been developed as a posh residential area some fifteen to twenty years previously, and now was accepted by many of the older Tampa families as an address of distinction.

"Mr. Hurst's residence," a voice said.

"This is Mr. Morris," Kirby said in a firm and formal tone. "I would like to speak to Mr. Hurst."

"Just one moment," the maid said dutifully. "I'll see if Mr. Hurst can be disturbed."

Kirby had visions of the old lawyer asleep on the living-room couch with a partly filled brandy snifter on the low table next to him.

Kirby's fantasies were interrupted by Hurst's low-pitched voice.

"G. Markham Hurst," he announced formally.

"G. Markham, this is Kirby Morris. We're back from Connecticut and we brought Caton's body. What do we do next?" Kirby looked at Pat as if to extract from her eyes the theme of the next question.

"I suggest you bury him," said G. Markham somberly. He was obviously not pleased about being called to the phone at home for another Caton-Morris problem.

"Spottswood in Orangeburrow will take care of that to-morrow, thanks," replied Kirby equally sternly. He knew that old Hurst did not like a business call at home, but damn it, he got nearly all of Ruscaton's legal business, and that should guarantee a little service once in a while. "I mean about the insurance papers," said Kirby. "Do we have to come in and sign any more to make the claim?"

"You can attend to that in the morning at the office if you wish," said G. Markham. "But I suggest that you proceed slowly with the claim concerning Mr. Caton's death."

"Why? What's wrong?" asked Kirby.

Pat spilled her drink in a frantic effort to get closer to the phone.

"If the death certificate says suicide, the company will balk about paying off that policy within two years of the date of issue." Hurst paused to let Kirby savor that legal pearl. "As a matter of fact, they might not want to pay off at all."

Kirby's face dropped as he whispered, "Holy shit."

Pat took the phone from his suddenly limp hand and said, "What's going on, G. Markham? Kirby's just had a stroke."

"Give him a drink and put him to bed, Pat dear," said G. Markham softly. "All I said was, 'The insurance people might not want to pay off on a suicide.'"

Pat's phony smile froze on her face and then fell away

in pieces. G. Markham Hurst's voice became weaker and fainter as he said, "But don't worry, you've got our law firm and we'll do everything that is possible to—" as Pat put down the phone, stunned.

10

Pat had broken out of her basic black and moved up to a trim, gray suit. Spottswood hovered nearby, attired in a less-than-crisp black suit and a white shirt. He looked toward the casket and admired the exposed face of Myrl Caton. The facial coloring—carefully redone to correct the Connecticut shade—was, in his humble self-appraisal, no less than perfect.

Some of Caton's friends and drinking buddies approached the casket and looked in, looked away just as fast, and retreated into small groups at the rear of the funeral parlor to talk about better days. A couple of them approached Pat and offered condolences which she accepted mechanically.

The Reverend Billie Alford, complete with small black book with ribbons, came up to the mourners with lengthy strides and a yeoman handshake. "Morning, folks," he offered in a voice louder than one would anticipate for the front viewing room. Spottswood offered the introductions between the cleric and the laity.

"Reverend Alford," Pat said, "I do hope you will be

considerate enough to keep the services as brief as Mr. Caton would have wanted."

"It doesn't take long to ask the good Lord for his blessing," assured Reverend Billie. He beamed a wide smile which showed a missing pre-molar and opened his Bible to a ribboned page. As he did, Kirby joined the group, nodded to Pat and Spottswood, and looked over the shoulder of Reverend Billie. "Looking for an appropriate text to cite over the body?" Kirby asked. Reverend Billie looked backward at Kirby and nodded gravely.

"It is important to select one's scripture with care befitting the man and the occasion," he intoned somberly. "I had in mind John 11:25. 'I am the Resurrection and the Life.'" As a matter of fact, the Reverend Billie expounded on that text at every funeral to which he was summoned.

Kirby moved easily to Pat's side. "G. Markham is coming in behind me," he whispered in her ear.

She whirled around to face the door and saw the stately frame of the old lawyer enter the room. He nodded silently to Pat, signed the guest register, and went to Caton's body. He gazed on the cosmetized face for a long time and may have prayed. Kirby and Pat watched closely. Kirby presumed that G. Markham was offering mental good wishes for the happy repose, while Pat was sure that his whole stance was a performance for two clients.

G. Markham turned from the casket, approached Pat, and offered his condolences. She accepted them silently.

The Reverend Billie had assumed a position behind a small, draped lectern. Without warning, he began his services.

"Oh merciful Lord," he half sang, eyes cast heavenward and hands uplifted. "We are gathered here today to commend to you the spirit of our dear departed friend, Myrl Caton." He paused to let his words echo down the empty corridor of the funeral home. "You know, Lord, his wrong doings and his good works far better than any of us. We ask that he be forgiven for all of his sins and that you find a place for him near your heart forever. He will be missed in this community by those of us who knew and loved him."

Pat moved two steps closer to G. Markham Hurst, who stood respectfully. "Did you get hold of the insurance people?" she whispered in his ear.

"This morning," he whispered back.

"Our hearts will be heavy on those days when we reflect on the hard fact that he has been taken from. . . ." Billie droned on.

"What did they say?"

"We have to file claim."

". . . his death, a reality, we can accept more easily knowing that you, dear Lord. . . ."

"When?"

". . . and the hope of an afterlife. . . ."

"As soon as possible—today maybe."

". . . with the angels and the dear departed loved ones from ages before. . . ."

"Do I have to sign anything?"

"No, I'll take care of it for you."

". . . am the Resurrection and the Life, he who believes in me, though he may die. . . ."

"Do you think there will be any trouble?"

"Hard to tell."

"Shhhh," said Spottswood softly.

". . . forever in a cool place up above. . . ."

"What about the death certificate?"

"It says 'suicide.' "

". . . without continuing our sadness and remorse. . . ."

"Who's got it?"

"Spottswood."

". . . but death has lost its sting. . . ."

"What are you going to do?"

"File the claim anyway."

". . . Amen."

"Amen," said a chorus of Pat, Kirby, Spottswood, and G. Markham Hurst.

"We will be ready for the interment in about an hour,"

advised Spottswood softly. The cemetery had advertised above-ground mausoleum entombment, burial, or cremation. Pat had chosen traditional burial and purchased a concrete vault to line the grave for two hundred dollars. Spottswood disclaimed responsibility for the grave and vault and said that he only passed along costs.

The attendants closed the casket after Spottswood offered Pat a final opportunity to touch the body. She recoiled in subdued horror at the suggestion. The casket was wheeled into another room with somber cadences and the door was closed. The attendants, safely hidden in their own back room, attacked the casket lid with screwdrivers and bolted it shut.

"That ought to hold him," one of them said as he wiped his brow with the back of his coatsleeve.

"Never heard of any of them climbing out, did you?" asked the other, chuckling. They wheeled the casket to the back platform and rolled it noiselessly into the Spottswood Cadillac hearse. The faithful were still gathered together inside the front viewing room.

"If you don't mind, Mr. Spottswood, I'd appreciate a copy of the death certificate," said G. Markham.

"Certified copy?" asked Spottswood.

"Yes, I think so," said Hurst.

"Then you'll have to wait until I send for one from the Health Department in Middlebrook, Connecticut. They have to stamp it and put on a state seal to make it a valid copy," explained Spottswood. "Course, if you just want a copy of the information . . ."

"No, a certified copy will be required," said G. Markham quickly. "Send one to my office." He offered his card.

"Would you let me see your copy, Mr. Spottswood?" asked Kirby.

The funeral director nodded in agreement and disappeared into his office. He reappeared with a small white paper marked Certificate of Death, State of Connecticut. The transit form, authorizing interstate shipment of the body, was attached.

"Is this the same certificate you read to me over the phone this morning, Mr. Spottswood?" asked G. Markham.

"Yes, sir," he replied. He handed both documents to G. Markham. Pat and Kirby huddled close to him to get a better look at the forms. The death certificate gave the name of the deceased, his race, sex, address, marital information, and occupation as well as other background information. The cause of death was listed in the center of the form as "gunshot wound of chest, self-inflicted." A small box indicating suicide rather than homicide or accident was checked off. The bottom of the form bore the signature of Alberto Fortunelli, M.D., Coroner, Middlefork County, Connecticut.

"Suicide," whispered Kirby and Pat, reading in unison.

"I wonder," G. Markham said blankly. Pat and Kirby turned abruptly to him and appeared surprised. Noticing this, G. Markham continued his statement, but in a more positive tone. "—if you'd mind making me a Xerox of this certificate—to use until the official copy comes from Connecticut?" He handed the document back to Spottswood.

"Not at all," said Spottswood. "But could it wait until after the gravesite ceremonies?" He motioned them toward the door with a graceful sweep of his hand. G. Markham did not reply, but took Pat gently by the elbow and, laying her arm on his, led the brief procession to the Spottswood family limousine waiting under a roofed drive outside.

"That reminds me," said Pat as she entered the rear of the oversized car ahead of G. Markham. "What about Myrl's car in Middlebrook?"

"Took care of it," said Kirby.

"What do you mean, took care of it?" she asked.

"I hired the Hitchcock Funeral Home to drive it to Tampa. They send a kid down with the car—you know, at so much a day plus gas, and then we fly the kid back to Connecticut. Simple as that," Kirby explained smiling.

"Why didn't you tell me?" Pat asked.

"I wanted to see the look on your face when the car showed up in your driveway in Orangeburrow," Kirby laughed.

The Spottswood fleet pulled out onto the highway and headed for the cemetery. A sheriff's car preceded the hearse and the two family cars followed. There were few private automobiles in the procession. Each vehicle had its lights on, and the pace was kept to a safe but respectful fifty miles per hour. The sheriff's car turned into the cemetery and continued through, exiting by the back gate. The hearse pulled up to a freshly dug grave where the mound of new dirt had been covered by artificial grass. The square hole yawned inside the cement vault. The Reverend Billie hopped out of the second family car and stood at the head of the grave. He began to mumble immediately while Pat, Kirby, and G. Markham stood back to allow the attendants room to place the casket on the lowering straps.

"Tell him that's enough," Pat said to Spottswood as she gestured in the general direction of Reverend Billie. Spottswood hurried to the side of Reverend Billie and whispered in his ear. The man of the cloth looked up astonished, closed his book, and marched to the car like an angry boy.

"And now what, Mrs. Caton?" asked Spottswood self-righteously.

"Lower him," she said firmly. Spottswood looked first at Pat Caton, then at Kirby, who shrugged, and then at G. Markham, who looked at the sky. He motioned to his two attendants, and they began to crank the casket down into the vault space. Pat picked up a handful of dirt and threw it on the casket. She went to the car.

Kirby and G. Markham looked blankly at Spottswood. The three stared at each other briefly and then returned to the car. Somewhat more quickly than they had gone to the cemetery, the group drove back to the funeral home.

"I suspect that it will be several weeks until we hear from the insurance company," said G. Markham, as he stepped out of the funeral car and headed toward his own. "I'll definitely keep in touch."

"We're counting on you," said Kirby. As Kirby said "we," Pat turned to look at his face.

"Don't make this too much of a partnership," she said. "I thought I was the biggest beneficiary on that insurance deal."

"You are, Pat, you are," he assured her. "I meant all of us—you, me, the business, the people out at Ruscaton . . ."

"They would have knifed Myrl any night if they thought they could get away with it. Now I suppose that I'm going to worry about their welfare. I'll tell you one thing, Kirby. You don't have a man on the road to hustle those damned tomatoes anymore. You won't be able to sit on your ass in the office and split the profits. I'm going to take my insurance money and then I'm taking my half of that stinking company, and I'm moving out to Miami Beach or Barbados or somewhere."

"You might need some of these people you crap on some day," warned Kirby.

"That will be one hell of a day," said Pat, laughing. "Let's see if this Mixmaster of yours will make it over to my place for a drink." Kirby climbed in the driver's side of the red Porsche and gunned it across the narrow parking lot.

11

It was a few weeks later when G. Markham Hurst and his younger associate, Paul Erickson, reached the office of Mark Campbell, M.D., in the Department of Pathology of the University of South Florida School of Medicine. A young secretary brightened when Paul Erickson inquired about their appointment. Erickson's blond hair was beginning to gray, but, at thirty-four he held his youthful looks quite well. Mark Campbell's secretary immediately joined the ranks of Erickson's female admirers when he stood in front of her desk in a pale blue shirt, narrow-cut green sport jacket, off-green striped trousers, and brown desert boots.

"You may go right in," she said pleasantly.

"Thank you very much," Erickson said directly and very personally to her. He opened the door which read Mark Campbell, M.D., Forensic Pathologist. The office was spacious and carpeted in a deep green shag. There were black leather-covered chairs and sofas in small groups, while in the center of the front wall stood a massive carved Spanish desk. Behind it sat Mark Campbell.

He stood up and offered his hand first to G. Markham Hurst.

"Mark, this is one of my trial associates, Paul Erickson," said Hurst.

"Mr. Erickson's reputation has preceded him," said Mark Campbell.

"Dr. Campbell, it's entirely my pleasure," said Erickson. "I have read several of your articles on the proof of sudden death and the identification of gunshot wounds."

"Those were submitted to fill space in the forensic-science journals to let the medical world know that the medical examiner's office still functioned," Campbell minimized. His articles were accepted as among the most careful studies of medical-legal topics by both doctors and lawyers alike.

"You wrote those when you were still in Denver, didn't you, Mark?" asked G. Markham. "Before they made you full professor here, right?"

Campbell smiled broadly and nodded. "Couldn't resist this job when they made the offer. It's different, not being tied up in day-by-day medical examiner's work. Teaching medical-legal material to the medical students and doing forensic science research is a refreshing change after all these years," Campbell explained.

"It's easier to perform an expert service than to teach it, isn't it, Doctor?" asked Erickson.

"Very much so," agreed Campbell. "These medical students have longer to question me than you lawyers do in court."

"And they know what the big words mean," Erickson chuckled. "That gives them a decided advantage."

"I'll bet not many medical terms slip by you, Mr. Erickson," said Campbell.

"Paul knows more medicine than some of the doctors practicing in Tampa," agreed G. Markham Hurst, "as a lot of them found out in Miami when he represented some angry patients against their hospitals."

Erickson shifted uneasily in his chair.

"I suppose that Mr. Hurst has given you some of the

75

background information on our case," he said, pointedly steering the conversation to the Caton matter.

Campbell nodded and opened a thin manila folder in front of him. "He gave me most of it, I guess, and I've read all that," said Campbell. "But I'd like to hear your version of the story and what you intend to prove." He sat back in his high-backed rocker.

"Well, here's the way I see this whole mess," said Erickson, opening his black attaché case. "This vegetable farmer, Caton—"

"Tomatoes," interrupted G. Markham softly.

"—tomato farmer—goes to Connecticut to pick up next season's orders. He's kind of a wild guy who has a history of trouble. He has a fight with the vegetable—I mean tomato—wholesaler in Connecticut over some woman both of them have been seeing. The next day he's found in his motel room, shot in the chest. The gun is on the floor and the door is locked. The local police up there call it a suicide." He paused and looked at Campbell. "The cops in Connecticut check out the scene, shoot some pictures, and the local coroner pronounces him dead—but there's no real body exam or autopsy, you understand."

Campbell nodded silently.

"So they clear the scene as a suicide, the doc signs him out, the body is shipped home and buried. We file a claim against the insurance company and they send it back unpaid."

"Too young a policy?" asked Campbell anticipating.

"Exactly," said Erickson, pulling another small packet of papers from his case. "Under our Florida statutes, the insurer has two years from date of issue to contest the cause of death. After that, he is stuck with it, suicide or not. That's to prevent some bird from buying a big policy and then shooting himself right after he signs it."

"In Colorado, it was one year, I think," said Campbell.

"I have it here, Paul," said G. Markham. He pulled a pad from his inside jacket pocket, adjusted his glasses, and began to read aloud. "Florida Statutes Revised. Chapter

627: Insurance Code: Rates and Contracts, 627.0204. Incontestability: There shall be a provision that the policy shall be incontestable after it has been in force during the lifetime of the insured for a period of two years from its date of issue, except for nonpayment of premiums, and except, at the option of the insurer, as to provisions relative to benefits in event of disability and as to provisions which grant additional insurance specifically against death by accident or accidental means." He took off his glasses and silently returned the floor to Erickson.

"The problem here, Dr. Campbell, is that the policy does indeed have an accidental-death provision, but suicide is not satisfactory for either that portion or for the basic benefit, since the date of issue is so recent," Erickson supplied carefully.

"So you need the death to be something other than suicide," said Campbell.

Both Erickson and G. Markham smiled broadly.

"A determination like that would be an invaluable aid in this case, Doctor," said G. Markham somberly.

"You sent me a copy of the death certificate," said Campbell. "Do you have copies of the scene photographs?"

"We have requested copies from the Middlebrook Police Department, and I expect that they will be along any day now. When they get here I'll have big blowups made of each one so that you can see the details," said Erickson. Big blowup photographs in the courtroom were almost an Erickson trademark by now.

"Be sure that they send copies of all their pictures. We don't want some ace-in-the-hole sprung on us in court."

Erickson was elated at Campbell's use of the word "us" so soon in the case, but he contained his joy with a poker face.

"We have also requested that the gun be returned to us and that the ballistics report from Middlebrook be supplied," said G. Markham.

"The interesting twist in this case," explained Erickson, "is that it is the insurance company's burden to prove the suicide. We will file a death claim and allege accident, homicide, or unknown. Then the insurance company will have to come back and prove that it was none of these, but in fact a suicide."

"That's a different point of view from the usual plaintiff's case, isn't it?" asked Campbell.

"So really all you have to do is to study their proof and help me criticize it sufficiently that the jury is not convinced," said Erickson.

"Beyond a reasonable doubt?" offered Campbell.

"No, not that far," corrected G. Markham. "This is a civil case, and as such, one need only prove it with the preponderance of the evidence rather than beyond a reasonable doubt."

"If the jury believes something is 49% white and 51% black, black wins," added Erickson. "The reason for this lesser quantum of proof is that only money is involved. In a criminal case, someone's life may be at stake, and the court wants the jury even more convinced."

"How much money is involved here, gentlemen?" asked Campbell straightforwardly. While the medical expert was not allowed to base his fee on whether or not the plaintiff wins or on a percentage of the recovery, as the lawyers do, he could legitimately take into consideration the amount at stake and thereby pace his efforts more reasonably. It would be ruinous to put in six months of effort to help a client prove a medical point if the maximum anticipated award was a token amount.

Erickson and G. Markham looked at each other blankly. It was not the policy of their firm to disclose the amounts of insurance coverage or offers of settlements to persons other than their clients. G. Markham nodded almost imperceptibly to Erickson. "In excess of $300,000," he said softly.

A low whistle came from the forensic pathologist. "I'll try to keep my fee less than that," he said, laughing.

"Considerably less, if you don't mind," said Erickson, and smiled.

"I will also need the coroner's report," said Campbell.

"All I have is a brief comment in your copy of the police report."

"That's all there is," said Erickson simply.

"You mean that there is no full coroner's report?" asked Campbell.

"The police in Middlebrook say that all they get from their doctor in this kind of case is a phone call and a death certificate. If they are really lucky, he might send them a ten-word letter stating the cause of death, but usually he reserves such careful work for homicide," said Erickson.

"That's the type of forensic science that makes my job so difficult," moaned Campbell. "In the United States today, most medical-legal autopsies are performed by persons who are not properly trained in medical examiner's cases or who are not even pathologists."

G. Markham looked mildly surprised.

"In many of the larger cities," Campbell continued, "there are well-organized medical examiners or coroners, but outside of these metropolitan areas, a dead body, if it is examined at all, will be seen by the local physician. And he may never have seen a similar case previously."

"That seems to be the state of the art in Middlebrook, Connecticut," said Erickson. "At least their coroner did not do much in this case."

"Where is the bullet now?" asked Campbell.

"In him somewhere, I guess," said Erickson.

"In him?" asked Campbell, astonished. "But you said the weapon was a .45!"

"It was—an Army automatic," supplied G. Markham.

"Then the chances are that it came right out through his back somewhere," announced Campbell.

"But, Doctor," protested Erickson, "the police report states that there was no exit wound."

"No exit wound," the pathologist repeated simply.

"All they recovered was the shell from the shot that was fired," said Erickson.

"Where was that?" asked Campbell, his interest growing.

79

"It was standing on its base at the head of the bed," said Erickson.

Campbell closed his eyes and tried to visualize how Myrl Caton could have held his .45 automatic so that when he fired at his own chest, the ejected shell would be thrown above his own head and land in the position described by Erickson. "Doesn't sound too likely," he said as he made mock gripping movements with his hands on his own chest.

"What's not likely?" asked Erickson.

"That the shell would land at the head of the bed like that," Campbell said.

"Are you sure?" asked G. Markham Hurst.

"Reasonably," said Campbell, "but what you need is your own ballistics man."

"Do you know one?" asked Erickson.

"Most of the ballistics people I know are connected with police departments around the country," Campbell supplied.

"Would they testify against another police department's findings?" asked Erickson.

"By and large, they are pretty objective forensic scientists. I don't think they would be influenced by the fact that they were opposing some other police department. You have to get someone as an expert. The judge will never let me as a pathologist express opinion concerning the path of that ejected shell. Somebody will have to come in with at least the paper qualifications as to his expertise in ballistics and firearms identification."

"Like whom?" asked G. Markham precisely.

"Well, let's see," said Mark Campbell as he opened the current roster of the American Academy of Forensic Sciences, an organization composed of forensic pathologists, medical-legal psychiatrists, criminalists, toxicologists, and police scientists. "With three hundred thousand at stake, you can afford to spend a little on travel and expenses," Campbell noted, paging through the small directory.

"We need a competent and cooperative ballistics man," agreed G. Markham.

"It seems to me that Milan Havlicek might be your man. He was professor of criminalistics at the University of Indiana, and has umpteen years of army and police ballistics experience. He used to be the gun man for the Chicago Police Department." Campbell settled on a page in the directory. "Here he is, Milan Havlicek, Associate Professor, Department of Sociology (Police Science), University of Indiana, Bloomington, Indiana (Retired), Fellow, Criminalistics section. That's in the Forensic Academy," explained Campbell.

"They give phone numbers there?" asked Erickson as he made hurried notes.

"Yes," said Campbell simply, "but I'm sure my girl could get him for you." He depressed a lever on his intercom and said to his secretary, "Estrella, get me Milan Havlicek at Sun City, will you?"

"Sun City, Florida?" asked Erickson. Campbell nodded.

"Doctor, if this man has been already embalmed and buried, would there be anything left to examine? I mean if we dug him up?" asked Erickson.

"The term is 'exhumed,'" corrected Campbell, smiling gently.

"OK, if we were to exhume the body," said Erickson, pronouncing the word with mock precision, "what kind of shape would it be in now?"

"I suspect that there would be some drying of the fingers and toes, partial liquefaction of the brain, some gas formation in the solid organs of the abdomen, and general preservation of most body structures," said Mark Campbell. He had seen dozens of exhumations during his career as medical examiner and was quite aware that the degree of preservation depended on the adequacy of the embalming plus the conditions of the grave. Where the ground is frozen most of the year, a body may be strikingly well preserved long after interment. But where the ground is wet and warm, decay may proceed rapidly despite the embalmer's promises to the bereaved.

"But what would we gain for our side of the case?" cautioned G. Markham Hurst. "We already have the Connecticut coroner's statement in the police report which says that it is a suicide by gunshot."

"But that's just what they *thought*, Mr. Hurst," pleaded Erickson. "To the Connecticut cops, it was an open-and-shut case. Locked door, gun on the floor—suicide. No need to examine the body further. Ship it to Florida and get it to hell out of Middlebrook. That's all they wanted. We have damn little to lose by digging him up and letting Dr. Campbell here have a look at him. What if the bullet isn't even a .45?"

"Then where is the shot fired from Caton's .45?" Campbell asked. "You still have the empty shell to account for."

"OK—so Caton shot at his assailant, missed, and the shot went out the open door into the motel courtyard," Erickson offered.

"By that theory, Caton was killed by some other person who came through the door?" asked G. Markham incredulously.

"Maybe—maybe not." Erickson said. "Maybe the murderer shoots Caton at the door or through the space allowed when the door is opened against the night chain."

"Could he make it back to bed if he were shot at the door, Mark?" G. Markham Hurst asked.

Campbell puffed on his unlit pipe and nodded slowly. "It is safe to say that any given individual, no matter how badly shot, could dance across a room, whistle *Yankee Doodle*, sign his last will and testament, and finish his tea, before actually dying of frankly lethal wounds. In any group of such cases, the odds will be against such activities, but I've long ago given up stating what a fatally wounded man can or cannot do before dying. Just as soon as I pontificate on such an impossibility, the other side parades in some expert who knows of one case to refute me. War records are filled with reports of combat victims running several yards and performing impossible feats even though they had sustained a wound obviously causing 'sudden death.' "

"So he could get shot at the motel door and then stumble backward into the bed," suggested Erickson.

". . . and fire his own .45 out into the courtyard—" contributed Hurst.

"Or into the assailant," Erickson interrupted.

"—drop the .45 on the rug, sprawl across the bed, and die quietly enough that no one in the whole motel heard a shot," continued Hurst.

"I'll accept the fact that no one in the motel heard the shot," said Campbell. "Lots of people sleep soundly enough that irrelevant noises do not wake them or register in their memories. But why do you need to shoot Caton at the door? Why not shoot him from the door as he sits on the bed?"

Erickson beamed wildly and joined eagerly with Mark Campbell as their imaginations raced to synthesize some plausible explanation for the death of Myrl Caton other than the suicide.

"I suppose too, Dr. Campbell, that a nimble burglar could hook or unhook that chain latch with a bent coat hanger from the outside. That way he could shoot him from inside the room, latch the chain with the coat hanger, and run," said Erickson.

"But he'd have to stand out there on that front sidewalk fiddling with some bent coat hanger, in full view of the motel office, not knowing whether or not the shot was heard." G. Markham Hurst shook his head sadly. "No, gentlemen, I cannot conceive of such a cool character as this. If he wanted his money he could shoot Caton, rob him, and run out the door. If it's an argument, he could shoot him and run—he could even take Caton's car. But to ask me to believe that he shot him and then calmly stood outside the door and fussed with a bent coat hanger until he latched that chain! Too farfetched, gentlemen, too farfetched." G. Markham stood up, walked to the window, and looked out on the University of South Florida medical school campus.

"Dr. Campbell?" a female voice asked from the intercom on the desk.

"Yes, Estrella."

"Professor Havlicek is on line two, sir."

Campbell picked up the phone and swiveled his chair around to allow his feet to rest heavily on the corner of the desk. "Milan?" asked the pathologist in a friendly tone. "This is Mark Campbell ... I'm fine. And you? ... No, not since the convention in Chicago.... No, you were the one who was drunk; *I* was merely a little stoned." Campbell laughed loudly, and Erickson grinned with empathy.

"Milan, we've got a problem case here that you may be able to help us with," said Campbell. "We've got an alleged suicide with a .45 army-style automatic which the police say was held to the chest of a man who was lying on a bed. Yeah, that's right, lying on his back. Now, Milan, what we want to know is, if the gun were held in that position, where would the ejected shell go?" Campbell paused and listened intently, nodding his head occasionally as if to follow the conversation being poured into his ear. Campbell pulled a small pad into the center of his desk and began to sketch a rough diagram of a .45 automatic pistol, pointed downward and ejecting an empty shell forward along a gently curving arc.

"So it could end up somewhere above his head, Milan?" asked Campbell with a tone of disappointment. He looked at Erickson and shrugged as if to glean from the young lawyer additional questions for the ballistics expert.

"Ask him if Caton could have depressed all those safety levers on the .45 with it held like that," urged Erickson. Campbell nodded. "Milan—could the man have held down the proper combination of safety levers to fire the .45 in that position?" Campbell asked into the phone. After a brief pause, he nodded affirmatively to Erickson.

Erickson shot his eyes to the ceiling, jammed one fist into his other palm and abruptly stood up.

"I don't know, Milan, some sort of an insurance beef concerning the proof of death. You know, suicide or accident—" Campbell was obviously interrupted by the voice on the phone. "—couldn't be accidental?" Campbell parroted. "Too awkward to accidentally depress all the safety devices and the trigger at the same time, he says," Campbell explained to Erickson.

"How about murder?" prompted Erickson.

"How about murder?" echoed Campbell into the phone. "How 'bout your ass too, wise guy," laughed Campbell. "Milan, it's good talking to you. I'll have these lawyers send you a modest fee—" He paused as if interrupted. "Because a modest fee is all you're worth, bullethead. If they want your full act, they'll call you. Stay sober. And give my regards to Marta." There was another pause and chuckle. "Marta Havlicek, your wife, that's which Marta. See you, Milan." Campbell hung up still laughing and looked up in time to see G. Markham Hurst and Paul Erickson exchanging somber glances.

"I'm going out to soak up a big dry martini," announced Erickson as he gathered his papers and stuffed them into his attaché case.

"I'll buy," said G. Markham Hurst ponderously.

"You guys are born pessimists," said Mark Campbell, smiling. "Go get your gin and call me when the scene photographs come in," he said as he opened the door to the outer office.

Erickson and then Hurst shook his hand silently as they left the forensic pathologist's office. Erickson searched the doctor's face for a clue, but the devilish grin hid everything.

"Your wheels are spinning, aren't they, Doc?" asked Erickson.

"They never stop, Paul," Mark Campbell said as he closed his office door.

12

The body of Myrl Caton had been buried in Orange-burrow for several weeks now, and Hervey Higgs could not help wondering what it looked like inside the casket. He sat at his desk rereading a slim stack of legal-sized papers and trying to figure out what sort of a plan had been hatched by the brains of G. Markham, et al. He looked up at the ceiling as if to see through the intervening several floors of The Bank of Tampa building into the offices of Chatam, Kellogg, Hurst, Mitchell and Rodriguez. His glasses were cocked up onto the prominence of his slightly bulging forehead. He rubbed his pudgy hand across his bald head and scratched meditatively at the brief rim of hair above his ears.

"What the hell are you up to this time, G. Markham?" Higgs inquired of the blank ceiling.

"They just want to beat us out of a couple of hundred grand," answered Red Spencer, his co-counsel for the Tampa region of the Insurance Group. Red was a night-school lawyer from Atlanta who thought like a cop and practiced like a street fighter. To Red, everyone's claim was a phony; he would be willing to doubt the authenticity of his own mother's marriage license. He stood looking out the window at the lights of the city below him. From that floor of the bank building, Tampa with its tinsel of colored neon could have been a section of Atlanta. But at ground level, the level at which Spencer worked best, it was plain old Tampa to him, even after twelve years in this assignment.

"Our position has to be that they took a perfectly obvious suicide, dressed it up with some classical doubts and questions, and are now slapping us with a claim for full accidental benefits," he said.

"Did you make them an offer?" asked Higgs.

"Offer, my ass," said Red. "If they want to squeeze us on this one, they'll have to take it to the Supreme Court."

"Red, you know, and I know, and they know, that we'll pay for something rather than fight it out."

"Not this time, Hervey. The home office said 'No more sell-out settlements.' They want us to crack down and try a few. The State Commissioner won't let the company raise the rates to make up the difference. So if we pay them, it's money down the drain."

Higgs turned to his partner. "Okay, let's look at what they've got. Here's some slob up in Connecticut with a suicidal gunshot wound—or at least so says their police department. The burden of proof for the suicide theory is ours, Red, and we haven't got squat on which to base a fighting case."

"We've got the police report and the coroner's certificate," Red offered.

"Sure—and we've got a still-cocked .45 automatic with an empty shell standing on its end at the head of the bed. You and I and every reasonable man in the world knows that a dead man in bed in a locked motel room is a suicide under these circumstances. But who knows what some jury is going to think?" Higgs argued. "Where's our motive for suicide?"

"He'd just lost a big account in Connecticut. Everybody at the Country Club knows how his wife plays

87

around with his partner. Besides, he drinks like a fish and you never need a suicide motive for an alcoholic," Spencer said, counting on his fingers.

"Come on, Red, you saw the police pictures of the scene."

"Saw them? Shit, I've memorized them! I know damned well they could cost us the whole case." Spencer charged across Higgs's office and took a stack of photographs from behind a file cabinet. There were six photos, and each had been enlarged to 18 by 24 inches. Some of them were spot enlargements of selected portions of other pictures.

"Look at those bloodstains," said Spencer dejectedly. "Do you think that Hurst and that vulture Erickson are going to miss the direction of those stains? Or that we could waltz into federal court and convince the judge and jury that blood flows uphill in Connecticut?" He paused to grind out his cigarette in an oversized ash tray.

Higgs took one of the spot enlargements from Spencer and studied it again. In the photograph, Myrl Caton was sprawled across the bed, face up. His shirt was partly pulled up and there was a bloody area on the left chest. The photographs were black and white, but all the spots that looked like blood had a similar appearance which helped to distinguish them from other stains on the shirt.

Red Spencer reached forward and pointed with a poorly-manicured finger at a particular batch of blood stains on the shirt. "Look at those, Hervey-boy. See how they run? All down. Down toward the feet! He had to be standing up or sitting up when he was shot."

"Or else he got up after he was shot," offered Higgs.

"Oh, bullshit, Hervey," said Spencer. "This guy's got a .45 in his heart and you want him to get up and dance a jig before he has the common courtesy to flop down and die."

"We've got to dig him up. No autopsy—no heart wound," said Higgs mechanically. "Chest wound, OK. But not heart."

"Dig him up—dig him up," said Spencer in an impatient sing-song. "You sound like a goddam ghoul with your shovel ready behind the door."

"What do we have to lose?" inquired Hervey Higgs with practiced patience. "If the entrance wound shows powder burns, our case for suicide will be strengthened. If there aren't any powder burns we'll argue that the shirt caught all the powder. And remember, Red, the Middlebrook police allowed the undertaker to burn all the clothes along with the bloody sheets and mattress."

Red Spencer nodded in agreement. He had already agonized over the situation created by the Middlebrook police, who allowed most of the real evidence to be destroyed. "At least they could have inspected the sheet and mattress under the body for a bullet hole."

"What for?" mocked Hervey Higgs. "The Hitchcock Funeral Home post-mortem experts swear there was no exit wound!"

"Yeah, but you know what Dr. Leatherman says about that," said Spencer.

Dr. Leatherman was the chief medical examiner in Miami. He had probably seen more gunshot wounds than any other man except the medical examiner of New York City. An excited, slightly balding man in his mid-forties, Jerry Leatherman was ranked by his forensic colleagues as among the best in the country. When the Miami office was established, he became its first chief medical examiner and had held the job ever since. Junior associates universally found him difficult to work with because his own extraordinary energy and near-genius intelligence kept him constantly involved in cases that they considered "theirs." Leatherman also had a weakness for collecting mementos of his cases. His office was a junkheap of bullets, homemade cannons, miswired electrical appliances, food canisters with rat poisons, photographs of flaming automobiles, pictures of floating, half-eaten bodies in Biscayne Bay, bones and broken teeth, shattered glass from automobile headlights, and a tightly bound group of dynamite sticks.

Given the slightest encouragement, Jerry Leatherman, M.D., would launch into a thorough explanation of the whole case surrounding each item in the collection. In their first meeting, Red Spencer had discovered this; but not before he had been treated to an hour-long explanation of how an antitank gun had come to be confiscated in the apartment of two University of Miami marine-biology co-eds. The insurance lawyer was finally able to keep Leatherman to the circumstances surrounding the death of Myrl Caton long enough to sift several pertinent observations from the verbal mountain of forensic garbage Leatherman showered upon him. Among the more interesting facts were the observations that Leatherman considered it highly improbable that the .45-caliber bullet had not exited—he knew of hundreds of gunshot wounds of every conceivable caliber, including an industrial stud gun which shot fatal rivets; he attempted to describe most of them—and possible that Caton had indeed shot himself while lying on his back in bed only to sit up, afterward, bleed downward on his shirt, and then collapse—he recalled several men, women, and children who had been shot, stabbed, bludgeoned, or otherwise fatally injured who had walked, run, staggered, ridden bicycles, taken elevators, or performed other implausible gymnastic feats prior to performing the expected courtesy of lying fatally still.

"From what you said, Dr. Leatherman was not too impressed by the police photographs," said Hervey Higgs, leaning back in his chair.

"At least he didn't think that those damned downward bloodstains indicated that Caton had to be standing up or sitting up at the time he was shot," agreed Spencer. "Do you think that old G. Markham and Erickson the Viking spotted those stains?" Spencer forcefully scratched his behind without embarrassment.

"Like an eagle spots a rabbit running across the desert," Hervey Higgs assured him.

"He didn't mention it or anything, did he, Hervey?" asked Spencer in a tone which already suggested a negative reply.

"My dear Red," began Hervey Higgs slowly, "G. Markham Hurst would not mention it if he personally witnessed the Statue of Liberty piss in the harbor. The only thing more taciturn than that crotchety old bastard is a deaf-and-dumb priest leaving a confessional."

"But they must have some angle on this case that we're missing," worried Red Spencer. "I mean, they couldn't file this suit on just these few facts. Could they?"

"Paul Erickson is a guts-ball player. My guess is that he will go for a settlement based on our inability to prove the damned suicide. I'll also bet that G. Markham is along for the ride, since his firm represents Ruscaton Incorporated anyway. To me, this is an Erickson production all the way."

"Except for good old Pat."

"Dear, loving, and devoted Pat is pushing Erickson against the wall at every turn, I assure you. I'll bet that she has poor old G. Markham doubling his tranquilizer dose before the case is half argued."

"And has Erickson in bed before a jury is picked," added Spencer.

"Hell, she bedded him before the case was filed," said Hervey Higgs with a knowing grin. "You be careful that she doesn't get you."

"Not for me," said Spencer with a wave of his hand. "I'm not the Palma Ceia Country Club type. I like them barefoot, stupid, and comfortable. When I'm with a broad, I don't want to be entertaining too."

"What you want is an Eskimo squaw," offered Hervey. "Besides, what makes you think that Pat Caton is Palma Ceia stock? The only thing that got her in there was a pile of money and Kirby Morris. It certainly was in no way due to the social graces of Myrl Caton."

"Hell, Caton didn't even know where the Palma Ceia was."

"And vice versa," added Higgs.

Red Spencer turned to the window and continued to watch the lights of the city. "Who the hell ever heard of Middlebrook, Connecticut, anyway? I'll get as much out of those Yankees as Ho Chi Minh cross-examining the Pope."

"When you get up there, Red," advised Hervey Higgs with a chuckle, "just remember that Negro is spelled with one G."

13

A light Connecticut fall snowstorm had powdered the streets of Middlebrook, and an aged janitor was sweeping the high steps of the County Courthouse when Paul Erickson mounted them in twos. He glanced at his watch to reassure himself that it was still prior to nine o'clock as he pushed the large double door and entered the building. A high, rusty radiator hissed at him as if to announce that it had all it could do to heat its appointed portion of the hallway without repeated gasps of chilled New England air being let in by arriving lawyers and witnesses. Erickson found the entry labeled Witnesses Waiting Room and proceeded further down the corridor. The knob worked with a loud clack and the door swung open to expose the opposing counsel, Red Spencer, a court reporter, and Lt. Casper. Paul Erickson thrust his hand forward to Red Spencer and offered a wide smile.

"Damned cold up here, Red," he announced.

"It's not Atlanta in June, Paul," agreed Spencer in a drawl that sounded somehow more Southern with the Connecticut snow falling outside. "This is Lt. Casper of the local police department. And this is Ann Kane, the court reporter."

"Pleased to know you, Lieutenant," said Paul Erickson, shaking the policeman's hand. "Miss Kane," he added pleasantly. He put his briefcase on the nearest chair and unbuttoned his topcoat.

"We set up the depositions here, Paul, so that you and I and the court reporter wouldn't have to run all over town to see these people. There's nothing on the local court schedule for a couple of days and the judge said we could use the witness room," explained Spencer.

"Nice of him," said Erickson, glancing around the barren room. It had a 12-foot ceiling which sported a bare 60-watt bulb on a short hanging cord. The string to the light was dirty, limp, and too short by at least a foot. There were about eight captain's chairs surrounding a long, heavy, dark brown oak table which held a few worn copies of the *American Legion* magazine and a single issue of *Life*, two years old. On the wall were a few Currier and Ives prints which had been inserted into wide wooden frames obviously made for something a little larger. The glass in each picture was sticky with old fingerprints.

Erickson took a chair at the middle of the long table opposite Spencer's pile of yellow pads and papers. The police lieutenant took the seat at the head of the table and the court reporter began to test her stenotype machine with a series of stiff-fingered jabs.

"Off the record," Spencer said matter-of-factly to the court reporter, "Lieutenant—you understand that this deposition is being taken both for the purposes of discovery and for possible introduction into evidence at any trial which may later follow in Tampa. You are to answer the questions just as you would if you were actually in court, even though there is no judge or jury present."

The police lieutenant nodded knowingly.

"And from time to time, Mr. Spencer and I may get to objecting to what either of us says—so we'd appreciate it if you'd hold your answers just long enough for us to get that objection into the record before you bust out with an answer. All right?" added Paul Erickson.

"I've been deposed before, gentlemen," said Lt. Casper, adjusting his uniform jacket.

"Good! good!" said Red Spencer in a mocking tone. "OK, young lady, swear him in."

The court reporter stood and raised her right hand, and Lt. Casper did the same.

"Do you solemnly swear that the testimony you are about to give is the truth, the whole truth, and nothing but the truth, so help you God?" intoned Miss Kane limply.

"I do," affirmed Lt. Casper solemnly.

"You may be seated," said Miss Kane. Following her own invitation, she sat heavily in her chair and pulled the stenotype machine closer to her knees. Ann Kane was probably forty and wore a green sweater and a coarse brown wool skirt. Her stocking were cotton and wrinkled. On a nearby chair, she had parked her enormous shoulder bag. Paul Erickson had just finished thinking, "At least she doesn't chew gum," when she unwrapped a stick of Juicy Fruit, folded it twice, and put it in her mouth.

"State your name, please," Red Spencer said mechanically.

"Harrison Casper."

"Where are you employed?"

"I am a lieutenant with the Middlebrook police department."

"Were you so employed on July 15th of this year?"

"Yes, sir, I was."

"How long have you been a policeman?"

"A total of twenty-three years—including the service."

"What special training, if any, have you received during those twenty-three years with the police department?"

"I have taken six weeks at the FBI Academy at Quantico—that was before I was made a lieutenant—and two short courses in crime investigation at Northwestern University in Chicago," Casper said with noticeable pride.

"Are you also involved in the training of junior officers here in Middlebrook?"

"Yes, sir, I am responsible for twelve lectures on crime scenes, trace evidence, interrogation of suspects, transfer of prisoners, and report-writing for our rookies," announced Casper.

Red Spencer cleaned his fingernails with the smallest blade of his combination pocket knife and cigar trimmer as the lieutenant answered his questions.

"How many men do you have under you at this time, Lieutenant?" asked Spencer.

"Twenty—including all three shifts."

"Are these all assigned to homicide?"

"Well, homicide, rape, and robbery," said Casper somewhat apologetically. "We aren't quite large enough to assign entirely separate details for each area of activity. We group them into 'crimes against persons.' "

"In any event, Lieutenant, you are in charge of homicide, are you not?"

"Actually, Capt. Dunsmore is in charge, but he defers everything to me. In fact, I'm up for promotion to captain. Dunsmore is retiring."

"I see," said Red Spencer, making a note on a yellow pad. "But Capt. Dunsmore did not investigate the Caton case last July?"

"No, sir. I handled that one myself, and then submitted my report to the captain."

Red Spencer drew a small pad of yellow sheets from his briefcase and leafed through the upper few pages. There were multiple notes on each page, written in a large, bold hand with a felt-point marker.

"Lieutenant, I direct your attention to July 15th, and specifically to the Caton case. You may use your notes to refresh your recollection, if you wish."

The lieutenant glanced automatically at Paul Erickson, who nodded approval. The lieutenant took a folded Xerox copy of a report from his inside jacket pocket.

"Where were you on July 15th, Lieutenant?" inquired Red Spencer.

The stiff fingers of Ann Kane clumped rhythmically on the little keyboard, and the coded gibberish printed itself on the narrow paper folding into an attached tray.

"At police headquarters."

"Do you recall getting a call from the Brownstone Motel regarding a dead body?"

"Yes, sir."

"About what time was that?"

"It was three o'clock in the afternoon," said the lieutenant, glancing at his folded report. "I got the call from a uniformed officer who went to the scene."

"Is that your usual procedure?" asked Spencer.

"Yes, sir—a uniformed officer is sent out on all such calls, and if he feels that there is really something to investigate, then he calls homicide and we got out and take charge," explained the lieutenant.

"Where did you go when you got the call?"

"The Brownstone Motel."

"Would you describe what you saw there, Lieutenant?" Red Spencer lit a cigarette and blew the smoke toward the chipped ceiling.

"I was met by Mr. Clyde Peabody, the manager, who said—"

"Excuse me, Lieutenant," interrupted Paul Erickson. "You have to confine your remarks to what you saw and what you did. Please do not tell us what someone else told you." He smiled pleasantly.

Red Spencer nodded in reluctant agreement. His impatience was quite visible. The police lieutenant adjusted his notes and cleared his throat like a moose in heat.

"Mr. Peabody directed me to room 15, where I observed the body of the subject, a Mr. Myrl Caton. The body was lying on the bed, face up. He had been shot." Casper paused as if to invite questions.

"Was the door to the room locked, Lieutenant?" asked Red Spencer.

"Mr. Peabody had busted the chain before I got there."

"Objection," said Erickson softly. "Lieutenant, if you

didn't see Mr. Peabody break in the door, please don't attempt to testify to that fact."

"OK," said Casper. "The door chain was broken off the wall when I got there. The door was open."

Erickson smiled gently.

"What did you do then, Lieutenant?" asked Spencer.

"I carried out a routine crime-scene investigation and called for the coroner since there was a dead body involved."

"That was Dr. Fortunelli?" asked Spencer.

"Yes, sir, Dr. Fortunelli," echoed Casper softly.

"And did he in fact come to the motel room?"

"Yes, sir. He pronounced Mr. Caton dead and said—"

"Oops!" interjected Erickson. He raised his eyebrows and a finger in the air to warn the police lieutenant again.

"Sorry," said Casper softly.

"What else did you do, or direct to be done, to clear the scene?" asked Spencer.

"I ordered my technician to shoot pictures of the scene and then released the body to Hitchcock's Funeral Home." He gestured to indicate the general direction of the funeral home.

Red Spencer reached for a packet of photographs and offered them to the policeman.

"Are these the pictures that were taken at the scene?"

"Wait a minute," cautioned Erickson. "He had already said that he didn't take these pictures, so I object on the ground that they are hearsay to the lieutenant."

"But Paul," said Spencer, "we can subpoena the police technician to identify the pictures if you insist. All I want from the lieutenant is an admission that they generally represent the scene as he recalls seeing it."

"OK," said Erickson pleasantly. "Let him comment on the pictures as representing the scene as he recalls it, but not for the purpose of identifying the photographs as those actually taken by the police tech."

"Go ahead, Lieutenant, look at the pictures. Mark them defendant's exhibits one through six, Miss Kane," Spencer said.

The reporter stamped the back of each photograph and numbered them.

The police lieutenant examined each picture. "These are photographs of the scene inside room 15 at the Brownstone Motel. They show the body of Myrl Caton on the bed. This one shows the gun on the floor. This one shows the clothes on the floor and the chair. This one shows the entrance to the bathroom. This one shows the door to room 16." He placed the photographs in a stack as he reviewed them.

"Did you identify whose gun that was?" asked Spencer.

"It was Caton's," said the lieutenant before the objection could even form in Erickson's throat.

Erickson arched his eyes toward the ceiling in frustration. "Lieutenant," he said patiently. "If you didn't personally check out the ownership of the gun, please reserve your comments on ownership."

"Do you know of your own knowledge that the gun belonged to Mr. Caton, Lieutenant?" inquired Spencer.

"No," said Casper softly.

Erickson made a cryptic note on his yellow pad.

"What did you do next, Lieutenant?"

"I examined the bullet hole with the doc and then cleared the scene."

"How did you examine the bullet hole?" asked Spencer.

"You know—we looked at it and poked at it with a pencil. The doc wasn't too interested. What the hell, the guy was cold and dead. It was an open-and-shut suicide."

"Oh, Lieutenant!" said Erickson, as if he had been personally injured. "Please!"

"Well, at least it was until you guys started to ask a lot of questions about the case," defended Casper.

"Is it less certain now, Lieutenant?" asked Erickson playfully.

"Please, Paul," said Spencer. "You'll get your chance." He turned again to Casper. "Did you interrogate anyone else in the case, Lieutenant?"

"I talked to the folks over at Connecticut Valley Produce." He looked at his notes and then announced, "Vincent Irafino and Angela Gaito."

"Did they know Caton?" asked Spencer.

"Object."

"OK, I withdraw the question." Spencer looked at his notes and then at Lt. Casper. "Did you see any powder marks around the wound, Lieutenant?"

"Object on the basis that it is leading and that there has been no predicate laid to demonstrate the lieutenant's expertise in the identification of powder from other stains," droned Erickson.

"But we're here mainly for discovery, Paul," said Spencer.

"Sure, and if I don't object, you'll slip it into the trial," Erickson answered.

"OK, Lieutenant, you can go ahead and answer the question." The objection would be officially ruled on by the judge at the trial, and then the answer could be suppressed if the objection were sustained.

"There was powder on the shirt all around the entrance wound," said Casper. "It was a circle about so big," he said, indicating with his finger and thumb.

"Let the record reflect that the Lieutenant is indicating a circle about one inch in diameter," said Spencer mechanically. "Would the presence of this powder burn indicate a close-range shot, Lieutenant?"

"Same objection," said Erickson.

"Go ahead," Spencer urged the lieutenant.

"Very close. Probably a contact wound," said the policeman.

"What do you mean by 'contact wound,' Lieutenant?"

"I mean the muzzle of the gun was probably in contact with the shirt when it was fired," explained Casper.

"And what conclusion did you draw from the total circumstances of the case, Lieutenant?" asked Spencer.

"Suicide," said Casper dryly.

"Your witness," Spencer said to Erickson.

"Lieutenant," Erickson began gently, "did you dust the gun for prints?"

"No."

"Did your technician dust the gun for fingerprints?"

"No."

"Did you find an exit wound in the body of Myrl Caton?"

"No."

"Did you look?"

"Well, not exactly," said Casper uneasily. "But Hitchcock said—"

"Oops—careful, Lieutenant," cautioned Erickson. "Did you look?"

"No."

"Where is the gun now?"

"Still in the police property room. We wrote to Mrs. Caton requesting a release, but she didn't reply. Lots of times the widow don't want the gun back. You know," explained Casper.

Erickson made another note on his yellow pad. So did Spencer.

"That door to the adjoining room, Lieutenant—was it locked?"

"I don't know," said Casper softly.

"Pardon me?" asked Erickson.

"I don't know, sir. I've looked through our reports to see if anyone checked that damned door and I can't find any note on it. I'm sure I didn't lock that door."

"So someone could have entered the room through that door?" asked Erickson.

"I suppose it's possible," said Casper.

"Did you check to see if that room had been occupied?"

"I did later," said Casper.

"And?" asked Erickson. Both lawyers leaned forward with suddenly renewed interest.

"Angela Gaito had that room."

Erickson emitted a soft, low whistle.

"Angela Gaito from Connecticut Valley Produce?"

"Ayah," said Casper, unconsciously reverting to his New England twang.

"Did you check her out?" asked Erickson.

"I had a long talk with Miss Gaito and satisfied myself that she used that room only to shack up—er, pardon me, Miss Kane—stay with Mr. Caton that night."

"Did you expect her to say she shot Caton?" asked Erickson sarcastically.

"Come on, Paul, be fair," Spencer chided.

"She was a hell of a lot smaller than Caton," argued Casper. "Besides, if she did it, why didn't she scram right after shooting him and take the gun with her?"

"Didn't she?" Erickson asked.

"You don't have no right to talk like that about Angela. I mean, she's a stupid bitch and all that, but she's clean in this case," Casper said excitedly.

"You seem pretty sure of that," Erickson taunted.

"Yeah—well, that's the way it is," Casper replied, defensively.

"You knew Angela Gaito before?" Erickson probed.

"Before what?"

"Before this case."

Casper hesitated. "Yeah. OK. So what? So I knew Angela Gaito. But that's all gone by now. Water over the bridge."

"Under," Erickson teased.

"Huh?"

"Under the bridge. But your knowing Angela Gaito didn't interfere with your objective investigation of this death, did it, Lieutenant?" Erickson's tone was almost insulting.

"No. No. Nothing like that. It was suicide. Open and shut." Casper's knuckles were white where he grasped his chair. "Is that all?"

"Almost," Erickson said. "Who authorized the burning of the mattress and the clothes?"

"I did," Casper said almost inaudibly.

"Please?" asked Miss Kane.

"I did!" the lieutenant shouted.

"Thank you, Lieutenant. That's all I need at this time," Erickson said, smiling.

"One more point," said Red Spencer. The lieutenant, who had half stood up, sat down again. "After questioning Angela Gaito, did you think there was any reason to alter your conclusions in this case?"

"No, sir," said Casper firmly.

"Still suicide?"

"Suicide," said Casper, nodding.

"You can waive the reading of this deposition or you have the right to review it before signing it, Lieutenant," explained Spencer.

"I waive," said Casper simply. He stood up, collected his notes, shook hands with each lawyer, and left the room.

"Angela Gaito," muttered Spencer.

"How about spaghetti for supper?" asked Erickson, grinning.

"Stick it up your ass," mouthed Red Spencer silently, covering his mouth so that Miss Kane could not see.

"Who's next?" asked Erickson. He glanced at his watch.

"Mr. Peabody and then his maid," said Miss Kane officially. She loaded her stenotype machine with new paper and cracked her knuckles loudly.

14

The depositions of Clyde Peabody and his maid, Ruby Green, went quickly. Spencer established the fact that Peabody had broken in the chained door after Ruby unlocked it with the passkey. Erickson saw to it that Peabody was unable to confirm the presence or absence of an exit wound or a hole in the mattress. Ruby's testimony contributed little of substance. No other testimony was scheduled for the first day of depositions, and the session broke up earlier than either lawyer had anticipated.

"Need a ride back to the motel, Paul?" offered Spencer.

"No thanks. I think I'll walk around the town a little," said Erickson.

"Careful. I think they still shoot Rebels up here."

"I'll keep my mouth shut."

"That will be the day," said Spencer.

"See you tomorrow, Red."

"Want to get together for dinner tonight?"

"Maybe. But don't count on it, Red. I've got some homework to do before we tackle the rest of these characters tomorrow."

"You plaintiff's lawyers run on nothing but nervous energy and guts. Why don't you get yourself a nice soft job defending some insurance company? It's easier on your stomach lining."

"Why ask some insurance company to pay me every month when I can steal enough from them to keep me happy?" Erickson slipped on his topcoat and said goodbye to the stenotypist. He winked at Red Spencer and left the witness room.

The door opened again suddenly; Spencer stuck his head into the corridor and watched Erickson disappear into the street.

Paul Erickson felt refreshed by the time he arrived at his room at the Brownstone Motel. He had walked the two miles from the courthouse, and the soles of his shoes were wet from the snow. By prior arrangement with Clyde Peabody, he had managed to be housed in room 15. The room was freshly painted and had a new mattress, but otherwise it was in the same condition as when it was occupied by Myrl Caton. Erickson unlocked the room. With the door swung wide, he stood in the doorway and tried to see the motel office. The maple tree partly obscured his view. He tried to imagine the tree loaded with leaves in July.

He put his briefcase on the dresser and kicked the door closed. With a sigh, he sat in the corner chair and tried to visualize Myrl Caton's body lying heavily on the bed. He took the 8-by-10 copies of the photographs from his briefcase and reviewed them again, carefully comparing each detail in the pictures with those that still remained in room 15. He walked to the adjoining door and opened it. The connecting door to room 16 was locked from the other side. Erickson turned suddenly, put his topcoat on again, and quickly left the room. He walked rapidly to the street and turned left. After about two blocks, a cab came along. Erickson hailed it and got in.

"Where to, pal?" the cab driver asked over his right shoulder.

"Take me to 2036 West Colazzi Street."

Erickson sat back in the seat and wondered what she

would be like and how she would accept his visit. She had been unwilling to meet him at Connecticut Valley Produce and had told him to meet her at her house.

He thought of a dark-haired woman, a little overweight, wearing a simple print dress, answering the door. Somehow, she would have to look a little like Anna Magnani and speak with a definite Italian accent. Erickson imagined a bowl of fruit on the dining-room table and the odor of some spicy Italian dish simmering on the stove.

"This is it," the driver announced. "Four-twenty." Erickson gave him a five and told him to wait until he waved him away from the door. The driver winked, gave a sly, knowing smile, and agreed. Erickson got out of the cab and proceeded toward the duplex. A blue Pinto stood in the driveway.

He adjusted his tie and knocked on the door. After a short wait and another slightly louder knock, the door opened. Angela Gaito stood in the doorway. Erickson's thoughts of Anna Magnani vanished.

"Mrs. Gaito?" asked Erickson softly and pleasantly.

"It's Miss Gaito," Angela corrected him. She was wearing black stretch pants which accented her generous buttocks, an African print shirt laced near the neck, and no shoes.

"I'm Paul Erickson," he said, extending his hand and smiling gently. "The lawyer connected with the Caton case."

"Now what is it you want from me, Mr. Erickson?"

"Miss Gaito, I have just a few questions to ask you. A few points to clear up in my mind before we take your deposition." Erickson removed his coat and sat on the edge of the sofa.

Angela sat formally in a chair with her hands folded in her lap. "I thought you lawyers were going to ask me all the questions down at the courthouse. At least that's what that legal paper said."

"Still true," said Erickson smiling. "But I wanted to ask you a few questions before we got to the courthouse. I represent Mrs. Caton in this case, and as you know, we are contesting the cause of death. The other side is the insurance company."

Angela nodded silently.

"Do you recall Mr. Caton's last visit to Middlebrook?" he asked.

"Yes," she said flatly.

"Did you know Mr. Caton well?"

"Reasonably well." Caton had been wet with sweat when he held her. Her hands were now almost as sweaty.

"Would it be fair to list you as among Mr. Caton's friends?"

"I think so," she said softly.

"Did you see him alone during his visit?" Erickson probed gently. Angela nodded and lowered her eyes. Erickson recognized the gesture instantly, and regrouped for a better approach.

"Miss Gaito," he began reassuringly. He reached toward her and placed his hand gently on hers. "I don't want to pry, and I don't want to bring back unpleasant memories. But you understand how important it is for me to know the facts. Our case will depend on knowing all the facts. It's the only way that we will be able to provide the best representation for Mr. Caton's widow." Angela withdrew her hand quickly as "Caton's widow" was announced. Erickson quickly added, "Not that Caton would have given a damn about her welfare."

"Myrl and me was real good friends. Real close," Angela said.

"Real close?" probed the lawyer.

Angela nodded, but this time did not drop her eyes.

"Miss Gaito—may I call you Angela?" Erickson warmed.

"Please," she responded.

"Angela, I know all this is tough for you now. He's gone and none of this is going to bring him back. We all loved him, Angela." Erickson, in fact, had never met Caton.

Angela nodded, and wiped a tear from her right eye with a blunt index finger.

"He was a great guy," she announced.

"A *great* guy," emphasized Erickson, sounding like a sports announcer at a testimonial for a deceased football coach.

"You want a glass of wine or something?" asked Angela suddenly. He nodded. She got up and went into the kitchen, dabbing at her wet eyes.

"How drunk was Caton that night?"

Angela came to the kitchen doorway and stood there without speaking. She held a glass in one hand and a quart of red Italian wine in the other. She stared at Erickson and then smiled broadly as she poured herself a glass.

"OK," she said admissively. "I was there. I already told the cops, you know." She drank the wine in a single gulp and refilled it.

"You were where?" asked Erickson, looking surprised.

"There—with him. In his room."

"The night he died?"

Angela nodded. "But not *when* he died, you understand. I left before he shot himself. I came over there to see him with Vincent Irafino when he first got in town. We had a couple of drinks and then I went back to see him later." She gulped her Dago red nervously.

"Easy," cautioned Erickson, "let's not get too free with that 'shot himself' bit."

"Shit," said Angela. "Who the hell you think shot him if he didn't? Me?" She laughed, but the laugh froze when Erickson didn't move a muscle.

Erickson raised his hands in a disarming gesture. "I'm not saying that anyone we know killed Caton," explained Erickson. "All I know is that suicide hasn't been sufficiently proved, and I'm betting that the insurance company won't be able to do so."

"So you want to stick me with the rap just so you can collect a few thousand bucks for his widow."

"I don't want to stick you or anyone else with the rap, Angela. Believe me, we're all on the same side in this case. All I want is your help to find out what happened."

"You're wasting your time if you think that anyone is going to believe that crap. Nobody in Middlebrook would

108

believe that I shot Myrl. You've got to be kidding, lawyer-man." Angela laughed and sipped again from the red wine.

"I think I'll have a glass of that wine with you." Erickson pointed at the bottle of Roma. Angela handed him the quart and quickly produced a stemmed glass from the cabinet in the dining room. She poured Erickson's drink and refilled her own kitchen tumbler.

"You're pretty damned clever," she said looking at the Tampa lawyer. "You come up here and mess around in this case until you get everybody all stirred up and then you'll go back to Florida and forget about us."

"Not so, Angela," protested Erickson. "I'm not going to run out and leave this case up in the air or ruin anyone along the way. All we need to show is that there is some reasonable explanation for Caton's death other than suicide. And I think we can do it. If you will help."

"Why should I?" Angela asked teasingly.

Erickson sat back on the sofa more comfortably. He loosened his tie and took a slow sip on his wine. He held the glass up to the light of the window as if he were examining a fine vintage. "To keep the court from getting too interested in Angela Gaito and where she spent the night of Caton's death," Erickson said coyly.

"You bastard," said Angela softly. Erickson shrugged and drank half of his wine, repressing the shudder that it generated inside him. "You are out to hang me."

"Look," he said suddenly and firmly. "You help me, and I'll help you. You need an alibi for that night and I need some facts to throw up against this suicide theory."

Angela paused and looked into her wine.

"Give me some time to think it over," pleaded Angela gently. Erickson nodded, finished off his wine, and stood up.

"Take all night," he said simply. He struggled into his coat and buttoned it. "I'm staying at the Brownstone. Call me if you think of anything to talk about." He moved to the door.

"What room?"

"15," he said softly with a grin.

"You son of a bitch," sighed the suddenly aging Miss Gaito. The telephone rang and they both looked at it. Angela walked across the room to answer it as Erickson waited at the door. She picked up the phone.

"Yeah?" Angela answered flatly. She looked blankly at Erickson for a moment as she listened. Her expression changed to overt hostility as she continued to stare at Erickson.

"He's already here," she said to the caller in a resigned tone. "He's worse than that, Harry. Right. I'll watch my step. No, nothing yet. But he's tricky. Right. Thanks for calling." She put down the phone.

"Casper?" asked Erickson. He quickly opened the door and left the duplex before the quart of Dago red smashed onto the front step.

Angela had suddenly achieved her Anna Magnani.

15

"I do," said Vincent Irafino after the stenotypist administered the oath. He sat down in the witness chair and watched nervously as the opposing lawyers shuffled their papers. Irafino took a loud sip from his paper cup of machine coffee.

"State your name," said Paul Erickson mechanically.

Irafino responded carefully and slowly, but Miss Kane still asked him to spell it.

"Where are you employed?"

"Connecticut Valley Produce."

"How long have you been so employed?"

"Nineteen years."

"Where were you born?"

"Right here."

"Did you know Myrl Caton?"

"I did."

"For how long?"

"Oh—" Irafino paused to inspect the ceiling of the witness room. "I guess about ten years or so. For as long as he's been coming up here to sell tomatoes."

"Caton sold tomatoes to you?"

"Hell, yes. What's a matter? Don't you guys know nothing about all this?"

"Mr. Irafino, what we know is totally immaterial. We are trying to build a record based on testimony of witnesses such as yourself. Some of the questions may sound silly or obvious to you, but we must have your complete answers." Red Spencer seemed unusually patient as he explained the procedure to the big Italian in his slow Georgia accent.

"OK, OK," said Irafino, looking at his watch.

"And we will be finished just as soon as we possibly can," added Spencer with deliberate and annoying slowness.

Irafino threw an exasperated gaze out the window and adjusted his position in the witness chair. "This is all you guys got to do," Irafino said.

Erickson looked up and smiled. He had not followed the Irafino-Spencer exchange until that remark. Now he waited expectantly for Spencer's rejoinder.

"You will be free to return to your vegetable bin in a few minutes," said Spencer acidly.

"The biggest goddamned produce market outside of Hartford and New Haven!" blurted Irafino. "Vegetable bin!" The big Italian was red-faced.

Erickson couldn't repress his laugh any longer. He began to whistle "Dixie" while fixing his gaze sternly on his papers.

"Now we don't need to fan the fire," said Red Spencer with a smirk. "Mr. Irafino will find enough to dislike about me without your counsel, Mr. Erickson."

Irafino looked at both lawyers blankly. The deposition settled down to the boredom of businesslike interrogation. After about three-quarters of an hour, Red Spencer had extracted the fact that Vincent Irafino had had a fight with Myrl Caton the afternoon before he was found dead; that Irafino had fired a shot from Caton's gun; that Irafino had denied all ill will against Mr. Caton; that the Middlebrook police had questioned and cleared him after Caton's death; that Irafino had welcomed and squired around Mrs. Caton and Kirby Morris when they came to claim the body; that neither Irafino nor Connecticut Valley Produce had anything to gain by Caton's death.

"Your witness," said Red Spencer. Paul Erickson shuffled his papers for a while longer and then rose to look out the window.

Miss Kane flexed her tired fingers and two of the knuckles cracked.

"How long have you been sleeping with Angela Gaito?" asked Erickson in a sudden turn from the window.

"I never—" began Irafino quickly. He was interrupted by an irate Red Spencer.

"Paul—dammit! What kind of crap is that? I mean, after all. You've got better sense than to screw up this depo with that kind of shit." Spencer pointed a shaking finger at the stenotypist. "Off the record, Miss Kane. Don't take none of this down."

"On the record, Miss Kane," said Erickson firmly. Irafino was on his feet and coming toward Erickson.

"I'm going to kick your ass out that window, mister," threatened Irafino. Red Spencer stepped between them.

"Wait a minute there, fella," Spencer admonished. "If there's any rough stuff going on here, I want to mix with you first."

"Come on," invited Irafino.

Erickson grinned widely. "Next?" asked Erickson over Spencer's shoulder, as if to make an appointment. Miss Kane continued to type furiously as she ducked partially beneath the table.

Irafino reached over Spencer's shoulder and grabbed the front of Erickson's shirt and tie. "Lawyer or not, you're going to get yours," said Irafino. He pulled Erickson toward Spencer, who maintained his battle station between them. The struggle without blows continued like a dance as the door opened and a thunderous voice shook the air.

"Gentlemen, please!" The godlike tone stilled the bristling air, and all three turned toward the door to see the arched eyebrows and horrified expression of the impeccable

G. Markham Hurst. Irafino, not fully understanding why, unhanded the shirtfront of Paul Erickson and backed away from the partially crumpled Red Spencer. The two lawyers looked sheepish and returned to their places at the table. Each extended a silent hand to G. Markham. The senior lawyer shook the hands ceremoniously and put down his ancient briefcase.

"Is this a deposition or a street brawl?" Hurst asked reproachfully.

"I'm sorry, sir," said Erickson, adjusting his clothes. "It was all my fault." He extended a hand to Vincent Irafino apologetically. Irafino shook the lawyer's hand and sat down, still visibly disturbed.

"We didn't expect you, Mr. Hurst," said Red Spencer. "But, welcome to Middlebrook, and all that."

"I'm rather glad I came," said G. Markham, looking around the room. "Where is the court reporter?"

"Here I am," said a weak voice from under the table. Miss Kane struggled into her seat, still typing.

"Well, my dear, you needn't be afraid," said G. Markham reassuringly. "But whatever you do, miss, do not read back the last question." All three lawyers joined in a genuine laugh.

Through it Paul Erickson said, "No further questions." The lawyers continued to enjoy their laughter.

Irafino looked at each of them with an expression of complete confusion.

"You can go, Mr. Irafino," said Red Spencer. Deliberately, he had pronounced the name Ira-fine-o.

"Go?" asked the confused Irafino.

"Yes, go. Go, Mr. Irafino. Go," said Erickson in a childish chant. He waved his hand toward the door in a grand sweep.

"All you lawyers is nuts. Completely nuts," said Irafino as he went toward the door.

"Do you waive reading and signing?" Miss Kane called after him. Her question was met by gales of renewed laughter from the lawyers, who now stood with their arms around each other and with tears streaming down their cheeks.

"Miss Reporter, there is no alternative than to recess for lunch," said G. Markham Hurst, partially regaining his composure.

"The defendant concurs," said Red Spencer. He stuffed his papers into his briefcase and still emitted an occasional laugh.

"And it's on the plaintiff," said Erickson, in an equally pleasant mood.

"I rather think that that might prove somewhat awkward," said G. Markham.

Erickson and Spencer looked at him quizzically.

"I brought along Dr. Campbell," announced G. Markham. "I had hoped that he would have time to lunch with us and view the room before he had to fly back to Tampa. You understand, Red."

"Of course. Of course," said Red Spencer. His mental gears were in full mesh and all wheels were spinning.

"Is he here?" asked Paul Erickson excitedly.

"No. He's over at the motel," said G. Markham. "We're meeting him there after I run a small errand at the police station."

Red Spencer stopped stuffing papers in his briefcase and looked up in genuine surprise.

"Police station?" asked Spencer.

"Yes. I want to retrieve an item belonging to one of our clients," said G. Markham Hurst. He reached into his inside jacket pocket and produced a legal-sized paper. He handed it to Red Spencer as he turned to move Erickson out the door.

"My client, Mrs. Caton, would like to have her late husband's gun returned. I think you'll find that the court has agreed with her reasonable request," said G. Markham with feigned disinterest. He took Erickson's arm and urged him out of the room as Red Spencer read the document silently.

16

When Paul Erickson and G. Markham Hurst arrived at the Brownstone, Dr. Campbell was busily measuring the room: the distance from the door to the middle of the bed; the angle from bed height to a place about forty inches above the floor at the doorway. He arranged tape measures along the floor in several of these areas and photographed them with his 35mm. Minolta.

Erickson stood in the doorway and watched the pathologist at work.

"Did you find that big clue to cinch the case for us, doctor?" Erickson asked pleasantly.

Campbell paused, looked toward the door, smiled, and shook the young lawyer's hand.

"G. Markham thought you'd need all the help you could get," joked Campbell.

"He certainly brought the best," said Erickson genuinely. The pathologist smiled and returned to his measurements near the bed.

G. Markham entered the room slowly and silently. "Find anything, Mark?" asked the senior lawyer.

"Oh, hi. You're back from the arena. Did you get the

gun?" asked the pathologist, pausing only long enough to glance up from the floor. G. Markham nodded and held up a paper-wrapped package about the size of a loaf of bread.

"They let me have it, but remember the terms of that motion. We only get custody long enough to get a ballistics check and then it has to go back to the court."

"We can have the gun examined and test-fired back in Tampa. Just be careful not to break that police seal on the package until we get the ballistics check set up," cautioned Campbell. He continued to work at his measurements and photographs as he spoke.

"Just what are you sizing up, anyway, Dr. Campbell?" asked Paul Erickson.

"I want to know what the angle and distance is from that doorway to the left chest of a man sitting up in bed."

"Sitting up?" asked Erickson.

"Well, we don't know he was sitting up, but we can be sure that he wasn't lying down when he was shot by your burglar at the door," explained Campbell.

"We can't use that theory. Nothing was stolen," Erickson protested.

"So, the burglar was too scared to complete the robbery after he shot Caton," theorized the pathologist.

Erickson wrinkled his nose to indicate that the story sat uneasily with him.

"Paul," said Campbell slowly, "we really don't need a burglar. What we need in this case is smoke. The burglar idea is only one of the several theories we may be able to come up with."

"OK," said Erickson, "but who puts the chain on the inside of the door after your burglar shoots Caton?"

"You can, if you like," said Campbell. "It was your own theory, Paul." He tossed Erickson a straightened coat hanger bent into a crude hook at one end. "Put the hook on the chain fastener and hold it level as you close the door." Erickson obeyed the instructions and closed the door partway.

"Like this?" Erickson asked.

"Now put the latch in the little slot on the doorframe."

Erickson manipulated the wire but he was unable to latch the chain.

"Here, let me show you," said Campbell. He took the coat hanger from the lawyer, stepped outside the room door, and hooked the chain into the slot without the slightest difficulty. "Practice," explained the pathologist simply. He gave the coat hanger back to Erickson and re-entered the room.

"OK, but wouldn't your man be seen from the motel office?" asked Erickson.

"By whom?" countered Campbell. "Do you know any night clerk that stands around watching the motel doors? If they aren't watching TV, they're asleep in the chair."

"Agreed," said G. Markham. "But I just don't see some assailant firing a large-caliber weapon like that .45 and then taking the time to hook up the door chain."

"You have to come up with someone," Campbell reminded them.

"A bogeyman at the door?" Erickson shook his head in disbelief. "How do you put the gun in the room?"

"Several ways," said Campbell. "One is to throw it in from the door or drop it as you leave. Another is to assume that the gun that killed Caton was not the one found on the floor."

"But if he wasn't shot with that gun on the floor, how do you account for the .45 caliber bullet in him?" asked Erickson.

"As you yourself pointed out, who says the bullet in him is a .45?" asked the pathologist. "For that matter, who says there is a bullet still in him?"

"Hitchcock, from the funeral home, does."

"Doesn't he have to at this point?" asked Campbell. "I mean, now that he had already corroborated the original police report, how can he change his story? There's a damned good possibility that Hitchcock never saw Caton's back."

"How about the coroner, Fortunelli?" asked G. Markham.

The pathologist shook his head sadly. "I had a talk with him by phone and he's not the sharpest bird I've ever crossed swords with."

"But a good GP?" asked G. Markham.

"Probably a drunk," offered Campbell. "Does a poor job as coroner, hands out lousy reports—or no reports at all."

"Why not let the killer come in through the adjoining door, shoot Caton in his sleep, go back through to the other room, and leave?" asked Erickson, steering the conversation back to the point.

"OK—but it's a little too shaky if you make it—what's her name—Angela coming through that door," said Campbell.

"Why the hell can't it be Angela?"

"Well, of course, it can be Angela," allowed the pathologist. "But somehow, I don't see her coming in his room in the middle of the night, shooting him, and then sticking around Middlebrook like nothing had happened."

"How about Vincent Irafino?" G. Markham asked, poking around in the bathroom.

"He shoots Caton?" Erickson asked, encouraging his senior partner.

"Why not? This Italian is not going to take a beating from some Southern tomato peddler—at least not in front of Angela Gaito," G. Markham said.

"Hot pants?" asked Erickson.

"At least hot blood," Hurst replied. "He would have to be mad as hell at Caton. Right, Doc?"

"Plausible," the pathologist said dryly. He squinted at the door frame again.

G. Markham Hurst squinted with him and began to reason aloud. "Let's assume that Irafino came back that night."

"To apologize?" Erickson asked testily.

"No, no," G. Markham said quickly. "He's had time to

119

lick his wounds and get really pissed off about the whole thing. He gives Angela a call and can't find her."

"And gets suspicious," Campbell added, warming to the theory.

"And charges over here, finds her car, and bangs on her door," Hurst said, nodding his head.

"But her door is locked," Erickson said.

"We don't know that, Paul," the pathologist offered. "Go on, G. Markham."

"Her door is opened—somehow. Irafino comes in her side, goes through the adjoining door, finds her in bed with Caton, and shoots him." Hurst held his hands wide to emphasize the simplicity of his explanation.

"With what?" Erickson asked.

"How about with Caton's own gun?" G. Markham said.

Dr. Campbell pursed his lips as if to test that point. "Irafino gets it out of Caton's Cadillac?" He did not sound convinced. He pointed his finger at an imaginary body lying in the bed and fired a mental shot. "Where is Angela all this time?"

"She leaps out of Caton's bed when Irafino busts into the room," Erickson suggested.

"But in a love squabble, the assailant usually shoots the girl too," the pathologist added. "Scenes like that don't get set up to look like suicides. They are straightforward homicides with both bodies left naked on the bed full of holes." He glanced around the room again as he shook his head. "We've got a lot of suicide angles to explain away in this case before we make it a triangle shooting."

"Good point, Mark," G. Markham conceded. "But Irafino had all evening to think about letting Caton have it somehow. When he finds Angela's car at the motel, that's all he needs. Instead of doing it in a blind rage, he decides to make it look like a suicide."

"How about a threat, and the gun goes off by accident?" Campbell offered.

"Still murder," Erickson said quickly.

"Yes, legally," the pathologist agreed. "But maybe

Irafino got Caton's gun out of the Cadillac and brought it in to threaten Caton with it. You know, he's going to tell him to leave Angela alone."

"Sort of poetic justice—his own gun," G. Markham commented. "Threatens him with the same gun they fought over that afternoon."

"He threatens Caton by putting the gun up close to his chest. There are your powder burns," Erickson added.

"Powder burns would certainly make it look like a suicide," the pathologist said.

"But it doesn't explain why Irafino is all that mad at Caton," G. Markham said, picking at his own explanation. "I mean, after all, he probably knew about Caton and Angela from some previous trip."

"Yeah, but what the hell," Erickson said. "No Italian guy is going to let an Italian broad double-time him and get away with it publicly. . . . Maybe he made her promise not to see Caton this trip."

"And then gave them an opportunity to get together? What's that? Some sort of lover's test?" the doctor asked.

"Why not?" Erickson asked. "He got pretty pissed off at the deposition when I asked him if he was still sleeping with her."

"Wouldn't you?" G. Markham asked. "Particularly if you had shot him?"

"I'd play a question like that a lot cooler, I think," Erickson replied, frowning.

"Right. But you're a lawyer and a lot better student of psychology than Irafino would be," Campbell said.

"How else can I make it as a shyster?" asked Erickson smiling.

G. Markham cringed at this playful attack on his beloved profession.

"Without psychology, you just cannot deal with people on any level," agreed Dr. Campbell.

"Even in your morgue?" chided Erickson.

"Even there," said Campbell, returning a grin. "Remember that all those corpses have families and family physicians—"

121

"And lawyers," added G. Markham with a sly grin.

"—and lawyers," agreed Campbell. He gave a little smile and puffed a few times on his pipe. It was out again, and instead of smoke, he evoked only a few bubbly sounds from the bottom of the briar bowl. He returned to his careful inspection of the room and was immediately lost in his own thoughts.

G. Markham recognized the intensity of the pathologist's attention and motioned Paul Erickson out of the motel room.

The two Florida lawyers felt the Connecticut chill explore their ankles and ribs.

"Give him a chance to go over the room by himself, Paul," suggested G. Markham. "I think we'll get more out of it."

"You're right, of course," agreed Paul Erickson. "It's just that I find the man fascinating to watch and talk to."

"You'll get your chance to talk to him in federal court."

"Yeah." Paul Erickson rubbed his hand together now, not from the cold but with enthusiasm.

17

Angela Gaito arrived at the courthouse in a Yellow Cab. She wore a black-and-white houndstooth wool skirt and a pink sweater. There was a charm bracelet on her left wrist that rattled every time she moved the hand across the oak witness table. To Erickson, nursing the raw edge of a gin hangover, each clatter of the bracelet sounded like a bombardment.

Angela smiled self-consciously at Red Spencer and took her seat. She carefully omitted looking at Paul Erickson.

"State your name," said Red Spencer suddenly.

"Angela Gaito," she said softly.

"Speak up so that the court reporter can hear you, Miss Gaito," suggested Spencer forcefully.

"Angela Gaito," she repeated louder.

"Excuse me," the court reported said, "I have to swear the witness." She raised her right hand to encourage Angela to imitate her, and led her through the formula.

"Thank you. Miss Gaito, I call your attention to the night of July 14th of this past year." Spencer continued, "Do you recall that date?"

"Uh-huh."

"And do you recall where you might have been on that night?"

"Uh-huh."

"Would you tell us in your own words everything you can recall about that evening?"

Angela shifted nervously in her seat and looked blankly at Red Spencer.

"Well, you know," she began, "I went to see him."

"See who, Miss Gaito?" asked Spencer.

"Myrl," she said softly.

"At the Brownstone?"

"Well, not at first."

"Where did you meet him then?"

"Well, you see, he called up that night and wanted to know if I wanted to go eat somewhere with him. I said, 'OK,' and he says, 'Where would you like to eat?' and I says, 'How 'bout Geraci's?' and he says, 'OK, come get me'."

"He said to you, 'Come get me'?" inquired Spencer.

"Yeah, he was kinda drunk and he wanted to go in my car."

"And did you?"

"Well, not exactly," Angela said. She hesitated.

"What do you mean, 'Not exactly'?"

"He said he'd meet me across the street in Fitzpatrick's, so I said, 'OK'."

"Fitzpatrick's?"

"The little bar across from the Brownstone," she offered.

"Continue, Miss Gaito," said Spencer.

"Well, that's about it. He was at the bar in Fitz's when I drove over. We had a couple and then left."

"To go eat?" asked Spencer.

"Well, Myrl said he wanted to get something from his room first."

"Where did you park your car?"

"On the other side of the motel. In front of the next room." She looked down at the table and waited for the next question.

124

"Why did you do that? Why not park next to Caton's Cadillac?"

"Because we didn't want to cause a lot of fuss."

"Fuss? Who would cause a fuss?"

"You know. Vincent."

"Vincent Irafino?" asked Spencer.

"Yeah. He can get pretty nasty sometimes, and I didn't want him to get any funny ideas. So I put my car on the other side, in front of the next room."

"How did you get into Caton's room, then?"

Angela remained silent for a moment, hoping that some additional question would help her with the answer. No help came from Spencer or Erickson.

"Myrl had already rented that next room for me. He told me about it at Fitzpatrick's. He said he booked it under some phony name so that Vincent wouldn't find out."

"Caton rented the room adjoining his?"

Angela nodded her head. "He got the key from the night clerk."

"He gave you the key?"

"At Fitz's."

"And you let yourself into that room?"

"Uh-huh."

Spencer and Erickson leaned forward in unison as their interest increased.

"Did he unlock both doors?"

"Between the rooms?" Angela asked.

"Yes, between the rooms."

"I guess so," she said. "They was both open when I got there."

"What was Caton doing then?"

"He was in the bathroom."

"Taking a bath?" pried Spencer.

Angela hesitated. She looked at Miss Kane, who flexed her fingers and then resumed her expectant pose.

"He was sick," she said softly.

"To his stomach?"

Angela nodded gently. "All that booze," she said.

Erickson nodded sympathetically as Red Spencer grinned at him.

"What happened then?" asked Spencer.

"Myrl flopped on the bed and began talking crazy."

"About what?"

"Oh, his wife and her friends at some country club . . . his partner back in Florida . . . stuff like that."

"Did he seem upset about his wife and partner?"

"Now, hold on, Red," Erickson said with a deep voice. "Let's not get too far out in this hearsay testimony. I'll be cooperative, but don't push it too far."

"OK," said Spencer, rechecking the notes on his yellow pad. "What, if anything, did you do next, Miss Gaito?"

"I laid down on the bed with him and talked a while," she said simply.

"Did you stay with him all night?"

"He got a little hard to handle after a while."

"How do you mean?"

"Well, you know," she explained. "He got kinda grabby and stuff."

"But you had been with him before, hadn't you, Angela?" Spencer asked tauntingly.

"Yeah, but I never let him do nothing when he was drunk."

"Why not?"

"Because he got mean when he was drunk, that's why," she announced.

"Was he mean that night?"

"A little," she said.

"What do you mean, 'a little'?" he urged.

"Oh, he started to pull at my skirt and stuff, but I didn't want any part of him."

"Then why did you come to his room?"

"I had to help him back to the motel," she said genuinely. "I couldn't just leave him at Fitz's, could I?"

"What did you do after that?"

"I told him to leave me alone and that if he would take a nap, I'd wake him up later and we could go get something to eat," she said.

"What time was it then, Angela?"

"About ten or ten-thirty, I guess. I don't know. Somewhere around there."

"Did Caton agree to that?" asked Red Spencer.

"Yeah, after a while, he did. He was pretty sleepy, I guess. I sat and talked quiet to him for a while and he stopped fooling around. Then he fell asleep and started to snore."

"Did you go to sleep, too?"

"Yeah, but not with him. I went back to my room and locked my side of the double door. He snored so loud you couldn't stand it. I figured I'd lay down a little while and then go out with him for a pizza about midnight."

"What happened next?"

"Well, I must have been tireder than I thought. I slept longer than midnight, and when I woke up, his side of the door was locked."

"Was he still asleep?"

"He wasn't snoring. I didn't know whether he was there or not. I figured I'd leave well enough alone, so I went back to bed and slept through till morning."

"Did you hear any noises during the night?"

"Like what?"

"Like anything. A fight—a shot—anything," prodded Spencer.

"I didn't hear nothing," she said. "When I sleep, I sleep like a dead man." She stopped suddenly and put her hand to her mouth as if to recapture the words.

"When did you first find out that there was a real dead man in the next room?" asked Spencer.

"From Harry Casper."

"Lt. Casper?"

Angela nodded her head.

"When did Lt. Casper talk to you about Caton?"

"After they found the body. The next afternoon."

"What did you tell Casper?" asked Spencer.

"Red," said Erickson softly, "objection."

Spencer glanced at Erickson and quickly returned his attention to the witness. "Did Casper know about you

127

and Caton. That you were seeing Caton . . ." Spencer paused, and added, "Socially."

"Oh, I guess he probably did. Casper makes it his business to know everything in this damn town."

"Didn't he inquire about what you had heard or seen that night at the Brownstone?"

Angela shook her head. "Harry said that since Myrl's death was a suicide, there was no need to stir up a lot of trouble and get me involved. I thought that was kind of nice of him."

"When did you see Caton again?" asked Spencer.

She fumbled in her bag for a crumpled Kleenex and dabbed at her eyes. "I didn't."

"You never saw the body at the Brownstone?"

Angela shook her head and blew her nose.

"Was Caton's car in front of his room when you left the motel the next morning?" asked Spencer.

"I don't know. I went out my side and I didn't go around to look."

"What time did you leave?"

"I guess it was about six or half past six in the morning. I ain't got a watch." She held up her wrist to demonstrate, and the charm bracelet fell down over her forearm.

"Did you recognize anyone or speak to anyone as you left?"

She shook her head. "Nobody."

Spencer flipped a few pages of his yellow pad and checked off some of the paragraphs written there.

"Your witness, Paul," he said simply.

Erickson sat quietly and looked at Angela Gaito intently. She lowered her eyes and picked at some ageless initials carved in the top of the witness table.

"Angela," he said softly, "do you know who shot Caton?"

"He did, I guess," she offered quickly.

"Do you know why he'd do a thing like that?" asked Erickson.

Spencer interrupted. "Paul, that calls for a conclusion and I don't think I'll allow that as evidence. But go ahead, Miss Gaito, answer the question for the purposes of the transcript."

Confused, Angela squirmed in her chair. "I don't know. He was a funny guy anyway."

"Funny? How funny?" Erickson asked.

"Oh, you know. Kind of wild, sometimes. Got into fights with guys. He told me about that kind of stuff."

"Who did he say he fought?"

"Nobody in particular. Sometimes he would talk about beating up a Mexican or a nigger down there on his place in Florida."

"Caton said that?" Erickson urged.

"Uh-huh. And he even got into a fight with Vincent Irafino."

"You mean a fistfight?"

"Uh-huh. But it wasn't all Myrl's fault. Vincent went over there looking for trouble," she said. "You've got to know Vincent. Once he makes his mind up on how something is going to be, he don't back off."

"Paul," Spencer said gently. "Let's not clutter up this depo with too much hearsay."

"OK, Red, but we've come a long way up here on this fishing expedition, and I think we ought to get our money's worth," Erickson replied cordially. "We can clean it up before the trial."

Spencer shrugged and looked at his watch.

"Do you know what they fought about, Miss Gaito?" Erickson continued.

"Oh, mostly me, I guess. Well," she interrupted herself, "that fight was over Vincent's shooting Myrl's gun, but Vincent went over there with a chip on his shoulder on account of I had told him I wouldn't be friendly with Myrl Caton this trip."

"You promised Irafino that you would not see Myrl any more?" Erickson was trying to understand her mixed loyalties.

"Uh-huh. And Vincent threw us together just to see what would happen. Kind of a test, I guess."

"And what did happen, Miss Gaito?" Erickson pushed.

"Vincent picked a fight and shot off Myrl's gun," she said simply.

"When exactly was this?" Erickson asked.

"The day that Caton got to Middlebrook."

"You mean the day before they found his body?" Erickson asked.

"Yeah. We had a couple of drinks, and Vincent—just fooling around, you know—got Caton's gun out of the car and accidentally shot the doorstep of the motel room. Nobody got hurt or nothin', but Caton called Vincent some names, and they got into a fight. Well, Vincent ain't much good at fighting so he took off." She paused to see if her story was being followed.

"Was Vincent mad at Caton after that?"

"Object," Spencer said, mechanically.

"Did Vincent seem upset after he left the motel?"

"Same objection."

"Did you leave with Vincent?"

"Sure, I did," Angela said quickly. "And he was p.o.'d at Caton." She snapped her hand at the wrist for emphasis.

Spencer threw his hands into the air in frustration. "Move to strike the last phrase," he said flatly.

"Did you ever hear Irafino threaten to get even with Caton?" suggested Erickson.

"Oh, what the hell," said Spencer with exasperation.

"I never did," said Angela.

"But Vincent knew that Caton kept the gun in the Cadillac?"

"Uh-huh."

"And he knew about you and Caton from previous dates?"

"I guess so," she said softly.

"Did you date Vincent Irafino too?"

"Uh-huh."

"Regularly?"

"What do you mean by 'regularly'?"

"Whatever you want it to mean, Angela."

"I date him some," she admitted.

"Did you sleep with both of them, Angela?" Erickson asked gently.

She remained silent and looked at the top of the table.

"Angela?" Erickson asked.

"Do I have to answer all these questions?" she asked.

"It's just like you were in a court of law," Spencer said.

Erickson nodded his head.

She looked from one lawyer to the other but found no help. She sighed loudly. "Uh-huh." She glanced at the court reporter as her answer became recorded by a single clump on the stenotype keys. "But not together!"

Erickson smiled. "I know—not together, Angela. I mean sometimes. You know. On different dates."

She nodded silently.

"You promised Irafino that you wouldn't date Caton this time?" Erickson probed.

"I wouldn't call it a promise," she said solemnly.

"But something like that?"

"Uh-huh."

"Did he catch you with Caton that night?" Erickson asked slyly.

"Who?"

"Vincent. Who else?" Erickson supplied, hopefully.

"No. After the fight, I told Vincent that it was all over between Myrl and me," she said. "I guess I was kind of mad at both of them."

"You said that Lt. Casper told you about Caton being found dead," Erickson said. "How well do you know Lt. Casper?"

"I know him pretty good, I guess."

"You date him, too?" Erickson fished.

"Not no more, I don't."

"You used to?"

"A while back. He was only a sergeant then." She fidgeted and Erickson caught it.

"Not since Caton's death?" he probed further.

She looked from face to face again and then watched Ann Kane chew her gum. Angela's mouth felt dry.

"No," she said quietly.

"Did he know about you and Caton?" Erickson asked.

"Who?" she asked nervously.

"Lt. Casper."

She wrinkled her nose and bit her lower lip gently. "No. I don't think he did."

"What about Vincent Irafino?" Erickson asked.

Angela shook her head. "Vincent didn't get along with Casper too good." She twisted the crumpled Kleenex into a paper cruller.

"Did they ever fight over you?"

"Nothing like that. Just didn't like to be around each other. Vincent was always throwing Casper up at me. So I figured I'd stop seeing Casper. It was more peaceful that way. Besides, Harry's wife was a real bitch and he was afraid she'd find out."

"You're kind of popular, aren't you Angela?" said Erickson with a friendly, disarming smile.

"Some people like me, I guess," she replied openly. "I get along."

Erickson asked, almost absently, "Could you shoot a man if he was really hurting you?"

Angela paused. "You mean if he was being mean and grabbing me and stuff like that?"

Erickson nodded affirmatively.

"I suppose I could, Mr. Erickson." She paused and then added, "I suppose any girl really could if she had to."

"Thank you, Miss Gaito," said Erickson. "Anything more, Red?"

Spencer shook his head and packed up his papers. He looked unhappy and Erickson was delighted.

"We can make the plane to Tampa if we hustle," he said.

18

"I'm very pleased to meet you, Mr. Havlicek," said G. Markham Hurst, welcoming the gun expert to his office in the Bank of Tampa building.

"And I am happy to meet you, Mr. Hurst. Mr. Erickson here has told me about you." Havlicek had a slight Middle European accent which to Hurst and Erickson, both native Southerners, was reminiscent of Bela Lugosi.

Havlicek took a chair in front of Hurst's desk and attempted to light his pipe with small wooden matches from a sliding-type box.

"I suppose that Paul told you about the gun problem we have in our case," said G. Markham.

Havlicek nodded and puffed on the balking pipe.

"I told him the highlights, but I thought I'd wait until we were together to go into detail," added Erickson.

"We are expecting Dr. Campbell in a few minutes," explained Hurst.

"Good! Good!" exclaimed Milan Havlicek. "I haven't seen Mark Campbell for a year now. You know, it's funny. When I was still at the University of Indiana—after I retired from the Chicago police force—I used to see

Dr. Campbell a couple of times a year. He was always at the Forensic Academy meetings. But now, now that I'm retired and living right here in Sun City, we never seem to get together." Havlicek chuckled to himself. The others nodded knowingly.

"I'm afraid that is the way of the world, professor," said G. Markham.

"But you can be sure that you will hear from me," announced Paul Erickson enthusiastically. "Before we get through with this Caton case, I want to know all there is to know about ballistics, bullet holes and, in particular, the U.S. Army Colt .45 automatic."

"About the Colt .45 and the ballistics, I can tell you a lot. About the bullet holes, I think better you should ask Dr. Campbell," said Milan Havlicek.

"We will ask both of you," pacified G. Markham.

"How do you define the Colt .45, anyway, Prof. Havlicek?" probed Paul Erickson.

"It is an automatic, gas-operated, hand-held weapon which fires .45-caliber ammunition. The weapon weighs about two and a half pounds, carries seven cartridges in the clip, and has a muzzle velocity of 830 feet per second."

"OK, but when you shoot someone with this gun—"

"Pistol," corrected Havlicek.

"OK, pistol," continued Erickson, "how much damage can you expect?"

"That's a question for Dr. Campbell," said Havlicek. "Of course, I have seen a great many such wounds, but in forensic science, we like to split up the subject into the science of the weapon itself, and the pathology describing the wounds."

"But, if we were to show you this gun—er, pistol—could you tell us if it were the one which killed our client?" asked Erickson.

"Possibly. I would need also the bullet."

"The bullet that killed him?" asked Erickson.

"And another one to test-fire from the same weapon," explained Havlicek.

"You could compare these bullets, then?" asked G. Markham Hurst rhetorically.

"Precisely," said Havlicek. "You see, the Colt .45 automatic has six grooves, all rifled to the left." He paused to find Paul Erickson somewhat puzzled.

"The Smith and Wesson revolver, for instance, has five grooves, rifled to the right," he offered, still watching Erickson's face for a sign of understanding.

Paul shook his head gently.

"Inside the barrel of the weapon, there is a series of carefully cut grooves which spiral all the way from the place where the bullet goes in—to the muzzle—that's the hole where the fired bullet comes out. OK?"

The two lawyers nodded in unison and listened carefully.

"These spirals are cut by the manufacturer to give the bullet a spin as it comes up the barrel after being fired."

"Why do you want it to spin?" asked Erickson, following intently.

"The spin stabilizes the bullet in flight and prevents it from tumbling. It increases accuracy," said Havlicek.

"OK, go on."

"The lining of the barrel between these grooves is therefore arranged in a series of spiral raised areas—raised above the bottoms of the grooves—" He gestured with his fingers. "—called 'lands.' "

"Lands and grooves," repeated Erickson.

"Right. Six grooves and therefore six lands." Havlicek looked at G. Markham and then at Erickson to assure himself that they followed.

"As the bullet comes roaring up the barrel, pushed by the gas from the explosion of the powder, the sides of the bullet are held firmly by these lands, which form the actual inside of the barrel itself. The contact with the sides of the hot bullet cause tiny etchings to be made. The Colt .45 makes these markings twist to the left, while most other weapons show these markings slanted to the right."

"So that by looking at the bullet itself, you could tell if it were fired from a Colt," said Paul Erickson excitedly.

"Probably," said Havlicek cautiously. "There are some other handguns which are rifled to the left, but they are not often used in the United States. In fact, even most of the European weapons are rifled to the right like the other American-manufactured weapons. For instance, the Italian 7.65mm. Beretta is rifled to the right."

"Why do you call some of them 'millimeter' guns and others 'caliber' guns?" asked G. Markham.

"Mostly convention," said Havlicek. "The Americans like to use inches to measure things, and the Europeans use millimeters. That's all. A .45 caliber simply means that the bullet measures 45 hundredths of an inch across."

Erickson and Hurst looked at each other and nodded knowingly.

The door opened and Mark Campbell walked in briskly, apologizing for being late, and throwing perfunctory greetings to both lawyers as he warmly shook Milan Havlicek's hand.

"Milan," he said tenderly. "It is really good to see you."

"My dear friend," said Havlicek genuinely.

"Retirement hasn't killed you yet?"

"Almost." Havlicek smiled. "This consultation may have saved me from falling asleep and drowning while fishing."

"Well!" said the pathologist, rubbing his hands together and looking from one lawyer to the other. "Has Milan told you all about his world of firearms?"

"Prof. Havlicek is a walking encyclopedia," said G. Markham, smiling expansively.

"A shooting encyclopedia," corrected Campbell.

"He has been telling us how the lands and grooves inside the Colt make identifiable marks on the bullet," said Erickson.

"If anyone can, Milan can," Campbell said. He placed his hand on the firearms expert's shoulder.

"Prof. Havlicek defers to you for the wound pathology, Mark," said G. Markham Hurst.

"Dr. Campbell is a well-recognized authority in traumatic pathology," said Havlicek. "There is no way that a body can be shot, stabbed, broken, or blown apart that would be new to him."

"How about the wound in this case, Dr. Campbell? What would you expect it to be like?" asked Paul Erickson rapidly.

"Well," said the pathologist thoughtfully, "if the weapon really was a Colt .45 automatic at close range, I suspect that there would be a rather prominent inshoot wound in the chest and a good-sized, irregular outshoot wound in the back."

Milan Havlicek nodded vigorously in agreement.

"Couldn't the bullet stay inside the body?" asked Erickson.

"Only if it struck bone or was shot from further away," explained Campbell.

"The further the bullet has to travel before it hits its target, the more energy it loses, and it therefore becomes less capable of passing all the way through the body," added Havlicek.

"But Caton was shot inside the motel room," said Erickson.

"As far as we now know," cautioned G. Markham Hurst.

"Right!" said Erickson. "Maybe the motel door was open and he was shot from further away than we have thought. The night clerk shot him from the motel office?" Erickson suggested facetiously.

Everyone but Havlicek chuckled.

"I really don't care who shot Caton as long as he didn't shoot himself," said Erickson.

"The hunger for truth," said Hurst with a slight frown.

"Bullshit," said Erickson. "Let Spencer and Higgs hunger for the truth. I've got a client to protect."

"And a fee to collect," Campbell chided.

"Fee first, justice will follow," Erickson said. He totally ignored the deepening frown on the troubled brow of G. Markham Hurst.

"I wonder," Hurst said, clearing the air by his very tone of voice, "if you gentlemen would be kind enough to examine these photographs of the scene and to comment. You have seen them before, Dr. Campbell, but perhaps if you looked again with Prof. Havlicek, some new thoughts might come to mind." The elder lawyer produced the enlargements from behind his desk and handed them to the pathologist.

"There's too much blood on the shirt to see if there is a great amount of powder burning," offered Havlicek. "Where is the shirt now?"

"Gone," Erickson said simply. "The cops in Connecticut had it burned."

Havlicek's expression changed to one of pained disbelief. He sighed and shrugged. He ran his finger over the photographs to gauge the distances in the bed by comparing the length of the barrel of the .45.

"The Colt has probably been fired," said Havlicek. "The hammer is back and it is ready for the next round." He pointed to the weapon on the floor of the motel in one of the photographs.

"Maybe it was empty," Erickson suggested idly.

"I doubt it," Havlicek said quickly.

"Why?" Erickson pressed.

"Because the Colt automatic locks open when it fires its last shot. If empty, the owner would have had to release the slide and cock the hammer." He shook his head for emphasis. "That's not likely. It's loaded and ready to fire again."

"If we give you that gun, Mr. Havlicek, would you examine it and give us a report?" asked G. Markham Hurst.

"I would be happy to examine the weapon for you, gentlemen," said Milan Havlicek. "But I strongly urge you to put off that examination until Dr. Campbell has had the opportunity to recover the bullet from the body for comparison studies."

Campbell shook his head slowly. "There is not going to be any bullet in him, Milan."

"But the undertaker—" Erickson offered.

"I don't care what the undertaker and the coroner said," lectured the pathologist. "If this .45 was fired inside that room, the bullet went all the way through."

"Unless it struck bone," Erickson reminded.

"OK, I'll buy that as a possibility. But only a possibility," Campbell said. "But Milan is still right, of course. We must complete the anatomical study before he spins his wheels over the gun."

"You're all set for exhumation then, Doctor. Your mind's made up?" G. Markham Hurst asked, quite seriously.

"What else can we do?" asked the pathologist.

"We can let *them* dig him up," Erickson said suddenly.

The room became silent and the other three men looked at the younger lawyer.

"Who? Higgs and Spencer?" G. Markham asked.

"Right!" said Erickson. "They are the ones who have suggested this disinterment from the beginning because they have the burden of proof. We don't have to prove a murder. They have to prove a suicide."

"But you told Mrs. Caton not to consent to the exhumation and autopsy," argued Hurst.

"I know," Erickson said, grinning. "I wanted them to do it by court order. It will look better to the jury."

"What if Higgs doesn't go for it?" asked Hurst.

"He will," Erickson assured. "And, if he doesn't, or if Spencer doesn't force him into it, we can always reverse our ground and dig him up ourselves."

"Who will they get to autopsy the body?" Hurst asked Campbell.

"Leatherman," said Campbell quickly. Havlicek nodded in quiet agreement.

"Leatherman from Miami?" asked Erickson.

"Either him or Irving Lefshay from Pittsburgh," said Campbell.

"It will be Leatherman," said Havlicek. "Why go all the way to Pittsburgh when a good man like Leatherman is available in Miami? Besides, how could you keep Leatherman out of the case? He'll want to save the stink-

ing casket and stand it up in the corner of his office."
They all joined in the laugh.

"I'll give Leatherman a call later in the week just to see
if the insurance people have contacted him," Campbell offered. "I won't show too much interest," he reassured the
frowning lawyers. "I call him every now and then about
other things, so I don't think he will be too concerned if I
inquire casually."

"In the meanwhile, I want you to have these photographs and Connecticut reports so that you and Havlicek
can confer about them at your leisure," said G. Markham
Hurst.

"Keep track of your time," said Erickson.

"Fees first," said Campbell and Havlicek together,
laughing.

"Up yours," said Erickson, grinning.

19

Fog filled the hollow in the road just below the cemetery but allowed the hill itself to emerge into the early sunlight like a bald pink head surrounded by a halo of fluffy white hair. Hillsborough Gardens was entered from the highway through a double wrought-iron gate. A large, well-lettered sign announced that the cemetery was closed at sunset and that all who entered after that time would be subject to prosecution as trespassers. In fact, vandalism had not been much of a problem at Hillsborough Gardens, although other cemeteries in Tampa had suffered toppled headstones and motorcycle races. In Orangeburrow, the only thing violated repeatedly in the cemetery had been juvenile virginity.

Spottswood's hearse moved almost silently through the haze and slipped out of the early morning Tampa traffic with a polite left-turn signal winking to the tank trucks. Spottswood dozed in the front passenger seat as his driver nudged the sleek black machine across the oncoming lane and into the macadam driveway of Hillsborough Gardens. If the hearse didn't know the way by heart, as the driver secretly supposed, its springs and shock absorbers at least were familiar with the bumps. Behind the hearse, another official Spottswood vehicle kept the somber pace and followed to a newer section of the cemetery.

In this section, the names were not as traditional as the more established corners of the Gardens. Instead, there were Brodys and Kleins and even Catons. At least one stone read Caton. It was located about seven rows inland from the fresh diggings, and the original sod had regrown over the still-higher-than-normal mound.

The vehicles stopped in the driveway and Spottswood's men got out. From the rear of the hearse, a few shovels were produced. Spottswood cringed and shushed the men as two of the shovels clanged together in the otherwise still, foggy morning. His abhorrence of shovel noises in the cemetery was strictly professional and in no way esthetic. In fact, when conditions permitted, he would even authorize the clandestine use of a Ford backhoe to open a new space. Provided, of course, that there were no mourners in the Gardens and that the family was not told.

Two of the passengers in the following car were long-time employees of Spottswood. Each had distinguished himself by faithful and expert spadework on the company azaleas as well as by tending to openings and closings. The qualifications for these positions were limited to strong backs, non-inquiring minds, and the ability to be invisible while working. The diggers were forbidden to speak to the bereaved or others except to give directions (hat in hand) to the front office. Neither was required to be Negro to hold his position. Since, however, Spottswood's was a long-established, smalltown, Southern funeral company, the fact that both of the spade men were black was considered to be fortuitous. At least that's what Spottswood has told the representative from the OEO the year before.

Spottswood remained in the hearse, listening to the radio news and attempting to read the metropolitan section of the *Tampa Tribune* by the gray morning light. The spade men had already obscured the name of Myrl Caton by draping their jackets over the headstone, and were carefully slicing the sod into replaceable squares. Spottswood supervised with an occasional squint in the general direction of the digging. Two other Spottswood employees, dressed in basic black, were careful not to get fresh earth on their well-shined shoes or to assume too casual a pose while on duty. Following a postwar relaxation of the traditional Spottswood rules, and since there was no family present, each of them silently smoked a cigarette. Most of the time, the smoldering cigarette was backhanded out of sight by a smooth, buttoned, gray glove.

When the spade men had piled a large mound of dirt onto the canvas they had spread next to the grave, Spottswood called a rest period.

"OK, you guys can let up for a while or go take a leak or whatever," he growled from the half-lowered hearse window.

The spade men pushed their tools into the sweet-smelling pile of dirt and disappeared toward the rear of the cemetery, fumbling with their zippers.

"I ain't ever met a nigger yet who don't want to pee the minute he puts his shovel down," Spottswood said to the two immaculate assistants. Both nodded with philosophical and historical agreement, although neither was older than twenty-five, and one had come to Orangeburrow from Ohio only three years previously. But a job was a job.

"Have they got to the top of the box yet?" asked Spottswood.

"Just about, sir," replied one of the assistants.

"Have 'em hold up before they hook the lifting ring to the handles. I want to give that damned insurance company time to get their blessed expert here," he fussed. "At least that's what they insisted on. I suppose we will have to wait all morning for this pathologist bastard to show up."

He reached under the seat and produced a heavy silver vacuum flask, unscrewed three of its interlocking cups, and poured coffee for each assistant and himself. They sipped the steaming coffee carefully as the two black diggers returned, glanced, and went silently back to work. The boy from Ohio felt a twinge of self-consciousness, but was able to repress it as he casually strolled to the opposite side of the hearse.

Headlights flashed as another car came across the drainage tile at the cemetery gate. Spottswood glanced in his mirror as the lights danced around the front seat of the hearse.

"I suppose that's them," he announced wearily as he stepped out of the hearse and straightened his tie.

Spencer's Buick pulled up behind the second Spottswood vehicle, stopped, and put out its lights. The inside lights went on briefly as the two front doors opened and slammed shut almost in unison. Spencer and Leatherman crunched their way through the loose gravel along the asphalt driveway and approached the hearse.

"Mr. Spottswood," announced Spencer, leading the pathologist forward like the father of the bride, "this is Dr. Leatherman, from Miami."

"Glad to meet you, Doctor," said Spottswood, gently shaking the pathologist's hand. "My boys have just about got the box exposed for you." He pointed with his head in the direction of the digging.

"Fine, fine, Mr. Spottswood," said Jerry Leatherman, reclaiming his hand.

"Have some coffee?" Spottswood offered loudly to the lawyer and the pathologist. One of the diggers paused briefly, wiped his brow with the back of his hand, and continued to dig.

"Thanks, no. We had some at a coffeeshop downtown," Spencer said. "As a matter of fact, I think I'll leave Dr. Leatherman with you and get on to the office."

"Are you busy or chicken?" Leatherman asked.

"To be honest, graveyards aren't my favorite places."

Spottswood frowned painfully to hear the lawyer refer to the well-manicured Hillsborough Gardens as a "graveyard."

"There's no one here to hurt you or complain," Spottswood offered.

144

"Except the bats, the ghosts, the ghouls, and the little winged creatures that shriek in the night and disappear at sunrise," Leatherman said in a tone suitable for a TV horror matinee.

"That does it. Call me when you've finished. I'll be at the office." Spencer returned to his car, started it, and backed down the driveway. In a moment, the gray Buick was speeding back toward Tampa.

Spottswood and Leatherman walked to the graveside and watched the diggers attach the block-and-tackle ropes to the concrete lid. One of the workers turned a small crank, and the ropes tightened on the loops in the lid. The lifting apparatus dug its feet into the sod bordering the grave as it began to contest the weight of the cover. With a loud creak from the ropes and pulleys, the concrete platform lifted free and rose a few inches above the box. Small clumps of new earth were shaved from the sheer sides of the reopened grave as the lid rose slowly to ground level and then knee-high. The lever on the crank was forced into a reverse position, and as the workers applied their weight to the side of the lid, the concrete slab was lowered, one gear tooth at a time, to a resting place next to the grave.

The casket sat quietly within the concrete box below. Occasional fragments of dirt dropped onto the top and rolled off to the sides. The floral spray that had been added as a traditional last gesture now, after three months, appeared limp and grotesque. Most of the coffin lay in semi-darkness, since the rising sun cast rays only to half the depth of the grave.

The diggers quickly detached the lifting hooks from the concrete lid and fastened them with slight difficulty to the casket handles along its sides. To accomplish this, one digger had lowered himself carefully into the grave and stood with a foot on each side of the concrete grave liner.

"Shall we wait for the other pathologist?" asked Spottswood, looking at his watch.

"Oh, I'm sure that Mark won't object to our lifting the casket out. He's meeting us at the funeral home, and we'll wait for him to arrive before we actually open it," Dr. Leatherman said.

Spottswood motioned to his workers and the crank was again slowly turned, each gear tooth snapping the retaining lever like an old, worn, clock. The ropes straightened and strained under the weight. The casket slowly rose from the concrete box and was lifted just above ground level. Several three-by-eight planks were slid across the open grave under the suspended casket. The diggers lowered the casket onto this temporary platform and unhooked his lines.

"You might as well put him in the car, boys," announced Spottswood.

The well-dressed attendants went quickly to the rear of the hearse and opened its large door. They adjusted the rollers along the floor of the hearse to accept an entering casket, and returned to the graveside to assist the diggers. Each of the four men took a position on the side handles and, at a silent, professional nod from Spottswood, lifted the casket gently. The walk from the grave to the hearse was unhurried and smooth. Even with no audience of mourners, their demeanor was somber, silent, and funereal. The casket slid effortlessly into the depths of the yawning hearse. The floor rollers were locked to hold it in transit, and the large rear door was gently closed with a heavy click.

One of the attendants opened the right front door for Spottswood and Leatherman, and then went around to the other side to become the driver. The diggers and the other attendant—the one from Ohio—got into the second car and backed down the driveway. At the gate, the second car backed into a cul-de-sac to allow the hearse to precede them into Orangeburrow.

Shovels and the lifting machines were left at the gravesite now marked by a small metal sign identifying the work as that of "Spottswood's—Orangeburrow."

The sun was a little higher in the sky now and the fog had all but burned out of the low places. A timid robin flew from a nearby headstone to the pile of fresh dirt and surprised an earthworm.

20

The brief Spottswood parade returned without delay to the white framed dwelling that had been converted into Orangeburrow's oldest funeral parlor. The vehicles went directly to the rear of the establishment and the hearse was backed up to the loading platform. One of the attendants opened the rear door of the Cadillac and unlatched the locks on the rollers beneath the casket. The box slid easily onto the platform. The attendants, assisted by the two diggers, lifted the casket by the handles once more and carried it into the preparation room. They placed it on the floor and looked inquiringly at Spottswood.

"Better leave it be, boys," directed Spottswood, glancing at Leatherman.

The Miami pathologist nodded in agreement. "I am sure Dr. Campbell will be along shortly," said Leatherman. He put his small black bag down on the casket lid as Spottswood inwardly recoiled. "Nice prep room you've got here, Mr. Spottswood."

"Thank you, Doctor. Here, let me show you the rest of the place."

Spottswood led the pathologist toward the public por-

tions of the funeral home. The furnishings were an assortment of real and reproduced antiques that failed to recapture any particular era. Some were Victorian, some were
Colonial, but all were worn by years of use. Spottswood
slid a heavy door into the wall and welcomed the visitor
into a large room with an equally large sweep of his hand.

"Our chapel," he announced with a near-theatrical dignity.

"Very nice," said Leatherman in an appropriately
hushed tone.

The chapel was carefully nondenominational. The folding chairs stood empty and waiting behind the several
rows of wooden pews which Spottswood had purchased
years before when a Baptist Church was remodeled. The
lectern that the Reverend Billie had used so many times
stood ready at the front.

"Very nice, indeed," said the pathologist, leaving the
chapel. He followed Spottswood to a small room which
had been furnished as an office. Leatherman expected a
rolltop desk, and was surprised to see a modern, formica-
covered table with clean lines and built-in drawers. The
top was orderly, far more orderly than anything Leatherman was accustomed to, and a small Kiwanis bell occupied a prominent front-and-center position. The engraved
plaque at the base of the little brass bell announced that
Spottswood had performed a great community service by
organizing the Easter sunrise worship five years before.

Leatherman looked around the room. Impressive certificates and photographs of small groups of smiling men, one
of whom was invariably Spottswood, covered the walls.
Leatherman had seen similar self-lauding certificates in every funeral director's office in Miami and felt no urge to
read the Orangeburrow edition. He glanced at the mock
Bavarian cuckoo clock and noted that it was exactly
nine. The clock did not strike and no cuckoo appeared.
He assumed that Spottswood had emasculated the clock
to eliminate the cuckoo during funeral services.

Spottswood's phone rang softly.

"Yes?" he inquired with a professionally somber tone.

"Dr. Campbell is here," said one of the attendants.

"We'll be right there," said Spottswood. He replaced the phone. "Dr. Campbell is in the prep room."

The two men left the office and retraced their steps down the carpeted and frequently creaking hallway. Spottswood opened the door at the end of the hall. A carved plastic sign on the door said "No Admittance. Employees Only."

"Mark, how are you?" Leatherman smiled and pumped Campbell's hand.

"Fine, Jerry, and you?"

"Never been better. Do you know Mr. Spottswood, here?"

Campbell shook the outstretched hand of the funeral director and was reminded of how it feels to hold a dead fish.

"I've heard a great deal about the wonderful things you're doing at USF," Spottswood said solicitously.

"Thank you. It's fun to organize a forensic pathology department in a new medical school. But Dr. Leatherman's department in Miami was famous all over the country before our university was even opened," Campbell announced.

"And now you've got all the new equipment," lamented Leatherman.

"Well, when you don't have anything at all, you have the perfect opportunity to buy new stuff."

"All I can do is wait for a juicy homicide or some sex assault on a child and then cry for a new machine when the newspapers and TV cover the case," Leatherman laughed. "That's called applied public psychology."

"It's also called chiseling," Campbell contributed. Spottswood smiled to be one of the group, but his laughter was an unusual sound for the white-tiled prep room.

Leatherman lifted his small black bag from the casket and moved it to a nearby countertop.

"My tools," he said simply. He opened the bag and began to arrange the stainless-steel instruments in a neat row along the counter.

"I didn't bring any," Campbell confessed. "I figured that Mr. Spottswood might let me borrow a blade holder if I needed one."

"You're welcome to anything we have, Dr. Campbell," said Spottswood, gesturing toward the glassed-in cabinet that stood in the corner of the room. The cabinet exhibited the artery hooks, scalpels, and clamps that made up Spottswood's professional instruments.

"Thank you, Mr. Spottswood. I'm really assigned the role of observer here this morning. Dr. Leatherman has to do all the work."

"Bullshit," said Leatherman. "If you think you're going to sit there, neat and clean, while I bust my ass cutting into this rotten corpse, you've got another think coming. You just might as well get your gloves on now, because I guarantee you that this is going to be a joint enterprise."

"I was afraid of that." Campbell took off his coat and hung it on one of several hooks protruding from the wall. Other hooks held several stained and spotted plastic aprons. Campbell selected one and carefully inspected it to determine which side the stains were on. To Spottswood's surprise, Campbell continued his undressing by removing his tie, shirt, and undershirt before putting on the apron.

Leatherman busied himself with his instruments and snapped new number 22 Bard-Parker blades on each of the four red plastic scalpel handles. The scalpels looked more like those used for building models than they did like surgical instruments. Since autopsies did not require sterile instruments and often were lengthy, Leatherman had long ago adopted the broad stubby handles that fit more comfortably in his hand.

"Would you like us to open the casket now?" asked Spottswood. His well-dressed assistants stood ready with screwdrivers.

"OK with me. How about you, Mark?" asked Leatherman. He rolled up his shirtsleeves and took out a new disposable plastic apron from his traveling tool bag.

"Whenever you're ready," Campbell said. "But I suggest that you turn on your fan, Mr. Spottswood."

One of the attendants jumped toward the switch on the wall and flicked it on. A large exhaust fan in the wall roared into action, lifting the small louvers which covered the exterior opening.

Spottswood motioned silently in the direction of the casket and the two attendants began their attack. They turned the locking screws in the front part of the casket just below the lid and lifted the cover. A flat wooden cover still closed the box after the lid was hinged back fully open. The attendants began the slightly longer task of removing the several screws which held this tight against its rubber lip along the edges of the box.

"I remember opening one of these after it had been buried a good while, and when the boys loosened the last screw on the lid, the whole thing blew up in their faces from the gas inside," Leatherman commented.

"And inflammable, too," Campbell added. "Better not be smoking when you pop one of these sealed caskets."

"Did you ever light the gas that comes out of a floater?" Leatherman asked.

"I've thought about it, but I have always been too chicken. I was never sure that the whole body might not blow up," Campbell said.

"Naw. All that happens is that the belly gas shoots up in a big blue flame when you make the first cut. And boy, does that cut down on the stink!" Leatherman said.

The attendants had stopped loosening the screws during this exchange between the pathologists, but Spottswood urged them on with a few impatient motions.

"The next time they pull one out of the Hillsborough River, I'll give it a try," Campbell promised.

"It really works," Leatherman said.

The sealed lid was pried loose with the screwdrivers and lifted from the casket by the attendants. They were somewhat disappointed that there was no rush of escaping gas as Leatherman had forewarned. A distinctive, musty odor immediately filled the room as the fully dressed body of

Myrl Caton lay exposed in the casket. His hands, blackened and leathery, lay folded across his lower chest. The eyes were sunken and the cheeks were hollow from partial dehydration. From each nostril a small cone of white, delicate fungus grew like foam. The hair was still neatly combed; the younger attendant looked at it carefully, fully expecting that it would have grown to a great length after death, but it hadn't.

The face was darkened along the left side, which lay a little lower than the right. The head had probably turned slightly during the transportation and burial, allowing more of the internal fluids to collect in the dependant portions.

"At least there are no maggots," Leatherman sighed.

"What do you use to kill those little bastards when you get a body that has been locked up in a house for a week or two?" Campbell inquired.

"We've tried everything," Leatherman said. "We avoid most of the usual liquids because we're afraid we might foul up our toxicology."

"Have you tried the dry-ice fire extinguisher?" Campbell asked.

"We have. But the maggots seem to wake up after being frozen for a while and crawl all over the damned morgue."

"The trick is to keep them frozen long enough to finish the post," Campbell said.

"You can also put a formaldehyde-soaked towel in the crash-bag, zip it back up and let it sit for a few hours. The fumes kill the maggots but the blood doesn't absorb enough formalin to screw up the alcohol tests," Leatherman advised. He removed Caton's shoes and dropped them back into the casket without ceremony. With a pair of sharp surgical scissors, Leatherman cut along the entire length of each trouser leg, joining the two cuts at the crotch. He unbuckled the pants and then repeated the clothing cutting along the arms of the jacket. The shirt, neatly buttoned, was quite greasy along the back and sides from fatty tissue which had broken down and seeped through.

Leatherman cut the shirtsleeves and unbuttoned it along the front. Myrl Caton, nude except for his undershorts, lay quietly in the remnants of his new suit. The shorts were quickly snipped, and the once-proud organ of the tomato king lay exposed, shriveled, dehydrated, and limp.

"Let me get a few pictures before we move him," said Leatherman. Both pathologists began to fire 35mm. color slides of the body. They moved around the casket and took turns standing on a small stool to improve the angle for the photographs as sudden bright flashes from their battery-powered strobe units filled the gleaming prep room repeatedly.

"You want to get a shot of that entrance wound now, Mark, or after we get him on the table?" asked Leatherman.

"I think the ones I just got will be sufficient until we lift him out," said Campbell.

The attendants had put on rubber gloves and somewhat reluctantly assisted the two pathologists in lifting the heavy body from the casket. The two diggers had long before found other chores to do and were noticeably absent when the casket lid was unscrewed.

The body was no longer stiff; it tended to fold at the hips as they struggled against Caton's weight. The greasy condition of the back added to the difficulty and Myrl almost fell to the floor before he was made secure on the ceramic preparation table.

"Sure looks like a .45 inshoot," remarked Campbell as he closely inspected the large circular hole in the left side of Caton's chest.

"And close, too," added Leatherman. "Look at all that powder splash around the wound." He pointed to an oval area of blackening which extended from a portion of the wound edge toward the skin of the left chest for a distance of half an inch.

"I'll go as far as admitting that it's blackened, but not as far as identifying it as powder," Campbell said, smiling.

"You're really going to earn your fee, aren't you?" Leatherman chuckled. "If you weren't on the widow's side in the case, what would you call the black stuff?"

"I'd probably wonder if it was powder," Campbell said. "But look closely at the hairs. None of them is burned."

Leatherman took a small magnifying glass from his black bag and inspected the chest hairs at the edge of the wound.

"You're right," he said, handing the glass to Campbell. "I guess his shirt absorbed most of the flash."

"And the shirt was destroyed," Campbell remarked with a wink.

"Along with the mattress," moaned Leatherman.

The remark about the mattress triggered the same thought simultaneously in each pathologist's mind. Without speaking and yet fully understanding the other's intentions, Leatherman and Campbell rolled the body onto one side and gave an arm to one of the attendants to hold for stability.

"Son of a bitch!" Leatherman said.

"No exit," Campbell said.

They allowed Caton to flop back onto the table. The two pathologists looked at each other as Leatherman tapped his finger in meditation on Myrl Caton's abdomen.

"It has to be in a bone," Leatherman theorized.

"Seems so," Campbell agreed.

"Well, it shouldn't take us too long to find out," Leatherman said.

Each of them took additional pictures from various angles and distances and then put their cameras on the counter as Leatherman made the initial deep incisions in the chest. He began at each shoulder and brought his scalpel blade down quickly to the bone as he joined the two cuts at the upper portion of the abdomen.

Without speaking, Campbell continued the incision along the abdomen to just above the pubic bone. In minutes, the thick chest muscles of Myrl Caton were flopped backward onto his face as the skin of the chest was dissected free. The intestines lay coiled in short loops, punctured in many places by the embalmer's trochar.

Leatherman noted the intercostal space through which the bullet had passed, and then crunched each rib with his strong cutters. The instrument was like a wire cutter, with a curved lower blade designed to slip under the rib when the sharp upper blade sliced easily through the bone and cartilage.

"Right through the heart," Leatherman said as he removed the chest plate and exposed the chest organs. The pericardial sac was torn along its left side; a ragged hole gaped in the left ventricle of the heart. Several clumps of clotted blood lay beneath the heart and in the left chest cavity. The left lung had shared in the injury; the portions of the upper lobe closest to the heart showed a penetrating wound and hemorrhage.

Leatherman dissected the heart from its attachments to the vena cava and arteries and lifted it out of the body. He pushed his gloved finger through the wound and wiggled it at Mark Campbell. The Tampa pathologist made a playful pass at the finger of his colleague with a hemostat.

"Think he ran around the room with this hole in his heart?" teased Leatherman.

"You wouldn't want to make that a congenital defect, would you, Jerry?" Campbell kidded.

Leatherman squinted at Campbell and allowed the heart to slide off his finger onto the dissecting board which Caton dutifully supported on his thighs. The heart was brown from the embalming and the post-mortem drying. The blood trapped within its chambers was no longer liquid, but now dropped to the cutting board as small fragments of red-brown clay.

"Can you see the bullet?" asked Campbell, standing on a small stool to look into the gaping chest.

Leatherman shook his head. "I think it's in one of the vertebrae," he said. He moved the left lung aside and Campbell slid his hand beneath it. His experienced fingers felt their way along the surfaces of the vertebral bodies until they found a round hole with rough edges.

"I think I've found it," said Campbell.

Leatherman slid his hand along Campbell's until his fingers found the hole. He smiled across the table at his colleague.

"Let me lop out that lung and we can see where it went in," said Leatherman.

Campbell removed his gloved hand as Leatherman applied the edge of the scalpel blade to the lung attachment. The bronchus, large arteries and veins, and several lymph nodes, blackened by years of dusty breathing, were quickly severed by Leatherman's single stroke. The left lung fell free into the pleural cavity. Without speaking, Campbell reached in and lifted the lung out. He inspected the bullet track through its medial portion and placed the lung on the dissecting board beside the heart. The lung showed similar drying effects from the months in the grave, and it no longer gave a wet-sponge effect when handled.

Leatherman scooped a red, claylike clot from the left chest space and dropped it in the plastic bag which lined a metal pail beneath the table. It broke into smaller clayey pieces when it hit the bottom of the bag.

"It looks like it's in T-6," Leatherman commented, identifying the vertebral bone which bore the apparent bullet hole.

Campbell adjusted his camera for the depth and flashed a slide of the bone and wound.

Leatherman removed the uninvolved right lung and put it on top of the other two organs on the board. Then, with several quick strokes of his scalpel, he dissected behind the diaphragm and across the lower end of the colon to remove all the abdominal organs in one anatomical block. Both he and Campbell would dissect these organs later, before replacing them, oddly assorted, within any available body space for final burial.

Campbell prepared the vibrating saw that Leatherman had brought and plugged it into the wall. Silently, he placed the instrument in Leatherman's hand and held the electric cord out of the fluid that had collected on the out-turned flap of chest muscle and skin.

The vibrating saw whirred like a milk-shake machine. The saw blade began to kick up bone dust and produce an odor reminiscent of a tooth being drilled. The spongy bone of the vertebral body melted easily under the blade of the saw, and in a few moments, Leatherman had made incisions below and around the hole.

"Just my luck, I'll saw the damned bullet in half," Leatherman said. His brow was beaded with sweat as he worked; Spottswood reached over and quietly mopped it dry with a folded towel.

"Thanks, Spottswood," said Leatherman. "You'd make a good scrub nurse." Both he and Campbell chuckled as Spottswood looked a little flushed. The younger attendant almost giggled, but his expression became stony when Spottswood glanced angrily in his direction.

"I can just see the edge of the bullet," announced Campbell, squinting into the depths of the gaping hole which once was Myrl Caton's chest. He pointed at a small glint of gray metal which peeked from the space in the vertebral bone.

Leatherman nodded and put the saw down. With a small chisel and hammer, he made a series of short, stabbing thrusts at the edge of the remainder of the back bone. The bullet was now exposed, and Leatherman wrenched it free with his fingertips. He was careful not to bring any of his metal tools into contact with the bullet, because he wanted to be able to testify that all the markings on the missile had come either from the gun, the victim's bone, or something in between.

Campbell extended his hand, and the Miami pathologist dropped the bullet into his palm. The lead-colored bullet was flattened along its nose, but was otherwise in good shape.

"You think the ballistics boys will be able to work with that?" Leatherman asked, as he made a few cuts into the organs of the abdominal block.

"Oh, yes," said Campbell, almost lost in thought. "They'll have a field day with this one." He rotated the bullet in his fingers and carefully inspected the markings along the sides of the bullet. "A field day," he repeated almost to himself.

Leatherman took the bullet from Campbell and carved his initials in the base. When he had finished this micro-engraving with the skin needle, he held the bullet close to his eye to inspect it. "JL," he said with self-satisfaction. He took a test tube from his traveling tool bag and stuffed cotton in the base of it to cushion the bullet. Leatherman then dropped the bullet onto the cotton, added a small label to identify the contents of the tube, stoppered it with a rubber cork, and put it in his shirt pocket. "I suppose the lawyers will figure out when your ballistics expert can get a chance to examine the slug," Leatherman said.

"I suppose," said Campbell. He examined the abdominal organs which Leatherman had sliced and found no gross abnormalities. The liver was brown, and a few small gallstones rolled from the gallbladder when Campbell poked at it with his forceps.

The kidneys were normal in shape and he agreed with Leatherman that there had been no significant urinary disease.

"The stomach is empty," remarked Campbell blankly.

"Either he didn't eat or the embalmer got it all out with his suction trochar," Leatherman observed.

Leatherman pushed the crumpled mass of chest skin out of his way. He combed the hair on Caton's head with the blunt handle of his scalpel to find a place for his next incision.

Leatherman made a sudden, deep incision across the scalp from ear to ear. He worked his hand and scalpel rapidly under the scalp until he was able to fold it forward and backward over the face and neck to expose Caton's smooth, white skull. The two attendants inched closer as Leatherman manned his saw and removed the skull cap. Caton's brain, still covered by the thick dural membrane, lay exposed like a giant blanched walnut.

Leatherman cut through the dura, and, supporting the badly softened brain to prevent its tearing free by its own weight, he severed its attachments and gave it to his colleague.

Campbell studied Caton's decaying brain now resting in his hands. "It thought. It wondered. It hoped. It imagined and feared," he murmured with hushed and genuine awe.

"It probably never prayed," Leatherman suggested as he removed the pituitary gland like an olive from a martini.

"Neither has yours," Campbell said. He smiled quickly and received a grin from Leatherman in return.

"It has too!"

"When?"

"Every time Eastern comes in for a landing with me on the passenger list," Leatherman said with a grin. "And once before a biochemistry exam," he added.

"It worked, didn't it?" Campbell asked.

"So far, I've survived all of Eastern's landings," he assured the USF pathologist, "but I flunked the exam."

"God's not a chemist," Campbell said simply, explaining this complex corner of theology.

Leatherman sliced the brain and showed each slice to Campbell. Neither was able to identify any significant pathological changes. There were several areas of post-mortem softening and cyst formation from gas-forming bacteria, but no wounds.

"Will you let me have a set of slides as soon as you're able?" Campbell asked. He looked deliberately at his watch.

"I'll have them out by the end of the week," Leatherman promised.

"Are you booked for lunch? Care to come out to USF and see the department?" Campbell offered. He stripped off his gloves and plastic gown.

"I'd like to, Mark, but I promised those insurance lawyers that I would hustle over and spend the afternoon going over the case with them."

"OK, have your skull session if you must," chided

Campbell. "I'm going to participate in a seminar on anoxic deaths with the third-year students, so I'll have to push on." He scrubbed his hands and forearms in a large drainage sink, looking surprisingly like a surgeon preparing for major surgery.

"Tell them about this suicide," Leatherman suggested. He picked up each sliced body organ and returned it to the gaping hole which now constituted the chest and abdominal cavity. The dissected heart lay awkwardly near the small intestine and both nestled intimately where the prostate used to be. With all organs replaced in random places, the well-dressed attendant, sleeves carefully rolled to the midforearm, began to sew up the abdominal incision like an elongated baseball.

Leatherman snapped off his rubber gloves and joined Campbell in scrubbing.

"Want to share reports?" Leatherman inquired gently.

"Better let the lawyers decide. Besides, I think yours will be the only official report in the case. Mine is only a critique."

"How much you going to charge 'em?" Leatherman asked, as he dried his hands on a new towel supplied by Spottswood.

"A bundle," said Campbell, putting on his shirt and coat. He shook hands with Leatherman and then with Spottswood. "Thank you, Mr. Spottswood. You have been quite kind to let us mess up your prep room like this."

"Glad to be of service," said Spottswood professionally.

"Don't forget to put him back," Leatherman said. He buttoned his shirt sleeves and tightened his tie.

"For good this time?" Spottswood asked with an uncharacteristic smile.

"If you're lucky," said Campbell with a wink to Jerry Leatherman. He picked up his camera and snapped the case closed.

"Hold it," said Leatherman quickly as he flashed a final picture of Mark Campbell, Spottswood, and the partly sewn Myrl Caton together for what he hoped would be the last time.

"I enjoyed it, Jerry," Campbell said. "I'll be in touch with you soon." He shook the Miami pathologist's hand briefly and turned toward the door of the prep room.

"Call me if you get down to Miami," called Leatherman. "Otherwise, I'll see you in court."

"Let's hope not," Campbell said. "Any settlement would be better than this trial."

"Tell your lawyers," Leatherman said.

"Tell yours," Campbell said. He winked at his colleague and left the prep room abruptly.

Leatherman looked at the dried, darkened face of the corpse. "What did you tell him?" he asked Myrl Caton. Caton's mouth, inadvertently remolded when the scalp was pulled forward, showed only a small, grotesque smile.

21

The foursome was inconspicuous among the many luncheon tables of businessmen, lawyers, and doctors that filled the main dining room of the Downtown Club. The two sets of opposing lawyers—Hurst and Erickson for the plaintiff, Higgs and Spencer for the Insurance Group's defense—seemed to be having an amicable time together.

The Downtown Club occupied the whole top floor of a tall building downtown and commanded an impressive view of the city and the bay. G. Markham Hurst could remember when the view was unobstructed, but now the horizon was obscured by the clouds of smoke and smog which settled over the industrial section and the docks like a ring around a bathtub.

"We're going to let you young tigers do all the snarling and snapping in the courtroom. We're going to sit back and take notes, right G. Markham?" asked Higgs.

"An equitable division of labor," said the senior partner of Chatam, Kellogg, Hurst, et al., smiling.

"I'll have the small chef's steak and the cottage cheese," Hervey Higgs said almost secretively to the waitress.

Erickson watched her buttocks move firmly beneath her tight black mini as she took the orders. "I'd rather have a piece of that," Erickson said with a straight face.

"Pardon me, sir?" she asked pleasantly. After a year or two at the Downtown Club, the better waitresses learned not to trade remarks with the customers and not to scream if an aged executive pinched her on the breast as she cleared the dishes. The girls that commented or made a scene were quickly replaced. The ones that only smiled frequently drove new sports cars and lived in better apartments.

"A piece of that roast beef that Seymour is carving." Erickson winked and pointed beyond the waitress's hip toward the serving counter where a huge round of beef was being expertly dissected.

"Yes sir, Mr. Erickson," she said professionally. She looked directly into Paul Erickson's eyes and said, "Whatever you want, sir." She continued to look straight into his eyes as Erickson broke into a small grin. The waitress took the menu from him and was careful to brush his hand with her fingers as she did so.

Spencer caught and savored the scene. He winked gently at Erickson. "An old friend?" he asked when the waitress had left.

"She's an old friend to a lot of guys," Erickson said. He grinned and adjusted the small packages of crackers in the basket in front of him.

"Well," G. Markham said, clearing the air gently but firmly. "What do you expect should be the order of witnesses?" The four lawyers returned to the purpose of the lunch. "I mean, each of us has subpoenaed damn near everyone in town and half of the State of Connecticut, but who are we really going to use?" he continued.

"The cop from Middlebrook, and the motel manager," Hervey Higgs began, counting on his fingers. As he spoke he looked across the table at his co-counsel for a nod of agreement.

"You don't want to put on the motel manager through

his deposition?" Erickson inquired. He was unsure of the manager's presentation and style.

"He's already scheduled to come down here at our company's expense, Paul. We may as well use him," explained Spencer. He was convinced that on the stand, the manager would come on stronger for the defense than for the plaintiff.

"And Dr. Leatherman, of course." Higgs folded away another finger.

Erickson nodded his head quickly.

"The girl from Connecticut?" Higgs asked Spencer, half counting the appropriate finger.

Spencer shook his head. "What can she add?" he asked.

"We may put her on, Red," Paul Erickson said softly. "We have both Miss Gaito and her boss, Vincent Irafino, on standby in Connecticut."

"She—they—might be able to offer some supportive testimony concerning the prior habits or character of the decedent," G. Markham said officially.

"Habits and character?" Spencer half shouted. He quickly lowered his voice and leaned toward the center of the table. "Bullshit," he stage-whispered.

"And Mrs. Caton, too, of course," G. Markham added softly. "Not only as the plaintiff, but as a character witness."

"With Judge Michael F. X. Haran on the bench, you'll have one hell of a time getting in all those character witnesses," Hervey Higgs warned.

"We have to try," Erickson said. "After all, you guys won't let us have your damned autopsy report, so we have to try something."

"Judge Haran agreed with us that Dr. Leatherman's report was privileged as part of our work product. Besides, you had your own pathologist there, so what do you need with our reports?" argued Spencer.

"Nobody but Judge Haran would have agreed with you on that point. In state court, we would have had a full copy of that autopsy and you know it," Erickson said, heating slightly.

"But this is federal court." Hervey Higgs shook his finger in an annoying gesture and Erickson was tempted to bite it.

"Don't we all know that," G. Markham lamented. In actual fact, he preferred the strictness of order and attitude that characterized federal court in general and Judge Michael Haran in particular. There would be no nonsense in his courtroom, and that satisfied G. Markham perfectly.

"What about the coroner?" Erickson asked almost too casually.

There was no rush to respond to the question. Spencer looked at his partner, and G. Markham at his.

"Fortunelli?" Spencer asked absently.

"Uh-huh," Erickson said, suppressing a grin.

"We had considered using just his death certificate and not actually calling him, Paul," Spencer said. His eyes were fixed on Hervey Higgs as he replied.

"We'd have to call him, of course," Erickson said in an indifferent tone.

"Oh?" Spencer inquired.

"He's on both our witness lists, so there has certainly been proper notice tendered," Erickson said. He found it easier and more effective to offer a defensive explanation before a question was raised.

"Oh, we agree, Paul, we certainly agree," Hervey Higgs said quickly. "But what do you propose to show by putting on Dr. Fortunelli?"

The minds of all four lawyers raced toward strikingly similar pictures of the inept physician on the witness stand. The question suggested its own obvious answer. The confusion that would be raised in the minds of the jurors by the expected testimony of a poor-caliber coroner would more than justify the expense to the plaintiff of bringing him to Tampa. Defense lawyers Spencer and Higgs had listed Dr. Fortunelli as a potential witness merely to be in position to prove the fact of the death.

The doctor who had pronounced the body dead would be the logical person to introduce the fact into the trial record if the death certificate was contested. But testimony beyond that fact was calculated by both sides to be damaging to the insurance company's position. Fortunelli would have to testify that he thought the death was due to a suicidal gunshot wound of the chest, but his inability to match wits and experience with Leatherman or Campbell would be quite obvious to the jury. The net result would be that Fortunelli would come on as the weakest link in the insurance company's claim of suicide and bolster Pat Caton's demand for a verdict of accidental death or homicide.

Paul Erickson poked at his cottage cheese with the edge of his fork. He allowed himself a slight grin while the question floated unanswered over the table.

"Dr. Fortunelli," Erickson began, announcing the name as if it were being called out to receive the Nobel Prize, "will be of great value in testifying about the circumstances surrounding the dead body. After all, he was the official police physician called in to investigate the scene for the state."

G. Markham stuffed half a roll into his mouth to suppress the laughter rising in his chest.

"But you will have his whole report," Spencer said. Almost as the words left his mouth, Spencer wanted to bite his tongue. He thought of the poor-quality report that Dr. Fortunelli had given the police.

"I understand that it was incorporated into the police report," G. Markham said heavily.

"It was. It was," said Higgs quickly. "And we will make all of that available to you."

"I really think we need to put on your Dr. Fortunelli to tie together any loose ends that might confuse the jurors," Erickson said. His tone was almost believable.

"Will that be all?" asked the waitress. She allowed the tip of her left breast to brush lightly against Erickson's ear as she reached forward to remove his plate.

Spencer relaxed with a grin. "It will be more than enough," he said directly to Erickson.

Hervey Higgs reached for the check but G. Markham Hurst had already quietly covered it with his hand.

22

Paul Erickson glanced at the traffic light. It was red against him, but since it controlled a one-way downtown street at 8:30 in the morning, Erickson decided to attempt a midblock dash. His square briefcase knocked against his thigh as he awkwardly changed his pace to glide behind a taxi that challenged him with an impatient beep.

The Jesuit Church across the street had just discharged its few faithful from the weekday mass. Erickson walked the half a block along Zack Street to the side entrance of the Federal Building and entered through the heavy glass doors that wheezed like one of the benchsitters out front. His footsteps clacked on the terrazzo floor and bounced back to him from the rows of closed Post Office boxes that lined the hallway.

Erickson took the worn marble steps in twos and emerged onto the middle portion of the second-floor corridor where there were a number of federal offices associated with the U.S. Public Health Service. Then he hurried up to the third-floor corridor and entered the courtroom.

The court clerk, wearing an unobtrusive and outdated

drab black suit, stuck his head into the room. "Excuse me. Are you Mr. Erickson?" He held his hand out in an official welcome.

"Right," Paul said, simply.

"The judge said you could make yourself at home. He will be along in about half an hour." The clerk walked with a slight stoop, acquired by his years of service at a low desk in front of the judge's bench in the courtroom.

The courtroom was ancient and the floorboards creaked. Each row of spectators' seats was formed by a pewlike bench without a center aisle. The front of this section looked more like a small New England chapel than a courtroom; there was even a belly-high red velvet cord to give it a communion flavor.

Inside the sanctuary, there were two modest wooden tables that provided a resting place for briefs and elbows, with three captain's chairs at each. Paul Erickson put his briefcase on the table nearest the jury box.

Erickson gazed at the empty jury box and wondered what twelve citizens would fill those seats. He had appeared twice before Judge Haran and was painfully aware that this particular jurist would not tolerate lawyers who attempted to question jurors. In state court, a judge expected and encouraged the lawyers to interrogate each potential juror, inquiring into prejudices and qualifications to sit as a trier of the fact; only rarely would a judge in state court interfere with this traditional method of jury selection or ask questions directly of jurors. But in federal court, it was the judge himself who asked almost every question to screen the jurors, leaving merely an occasional unexplored area for the lawyers to probe. As if to personify his own larger-than-life impressions of the federal court system, U.S. District Judge Michael F. X. Haran rode his trial lawyers without mercy. Other federal judges in the same district did not demonstrate the same intolerance for minor relaxations of the rules. The attitude was clearly his own: not federal, not judicial, not Irish-Catholic—just one hundred percent Haran.

The courtroom door squeaked open, and Erickson's opposition entered the arena. Spencer came in first, talking hurriedly over his shoulder to his co-counsel Hervey Higgs.

The older lawyer waved to Erickson. "Good morning, Paul," he called in a stage whisper. He glanced nervously at the door leading toward the judge's chambers and was relieved to see that the tiger of the bench had not yet appeared.

"Hervey, Red," Erickson said simply. He got up, crossed the room toward the two lawyers, and shook their hands.

"Nice day for it," Spencer said. He rubbed his hands together. "Where is G. Markham?"

"He'll be along after a while. But we won't wait for him. I'll start in on the jury selection as soon as they arrive." Erickson walked back to his own counsel table and sat down.

"You mean Judge Haran will start with the jury selection when he is ready," Spencer said.

"Don't cross him. He can be a real bastard," advised Higgs.

"Don't tell him, Hervey," kidded Spencer. "Let's let him throw Paul in the federal jail for contempt. Then we can pack up and go home." He winked at Erickson.

"Don't worry. I've been in front of him twice before. Besides, what do you think this is, one of those hippie trials?" Erickson retorted.

"If Judge Haran had presided over one of those civil-rights circuses, there would have been a lot less bullshit," Higgs observed, somberly. "Can't you see him putting up with some defendant calling him a fascist pig?"

"He'd have the guy in irons and shipped to some cell in about ten seconds flat," Erickson predicted.

"And then he'd quietly have a stroke," Spencer added. "I really think he sleeps in his robes."

"That's not all he does in them," Erickson whispered behind his hand.

The covering of the remark was fortuitous, since at that very moment, the tiger's den opened and Judge Haran swept into the room. His robes swished out behind him like a cassock as he strode briskly to the bench platform. He dropped one small pad and two law books noisily onto the bench and looked suddenly at the three lawyers. His gaze was stern as he continued to study the men standing silently before him.

"Good morning, gentlemen," he announced without warmth. The three barristers mumbled an essentially unspoken reply. "Who has been smoking?" the judge shouted. He leaned across the bench as his eyes wildly searched the room. He sniffed the air like an asthmatic bloodhound. "I don't allow smoking in my courtroom!" he shouted. "Truman! Truman!" he shouted.

The three lawyers glanced slyly at each other. Erickson cleared his throat as the court clerk reentered the room. "No one has been smok—" attempted Paul Erickson.

"Truman!" shouted Judge Haran. "See if any of these men have been smoking in my courtroom!" The clerk quickly approached and looked for an ashtray but found none on either table. He attempted to stand close enough to each of the three lawyers to determine whether there was cigarette smoke on any breath. There was none. "There does not appear to have been any smoking, your honor," the clerk announced.

Judge Haran continued to eye each lawyer suspiciously as he slowly sat down. He waved the clerk to one side with an impatient flap of his hand.

"All right," he said, more calmly but no more cordially. "Let me give you the ground rules. This is a federal court." He paused to let each lawyer savor that announcement. "Federal court, gentlemen," he repeated. He looked into the face of each lawyer, and said quite slowly and softly, "There will be no nonsense in this trial. Do you understand?"

The lawyers nodded silently. They were still standing.

"I have called you together before letting in the jury panel to make sure that we, as professionals, understand that in my courtroom there will be no statements or actions which do not reflect honor and credit upon the legal profession. This is not some state court, where a sideshow may be put on to confuse the jury and entertain the judge." He turned and pointed his bony finger at the carved official seal on the wall behind him. "We will refrain from any actions which might sully the image of the United States in the eyes of any juror, party to the case, or spectator. Clear?"

The lawyers nodded again. The session resembled a schoolmaster-pupil relationship. Erickson suddenly knew why G. Markham had chosen to be late. His age and stature in the legal community were sufficient for him to avoid a caustic comment from Judge Haran when he showed up later. G. Markham Hurst had never entertained the slightest intention of hearing the famous pretrial sermon from Judge Haran.

"Are there any questions, gentlemen?" he asked. His tone defied any of them even to think of one.

Spencer cleared his throat and Hervey Higgs kicked him gently in the shin. Spencer ignored his law associate and picked up a pencil as a prop. "Will you allow blackboard diagrams or charts to be used in the presentation of evidence, your honor?" he asked.

"I don't like that sort of thing, counselor. It makes the place look too much like a high-school classroom. I don't like any kind of theatrical props unless they are absolutely necessary for the jury's clear understanding. But I will allow those large photographs provided that they can be properly identified and introduced into evidence." He looked at each lawyer, as if to inquire whether there were still more ridiculous questions. There were none. The judge turned to his clerk, who was standing obediently at the courtroom door.

"Truman!" he snapped. "You may bring in the jury panel in ten minutes. In the meanwhile, gentlemen," he said to the lawyers, "you may stay in the courtroom or move about the building as you wish. But—there will be absolutely no communications, verbal or otherwise, between you, your clients, or any of your staff and the members of the jury panel. Is that quite clear?" He acknowledged the silent nodding with an additional grunt and picked up his small pad. He checked off several items written on the top sheet, and marched out of the courtroom without a further word.

"Why the hell didn't I become a dentist like my mother wanted me to?" Red Spencer asked. He put his arms around Erickson and Higgs, and the three attorneys, closer now than ever before, left the courtroom in search of an empty urinal.

23

Pat Caton found an empty parking space behind the Jesuit Church and easily maneuvered her Cadillac into it. She fit a dime into the meter and crossed the street to the courthouse. The dime would buy only the first hour and she fully expected a ticket under the wiper when she returned.

Pat was carefully dressed, and more than one male head turned to get another look as she rounded the corner onto Florida Avenue. She wanted to make sure her demeanor suggested the grieving widow. A widow, now many months after the death and therefore mainly recovered from the shock, of course, but nonetheless dressed in well-tailored black, with small accessories. The outfit had been suggested by Paul Erickson. A basic black ensemble, and a little expensive-looking: pure Maas Brothers.

In the massive stone archway above the front entrance, someone had carved UNITED STATES OF AMERICA in letters two feet tall. She was nervous, and she felt even less secure as she read these words and wondered why her trial was in federal court anyway. She made another mental note to ask Erickson about that, even though he had previously tried to explain diversity of citizenship—that several states were involved still hadn't sunk in to her head.

As she reached the heavy bronze doors, one opened spontaneously, and she found a grinning Kirby Morris standing behind it.

"Got yourself a soft government job, Kirby?"

"Good morning, Pat. Did you have any trouble finding the place?" He took her arm and led her toward the small stairway to the upper floors and the courtrooms. Kirby wore a light tan gabardine suit, complete with black-and-white saddle shoes and a Panama hat.

"You look like a goddamned strawberry farmer from Plant City," Pat said out of the corner of her mouth.

"That's just what I am, sweetheart," Kirby drawled. "A strawberry farmer turned tomato king."

Pat snatched her arm from Kirby's hand with obvious annoyance. "King? King shit!" said Pat derisively. "Just look at those Ruscaton books sometime, baby. Since Myrl died we've been outsold by every Mexican grower from Gainesville to Pahokee."

"Don't worry, Pat, when we win our lawsuit, we won't have nothing more to worry about. The tomatoes can just—"

"Our lawsuit? Why, you cheap bastard!" Pat stopped on the worn marble stairs and faced Kirby Morris, one step below. She looked directly into Morris's eyes. "Let's get one thing straight," she said loudly. Her words echoed through the stairwell. "This is my goddamned lawsuit. Got that? Mine, Kirby!" Her eyes were dilated as she warmed to the excitement.

"OK, OK," Kirby hushed her. He glanced nervously up and down the stairs, but saw no one. "Let's keep it down, honey. Ain't no need to make a public fuss." He smiled a half-smile of embarrassment.

"Then you just hush up your face. I don't want to hear any more talk like that again. You hear?" Kirby nodded silently. "Just because you were lucky enough to crawl into my bed sometimes when we was both full of gin,

175

don't get no funny ideas about half of this lawsuit being yours. The business will get its share of the insurance money. You remember how Paul went over that?"

"Oh—so now it's Paul?"

Pat was undisturbed by his inference. "Yes—Paul. What of it?"

"Nothing, nothing. Maybe next you'll be able to tell me what the 'G' in G. Markham Hurst stands for." Kirby grinned slyly.

"You're a rotten bastard, Kirby." She shook her head slowly. "I really mean it. A perfectly rotten bastard."

"Nobody's perfect," he said. " 'Specially you, Pat baby. If you want to walk up these courthouse steps all by yourself, you just say the word. Maybe you can answer some of those questions about Myrl's death."

"What's that supposed to mean?"

"If you drive me out of this case, you've got real troubles. You need all the help you can get in making a murder out of Myrl's death. After all, you gave him plenty of reason to shoot himself."

"You had as much reason to get rid of him as anyone. How else would you ever inherit a company?"

"You better leave the suspect-hunting up to those lawyers," Kirby said.

She did not return his tiny smile as he took her arm and led her through the doorway and into the third-floor lobby. They stopped to read the directory on the wall opposite the elevator.

The elevator door opened and Erickson and Hurst got out. There were mixed words of greeting as all of them spoke at once.

"Today's the day," Erickson said. "Are you ready, Pat?"

"The real question is, are you ready?" she returned.

"We are loaded for bear," Hurst said confidently as he opened the hallway door and allowed the members of his party to precede him.

As they neared the courtroom door, the U.S. marshal stepped in front of them and raised his hand like a traffic cop. Erickson and company halted at this silent command. Pat looked at Paul Erickson for an explanation. He put a finger across his lips and then pointed toward the hallway from the end of that wing. A small crowd of men and women came down the hallway, looking like a group enjoying a tour through a museum. It seemed to Pat that there were about thirty to thirty-five people in the group.

The marshal held the door open and they filed into the courtroom one by one. They sat in a loosely collected group in the spectators' seats and looked generally relaxed. From this group, a jury would be selected.

Paul Erickson guided Pat around the red velvet cord which separated the spectator section from the front part of the courtroom. He showed her a seat at the counsel table. G. Markham assumed the chair to her right, leaving the chair on her left for Erickson. Kirby looked a bit puzzled and slightly embarrassed that there was no chair immediately available for him.

"You will have to sit in the first row of seats behind the cord," Paul Erickson whispered to him.

"Why?" asked Kirby, disappointed.

"Because you are technically not a party to this lawsuit, and because we want to use you as a witness later," explained Erickson.

Kirby looked at the first row of empty seats and then at Pat Caton. She returned a triumphant grin.

"What's worse is you will probably be forced to miss the whole trial anyway," G. Markham said over his shoulder.

"Miss it? Why?" Kirby asked.

"The rule. We'll invoke the rule which will exclude witnesses for both sides from the courtroom when other witnesses are testifying."

"Sounds crazy to me," Kirby said.

"It's a good rule," Erickson said. "Without it we would stand a good chance of hearing the same testimony over and over."

"OK, I'll sit over there. But who are all those other people?" He indicated the crowd in the spectators' sec-

177

tion, where the clerk was calling roll. Erickson glanced in that direction.

"Don't talk to any of them, for God's sake, Kirby. That's the jury!" Erickson raised the volume of his whisper for emphasis.

"All of them?" asked Pat, obviously astonished.

"No—only twelve," said G. Markham.

Pat looked over the group in the spectators' section. "Which twelve?" she asked.

G. Markham slowly scanned the crowd as Kirby and Pat searched his face for the answer.

"We wish we knew," Paul Erickson offered quietly. "We actually choose thirteen. The last poor guy has to serve as an alternate," said Erickson.

"The thirteenth juror has to sit through the whole trial, listening just as carefully as the other twleve, but not taking part in the decision unless one of the others gets sick or has to be replaced before the case ends," G. Markham explained.

"That poor bastard," Pat said softly and sincerely.

"They're all poor bastards," agreed Erickson. "They only get a few bucks a day to hear the case, and if it was a criminal case, or maybe a very large civil case, they would also have to spend each night locked up in some hotel, without their families."

"And without TV, newspapers, or private messengers," G. Markham continued. "Most people don't realize how hard it is to serve on a jury and how much money some of them—businessmen, for instance—might lose while they serve."

Pat scanned the small crowd again. "Paul," she said.

"Yes, Pat?" He was sorting some of his papers.

"Will the judge talk to me?" she asked nervously.

"Only if you are a very bad girl," Erickson said. He slid his arm around her shoulders and gave her a reassuring squeeze. "It will all be all right," he said.

"I just wish it would start. We've been all this time getting here, and now I'm getting antsy," Pat said.

"Even Sir Laurence Olivier might be nervous on opening nights," G. Markham suggested paternally. He tapped her gently on the back of her wrist with his own soft, wrinkled scholar's hand.

"But he's not on trial for his life," said Pat. Her voice quaked slightly.

Both lawyers looked at her and then grinned at each other.

"Neither are you," said G. Markham. "This is not a criminal case. This is a civil action. Nobody is on trial for his life here, Pat. We don't need to find the murderer. All we need to show is that your husband didn't commit suicide."

"The only thing really at stake here is money," joined Paul Erickson.

"But it's my money," she said, a small grin returning to soften her expression.

"That's why G. Markham and I aren't nervous." Erickson smiled. Pat joined him in the grin and rubbed her palms together to get rid of the sweat that had suddenly appeared there. She turned in her chair to find Kirby Morris seated dutifully in the first row. Kirby sent back a friendly wink.

"Are all the witnesses here?" Pat asked Erickson.

The lawyer did not bother to divert his attention from his notes to the faces in the first row. "They don't have to be. Sometimes, the lawyers and the judges make the non-expert witnesses show up on the first day to be sworn in as a group and be lectured by the court on their duties and so forth. But we don't ask expert witnesses to go through all that just to come in and state their opinions. Most of the experts have been in court many times before."

Pat nodded as if she understood. She was totally confused, but she felt more secure when someone like Paul Erickson explained the situation to her. Even if his terms were incomprehensible to her, she liked the fact that he understood.

The door from the judge's chamber opened and Judge Michael F. X. Haran entered.

"All rise," said the U.S. marshal. He spoke in a carnival tone, but they all rose. The marshal watched as the judge assumed his seat on the bench and turned to face the people in the courtroom.

24

The U.S. marshal, quite somber in his styleless black suit, complete with identifying shoulder patch and breast-pocket badge, stood in center stage and quietly cleared his throat. He began his chant:

"Hear ye. Hear ye. Court is now in session. Anyone having business before this honorable court, draw near and ye shall be heard. God save the United States and this honorable court."

Everyone except Pat Caton sat down. A few seconds later, she realized she was still standing and self-consciously took her seat. She glanced at Judge Haran and felt that he was glaring directly through her. Judge Haran had actually focused his myopic gaze on the ancient, government-issue lithograph of Chief Justice Marshall which hung on the back wall of the courtroom.

"The Honorable Judge Michael F. X. Haran presiding," said the U.S. marshal in the same nasal monotone. He left the front of the courtroom and assumed his position of doorman, peacekeeper, sergeant-at-arms, messenger boy, and ineffectual bodyguard for Judge Haran.

Judge Haran adjusted his glasses and looked out into

the courtroom, slowly panning the nervous crowd scattered throughout the spectators' section. He frowned slightly as he studied each face. As he reached G. Markham Hurst, the judge raised one eyebrow. That would be the judge's friendliest sign in court and he had reserved it for the senior counsel.

"Ladies and gentlemen," he called to them in a raspy voice. "You have been called here to form a jury and to serve in this court. Each of you has been summoned to perform a most sacred duty in the system of justice that we, as citizens, enjoy in these United States. Each of you has been chosen because you possess certain required qualities that qualify you—qualities that you may share with others who have not yet been called." He paused to let each potential juror savor his tone, if not his words.

"You have already heard your name called from a roll by Mr. Fernandez, my clerk," he continued. Judge Haran glanced quickly at Truman Fernandez and received a practiced, almost imperceptible nod from the clerk. "I congratulate you all for being present and accounted for. Mr. Fernandez has also assigned each of you a number, and I have duplicate numbers in this box." He patted a small box in front of him on the bench. "As I draw out a number, Mr. Fernandez will call out the corresponding name. If your name is called, you will come forward and quietly take a seat in the jury box. We will ask some general questions of all of you before we start the actual selection. If, for any reason, any of you is chosen but then is later asked to leave the jury box, it will be only because I have determined that it would be better for you not to serve in this case. In addition, each side of this lawsuit will have three opportunities to reject any of you without stating a reason. If this should happen to any one of you, I want you to understand clearly that there is no personal inference intended. None of you is to feel insulted, slighted, or otherwise unqualified to serve. It is this method which preserves our system of justice in this country. Without it, none of us could feel secure in his constitutional guarantee to a fair trial." He paused and blew his nose into a wrinkled handkerchief which he kept in the sleeve of his robe. "Are there any questions, ladies and gentlemen?" Judge Haran searched the room slowly but found no raised hand, no questions, no comment. With Judge Haran, there seldom were.

Erickson busied himself with small notations on the margins of some of the depositions as the judge continued to inquire generally into the jurors' basic qualifications as a group.

Pat found herself interested in the judge's questions. She followed each question with a quick turn of her head to see who, if anyone, answered when Judge Haran asked if they were all citizens, all over twenty-one, none convicted felons, none under active medical care, none in the armed services, no doctors, no lawyers, no relatives of any of the parties or their attorneys, none engaged in vital community occupations which would prohibit their serving throughout the whole trial . . . Pat felt self-conscious when the judge identified her as "Mrs. Patricia Caton, the widow of the late Myrl Caton," and made her rise and face the prospective jurors for identification. The attorneys, Higgs, Spencer, Erickson, and G. Markham Hurst, were also identified, but no juror candidate acknowledged them as friend, foe, or business associate.

When Judge Haran had asked the crowd whether any of them had sued or been sued by any of the lawyers present, Pat looked quickly at Paul Erickson, searching his face for some sign of injury. She felt somehow affronted that the judge would ask such a thing, but each lawyer took it in professional stride, happy to acknowledge a prior client or adversary. But none came forward. No one on the jury panel had apparently had anything to do with them previously.

Nor had any of the jurors had dealings with the Insurance Group. In most lawsuits, one is seldom allowed to mention the fact that an insurance company is involved. The courts have kept up the myth that some injured party in an automobile accident case is actually bothering to sue some penniless defendant, even though virtually every member of the jury would be an insured motorist himself. But in Myrl Caton's case, the suit was directly against the insurance company. The suit had been filed to force the insurer, as defendant, to pay off on the policy, even though it was less than two years old. As defendant, the insurance company had no straw man to hide behind, no false identity to wear throughout the trial. The company was standing alone in the courtroom, a fact that gave Hervey Higgs a chill. He was well aware that with the parties to a lawsuit a pretty widow and a big insurance corporation, the company started off with one foot in the grave. It was obviously Myrl Caton's grave, even though he was back in it somewhere in Orangeburrow.

"Number seven," continued Judge Haran. He had already called five jurors to the box.

"Morris Ross," translated Truman Fernandez. Mr. Ross left his seat and awkwardly found his way to his assigned seat in the box.

"Number twenty-four."

"Catherine McGuire."

Paul Erickson smiled gently as the buxom, matronly, white female walked heavily toward the jury box. Hervey Higgs shared the same thought as Paul Erickson, but in reverse. Erickson, representing the plaintiff-widow, was pleased to see a woman reach the box; the previous numbers had all been men. As counsel for Caton's side he felt that a woman would be more sympathetic and more responsive to the human elements of the death experience. Spencer counted on having to use a challenge to get rid of Mrs. McGuire, and made a small mark beside her name. Erickson felt sure the lady would be bumped, but with a total of thirteen jurors to be finally picked, he was hopeful that more women would be chosen than Spencer had challenges.

As the numbers were drawn and each name called, the lawyers made little diagrams of the whole jury box and filled each slot with a name. Later, when there were no more empty seats, the judge would delve deeper into the age, marital status, birthplace, address, occupations, and any other qualifications of interest. The lawyers would then fill in the little jury diagram with personal facts and use them as the basis for picking out which jurors to bounce.

At every legal convention, lawyers lectured and argued the fine points of selecting a jury and who to get rid of promptly. Never allow a woman on a rape case, said one. Always put a woman on a jury in a rape case, said the next. No Jews. Always get a Jew on a small-crime case. Never put a Southerner on a murder jury unless the defendant is a black. Never a laborer if the crime is a white-collar theft, such as embezzlement, or if the damage award might reach six figures. Look out for retired army brass—too intolerant ... The formulas were endless, contradictory, and sacred. No one knew for sure, but everyone had his own method, learned from years of experience or from some senior counsel. But in later years, many lawyers began to have doubts about the reliability of their own systems. Nevertheless, through the doubts, each stuck to his own method, like an inveterate horse player.

Spencer and Erickson completed their jury diagrams simultaneously, as a heavy-jowled man with the collar points of his one-size-too-small starched white shirt pointing upward like suppliant hands puffed forward and amply filled the twelfth chair.

"And now, ladies and gentlemen, I want you to pay strict attention as I inquire further into your attitudes and associations with persons or things which might demonstrate preconceived points of view or otherwise render you less than perfectly objective in this case."

Each juror turned in his swivel chair and faced the judge as he spoke.

"I have generally introduced Mr. Paul Erickson, the lawyer for Mrs. Patricia Caton. Mr. Erickson is functioning as an associate of Mr. G. Markham Hurst, a senior partner in the law firm of Chatam, Kellogg, Hurst, Mitchell and Rodriquez." Judge Haran nodded politely in the general direction of the plaintiff's table, but Erickson carefully refrained from any sign of acknowledgment.

Each juror turned his head in the direction of the attorneys being described, and studied them like a patient being presented as an example of an obscure disease.

"We have already established that none of you ever had professional dealings with any of these gentlemen or with other members of their law firms. Is that not correct?" The judge waited as each juror studied the attorneys and began a slow shaking of the head to deny, at first individually, and then in unison, any prior connections.

"And none of you has had any dealing with the insurance firm here named as defendant?" the judge continued. "Or with Ruscaton Tomato Growers? That's a packing firm down in Ruskin that some of you may have seen as you drive south along Route 41." He watched each juror for a spark of recollection, but none came.

"How about you, Mr. Schatz?" Juror number five stiffened in his chair and focused on the judge attentively. "Your information card says that you are in farming."

There was no reply from Mr. Schatz.

"Is that correct, Mr. Schatz?" Judge Haran snapped in a patriarchal tone.

Schatz jumped visibly. "Yes, sir," he said nervously.

"Did you ever sell any tomatoes to the Ruscaton packing firm in Ruskin?"

"No sir."

"Or anything else?"

"No sir."

"What do you grow in your farming, Mr. Schatz?"

"Easter lilies, sir." The voice was weak and hesitant. There was a slight snicker from those prospective jurors still seated in the spectator section.

"Easter lilies?" asked Judge Haran incredulously. He was visibly unprepared for the occupation of the juror named Schatz.

"I presume that Ruscaton did not purchase any lilies from you, right, Mr. Schatz?" Judge Haran smiled one of his rare genuine smiles.

"No, sir."

The judge continued with each juror in turn, searching

for any prior associations with any of the parties or their lawyers, and specifically following any leads that the inquiry uncovered. In fact, he found that juror number nine, Mr. Morgan, had had an unsatisfied claim against his insurance company a few years previously, following an automobile accident. This had left a bad taste in Mr. Morgan's mouth for insurance companies in general. Judge Haran excused Mr. Morgan for cause, and replaced him with another middle-aged male whose number was selected from the box on the bench.

The judge's inquiry went on for an hour and a quarter. He retired another man who belatedly decided that he was a diabetic and therefore unsure that he would be able to last out the whole trial comfortably. Judge Haran admonished him and the rest of the prospectives that health conditions should be announced early in the examination to save time. The diabetic was replaced by a man who was either chewing something or eating the inside of his cheek.

When each juror had been examined by the inquisitive judge, he gave the lawyers a similar but unequal opportunity. He had left few areas to inquire into.

Paul Erickson stood up and addressed himself to each juror in turn. He thereby shared a personal experience with each juror which allowed him a gut judgment of the juror before he used his three peremptory challenges.

"Mr. Cannella," he said to juror number three. "If, as we go along in this trial, you find that there are people involved who are quite obviously Italian or of Italian descent—" He allowed a dramatic pause during which each member of the jury paid careful attention to him. "—would you be able to listen objectively to all the evidence and not be swayed one way or the other?"

"Eh?" said Mr. Cannella with a frown. His accent, limited here to a monosyllable, was obvious.

"Mr. Erickson wants to know if you would favor an Italian in this case over someone else who was not Italian," said Judge Haran impatiently.

"Naw," said Cannella, shaking his head athletically. "I give everybody a fair shake."

"Aren't there a great number of Italians in the fruit and vegetable business here in Tampa?" Erickson persisted.

"I think so," said Cannella.

"Some in your own family?" Erickson asked.

Judge Haran leaned forward over the bench to catch every word.

"I got a cousin," said Cannella softly.

"How's that?" snapped Judge Haran.

"I got a cousin."

"In the vegetable business?" asked the judge. Cannella nodded. He cast his head down gently.

Erickson smiled slightly and returned to his table without sitting down.

"Mr. Erickson, do you wish to inquire further of this juror?" asked Judge Haran.

"No, sir. I request that the court excuse Mr. Cannella for cause," offered Erickson. His voice was a practiced, matter-of-fact monotone, carefully underplayed.

"For being Italian, Mr. Erickson?"

"No, sir. For demonstrating that he has certain personal or familial connections with a business which may be intimately involved in the circumstances of this case." If the judge would not remove the Italian juror for cause, then Paul had earmarked a peremptory challenge for him.

The judge sat silently for several moments before he picked up his pencil and made swift movements on the paper in front of him. "Mr. Cannella, you may return to your seat at the rear of the courtroom," the judge announced. "Juror number thirty-one," he called. Another woman rose from the small crowd in the spectators' section and replaced Mr. Cannella.

Paul Erickson smiled to himself as the third female sat down. Now, he thought, Spencer will either have to blow all his challenges on the ladies, or accept at least one of them.

Erickson studied his jury diagram for a moment and

188

leaned across the table to confer briefly with Pat Caton.
He stood up abruptly and faced the judge.

"The plaintiff will excuse juror number ten," he said
simply. Since he was exercising one of his three challenges, he was not required to state why he was rejecting
the astonished juror. For some reason, which Erickson did
not explore, Pat Caton personally disliked something
about the pudgy, average-looking man who had filled jury
seat ten.

"Mr. Bailey," the judge announced after he had
checked his own diagram to determine number ten's
name.

The juror, appearing a little embarrassed, left seat ten
and returned to the crowd. Both Higgs and Spencer were
pleased to see that another middle-aged male, took the va-
cant seat without effecting any significant changes in the
jury.

Apparently the replacement did not displease Pat Caton, since she offered no further frantic comments to her
lawyer.

"Mr. Spencer," the judge said, "would you care to inquire?"

Spencer arose, adjusted his yellow legal pad and jury diagram, and approached the rostrum. Judge Haran was no-
torious for keeping every lawyer behind the small, erect
desk which faced the witness stand and the jury.

Erickson leaned closer to Pat Caton and cupped his
mouth to her ear. "Who was Bailey—juror number ten?"
he whispered.

"He got drunk and danced with me once at the Palma
Ceia. But I don't guess he remembers it," said Pat.

Erickson nodded distantly. "How come you do?"

"Because he stunk. He had on a twenty-dollar golf shirt
that day, but he smelled like a Ruscaton packer."

Spencer smiled at each juror with the plastic smile of a
used-car salesman before he began to speak.

"Mrs. McGuire," he announced softly. "I believe you
said you had three sons." The female juror nodded affirm-

atively. "And that two had served in the war." She nod-ded again. "And that one of them is buried overseas?"

"Yes, sir."

Spencer didn't really care whether the juror's sons had served in the war or not. He simply wanted personal contact with her so that he could decide whether he would keep her or bump her. Any personal question would do as long as it provoked conversation.

"Mr. Spencer," Judge Haran growled. "There is no need to go over material which has been already covered." Judge Haran had always considered himself to be far more capable as a voir-dire examiner than any of the lawyers who appeared before him. It has been observed by some-one that in court, every spectator wants to be a juror, ev-ery juror a witness, every lawyer the judge, and every judge a practicing attorney.

Judge Haran had never really recovered from the trauma of law school, where he had sacrificed his time and energy to score high on the exams. Even now, forty-three years after receiving his LL.B., cum laude, he could recall the grades he had received on insignificant midterm exams in obscure legal courses. For Michael F. X. Haran, the op-portunity to study the law was a sacred trust second only to the priesthood. Had his mother had her way, it would have been the priesthood. But somewhere in his formative years, he had been influenced by the old lawyer who walked the neighborhood and frequently visited with his father. On many mornings, before the world had awak-ened, it had been cornbread, bacon, and Prosser on torts for Michael Haran the student.

"Confine your inquiry to points that you feel were omitted, Mr. Spencer. We do not intend to be tied up in this case forever." He allowed himself a small smile.

"Yes, your honor," Red Spencer submitted. Only a neo-phyte attorney would tangle with Judge Haran for insig-nificant reasons or at premature moments.

"Your honor, the defense will excuse Mrs. McGuire and Mrs. Tucker." Red Spencer had played two peremp-tive trump cards and kept one as an ace in the hole.

Judge Haran cleared his throat and called two more numbers—both male.

"What's Spencer's game, Paul?" G. Markham asked.

"I think he's saving his last challenge to see what we will do with the two we've got left."

"What are you going to do with them?" Pat asked. She was wedged between the two whispering lawyers.

"Not much. G. Markham, you know Judge Haran. There really isn't anything left to present to get rid of anyone for cause, and I'm afraid of getting someone worse if I bump anybody on a challenge. What do you think?" Both of them studied the jury and compared the biographical notes Erickson had made on each to the actual face.

"Mr. Spencer, you may continue," said Judge Haran, still glaring at G. Markham Hurst.

"Thank you, your honor," Red Spencer said. "The defense accepts the jury." He glanced at Erickson, smiled slightly, and sat down.

Erickson looked a little surprised. Spencer had accepted the jury with one challenge left. Evidently, thought Erickson, the insurance lawyers expected that he would bounce someone else, thereby calling up some new juror, and that Spencer might need his last challenge for the new man.

"What do you think?" Erickson whispered to his partner.

"Anyone you can't live with?" asked G. Markham.

Erickson quickly scanned the jury box again. "Nope. They all look OK to me."

"Then leave them alone and you've kept your last woman on the jury."

Erickson grinned and stood up. "Your honor," he said. "The plaintiff accepts this jury." He sat down quickly and glanced at Spencer. The insurance team was visibly disturbed by this strategy.

"If it please the court," said Hervey Higgs, rising slowly.

"Yes, Mr. Higgs?"

"The defendant would like to exercise his remaining

191

challenge and excuse Mrs. Endicott." Hervey remained standing as the judge leaned forward as if to confide intimately with the lawyer.

"Mr. Higgs, your side has accepted this jury and the plaintiff has accepted them. It's a bit late for you to attempt to exercise a peremptory challenge, don't you think?"

"Since the plaintiff still has challenges left, your honor, I think it not unfair to allow the defendant this opportunity," Higgs argued gently.

"I'm forced to disagree with you, Mr. Higgs, but if you are so set on exercising your last challenge, you may do so by excusing my first choice for alternate." The judge smiled easily and drew a number from the box. "Number fifteen," he called.

"James Cassidy," announced Truman Fernandez. A youngish man, perhaps in his late twenties, came forward and took the alternate juror's seat. The judge quickly ran him through the questions that everyone in the courtroom had heard many times that morning and threw him to the lawyers.

Spencer arose and accepted Mr. Cassidy with obvious resignation. If he bumped this choice, Spencer had to chance another unknown from the crowd which still contained several more women.

Erickson quickly accepted the man after Pat Caton leaned over to him and whispered that she thought Cassidy was cute.

"Gentlemen," said Judge Haran, addressing the whole courtroom, "we have our jury. This court wishes to thank all you citizens who have served here this morning and cautions you again not to feel rejected or slighted if you were removed from the jury. You may have another opportunity to serve the court elsewhere in the building. The marshal will escort you to Judge Hagstrom's courtroom, where some of you may still be needed. If not, you are free then to go, and we thank you for your cooperation and patience." Judge Haran smiled at the remaining crowd of prospective jurors as the marshal ushered them out the courtroom door. When they had left, the judge turned to the thirteen citizens in the jury box and smiled warmly to them.

"Lady and gentlemen, we are about to begin our lawsuit between the plaintiff, Mrs. Caton, and the defendant, represented by Mr. Higgs and Mr. Spencer. I admonish you to listen as carefully as you possibly can and to weigh the evidence to the best of your abilities. If there are any questions concerning the law, I will supply you with the appropriate answers. From this moment on, you are not to talk to any of the parties in this case except as the occasion may arise within the courtroom. If any person, attorney or otherwise, should approach you outside the courtroom and attempt to discuss any facet of this case with you, you are to come immediately to me and report the incident. Until you withdraw to consider the verdict at the close of all the evidence, you are not to discuss this case among yourselves or to receive any information concerning it from newspapers, television, or any other source." He paused to let each juror consider his words.

"There will be further instructions before the testimony actually gets under way, and I may have additional comments to offer you at the end of the case. Now, before I grant you a well-earned fifteen-minute recess—with coffee, Mr. Fernandez, please—I want you all to stand, raise your right hands, and be sworn in."

Paul Erickson squeezed Pat Caton's hand. "We're on our way now, Pat."

"Should I stand up or something?" she asked.

She suddenly felt reminded of the Catholic wedding she went to many years before. Then, as now, she didn't know when she should sit, stand, or kneel.

"All you have to do is sit back and enjoy the ride," Paul said reassuringly.

Pat sat quietly for a moment and studied the jury. "That's what a police detective once told me to do if I thought I was going to be raped."

25

The lawyers had returned to the courtroom, but the jury itself was still out. There were a few real spectators now. Not prospective jurors but actual spectators, drawn from their small retirement apartments and rented rooms by the magnetism of the drama of a lawsuit. For parties caught up in a suit, there is always a fear that the whole community will assemble to devour every word, basking in someone else's scandal. But in fact, except for the rare sensational homicide, no one finds time to attend a trial except a scattering of social-security pensioners with nothing better to do, an occasional newspaper reporter, and the father of the youngest attorney.

Pat Caton glanced around the courtroom, a little less nervous now than she had been at the start. She knew the fluttering in her stomach and the dry mouth would return as soon as Judge Haran resumed the bench. But while there was a recess, she could at least appear calm.

Spencer and Higgs were consumed by a discussion they were carrying on over some portion of a deposition opened on the table in front of them.

The judge's door opened and the U.S. marshal entered.

"All rise," he called, and a few additional phrases which were lost in the rumble caused by the rising of the small crowd.

The judge walked through the open door and onto the bench. He occupied his restless hands with compulsive adjustments of the ordinary objects on his bench, his drab tie, his black robe, cuff links, and worn college ring.

Judge Haran motioned everyone to be seated. "Mr. Fernandez," he called. "Have the witnesses been sworn?"

"No, your honor."

"Well, get them up here."

Fernandez scrambled toward the first spectators' row and urged forward the few assembled witnesses for both sides like a sheepdog. Kirby Morris took his place in the short line of witnesses and dutifully raised his hand as he faced the bench.

Truman Fernandez faced the witnesses, his back to Judge Haran, and, raising his own right hand, he asked the group, "Do you swear to tell the truth, the whole truth, and nothing but the truth, so help you God?"

Each witness mumbled "I do" and lowered his hand. Kirby Morris turned to go back to his seat.

"Just a minute!" snapped Judge Haran. "I'll tell you when to sit down! And it's not yet."

Kirby returned to his place in line and meekly faced the judge. His heart pounded a bit and he felt a growing resentment as his shock wore off and his embarrassment increased.

"You witnesses will have an important part to play in this trial," the judge lectured. He looked directly at Kirby but spoke to them all. "You will wait in a room provided for you until it is your turn to testify. You will not—I repeat, not—talk among yourselves or to anyone else about your testimony before or after you have given it. You are not to enter this courtroom after the trial has actually begun except when called to testify. Is that clear?" He glared at the assembled witnesses and gave them about thirty seconds to think over his instructions.

There were no questions. Kirby stole a small glance at

Pat Caton and hated the familiar but almost imperceptible twitch of her lips that told him that under more
relaxed circumstances she would have been laughing out
loud.

"You may show these people to the witness room, Mr.
Fernandez," said Judge Haran. He watched as the clerk
ushered the group silently from the courtroom and down
the corridor. The judge then turned to the lawyers' tables.

"Are you gentlemen ready?" Judge Haran asked. He
rubbed his hands together like the father of the family
about to carve the Thanksgiving turkey.

Erickson bounced to his feet. "The plaintiff is ready,
your honor."

"The defendant is ready, your honor," said Spencer,
half-rising and immediately resuming his seat.

"Good." The judge said simply. "Mr. Fernandez, see
that the jury is brought in and we will get on with this
case." The U.S. marshal disappeared through the door
toward the jury room. "Let's hope, gentlemen, that we
can push on with this case at all times. We don't anticipate any delays." He stared directly at Spencer and Erickson as he spoke.

Both stood silently and faced the jury as the twelve
men and one woman entered and took their seats.

When the jury had been seated and the lawyers had
rearranged their yellow pads still another time, Judge
Haran folded his hands in front of him on the bench. He
turned to the jury box and made a brief announcement.

"Lady and gentlemen," he began—he obviously savored
each opportunity to say that—"each side in this lawsuit
will now have an opportunity to make a brief"—he emphasized the word—"brief opening statement. Let me re-
mind each of you that what you hear is not evidence. It is
one lawyer's interpretation of what he thinks he may be
able to prove during the course of the trial. If what he
says helps you to understand the evidence his witnesses
will present, so much the better. But if his statements
vary from what you think any witness says later, you are
to believe the witness and be guided by your own inter-

pretation and understanding." He paused and allowed a minimal smile in the direction of the jury. His face then froze in a stoical expression as he turned to Paul Erickson and nodded solemnly.

Erickson took his yellow pad and walked to the rostrum. He placed his notes on the rostrum, stood straight, quietly cleared his throat, and began to speak on behalf of the plaintiff-widow. The trial was on.

"Members of the jury," Erickson began, "this is a trial brought by my client, Mrs. Patricia Caton." He paused and half-turned toward the woman seated next to G. Markham Hurst. Pat twitched slightly in her chair. G. Markham Hurst reassuringly put his hand on hers. "As you will be shown in this trial, Mr. Myrl Caton, the plaintiff's late husband, met with an untimely death. He was part-owner and the managing partner of the Ruscaton Tomato Company in Ruskin. During one of his frequent selling trips up north, Mr. Caton was found dead in his motel room, the victim of a gunshot wound. And in the same room with him was his .45 automatic lying on the floor. Now, these facts are undisputed." He allowed himself a small gesture in the direction of the defense table. Both Spencer and Higgs appeared to be following his statement carefully.

"Mr. Caton was insured by the defendant insurance company under several policies through his tomato business. One of these policies, the one under dispute here today, was relatively new, since it had been purchased only a short time prior to his death. You will be shown that this was not an unusual insurance policy nor was it a strange business procedure for Mr. Caton's tomato partnership or other local businesses. In fact, we will show you that it is quite commonly done." Erickson paused and glanced into the faces of several jurors selectively to begin some personal rapport with them. He turned toward Pat Caton again.

"But when the plaintiff, Mrs. Caton, filed for payment of the benefits under that policy, she was refused by the defendant company." He turned toward Spencer and

Higgs, as if to identify the villains. The insurance lawyers carefully maintained their deadpan expressions as several jurors glanced in their direction.

"You will hear the insurance company claim, through their capable lawyers, Mr. Spencer and Mr. Higgs, that the company does not have to pay off this claim because of a Florida statute. That statute, members of the jury, is a good law. It was put there for a particular purpose, and every state has one just like it or similar to it." He adjusted the pages of his notes, running his finger down a selected page, and then continued.

"That statute, and I won't bore you with the citation or the heavy words that the legislature used to write it, says that if you kill yourself within two years of the date on which you purchased life insurance, the company does not have to pay off." He paused again for minor emphasis. "Now, that's a good law," he repeated. "It's a good law because it prevents some despondent or disturbed person from buying insurance and then killing himself at least for two years." Erickson smiled slightly and looked at his lone female juror to see if she followed. She did.

"I guess the legislature thought that after two years, a man who bought insurance on his life would kill himself for some reason other than the insurance benefits. In any event, the lawmakers said that even though the death may be due to suicide, after two years the company has to pay the beneficiary."

One of the jurors coughed several times and Erickson waited for him to finish without embarrassing the man.

"Now, in our case," he continued, "we have a slight variation on that theme. We will show you that Mr. Caton, the insured, was killed, not by a suicidal gunshot wound, but by some other means." Erickson pointed his finger into the air and shook it for emphasis as he spoke. "We will demonstrate to a preponderance of the evidence that there are several other possible explanations for Myrl Caton's death than his own suicide. And," he lowered his voice slightly as if to impart something confidential to the jurors, "a gunshot death due to homicide or accident is not sufficient to allow the insurance company to escape even if the ink on the policy is still wet."

Higgs winced slightly as he thought of the inaccuracy of Erickson's last remark, but refrained from voicing an almost unheard-of objection to another lawyer's opening remarks. In fact, he remembered a case where a man had been killed by a robber who came into the man's store in the middle of the insurance agent's sales pitch. The robber shot the store owner before the old man had actually signed the life-insurance application. The company had come forward spontaneously and paid the old man's wife the face value of the policy, not because they had to, but because of the favorable publicity it evoked nationwide. The company could have successfully argued that even if the old man had signed the application, the policy did not begin to be in force until the home office had accepted it. But, for a couple of grand, they decided, why not pay off the claim and look like heroes? They did, and came out smelling like roses. A million miles worth of favorable publicity for a few thousand bucks!

"We will offer you testimony by persons involved in this strange case, and by expert witnesses who will help you to understand it, that this death was not the obvious suicide that it has been claimed to be. Remember, we do not have to bring a murderer in here to confess the crime like some daytime television story." He waved his hand toward his adversary gently.

"Mr. Spencer hopes to show you how obvious this 'suicide' is, members of the jury. We intend to show you how unproved that claim really is. We will show you that the decedent, Myrl Caton, was a very angry man, and that men who are angry get into trouble. Mr. Caton had a fight while he was up there in Connecticut. We want you to consider that fact when you evaluate our opponents' claim of suicide.

"As we go forward in this trial, I wish that you will all pay careful attention to all the testimony that may be offered. And as you do, ask yourselves the question, 'How did Myrl Caton really die?' If, at the end, you are convinced that he shot himself, then you must find for the insurance company and uphold their nonpayment of the claim. But, if you are not convinced that this death was a suicide, then you are obliged to find for the widow, even if we fail to prove another mechanism of death." Erickson scooped up his papers and smiled warmly to the jurors. "I thank you for your kind attention."

He walked quickly to his table and sat down in the empty chair next to Pat Caton.

"Good, Paul," G. Markham whispered.

"Mr. Spencer," Judge Haran rasped, "do you wish to make an opening remark?"

"The defendant wishes to reserve his opening remarks, your honor," Spencer said, half rising. He was entitled to speak to the jury then or to wait until the plaintiff had presented all her evidence. Spencer chose the latter time, since he would then be in a position to use some of Erickson's evidence in his own opening statement. The tactic was a common one and his reservation came as no surprise to Erickson and G. Markham Hurst.

"Very well, then," Judge Haran said mechanically, "present your first witness, Mr. Erickson."

Paul Erickson rose and leaned forward on his knuckles. "The plaintiff calls Mr. Kirby Morris."

"Kirby Morris," the marshal echoed as he left the courtroom through the double doors and headed toward the witnesses' room. He called the name repeatedly as he went.

Kirby Morris felt his mouth go dry and his throat begin to ache as he followed the marshal into the courtroom and stood before the bench. He raised his right hand and faced the clerk.

"You've already been sworn, Mr. Morris," the judge snapped.

Kirby scrambled into the witness chair.

Pat Caton looked at Kirby and wondered if he had wet his pants. He had, slightly.

26

Kirby Morris glanced at Pat Caton as he seated himself in the witness chair. The seat was enclosed in a chest-high box which afforded a degree of modesty to females and a fair amount of security to all witnesses. His palms were uncomfortably wet while his throat remained painfully dry. Kirby wondered if everyone in the courtroom could hear the pounding of his heart as clearly as he could.

"State your name, please," Paul Erickson said from the attorneys' rostrum.

"Morris. Kirby Morris," he answered almost inaudibly.

"You'll have to speak up or get closer to the microphone"—he pointed to the small microphone on the flexible steel cable—"so that every member of the jury can hear you, Mr. Morris," Erickson said. He smiled at his nervous witness to bolster his spirits.

"Kirby Morris," he said more loudly, ignoring the mike. His voice did not quake as much as he thought it would, and that gave him some encouragement.

"And what is your address?"

Kirby gave the address of his apartment complex, including the zip code.

"And your occupation?" Erickson's preliminary questions came mechanically. The vital statistics concerning Kirby Morris, recounted only for the record, were easily extracted from the witness. Erickson then paused briefly to give Kirby a chance to relax, but the opportunity was ignored.

"Mr. Morris, in your capacity as full partner to the late Mr. Myrl Caton, did you have an opportunity to be intimately involved in the business affairs of Ruscaton Tomato Growers, Inc.?"

Pat Caton answered the question mentally and silently pointed out that Kirby didn't know a tomato from a hand grenade. Audibly, Morris stated that he was indeed, closely involved with all facets of Ruscaton affairs.

"Including the company's insurance arrangements?" probed Erickson.

"Yes, sir."

"Were you present when the insurance contract under dispute in this trial—" Erickson paused to hold up a folded document. "—was signed?"

"Yes, sir, I was. I signed a policy myself, the same day."

"And when was that?" Erickson asked.

Spencer stood up and made a small interrupting gesture. Reciprocating, Judge Haran motioned to Erickson and to Morris simultaneously.

"Your honor," interjected Red Spencer. "In the interest of the conservation of time, the defendant would be happy to stipulate to the existence and date of the questioned policy."

"The plaintiff appreciates the defendant's interest and spirit of cooperation, your honor," Paul Erickson said, "but the fact that this witness was present at the signing and knew of the policy limits may become important in this case later."

In fact, both lawyers were just verbally fencing. No one would dispute the existence of an insurance policy on the life of Myrl Caton after all this time and trouble, and conversely, Kirby Morris's interpretation of the normal or usual Ruscaton affairs would be of little probative value.

Erickson was afraid to inquire too closely into Kirby's alibi for the night of Caton's death. Kirby's connection with Pat could be enough to implicate her and keep the insurance company from paying off either of them.

"Proceed, Mr. Erickson," Judge Haran said.

Spencer sat down casually, expressing no disappointment or disagreement verbally or by his motions. He was quite aware that the jurors would follow every movement of each actor in the courtroom drama and continually make judgments on the basis of their impressions, correctly or otherwise.

"You may answer, if you can," Paul Erickson suggested. He counted on Kirby's inability to remember the exact wording of the question, thus providing him with a greater opportunity to be spontaneous. When allowed to be voluntary or spontaneous, a witness's testimony frequently included statements that were difficult to extract by restrained, direct questioning. And the opposing attorney was unable to anticipate what the witness would come out with until he had already testified. At that point, all the frustrated lawyer could do was suggest to the judge that the witness be admonished not to volunteer testimony and that the jury be instructed to disregard the witness's previous statement. Both instructions, even where painfully appropriate, were among the most useless commands in organized human experience. As one appellate judge had put it, you can't unring a bell.

Kirby Morris looked blankly at Erickson and then, as if recalling the scene more vividly, began to speak. "The insurance policies, you know, his and mine, were taken out the same day, about three weeks before he—" He paused, and looked at Pat Caton. She sat placidly, watching his every movement. "—died," he concluded.

"Three weeks before his death?" asked Erickson for emphasis.

"Yes, sir. Almost to the day. My own policy was taken out at the same time. That's how I can remember." Morris smiled uneasily at the nearest member of the jury and wondered if the man thought he was lying.

"You knew Mr. Caton fairly well?" asked Erickson.

"Yes, sir—for quite a few years."

"And his wife, Mrs. Caton, too?" Erickson nodded in Pat's direction. Morris glanced at Pat but turned quickly back to Erickson.

"Yes, sir. I know Mrs. Caton."

Erickson would have been happy to leap through the courtroom window had Morris described just how well he knew Mrs. Caton.

"Did Myrl Caton seem disturbed or despondent the last time you saw him, Mr. Morris?"

"You mean the day he left Ruskin for the trip up north?"

"If that's the last time you saw him, yes," clarified Erickson.

"He seemed OK to me," Morris said. He shrugged his shoulders and appeared to be thinking. "As far as I could tell, it was the same old Myrl. You know, a little rough, but nothing strange."

"What do you mean by 'a little rough'?"

"Oh, you know how he was. Myrl was never one for gentle words or softness. He complained a little about having to head up through the New England states alone again, but that was just the way he was. He wouldn't have let anyone go with him anyway. I didn't make anything of it when he left."

"When he left, Mr. Morris," Erickson asked carefully, "did you expect him to return?"

"Object!" said Spencer, rising quickly to his feet. "That calls for a conclusion from this witness and—"

"Overruled," interrupted Judge Haran. He nodded to Erickson to continue.

"Of course I did. We all did," Morris said.

"But you never saw him again?"

"Not—alive." Kirby suddenly recalled the cold, cosmetized face of Myrl Caton lying in the casket at Spottsswood's.

"Mr. Erickson," the judge said, "I believe you could

phrase your questions in such a way as to avoid leading the witness quite so blatantly."

"Yes, your honor," Erickson said cooperatively. He returned to the witness and glanced once more at his notes on the rostrum in front of him. "Mr. Morris, did you stand to gain anything from the death of your partner?"

"Gain? No, sir. Not directly, at least."

"Indirectly then?"

Kirby glanced at Pat Caton and hesitated momentarily. Erickson silently pleaded for him not to extend this incriminating pause. As if urged by mental telepathy, Kirby resumed his testimony.

"Well, you know. Without Myrl, I'm now running the whole show. I guess that makes me the boss. That's what I mean by 'indirectly.'"

Erickson nodded knowingly for the jury's benefit. While he and G. Markham had carefully reviewed all the pertinent points of the case with each available witness, they had not resorted to frank rehearsal with Kirby Morris. Erickson was torn between forcing Morris to conform to mechanical, precise answers that would surely lose the jury's interest and the uncertainty of his witness's inventiveness. He glanced at G. Markham and received a raised eyebrow in return.

"May I have a moment, your honor?" Erickson asked.

"Quickly, counselor, please," said the judge.

Erickson walked to G. Markham's side and bent over at his ear. "I don't trust this stupid son of a bitch. What do you think?" he whispered to his senior colleague.

"You've gotten enough out of him," G. Markham Hurst advised. "If he can survive the cross-examination, I'd say he has served his purpose. You've shown that he knew about the policy but wasn't the direct beneficiary. If he doesn't admit to an intimate relationship with Caton's wife, we'll be damned lucky." His whispered remarks were carefully hidden from Pat Caton despite her straining to hear them.

"I'll dump him," Erickson decided. G. Markham nodded in silent agreement. Erickson returned to the rostrum and looked quickly at his yellow legal pad. "Had anyone made any threats on Mr. Caton's life, Mr. Morris?" he asked quickly.

"Object, your honor. Object," said Red Spencer.

"Sustained."

"No further questions," Erickson concluded. "Your witness," he said to Spencer. Erickson took his notes to the plaintiff's table and sat down.

G. Markham greeting him with a surreptitious wink, but Pat Caton looked a little astonished. She had expected more from Kirby Morris, but didn't clearly know what it was.

"You may inquire, Mr. Spencer," Judge Haran directed.

Spencer scrambled quickly to the rostrum, pausing only to deliver a comment to Hervey Higgs's ear. He turned to speak to Kirby. "Hadn't the tomato business been failing during the several months prior to your partner's death, Mr. Morris?" Spencer asked without waiting to actually reach the rostrum.

"Failing?" repeated the surprised Kirby Morris.

"Yes, you know. In financial difficulties."

"In the tomato business, there are always financial difficulties, Mr. Spencer."

"Of course, sir. But what about those portions of the business that were directly under your late partner's control?"

"Well, just about everything was under his control when he was alive," Kirby said. "That's just the kind of man he was, that's all."

"Did you keep the books or did he?" asked Spencer.

"Really, neither of us did. Myrl—that is, Mr. Caton—was a lot closer to that sort of thing than I was, but even then his wife, Pat, and the accountant we had in Tampa did most of the books. I've only started fooling around with the books since I took over . . . after Myrl died."

"Then if there was a financial difficulty pressing Caton at the time of his death, you wouldn't have known about it necessarily. Right, Mr. Morris?" Spencer gazed at the courtroom ceiling as if to show that the answer was obvious and that Kirby was allowed all the time in the world to answer it.

"I suppose not, but—"

"Thank you, Mr. Morris," said Spencer, shutting off the answer. "And were you aware that Mr. Caton was known to carry a gun in his car?"

Kirby shot a glance at Erickson but received no instructions. Both Erickson and Hurst were too experienced to allow their own expressions to be seen by the witness and therefore by any interested juror. The time for instructions was prior to trial, not in the middle of uncontrollable testimony.

"Yeah, I knew that. Who didn't?" Morris said, somewhat defensively.

"Just answer the question," snapped Judge Haran.

"Did you ever see him shoot that gun?" Spencer inquired.

"Sometimes," he fenced.

"At what?"

"Well not at himself, it that's what you're getting at."

"Mr. Morris!" Judge Haran shouted menacingly. "You will confine your remarks to simple answers to the questions that are put to you. Is that quite clear, sir?"

"Yes, your honor," Kirby said. He swallowed nervously as the judge drummed a military rhythm on the bench.

"What did Myrl Caton shoot at, Mr. Morris?" repeated Spencer.

"Oh, cans and birds. Stuff like that."

"And road signs?"

"Sometimes." Kirby glanced uneasily at the judge. For all he knew, the judge would begin to write out a ticket to poor dead Myrl for shooting road signs. The courtroom was not familiar ground for him.

"And Mexicans?"

"I object, your honor," Erickson interrupted. "Myrl Caton is not on trial here. I fail to see what relevance this line of questioning has."

"Just where are you going with these questions, Mr. Spencer?" Judge Haran inquired.

"I'm attempting to show that Mr. Caton was quite familiar with his gun and that he often used it, even to intimidate other human beings."

"I think you should confine your questions to the actual familiarity with the weapon, if you wish to establish that point further, and leave out his selection of target," the judge ruled.

"But at any rate," Spencer continued, "Caton was not averse to shooting his pistol, was he?"

"No, sir."

"And he often carried it around, didn't he?"

"Yes, sir."

"When he went on business trips?"

"Yes, sir."

"In fact, he would never go anywhere without it, would he, Mr. Morris?"

"No, sir."

Erickson was in the act of rising to object but sat down again when Kirby supplied the answer. Spencer paused and reviewed his notes.

"Caton was a temperamental fellow, wasn't he, Mr. Morris?"

"How do you mean?"

"I mean he blew hot and cold, didn't he?"

"He had good days and bad days, if that's what you mean."

"And drank a lot, too?"

"You might say that." Kirby glanced at the jury and noticed that two of the men in the second row frowned simultaneously at that answer.

"Well, he came in drunk sometimes, didn't he?"

"Object—"

"Sustained."

"I'll rephrase that. Mr. Caton had days when he was unreliable, didn't he?"

"Same object—"

"Sustained."

"All right. Tell me this, Mr. Morris. Isn't it true that

Caton could be described as a great guy if he liked you and quite difficult to accept if he didn't like you?"

"I think that would be a fair statement."

"And didn't some of the men fear him?"

"You bet they did," Morris agreed, without restraint.

"Why, Mr. Morris? Why did some of the men fear Mr. Caton?"

"Because he was hell on wheels when he was mad, that's why."

"But then, he could turn right around and be the nicest guy you'd ever want to meet, right?"

"Right. Myrl was funny that way."

"Thank you, Mr. Morris. No further questions."

Kirby Morris felt uneasy about his answers when Spencer did not offer any more questions. He was not sure whether he had done Pat's case a favor or blown it sky-high. He looked helplessly at Paul Erickson, who was slowly getting out of his chair.

"Mr. Morris," Erickson began. "Myrl Caton knew a great number of people who had reason to be angry with him, didn't he?"

"Some, I guess," Kirby shrugged.

"And some of the men weren't too happy about his angry moments, were they?"

Kirby shook his head.

"You will answer so that the court reporter can hear you, sir," Judge Haran announced.

"No, they weren't," supplied Morris.

The court reporter struck combinations of keys without any outward sign of recognition.

"You spoke of Caton's moods. You have mood changes too, don't you?" Erickson asked slyly.

"Sometimes," he admitted.

"But you're not a psychiatrist, are you?"

"A who?"

"You've had no special training in the recognition of moods or the significance of mood changes, have you?" Erickson smiled softly to the jurors as he waited for Kirby's answer.

"No, sir?" Kirby Morris offered inquisitively.

"And since you have taken over as director of Ruscaton, you haven't uncovered any financial losses, have you, Mr. Morris?"

"No, sir."

"Business is generally pretty good, isn't it?"

"Generally, yes."

"And it was when Caton died, wasn't it?"

"About the same, I guess."

"Thank you, Mr. Morris. I think that will be about all," Erickson said. "May I have just a moment, your honor?" Without waiting for an answer from the judge, Erickson crossed quickly to G. Markham and began to whisper. "Anything else?"

Pat Caton leaned into the whispered conversation and said, "Ask him if he knew about that Italian girl in Connecticut."

Erickson recoiled like a horse that has seen a snake. "Shit no, Pat!" he said in a hoarse whisper. He turned quickly to the judge and said, "No further questions." He wondered if anyone had heard his last whispered remark, and noticed that Spencer was grinning.

27

Judge Haran called a lunch break after Kirby Morris's testimony. The marshal paraded the jurors down the block to a small, semiprivate dining room at the Jefferson Hotel.

Erickson wasted no time in getting down the stairs of the Federal Building and out onto the street. Across the street, in the entrance to the hotel bar, he found an empty pay phone and deposited a dime. He dialed a local number and watched a distinctive pair of female legs walk briskly by as it rang.

"This is Paul. We've quit for lunch. What's happening at the office?" He waited quietly. "Did you get hold of Havlicek and Dr. Campbell? Good. Make sure they both stand by for late today or maybe early tomorrow. I'll try to get word to you later so that you can give them a better fix on the time. OK. I'll call you later."

Erickson balanced the Tampa phone book on the edge of the narrow shelf and ran his finger along a page. He deposited another dime and dialed the Hawaiian Village. It was answered on the first ring.

"Room 318, please." There was a pause as the phone

was connected inside the plush, Polynesian motel he had called.

"Angela? This is Paul Erickson. We are in recess for lunch and I'd like to come out there to talk with you and to bring you to court. Have you eaten yet? OK. We have only till 1:30 to eat and get back, so call room service and order something that's quick. I'll be there in about fifteen minutes. OK? See you shortly."

Erickson had parked his car in a high-rise downtown garage. He took the elevator to the color-coded floor on his parking-ticket stub and easily found his two-door Lincoln.

He eased the machine onto the Interstate and headed west. The noonish traffic was never particularly heavy, and that Monday was no exception. He goosed the car from the lawful fifty-five to his more characteristic eighty-five. The few miles to the Hawaiian Village Motel melted away in a blur of slower vehicles and a rhythmic pockity-pock of the pavement.

Erickson's low-pressure tires screamed for mercy, but received none as he roared off the highway onto the busy north-south artery. This had been one of the better routes to the airport, and therefore most of the newer motels had been built along the strip.

The Lincoln crunched on the gravel of the Polynesian driveway and stopped in front of a pot-bellied South Sea character carved in volcanic rock standing over a tropical pool with Tampa Gas Company flames belching from its center. Whether the rock creation was guarding the pool or relieving himself at its edge depended on the angle from which the viewer saw him and how long the viewer had enjoyed the coconut-and-rum concoctions at the bamboo bar.

Erickson flipped his key pouch to a Cuban dressed in a Polynesian costume, then walked toward Angela Gaito's room. Room 318 was set in the middle of the third building of the two-story poolside motel.

Erickson tapped lightly on the door.

There was an energetic shout from inside. "Whata ya want?"

"Angela? It's me. Erickson."

The door was opened against the short chain, and a round Italian face peered out. Erickson glanced at the chain as Angela fussed to release it. The door virtually burst open as Miss Gaito triumphantly mastered the mechanical hurdle and smiled broadly.

"Come in. This is one hell of a motel, eh? Some place! Class. That's what it is, pure class. And a pool too!" she continued. "I should of brought my suit. Imagine! And there's still snow on the ground in some places up north. I phoned for some lunch. It will be right over, they said."

She paused, almost breathless.

"How was your flight?" Erickson asked, walking to the single upholstered chair.

"Not bad. A little bumpy. But I guess you always get that, huh?" Angela Gaito had flown exactly once before, from Hartford to Boston, to attend a family wedding.

"Usually. Did Irafino come on the same flight?"

"Yeah, he's here. Room 319." She cocked her head toward the wall to her right. "But he's over in the lobby building getting cigarettes."

"Did you tell him I was coming out for lunch?" Erickson asked in an unconcerned tone.

"Yeah, I told him. He tried to invite himself to join us, but I told him it was a private talk."

"Hell, you could have let him come. I wouldn't want him to get the wrong idea."

"He don't own me," volunteered Angela Gaito. She took a step closer to the lawyer and looked directly into his eyes.

"I mean about the trial. I wouldn't want him to think that I was here to suggest to you what I think your testimony should be."

"Testimony? I gotta appear in court?" Her tone was one of mock astonishment. She was not only resigned to the appearance, but had mentally rehearsed it for several weeks.

"I told you that."

"Yeah, but I thought maybe you could just use all

213

them notes that the girl wrote down when I answered all them questions in Connecticut."

"Oh, we could still use your deposition, Angela, but I'd rather that you told your story directly to the jury." He paused for a moment and then added softly, "It would be better for Myrl."

Angela nodded gently and stood silently as the phony memorial moment faded into the air of the motel room.

There was an official knock at the door that could only have been made by a motel employee. Police banged on a door in an effort to wake the dead, friends rapped in musical couplets, and clandestine visitors knocked as if a hotel detective was lurking behind every bush.

Angela threw open the door and stepped aside as a waiter carried in a large metal tray covered by a white cloth. He pulled a small table toward the center of the room and served the lunch.

The waiter took a stiff card from the pocket of his white coat and handed it to Paul Erickson. Erickson wrote 318. Angela Gaito, on the bottom of the card and gave it back to the unsmiling waiter.

"For you," Erickson said as he added a dollar in cash.

"Gracias," said the waiter. He took the card and left the room. At no time did he look at Angela Gaito or otherwise inspect the room or bed. Erickson mentally applauded his professional demeanor.

"I ordered Egg Foo Yung," Angela announced.

Erickson felt his already tense stomach tighten another knot. He managed a small smile. "Nice, Angela. I love Egg Foo Yung."

"And tea!"

"And tea," he sighed. He brought a chair closer to the table for her, but she was unused to being helped. She seated herself with enthusiasm and lifted the metal cover from her dish.

With a sick smile, Erickson uncovered his dish. He stared at the off-yellow food on his plate. "Almost my favorite," he added resolutely. He picked up his fork and looked at his luncheon companion. "We probably won't have too much time," he said. "There are a few things that I want to ask you about before we go downtown."

"Shoot."

"How close have you been to Lt. Casper lately?"

Angela dropped her fork and coughed a large fragment of egg onto the table near her plate. "What the hell are you getting at?" she asked menacingly.

"I want to know what you and that cop cooked up for Myrl Caton in this whole mess." Erickson looked directly at Angela and received a wild glare in return.

"You think we got to Caton? Shit. What would we want to do that for? You know Myrl and me was good friends."

"But only when he came up to Connecticut. You had Casper to please on other nights, didn't you, baby?"

"You rotten lawyer bastard," said Angela in a low animal growl. "You want me to sing you a pretty song down there in your courthouse and squeeze the insurance company for a few big bills for that bitch that Myrl married. Well, I'll come down there and tell all them cracker jurors how I seen Myrl blow his own head off. How would you like that?"

Erickson felt a devilish urge to put Angela Gaito on the stand just to have her lie about Caton's fatal scene. "Then you didn't see him shoot himself, did you, Angela?" Erickson said. "At last I can believe you." He stood up and moved toward the door and opened it part way.

"What time do I have to be there?" She knocked her chair over as she stood.

"Anytime you please, baby. But you'll wait one hell of a long time before I'll put you up on that stand." He smiled easily and stepped onto the sidewalk in front of her room.

"Then what the hell did you bring me all the way down here from Connecticut for?" Angela suddenly felt left out and uneasy.

"To keep that cop honest. If that's possible."

"You are really no good. No good at all," Angela said, shaking her head slowly.

"Sweetheart, this kind of a case does not make for high ideals or for lasting friendships among the witnesses." He kept his eyes on Angela Gaito as he backed down the sidewalk to a nearby room. He was still watching the Italian woman as he knocked loudly on the door.

There was a brief delay and then a large man appeared in the open doorway. "Yeah?"

"Casper?" Angela had poked her head out of her room.

"Oh, hi there, Mr—Mr—"

"Erickson. We met in Middlebrook."

"Yeah. Sure. How's it going? I mean the trial and all."

"I'll give you a ride downtown if you're ready." Erickson turned toward the police lieutenant and extended his hand.

"Yeah—I'm ready. Just let me get my coat." He disappeared briefly into the motel room. "Come on in," he shouted back to Erickson.

"We'd better get moving. The judge will want to crank it up soon." Erickson bowed formally in Angela's direction. She pulled her head back into the room and shut the door, but not before she had extended an obscene finger gesture to the lawyer.

Casper emerged from his room and adjusted his jacket as he closed the door. "What about Angela and Peabody?"

Erickson put his hand gently on the policeman's shoulder. "We won't need Angela right away," he said blandly. He led the cop toward the lobby entrance and the car. "Peabody will be brought down by my partner. They need to go over some details about the room lock and chain."

"You want me to call Irafino? He's over in the lobby."

"Let's leave him here with Angela for a while," teased Erickson.

Casper stiffened and then changed the subject. "You know, it's damned hot down here," he said as they approached Erickson's car.

"It will get a lot hotter," Erickson promised.

28

Erickson and Casper found G. Markham Hurst pacing nervously in front of the main door to the courtroom.

"Paul, I'm glad I was able to catch you," he said. "Judge Haran is about ready to start the afternoon session and Dr. Campbell called."

"This is Lt. Casper," Erickson offered.

The old lawyer and the policeman shook hands. "Nice to see you, Casper." G. Markham turned to Erickson. "It seems that Dr. Campbell is tied up in some new homicide downstate and wants to be put on the stand soon as possible."

"Now?" Erickson asked. He looked at his watch.

"Out of turn, of course, but I think that Judge Haran will go along with it if you explain the circumstances."

Erickson considered the effects of this unscheduled change in his proposed order of witnesses. "That will make you a bit late, Lieutenant."

The policeman smiled and shrugged as if to express his willingness to cooperate with the inevitable.

"Is he on his way down?" Erickson asked.

G. Markham nodded. "He should be here any minute."

"Well, let's get in there and get ready for our professional forensic expert." He turned to Casper and extended one hand toward the room reserved for plaintiff's witnesses. "You will have to wait in this side room, Lieutenant. You understand, I'm sure."

"Perfectly, Mr. Erickson. But who is this 'forensic expert' you are talking about?"

"Dr. Mark Campbell. He came up to the Brownstone Motel and measured Caton's room and looked it over for us."

"He did the autopsy for us," G. Markham supplied.

"Autopsy?" Lt. Casper was visibly astonished.

"Well, actually, the insurance company's pathologist, Dr. Leatherman, did the autopsy, if you want to be really technical. But Dr. Campbell was present and assisted in many parts of it."

"When did they do all this?" Casper asked. His tone seemed less jovial. His eyes flashed from Erickson to G. Markham and back again.

"Oh, hell, months ago now, I guess," Erickson said.

"Did they—did they find anything?" asked Casper.

"The usual half-rotten body."

"I suppose they couldn't really tell much, huh? I mean after being buried and all?"

Erickson pushed the conversation further, playing Casper's anxiety like a stringed instrument. "You'd have to hear Dr. Campbell describe it to believe just how much those two grave diggers were able to squeeze out of Caton's stinking coffin. Those guys can reconstruct a whole story if you give them a bone or a tooth to measure and examine."

"Yeah," Casper said somewhat pensively. "We have a few of those crime doctors in Connecticut. Work mainly with the state police. Amazing, sometimes; amazing."

"Well, make yourself comfortable in the witness room, Lieutenant, and I'll put you on just as soon as I can." Erickson urged the policeman toward the small room by gently pushing his arm.

The lieutenant obeyed silently and went into the room without looking back.

"Do you think he bought all that?" G. Markham asked quietly.

"I think we have him just about ready to climb the wall. Is Campbell really coming?"

"He's here. I have him standing by in the little law library at the end of the hall," said G. Markham.

"I wish to hell we could let Casper hear Campbell's testimony or get him to talk to Havlicek."

"We could have Havlicek wait in the witness room with Casper and let human nature take its course," G. Markham suggested slyly.

"You? The pillar of legal ethics suggesting such a maneuver?" Erickson grinned.

"It would be unethical to *ask* Havlicek to tell Casper what his testimony will be, but it is surely not unethical to put them in the same cage for a couple of hours, is it?"

"After instructing them not to discuss the case, of course," added Erickson.

"I believe such an instruction would satisfy the court and at the same time whet their appetites." G. Markham grinned. "And I wouldn't be a bit surprised if Caton's name came up."

"Where is Havlicek now?" asked Erickson.

"In the little witness room, probably introducing himself to Lt. Casper."

Erickson looked at the senior lawyer with open admiration and held the courtroom door for him to enter.

Pat Caton was already seated at the counsel table as the two lawyers approached.

"Have a good lunch?" Erickson asked pleasantly.

"Pure indigestion. I really don't understand how you lawyers can go through this kind of crap every day and still eat lunch."

"We don't do this 'kind of crap' every day, Mrs. Caton," G. Markham Hurst said soberly. "And you may find some consolation in knowing that some lawyers are not only too upset to eat lunch during trial days but actually grow ulcers."

"I can see how."

"Where's Kirby?" Erickson asked, looking around the courtroom.

"He said he was too sick to come back. He said that the courtroom made him too nervous," Pat explained without emotion.

"Left you to fight it alone, eh?" Erickson said.

"Hell, yes. That's Kirby. His idea of help is letting you send him a card telling him how it all came out. The son of a bitch."

G. Markham placed a hand gently on Pat's shoulder.

The minute hand of the courtroom clock snapped to 1:30 precisely as the door to the judge's chambers opened. At exactly that instant the clerk twanged, "All rise."

Judge Haran mounted the bench, took his seat, arranged his papers, adjusted his black robe, put on his glasses, motioned to the lawyers to sit down, and cleared his throat with a blast that announced that the United States government had ended its lunch hour and was now back in business. Lunch for the United States had been an apple and cream cheese on datenut bread sent over from the main kitchen of the Hillsboro Hotel by the maitre d'.

"Are you gentlemen ready?" Judge Haran boomed. Spencer nodded officially, half-rising from his chair.

"Your honor," Paul Erickson announced, "the plaintiff would like to approach the bench."

Judge Haran looked at Erickson over his glasses and nodded wearily. Erickson and Spencer walked silently to the bench while Hervey Higgs and G. Markham Hurst remained at their respective tables.

"Well, Mr. Erickson?"

"Your honor, the plaintiff requests the court's permission to call a witness out of turn so as to minimize the inconvenience to that witness."

"Inconvenience to the witness?" Judge Haran mocked with appropriate facial grimaces. The United States adjusted its robes.

"Yes sir. The witness is Dr. Campbell, and in deference to his busy professional schedule at the medical school and his—"

"Oh, all right, all right, Mr. Erickson. Get on with it. Get on with it." Judge Haran waved the lawyers away from the bench without allowing a word from Red Spencer although his mouth was opened and his lips were moving. "Let the record reflect that Mr. Spencer objects," Judge Haran added. He smiled stiffly at Spencer, who exchanged a mechanical expression of satisfaction.

"Bring in the jury," the judge ordered busily. The marshal led the short, silent parade of citizens from their small room to the confinement of the double-rowed box.

Judge Haran peered over his glasses and examined the plaintiff's counsel. Erickson looked up at the judge and waited for the court to say something profound, like "Go ahead, Mr. Erickson." An eternity later, Erickson realized that there was to be no verbal invitation to start. He stood up, gathered a few sheets of paper, and walked quickly to the rostrum.

"The plaintiff will call Dr. Mark Campbell," he announced flatly. The marshal disappeared through the courtroom door, calling the name.

The United States busied itself with notemaking at the bench.

With a professional air, Dr. Campbell walked quickly to the bench, raised his right hand, and immediately replied "I will" to the clerk's already-in-motion, toneless swearing-in prattle.

Mark Campbell sat down in the witness chair and adjusted the small microphone. He glanced along both rows of the assembled jurors.

"Would you please state your name?" Paul Erickson began flatly.

"Mark J. Campbell."

". . . and your occupation."

"I am a doctor of medicine, specializing in pathology."

". . . and where are you so employed?"

"The School of Medicine, at the University of South Florida."

"Tampa?" completed Erickson.

"Tampa."

Erickson adjusted his papers slightly and then looked pleasantly at his witness. "Dr. Campbell, I wonder if you would give the jury the benefit of your educational background."

"The defense will stipulate as to Dr. Campbell's qualifications as an expert in the field of pathology," Red Spencer volunteered, half-rising.

Erickson smiled slightly and turned to the judge, who had apparently paid absolutely no attention to the perfunctory defense offer and the anticipated plaintiff's refusal. The judge waited only for the next appropriate interval of silence to inform Paul Erickson that he could continue.

"I received my bachelor's degree and my medical degree from Queen's University in Kingston, Ontario. After that I served a full internship at the University Hospital at Toronto."

"Canada?"

"Canada," said Campbell with a wry smile. He frequently found humor in the lawyer's frantic compulsion to add to the record the most obvious of facts.

Erickson nodded, a wordless signal to continue.

"I completed a year of residency in internal medicine at the Massachusetts General Hospital in Boston." He paused and then added artfully, "In Massachusetts. I then served a four-year residency in pathology at the Massachusetts General Hospital on the Harvard Service and at the Mallory Institute."

"Is that also in Boston?"

"Yes, sir. All at the Mass. General."

"I see." Erickson made a few tiny check marks on his legal pad.

"I instructed in pathology at Harvard Medical School for one year before accepting the position of Assistant Medical Examiner for the City of New York."

"Was that appointment in the form of further post-graduate training, Doctor?"

"Yes, sir. That year qualified me to be examined by and certified by the American Board of Pathology in the subspecialty of forensic pathology."

"You were, of course, also certified in regular pathology, were you not?"

"Regular pathology?" asked Campbell testingly.

"Or whatever the proper term is. You know, the usual, hospital pathology," clarified Erickson.

Red Spencer stood up and gestured with his pencil. "I think Mr. Erickson could let his 'expert' witness develop his own curriculum vitae."

"If that remark is intended as an objection, Mr. Spencer, I'll sustain it," whined Judge Haran.

"It was, your honor," said Spencer.

"Lead more gently, Mr. Erickson," the jurist suggested.

Erickson nodded pleasantly. "Would you explain to the jury the difference between these branches of pathology?"

Campbell adjusted his position in the witness chair and turned to face the jury.

Both Spencer and Higgs recognized immediately this indicator of the witness's professional capabilities.

"Hospital pathology might be defined or explained as that portion of medicine which has to do with the laboratory examination of various body fluids and tissues, including a study of the tissue and cellular effects of disease, while forensic pathology concerns itself with the study of sudden death, death by violence, poisonings, accidents, homicides, and otherwise unexplainable deaths." He paused to run his eyes down each row of jurors to identify anyone who might not be comprehending. All seemed to be following him. "In some areas," he continued, "the forensic pathologist or medical examiner is also concerned with the investigation of rape and sex crimes." The female juror savored the announcement and raised her eyebrows.

"But you are a certified specialist in all of these branches of pathology, right, Dr. Campbell?" reaffirmed Erickson.

223

"That's correct," Campbell said simply.

"Please continue."

"After the year's training with the New York City Medical Examiner's office, I accepted the opportunity to become Assistant Coroner's Pathologist in Denver, Colorado, and held that position for approximately twelve years."

"But you didn't remain Assistant Coroner's Pathologist there, did you, Doctor?"

"No, sir. I became chief of the department and professor of legal medicine at the University of Colorado Medical School." Campbell paused for a moment and then added, "I came to the University of South Florida at Tampa from Colorado."

"What position were you asked to fill at USF, Dr. Campbell?"

"Professor of legal medicine at the new medical school."

"Are you also the medical examiner for Tampa?"

"No, sir. That office was allowed to remain at Tampa General Hospital and at the Hillsborough County Hospital. Only the interesting or instructive cases are brought out to the university."

"Dr. Campbell, are you licensed in this state?"

"I'm licensed to practice medicine in Ontario, Manitoba, Massachusetts, New York, Colorado, and Florida."

"And you belong to several professional associations?"

"Yes, sir—the state and national medical and pathological societies. I have held office in several of these. Would you like me to list each organization separately?"

"No, thank you, Doctor," Judge Haran said. "Proceed, Mr. Erickson."

"Dr. Campbell, what is an autopsy?" asked Paul Erickson. His tone was slower, more deliberate.

"An autopsy is an examination of the dead body, including a systematic dissection of the body organs in order to identify the changes left in these body structures by disease or trauma."

"Have you performed many autopsies in your career?"

224

Erickson turned slightly and faced the jury, one thumb in his belt.

"Several thousand, Mr. Erickson," minimized the pathologist.

"Including deaths due to gunshot wounds, sir?" Erickson continued. His gaze did not cease to search the jurors' faces as he probed.

"Yes, sir. A great many. Including, of course, suicidal, homicidal, and accidental gunshot wounds."

"Did you have an occasion to perform an autopsy on the body of one Myrl Caton?"

Pat Caton found her hand suddenly pressing against her lower lip.

"I assisted at one."

"Would you explain the circumstances, Doctor Campbell?" Erickson relaxed slightly and again half-turned to face the jury box.

"I was requested by your office to be present at the autopsy of Mr. Caton," Mark Campbell explained. "Dr. Jerry Leatherman of Miami actually performed the autopsy."

"Now, Dr. Campbell, can you explain why Dr. Leatherman was there to do the autopsy?"

The veteran witness withheld his answer for a brief but sufficient moment to allow any objection which might have been elicited by that question.

"Your honor," said Red Spencer nasally, rising from his chair. "The defendant will object to this line of—"

"Sustained," interrupted Judge Haran.

"But you say you 'assisted' Dr. Leatherman, is that correct, Dr. Campbell?" pushed Erickson.

"It was more a cooperative effort than a true assistance," said Mark Campbell.

"Did you join with Dr. Leatherman in the formation of an opinion regarding the cause of death in Myrl Caton?"

"Object," Spencer said without further comment.

"The witness may answer that question if he can, but he is specifically instructed not to attempt to express the opinion of any persons other than himself." The judge directed his remark straight at Mark Campbell.

Campbell readjusted his position in the witness chair to face Paul Erickson again.

"You may answer, Dr. Campbell," said Erickson simply.

"No, sir, I did not," said the pathologist positively.

"You did not?" Erickson asked in mock astonishment.

"No, sir."

"But you did form an opinion regarding that cause of death, did you not?" Erickson held his arms stiffly on the sides of the rostrum.

"Yes, sir, I did, but it was not formed cooperatively with Dr. Leatherman. It is entirely my own."

"All right, sir. Before I ask you to state that opinion, I'd like to inquire of you regarding certain other investigations you may have performed at my request."

"Yes, sir?"

"Did you travel, at the request of my office, to the Brownstone Motel in Middlebrook, Connecticut, some months ago?"

"Yes, sir, I did."

"What was the purpose of that trip, Dr. Campbell?"

"To familiarize myself with the motel room in which the body of Myrl Caton was found."

"Did someone identify that room to you, sir?"

"The motel manager."

"Do you recall his name?"

Mark Campbell frowned slightly and looked at the courtroom ceiling. "I believe it was a Mr. Peabody. I only met him once."

"What room did he identify to you, Dr. Campbell?"

"Number 15."

"And did you have an opportunity to examine room number 15 at the Brownstone Motel, Dr. Campbell?"

"Yes, sir."

"Tell us what you found, please," urged Paul Erickson.

"Object, your honor," said Red Spencer. "The doctor

has not been qualified as an expert in motel rooms or the examination of such places."

"Dr. Campbell is as qualified as anyone to describe what he has seen, your honor," argued Paul Erickson. "Mr. Spencer would do well to wait for some question requiring an expert opinion about the room before objecting."

"I'll object when I please," Red Spencer retorted, heating slightly.

"Overruled," said Judge Haran. He waved his hand at each counsel as if to brush a fly from his dessert.

"I found a single motel room with adjoining bath, moderately furnished, opening through one door to the outside and through an inside door to an adjacent room."

Erickson walked quickly to his counsel table and picked up several large photographs mounted on stiff cardboard frames. "Your honor, the plaintiff requests these photographs be marked for identification as consecutive plaintiff's exhibits." He handed the pictures to the clerk, who stamped the back of each and then proceeded to fill in the form blanks with the appropriate identifying notations.

"P-one through P-eight," the clerk said over her shoulder to the judge.

"Let the record reflect the marking of these exhibits for the plaintiff, as one through eight inclusive," Judge Haran said.

Erickson took the photographs to Red Spencer as a gesture of professional courtesy. The defense counsel examined each one and handed them back without comment. Erickson brought the photographs to Campbell. "I hand you what have been marked, for identification, plaintiff's exhibits one through eight and ask if you can identify them," said Erickson, speaking to no one but the record.

Mark Campbell looked quickly at the photographs, turning each over to view the identifying number. "Yes, sir, I can."

"What are these exhibits, sir?" Paul Erickson asked.

"These are photographs which show several views of

room 15 at the Brownstone Motel in Middlebrook, Connecticut, some of them showing the body and the gun."

"Have you had occasion to see these photographs before, Dr. Campbell?" asked Erickson.

"Yes, sir," Campbell said easily, "I took two of them, and the others are the police photographs."

"Thank you, Doctor." Erickson turned toward the judge and paused briefly. "Your honor, at this time, the plaintiff would introduce these photographs as evidence."

"Objection, Mr. Spencer?" asked Judge Haran.

"None, your honor," said Red Spencer.

"So received."

"I direct your attention to these photographs again, Dr. Campbell, and ask if you can identify the relationship of the bed in that room to the doors and to the bathroom. You may demonstrate for the jury, if you wish."

The pathologist took the photographs one at a time and indicated on each the positions of the doors, the chair, the dresser, the small bedside table, and several other items equally obviously displayed in the views. The purpose was, of course, to focus the jurors' attentions on the scene as well as to transcribe the verbal description into the record.

Erickson puttered around the witness box and his rostrum, eating up time and giving each juror the opportunity to satisfy his curiosity about the Brownstone Motel room and the body.

"Dr. Campbell," said Erickson pointing to the figure of Myrl Caton sprawled across the bed, "what do you make of those marks on the shirt?"

"If they are blood, the direction of flow indicates that some time after being shot, the body was erect—at least from the waist up."

"Or standing?"

"Possibly."

"But could he have stood up after he was shot, bled downward, and then assumed the position in which you see the body in the photograph?" asked Erickson.

"People who are shot can do most anything—provided

228

they do it quickly when they are shot through the heart."
Campbell handed the photographs to Erickson.

"I want to direct your attention to the autopsy, Dr.
Campbell."

The pathologist nodded and twisted slightly in his
chair.

Erickson returned to the rostrum and assumed a stage
pause to regain the attention of the jury. "Dr. Campbell,"
he began, "please tell the jury what you found during the
autopsy of Myrl Caton."

The jury leaned as one interconnected listening machine toward the witness box.

"I found a partly decayed body of a middle-aged white
male, fully clothed, lying within an exhumed casket."

"Why was that?"

"You will recall that the body was not autopsied until
three months after his death."

"How many months, doctor?"

"I recall it was just about three—three and a half."

"Where had he been during those three months?"
asked Erickson.

"Mr. Caton had been buried in Orangeburrow, Florida."

A juror readjusted his seat quickly.

"But doesn't burial destroy the body by decay, Dr.
Campbell?" led Paul Erickson.

"Partly. Of course, it is a factor of the ground tempera-
ture, the ground moisture, the rate of casket leakage, and
the efficiency of embalming," lectured Mark Campbell.

"You've examined exhumed bodies before?"

"On many occasions," said the pathologist simply. He
examined his fingernails.

"How would you characterize the amount of decay you
observed in your examination of the remains of Mr. Caton?" asked Erickson.

Mark Campbell glanced in Pat Caton's direction. She
was looking down but her ears remained sharply focused
on the exchange between her lawyer and the pathologist.

"There was moderately severe decay with some mummification of the fingers and toes and a generous amount of mold."

"Did he—did he smell?"

"Object as prejudicial," said Spencer.

"Overruled." The judge leaned toward the witness, his interest whetted by the macabre inquiry.

"Not too badly," said Mark Campbell. His eyes assumed an expression that pleaded with Erickson to get off that type of approach. Campbell's style was one of strict science with complete omission of the emotional aspects.

Erickson pushed on. He had an obligation to interest, inform, and often to entertain his jury. To accomplish this, Erickson was quite willing to push his witness to a fracture point, but not beyond. He saved that degree of thrust for cross-examinations of adverse witnesses, and even then only rarely.

"How badly was 'not too badly'?" pursued Erickson. He glanced at the jury and was gratified to see each of them straining for the answer.

Campbell thought for a moment and then gave the only answer that he knew would get Erickson off of the point and on with the case.

"He stank," said the pathologist in a matter-of-fact tone. Each juror sat back and displayed a facial expression which typified the mental image that was called up. Spencer gazed at the ceiling and adjusted his tie. Pat Caton gently closed her eyes. G. Markham touched her hand and Erickson inwardly jumped for joy.

"Did you then proceed to examine the tissues and organs of the body?" Erickson asked.

"Yes, sir. We did."

The judge leaned forward. "Just one minute, Doctor," he interrupted. He squinted at the alternate juror. "Mr. Cassidy," he called sharply.

All eyes in the courtroom shifted to the thirteenth juror. The young man was pale. He held his neatly pressed handkerchief to his mouth and sat stiffly upright. His eyes were closed but not tightly.

"Mr. Cassidy," Judge Haran called again. "Are you going to be all right?"

Truman Fernandez stood up and began to cross the courtroom toward the jurors' box. The judge raised his hand almost imperceptibly and held him off.

"Sir?" Cassidy said meekly. He had begun to perspire generously although none of the other jurors appeared overly warm.

"You've gotten quite pale, Mr. Cassidy," Judge Haran said clinically. "Would you like some water?" He motioned again to Truman Fernandez, and a tiny paper cup of not-quite-cold water was placed on the jury-box railing as if by government order.

"Thank you, your honor," the juror said. "I just felt a little strange when the doctor said—" He paused, apparently unwilling to permit his own voice to speak the same words. "—when the doctor described the body." He recoiled from the concept in his mind, and put the handkerchief to his lips again.

"None of us finds the subject matter too pleasant, Mr. Cassidy. I am sure that the doctor will be as delicate as he can with the required descriptions." Judge Haran's tone left little doubt in anyone's mind, including Mark Campbell's.

"It's all right," Cassidy said, recovering some of his poise.

"Were you in the service, Mr. Cassidy? Did you see anyone killed or wounded?" Judge Haran asked quickly.

"Heavens, no!" the young juror said. "I was a C.O." He sat up a little stiffer.

Michael F. X. Haran squinted at James Cassidy and studied him silently. He wanted to ask him if he were really Irish-Catholic, but knew that the circumstances would not permit it. The classic Haran pep-talk on Americanism, the flag, and keeping those little yellow-skinned Communists from landing on the California coast rose and faded instantly in the judge's brain.

"You're going to have to make up your mind that some of this will be distasteful, Mr. Cassidy," Judge Haran said.

There was just the slightest tone of contempt in his voice now.

"Yes, sir," Cassidy said meekly. "I'll try."

"All right, Mr. Erickson, you may proceed."

"Tell the jury what you found, Doctor," Erickson said, leaning forward on the rostrum.

"And Cassidy," Judge Haran added loudly, "if you're going to be sick, for God's sake feel free to leave the courtroom. You understand?"

The alternate juror nodded silently. Judge Haran activated Erickson again with a flick of his finger and Erickson threw the ball to Campbell with a nod of his head.

"There was an inshoot—that is, an entrance wound—in the left chest and considerable tissue destruction of the underlying lung and heart."

"Would you demonstrate on yourself the approximate location of this entrance wound, Dr. Campbell?" Erickson asked, playing to the jury.

The pathologist stood up in the witness box and placed his extended index finger against his left jacket flap in the area of Caton's wound.

"Was that the cause of death?" Erickson asked.

"Very probably," conceded Campbell without hesitation. "He was shot through the heart."

"Very probably? You mean there was a possibility of some other cause of death, Doctor?" Erickson again turned to face the jury.

"Objection, your honor." Red Spencer rose from his chair quickly.

"Overruled."

"Well, there was only softened brain substance left, and much of the liver, pancreas, and lung had been greatly altered by decay. So if there had been some other lethal pathology prior to the gunshot wound, it could have escaped my attention in some of these areas." The pathologist paused as Erickson's spirits soared. "Of course . . ."

"Yes, Doctor?" Erickson urged.

"Of course, I really don't think there is any doubt as to

232

the real cause of death here." Erickson crashed earthward. "Gunshot wound of the chest," said the pathologist with authority and professional poise.

"Could you identify any other areas of injury?"

"No, sir. I paid careful attention to the hands to see if there were any powder markings. There were none."

"What did the absence of powder markings on the hands mean to you, Doctor?"

"In this case, the absence of the powder markings meant essentially nothing. The presence of powder markings might have indicated that one of the hands had been close to the muzzle of the gun at the time the shot was fired."

"Meaning what?"

"Meaning more probably, suicide."

"But you didn't see these marks, right?"

Red Spencer was suddenly on his feet, face flushed. "Your honor, this is highly objectionable. Mr. Erickson is extracting from this witness prejudicial statements based on observations which the doctor says were not present and then basing further presumptions on those absences."

"Sustained. Mr. Erickson, please couch your questions in such a manner that the witness can describe what he saw or did not see and reserve your extraction of conclusions or expert opinions for your hypothetical structures."

"Yes, sir," Erickson said obediently. "Doctor, what other wounds did you find?"

"None, sir."

"No exit wound?" Erickson assumed his astonished pose for the jury.

"No exit wound, sir."

"Then you recovered the bullet," suggested Erickson knowingly.

"In fact, Dr. Leatherman recovered the bullet," the witness conceded.

"But you saw it and where it was found?"

"Oh yes. I examined it carefully. It was found in a vertebral bone—that is, one of the back bones—and was in fairly good shape."

"What did it look like, Doctor?" Erickson asked with nonchalance.

"It was moderately heavy, lead-colored, non-jacketed, and—"

"Do you have an opinion as to its caliber, Doctor?"

"Object!" shouted Spencer. "The witness has not been qualified as a ballistics expert and is therefore not qualified to answer that question."

"Sustained," said the judge. He stole a glance at his watch.

Erickson resumed his position at the rostrum and leaned forward toward his witness. "Did you perform a blood-alcohol test, Doctor?"

"Certainly not," chuckled Mark Campbell.

"Too much decay?"

"Decay—embalming—chemical changes due to many months in the grave—you just can't rely on any blood-alcohol results under those circumstances," the pathologist explained in a professional tone.

"Then, you really have no opinion as to Mr. Caton's sobriety or inebriety, correct?" Erickson pushed.

"Correct."

"Were there microscopic slides made of the tissues, Dr. Campbell?"

"Dr. Leatherman made slides of the major organs and the edges of the wound."

"Have you had an opportunity to examine these slides?"

"Yes, sir. I did. Dr. Leatherman made them available to me at his laboratory in Miami. I examined them with him."

"And what did you conclude?" Erickson looked over his jury.

"That the inshoot—excuse me, entrance wound—was quite close."

"Why 'quite close,' Doctor?"

"Because there were small particles of black material impressed into the skin edges of the wound and the subcutaneous fatty tissue."

"What was that black material?"

The pathologist paused and pouted his lips, apparently considering his answer before speaking. "I suppose that it was some fouling material from the inside of the gun barrel."

"You mean powder?"

"Maybe. More likely, hot, half-burned grease. Either way, something from inside the gun immediately following the bullet."

Erickson stepped to the side of the rostrum and leaned forward, lowering the volume of his voice to cause the jury to strain to hear the question. "You mean that the gun was that close to his skin, Doctor?"

"Well, I don't know how close you mean by 'that close,' but I mean that it was within a few inches of his chest," Campbell explained.

"Could the gun have been closer than a few inches? I mean, like hard contact?" probed Erickson.

"It's possible. But I personally doubt it."

"Why do you doubt it?"

"Because there was no actual burning of the skin edges of the entrance wound nor were there any singed chest hairs."

"So you don't think that the gun was held right on the chest when the shot was fired, right?"

"Right."

"But aren't suicides usually performed by holding the muzzle right on the skin?" searched Erickson. He gathered his notes and papers as he fired this question at the pathologist.

"Object," said Spencer in a bored, flat, self-confident tone.

"Sustained." Equally bored.

"No further questions," said Erickson as he sat down next to G. Markham Hurst.

Red Spencer conferred briefly with Hervey Higgs and then walked slowly, almost pensively to the rostrum, placed his papers on it, and returned to the counsel table.

"Erickson was too easy on him, Hervey," Spencer whispered. "I smell a rat."

Higgs looked at Erickson and Hurst, who were huddled in a whispered conference.

"I think you're right, Red," Higgs agreed. "Let's ask for a break and nose around. Maybe you can call up Leatherman and run Campbell's testimony by him before we launch into cross-examination."

"Where am I going to find him now?"

"In his cool, stainless-steel Miami morgue, where else?" Higgs nudged Spencer back toward the rostrum.

"Your honor," announced Spencer, "the defendant would like a brief recess."

Judge Haran glanced quickly at the wall clock. Without altering his gaze he announced, "All right, Mr. Spencer. Fifteen minutes." He stood up at the sound of his own gavel hitting the block.

"All rise," intoned the marshal, as the United States swept toward his chambers and disappeared through the door. Erickson looked at Red Spencer and made no effort to conceal the broad, self-pleased grin which threatened to split his face.

Spencer returned a small, courtly bow.

29

Spencer and Higgs dragged their heels in the hallway to give Erickson a chance to emerge from the courtroom. Spencer smelled more than a rat. Somehow the whole case had begun to have a slippery feeling. Not yet slimy, just slippery. He continued his stage conversation with Higgs as Erickson and Hurst came through the courtroom door and headed directly for the plaintiff's witness room. They had not yet reached it when Lieutenant Casper threw open its glass-fronted door. He looked somewhat pale and anxious.

"Hi, Lieutenant." Erickson really wanted to ask the policeman what was eating him. Not out of concern for the cop's welfare but to assure himself that Havlicek had infected the patient fatally.

"Oh—Mr. Erickson," said Casper with slight surprise. "I thought you were in court."

"Recess."

"Huh?" Casper was visibly concerned with another thought. His eyes searched the corridor.

"Recess," repeated Erickson. "Lose something?"

"Just looking for a pay phone," said Casper as he continued to look up and down the hallway.

"There's one down the corridor—near the elevator," offered Erickson without visible concern. "There's a booth downstairs near the blind stand if you need privacy."

"Where? Oh—good. Thanks." said Casper. He hurried off down the hallway and disappeared around the corner fumbling in his pocket for a dime.

Erickson smiled and winked at G. Markham Hurst. "Smell anything?" he asked.

"Worry," Hurst said.

"Maybe even panic. We are setting him up real tight and he knows it."

"Well, don't make it too tight, Paul," the older lawyer counseled him. "Remember, we're out to throw a fish to the jury, and he'll do just fine. But if you get in deep enough with this Casper theory, you'll end up in a murder trial. Judge Haran will see to that."

"Who knows? Maybe old Casper really did it," Erickson said.

"Who cares? Just as long as we convince that jury that Caton didn't do it himself. Besides, what valid reasons could we offer for Casper's knocking off Caton?"

"Girl problems, G. Markham," Erickson supplied. "You remember those."

The older lawyer squinted at the remark. He would admit to no longer being thought of as a man about town, but he didn't consider himself dead, either. "I think both Lt. Casper and I could handle our 'girl problems' without resorting to homicide."

"But you never caught your mistress in bed with some tomato farmer," Erickson said.

"The point is yours," Hurst conceded.

"Besides," Erickson said, "I don't want to actually prove Casper did it. I just want to waltz him around this civil courtroom for a while. Hell, I'd implicate Spencer and Higgs if it would win the case."

"Speaking of which . . ." Hurst said in a hushed tone. He directed Erickson's attention to the opposing lawyers standing near the door to the courtroom. The younger lawyers quickly avoided each other's direct gazes, and the senior lawyers muttered almost simultaneously, "That son of a bitch is up to something."

Erickson opened the door to the witness room and ushered G. Markham in before himself. Havlicek stood up, smiling.

"Happy to see you, gentlemen," Havlicek said. He gave each of the lawyers a stronger-than-necessary handshake.

"Milan," Erickson said, "I'm a little puzzled."

"Puzzled?" Havlicek asked with arched eyebrows.

"Casper," G. Markham supplied somberly.

"Yes! Lt. Casper!" Havlicek said excitedly. "He was very upset."

"We noticed. What's he bugged about?" asked Erickson.

"I really don't know," said Havlicek with his arms spread wide in a gesture of complete innocence. On him it even looked convincing.

"Did you talk to him at all?" asked Erickson with a phony naïveté that almost made G. Markham cough.

"Yes—yes. We have good talk. About police departments. About crimes. About guns."

"About Caton?" Erickson asked casually. He pretended to look for something among the pages of his yellow notebook.

Havlicek looked from Erickson to G. Markham Hurst and back again and his expression took on a sheepish character. "Maybe a little," he confessed.

Erickson smiled with relief. "What did you tell him?" he probed gently.

"We talk generally about this case—how interesting it is."

"And about the bullet?"

"Yes—yes. All about the bullet. I tell him how well preserved the bullet is. And what it looked like. Lt. Casper is an experienced law-enforcement officer. He knows much about such things." Havlicek's complimentary remarks had a genuine quality about them.

"Is that when he left?" inquired G. Markham.

"He said he had to make a phone call. It must have been important," Havlicek supplied.

"Well, Milan," Erickson reassured, placing his hand on the criminalist's shoulder, "I wouldn't be too concerned. Maybe he left the water running in his bathtub back home."

"Bathtub?" Havlicek asked with earnest concern.

"We'll try to get you on the stand later today, Milan," said Erickson, chuckling. "Spencer has to cross-examine Dr. Campbell, and then we'll be ready for you."

Havlicek stole a quick glance at his watch and emitted a small sigh of resignation.

"Anything that you wish to go over with us before you go on?" asked G. Markham Hurst.

Havlicek pursed his lips, frowned, and shook his head slowly. He and the two lawyers had been over his proposed testimony so many times that there were no areas of mystery or surprise left.

"Just one thing. My English is not so good. The lawyers—sometime they trick me," Havlicek said.

Erickson thought of the soft Hungarian accent and how his Chicago phrases would sound in court. "You'll do just fine, Milan. Just fine." In fact, Havlicek's bumbling manner in court often proved to be an asset. The jury was sympathetic to him.

Impulsively, Erickson opened the door of the witness room and looked out. Spencer and Higgs were no longer standing near the water cooler.

"Want to bet that Spencer is out pumping Casper?" Erickson offered.

"No bet," said Hurst. "Let's just hope that they find interesting things to chat about."

Pat Caton saw them looking up and down the hallway and wandered over like a cat investigating undefined movement. "Did you gentlemen lose something?"

"Not yet," Hurst said.

"We were wondering where our worthy opponents had gone," Erickson said.

"They took off after the cop. I think they all went downstairs." She indicated the general direction by a toss of her head which threw her hair across her face. She readjusted it about her ear. "What are they up to, anyway?"

"A lot, we hope," Erickson said.

"Don't give me that, Paul," she pleaded. "What the hell is going on?"

Erickson moved her toward the hall and shielded her with his own frame. He leaned closer to her ear and spoke softly so that only she could hear the conversation. "We are giving them the bait and letting them run with the line."

"What bait?" she said too loudly.

"Shhhh. It's not over yet. Let's wait for their offer," Erickson cautioned.

"Settlement?" asked Pat, astonished.

"You agree with an adequate settlement, don't you, Mrs. Caton?" inquired G. Markham Hurst.

"Yes, but—" She was speechless. She searched the two lawyers' smiling faces but received little information.

"It will all come out soon," said Erickson reassuringly. He reopened the door to the witness room and winked at Havlicek. "Hang loose, Milan. We'll get to you as soon as we can."

"I will remain here?"

"Yeah. And Milan—"

"Yes, Paul?"

"If Casper comes back, keep him entertained."

"Entertained?" Havlicek asked.

"You know—tell him stories about famous criminals you have known. All that stuff."

Pat Caton saw that the spectators were returning to the courtroom and tugged at Erickson's sleeve. "They're going in, Paul," she announced. Erickson looked over his shoulder and nodded.

"Take Pat back into the courtroom, will you?" he asked his partner. "I want to hang around out here for a few moments to see if Red Spencer bites."

G. Markham silently offered the arm of his gray Wolf Brothers' traditional to the widow Caton. Erickson shut the door to the witness room and began to fumble with his legal pad. To a casual observer, he might be searching for something lost in the notebook's pages. But his eyes monitored the hallway for the returning Spencer.

30

Pat Caton resumed her seat at the plaintiff's counsel table and tried to pry hidden facts from the lines on G. Markham Hurst's face. The senior lawyer held his cheekbones with his long thin fingers and stared straight ahead, his brain lost in the rapid review of the case.

At the defense table, Hervey Higgs sat alone, leafing slowly through the notes that Spencer had made during the direct examination of Dr. Campbell. Occasionally, Higgs looked over his shoulder at the courtroom door, hoping to see Spencer bounding nervously in.

The small door to the chambers opened and all rose as Judge Haran and his entourage entered to resume the trial officially. The judge motioned for the jury to be returned without looking at either counsel table. The clerk noticed the absence of both Erickson and Spencer and moved quietly to the judge's side, where he bent toward the ear of the United States and whispered. The judge looked immediately at the two empty chairs. He quickly motioned to Hurst and Higgs to approach the bench. The senior lawyers walked slowly and with practiced dignity to the bench where the judge leaned forward to meet them.

"G. Markham, Hervey," said Judge Haran in an intimate and not unfriendly tone. Each lawyer nodded and mumbled a barely audible greeting in return. Their collective years as members of the Hillsborough Bar Association afforded this infrequent opportunity for first-name salutations, carefully kept from the jury's ears.

"The fireballs seem missing from each counsel table," Judge Haran said with a small smile. "Do you old warhorses intend to carry on this battle personally, or are we to send the marshal out to search the men's room?"

Hurst and Higgs glanced at each other. Each deferred to the other for reply, and then both started to speak at once. Again they withheld their replies until, with a small wave of the hand, Higgs indicated that he would wait for G. Markham to speak.

"I don't know what Hervey's wishes are, Judge, but as for me, I'd prefer to wait for Erickson to return." He turned to glance at Higgs. "But since we are right at cross-examination, the defense had best make that choice."

"Your honor," Higgs began, "I would not like to delay the trial, but in fact, we had planned for Mr. Spencer to cross-examine Dr. Campbell."

"Well, where is he?" asked Judge Haran not unpleasantly.

"I think he may be in conference with Mr. Erickson," Higgs replied quietly. He half-turned to glance at the jury, now fully seated in the box.

"Do I smell a settlement?" Judge Haran inquired.

"That's always a possibility, your honor," said Hervey Higgs noncommittally.

"And a laudable one, too, gentlemen," Judge Haran said. He rubbed his hands together gently and with growing satisfaction. Every judge would prefer a satisfactory settlement to continuing an adversary procedure for jury consideration.

"That may be a moot point," Judge Haran suggested, looking beyond the two elder lawyers in front of him. The courtroom doors were swung wide as Erickson and Spencer marched briskly into the arena.

Erickson smiled gently at Pat Caton. Spencer remained silent and somber. The senior lawyers returned to their respective tables. Each table huddled and carried on a whispered conference as every eye in the jury studied their movements. Judge Haran occupied himself with a few papers requiring his signature that his secretary had sent out via the faithful Mr. Fernandez. After he had attended to these forms, he looked up and inspected each counsel table.

"Gentlemen," he announced. "Would you be so kind as to include this court in your conversations?" His tone had returned to the testy nasal twang that he paraded in front of juries and courtroom spectators. Gone was the warmth of the old school tie which he wore only in front of G. Markham and Hervey Higgs.

Erickson and Spencer looked up abruptly like two gazelles interrupted while drinking at the water hole.

"Your honor," Spencer announced. "The defendant is ready to proceed."

"To proceed—with cross-examination?" asked Judge Haran, somewhat astonished.

"Yes, sir."

"Then, Mr. Spencer, by all means proceed," said the judge. He glanced in the direction of the marshal and said, "Bring in Dr. Campbell." The marshal responded immediately and disappeared through the swinging doors.

Pat Caton was unable to contain her curiosity any longer. "Will somebody tell me just what the hell is going on?" she asked in a hoarse whisper.

"They're nibbling at the bait, Pat. All we have to do now is give them a little more line." Erickson offered a self-confident smile.

"Where do we get the line?"

"He's coming in the courtroom right now." Erickson motioned with his head toward the double doors just as the pathologist reentered the room and walked toward the witness stand.

"You do understand that you are still under oath, don't you, Doctor?" asked the judge.

"Yes, sir," said Mark Campbell. He assumed the witness chair and bent the microphone cable closer to his face.

Spencer rose slowly from his seat and walked even more slowly to the rostrum. "Dr. Campbell," he began. "I believe you testified that in cooperation with Dr. Leatherman, you recovered a bullet from the body of one Myrl Caton."

"Dr. Leatherman recovered the bullet," the pathologist corrected.

"All right, sir. But nonetheless you saw the bullet that was recovered, did you not?"

"I did."

"And did you see what happened thereafter to that bullet?"

"You mean immediately thereafter or subsequently?"

"Both, sir, if you know."

"Each of us examined the bullet. Dr. Leatherman marked the base, and then packaged it for further analysis."

Spencer walked toward the clerk's desk and picked up a small sealed test tube to which was attached a tag. He spoke briefly to the clerk and waited as the identifying stamp was placed on the back of the tag. He carried the vial to the witness stand and handed it to the pathologist.

"Doctor, I hand you what has been marked, for identification, defendant's exhibit number one, and ask if you can identify it." He stood close by as Campbell examined the tube and then the attached tag.

"I believe this is the tube that Dr. Leatherman put the bullet in." He paused to look at the defense attorney.

"You were there when Dr. Leatherman tagged the tube?"

"I'm really not sure, sir. I was there when he marked the base of the bullet, but I really don't recall seeing him tag this tube."

Spencer walked halfway back to the rostrum, stopped, turned, and appeared lost in thought. "Would you open the tube and describe what you find there, Dr. Campbell?"

Judge Haran looked at Erickson for the objection he was confident would explode momentarily. None came. The pathologist pulled the rubber stopper from the tube. The tube was filled with white cotton, with a firm, lead-colored metal object nestled inside the center like an orphaned egg of some rare and tiny bird.

"You may remove the contents, Doctor," urged Spencer. The pathologist gently lifted the bullet from its cotton cradle and held it close to his eye. He squinted carefully and silently at the base as he slowly began to nod his head.

"This is the bullet," he announced. Campbell looked at the nearest juror to be sure that his decision had been understood.

"And how do you know that, sir?" asked Spencer.

"I note the initials 'JL' on the base of the bullet. I take that to mean 'Jerry Leatherman.' "

"You saw Dr. Leatherman mark that bullet 'JL'?"

"Yes, sir."

Spencer took a rhetorical stance at the rostrum and studied the wall beyond and above the witness stand long enough for Judge Haran to readjust his robes, cuff links, and class ring at least twice.

"How would you describe that bullet, Doctor?" Spencer asked slowly.

Campbell glanced at Erickson and then at the judge. He was too straightforward and too professional to be soliciting instructions. He was only giving the plaintiff's attorney an adequate opportunity to object before he began his answer. After all, he had been declared incompetent on the subject of bullet identification when Erickson had asked him a similar question. But now the request came from the opposite camp, unopposed by any comment from Erickson. Evidently, Spencer had had a change of heart about letting Campbell's ballistic testimony hit the record.

"I'd say it was essentially undeformed, nonjacketed,

247

lead-colored, and of a moderately large caliber," the doctor replied.

"Do you have any knowledge of lands and grooves, Doctor?" Spencer pushed.

"Some. Only academically. No real or practical experience."

"Can you tell the jury about the lands and grooves on that bullet?" Spencer paused to study Erickson as he asked the question. He was disappointed to find Erickson not only totally unobjecting, but apparently delighted.

"You mean here and now?" asked Mark Campbell, somewhat puzzled.

"If you would not mind, sir." Spencer continued to study Erickson for even the slightest crack in his cast-iron face.

"We would need a comparison microscope before I could make any intelligent statement about the lands and grooves, Mr. Spencer. That type of data can be properly observed only with the use of high magnification, proper lighting, and hopefully another bullet from the suspect gun to compare it to."

"Mr. Spencer," interrupted Judge Haran. "Where do you intend to go with this line of questioning? I have waited patiently for Mr. Erickson to express some modicum of concern for your latest group of questions, and while he may be content to let you go on with this, I am not. If necessary, I'll enter the proper objections myself, in the interest of justice." The judge adjusted his robes, cuff links, and class ring. "I think you'd do well to save this line of inquiry for some other witness. I understand from our pretrial conference that there will be a ballistics expert called, is that not correct?"

"Yes, sir," said Spencer and Erickson simultaneously.

"Well, then, Mr. Spencer, let's confine our remarks to the doctor's area of specialization, which I believe is human pathology."

"Yes, sir. No further questions, Doctor." There was an audible murmur from the spectator section as Spencer gathered his notes and returned quickly to the defense counsel table. Somewhat astonished, Judge Haran directed his attention to Paul Erickson. Erickson smiled.

"Any re-direct, Mr. Erickson?" the judge asked.

"None, your honor," said Erickson.

"May this witness be excused, then, gentlemen?" The judge looked from one counsel table to the other and saw only four lawyers nodding in total agreement.

"Dr. Campbell, you are excused. The court thanks you for your testimony and cooperation." Judge Haran allowed Mark Campbell a tiny, noncommittal smile.

"Thank you, your honor," said the pathologist. He replaced the bullet in its cotton nest, put in the stopper, returned the small tube to the clerk's desk as he walked from the witness stand. On his way to the courtroom door, he carefully avoided looking at either counsel table.

Pat Caton turned as he passed and followed him with her eyes.

"Will you stop grinning like a pregnant buffalo and tell me what Spencer is up to?" she asked Erickson.

"He is biting on the bait, my dear," said Erickson.

"Why don't you pull him in, then?"

"Because I have to sharpen my hook."

"What is your hook?"

"A beautiful Hungarian named Havlicek," he replied.

"A Hungarian?" Pat was now totally confused.

"Why not a Hungarian? Do you know what a Hungarian is?"

"What?"

"A Hungarian, my dear, is a magnificently proportioned male from Gary, Indiana."

G. Markham Hurst looked personally pained.

"From where?" Pat Caton could not be made party to any humor that did not rest squarely on solid, earthy pornographic images.

"Ours is from Sun City," assured G. Markham Hurst.

"Mr. Erickson?" Judge Haran inquired in a firm tone.

"The plaintiff will call Milan Havlicek," Erickson announced.

31

Havlicek entered the courtroom looking like a through passenger on the Greyhound bus from New Orleans to Boston. His gray suit seemed permanently wrinkled, and his white shirt, overstarched that morning, was now limp and damp. The off-blue tie exhibited a knot that defied an identifying name. There were several papers stuffed into the jacket pockets and a larger-than-necessary comb protruded from the breast pocket behind an incongruously neatly folded three-point handkerchief.

The ballistics expert squinted toward the bench and walked slowly forward, exhibiting profound respect for the courtroom with every measured step.

Judge Haran found himself inspecting the retired police expert. The oath was administered to Havlicek and the judge motioned him toward the witness stand.

"You may adjust the microphone, sir," Judge Haran offered. "Be sure to speak directly into it. Do you understand, sir?" The judge's tone was one that he usually reserved for the enfeebled, but Havlicek accepted the directions graciously. Milan Havlicek understood that the man in the black robes represented power. Since he had spent most of his professional lifetime working with the police and testifying for the state, his attitude toward the court was closer to prudent, unquestioned cooperation, than fear.

Erickson rose, smiled easily at Havlicek, and took his legal pad to the rostrum. Havlicek sat stiffly upright and folded his wrinkled hands in his lap.

"Would you state your name, please?"

"Milan Havlicek."

"Where are you now employed?"

"I am retired. I live in Sun City, Florida." He gestured slightly with a half-raised hand as if to indicate the general direction to Sun City from downtown Tampa.

"What was your occupation before you retired, Mr. Havlicek?"

"I was criminalist with the Chicago police force for many years."

"And after that?"

"After that, I was professor of police science at the University of Indiana for three years."

"You did not continue your teaching?" probed Erickson, gently.

"I find that doing police science was something I like very much to do—as long as I can. But teaching ballistics to young college policeman was not my best line of work." Havlicek grinned self-consciously.

"Prof. Havlicek," announced Erickson with pride and a smirk toward Spencer's table. "Tell the court what your duties were when you were with the Chicago police department." He turned to face the jury and to study each juror's reception of Havlicek's pedigree.

"When I was with the Chicago police department, I was many things. I started as an assistant technician in the laboratory. It wasn't much in those days. Just raw fingerprints and some crude chemical tests."

"It's more sophisticated now?" probed Erickson.

"Now they have a Ph.D. in every section. You have to be a chemist just to read the labels on the reagent bottles."

"But you're not a Ph.D. are you, Prof. Havlicek?"

"No."

"Or a professional chemist?"

"No."

Erickson preferred to demonstrate any potential weak points in his expert's qualifications rather than leave them for Spencer to pounce on. When a weak qualification was demonstrated only by the opposition, there was always the danger that some juror would think that the witness wanted the unfavorable point concealed.

"What position did you hold when you retired from the Chicago police department?"

"Chief of Ballistics Section."

"Chief?" asked Erickson for emphasis.

"Yes, sir."

"Would you tell us what the ballistics section concerned itself with, Prof. Havlicek?"

"The ballistics section had charge of firearms identification, examination of firearms, examination of bullets, cartridges, and other explosives, storage of firearms and bullets for later presentation in court—" He paused to see if his rapid-fire answer had been sufficient.

"So it might be fair to characterize you as a 'gun expert'?"

"Object," said Spencer, half-rising.

"Overruled."

"You may answer," coached Erickson.

"A gun expert?" Havlicek asked with a minimal expression of displeasure.

"That would be fair, would it not?" Erickson wanted this to be the way the jury remembered his expert—not as a wrinkled Hungarian from Sun City.

"I suppose you could call me a gun expert."

"Have you ever written any articles or books on guns or ballistics?"

"I wrote an article on firing-pin marks and breech-block markings on cartridge cases for use in police training."

"Was that published?"

"Yes, sir. In the *American Journal of Police Science*."

"Any other publications?"

Havlicek squinted slightly and looked at the far wall of the courtroom. "I helped write the chapter on firearms for a textbook entitled *Crime Investigation*."

"All right, sir." Erickson paused and examined his notes. "Are you a member of any professional organizations?"

"I am still a Fellow of the American Academy of Forensic Sciences. I used to belong to a lot more police-science groups, but since I retired, well—"

"I understand. The American Academy of Forensic Sciences, is that the same organization of pathologists, criminalists, forensic psychiatrists, and toxicologists that Dr. Mark Campbell belongs to?"

"Yes, sir."

"And you know Dr. Campbell, do you?"

"I know Dr. Campbell for many years. I have much respect for him. He is a fine—"

"Object."

"Sustained."

"All right, Prof. Havlicek," Erickson continued in his friendliest tone. "You understand that you will not be allowed to testify as to Dr. Campbell's qualifications."

"Yes, sir."

Erickson took a stage pause and leaned forward on stiff arms, looking directly at the witness. "Did you ever have occasion to examine a bullet at my request, Prof. Havlicek?"

"Yes, sir."

Erickson walked forward and picked up the small tube from the clerk's desk. He brought it with slightly more ceremony than necessary to the witness stand. Erickson handed it to Milan Havlicek.

"I hand you what has been marked, for identification, defense exhibit number one and ask you to examine it."

Havlicek carefully inspected the small tube and hesitated before removing the rubber stopper.

"It's quite all right, Prof. Havlicek. You may examine the contents," encouraged Erickson.

Carefully, Havlicek removed the bullet and squinted at its base.

"Have you ever seen that bullet before, sir?"

Havlicek continued to squint at the bullet base, rotating the bullet in his fingers. He looked up at the fluorescent ceiling lights with an expression of exasperation and then resumed his study of the base.

"Yes, sir, I have."

One of the jurors breathed a silent sigh of relief.

"On what occasion?" asked Erickson.

"I went to Miami to see this bullet in the office of Dr. Leatherman."

"And he let you examine the bullet?"

"I had a letter from Mr. Spencer who said I can look at the bullet."

"Was that in lieu of a court order?" asked Erickson, hoping to clarify the point for the jurors.

"In where, sir?" asked Havlicek.

The sixth juror allowed a small smile to crack his somber face.

"You understood that the lawyers for both sides had agreed to let you examine the bullet, right?" Erickson began to wish he had left the point alone.

"I guess so. All I got was a letter from you telling me to go to Miami to look at this bullet and the letter from Mr. Spencer was stapled on the back." Havlicek looked at the judge to see if he was incurring the jurist's displeasure. Judge Haran exhibited an emotionless expression that even failed to disclose whether he was following the testimony.

"And then what happened?" urged Erickson.

"I looked at the bullet," said Havlicek haplessly.

"I know, Professor, but what exactly did you do to examine this bullet?" pressed Erickson.

"I looked at it carefully. I saw the 'JL' marked on the base like Dr. Leatherman told me. I look at the bullet under the microscope. I see the lands and grooves and the scratches along the sides of the bullet. I look it all over." Havlicek sat back.

"Did Dr. Leatherman tell you the origin of that bullet?" asked Erickson.

"Oh, yes! He said he took it from a body."

"Did he say what body?"

"Some man he autopsied in Orangeburrow."

Spencer rose slowly and stuffed his hands into his pockets. "The defendant will stipulate that the bullet came from the body of Myrl Caton, your honor."

"Thank you, Mr. Spencer," said Judge Haran.

"OK, then, Prof. Havlicek," Erickson resumed. "After you examined the bullet, what conclusions did you draw? What did you think?"

"I thought they gave me the wrong bullet," Havlicek replied simply.

"The wrong bullet?" Erickson emphasized.

"Yes, sir."

"Why 'the wrong bullet,' Prof. Havlicek?" Erickson watched the jury as each member leaned forward to catch every word.

Havlicek allowed a small smile and a shrug. "Because, before I go to see the bullet, I hear about the case from you and Mr. Hurst, and you tell me that the man was shot with a Colt .45 automatic. U.S. Army type."

"Did anyone else tell you a similar story?" urged Erickson.

"Dr. Leatherman told me all about the autopsy and the gun. He talked all the time I was in Miami."

"But why did you think he had given you the wrong bullet?"

"Because when I see this bullet—" He held it up in the air between his thumb and his index finger. "—when I see this bullet, I say to myself, this is not a .45."

"Not a .45?" asked Erickson, feigning astonishment. He paused to let the jury savor Havlicek's announcement.

"No, sir."

"Why did you doubt that the bullet was a .45 caliber?"

"Because it was too light, the wrong size, not jacketed—" He nodded to himself to show he was completely satisfied with his conclusion.

"Did you tell Dr. Leatherman about this?" asked Erickson.

"No, sir." His answer was firm and unflinching.

"Why not, Prof. Havlicek?" asked Erickson with apparent innocence.

"Because you tell me before I go to Miami not to discuss the bullet examination with anybody—not even Dr. Leatherman. So I didn't."

"Who did you tell?"

"Just you and Mr. Hurst—when I got back."

Spencer was squirming in his seat, unable to find a comfortable spot on his chair. Higgs stared straight ahead but kept his eyes gently closed. Erickson stood comfortably at the rostrum.

"Well," Erickson began happily. "If you did not feel the bullet was a .45, what did you think it was?"

"A .38."

"A .38?" echoed Erickson, playing to the jury.

Havlicek nodded.

"But, Prof. Havlicek, let me show you one of these photographs." Erickson picked slowly through the stack of enlargements and selected one. He presented it to the witness as two jurors arched their necks to see which one he had chosen.

"This is plaintiff's exhibit number five, Prof. Havlicek," Erickson announced.

"Yes?" said the witness noncommittally.

"Do you see a gun in that picture?"

"Yes, sir. A U.S. Army Colt .45 automatic."

Spencer walked to the end of his appointed table to get a better look at the photograph. He leaned gently against the end of the counsel table with his back toward the grieving Hervey Higgs.

"What do you observe about the gun in the photograph, Professor?" asked Erickson.

"Well, it is probably ready to fire," said Havlicek.

"Why do you say that?"

"Because you can see that the hammer is drawn back

256

and the slide is closed." He indicated these observations on the pistol in the photograph.

"Does that mean that the .45 has just been fired?" pushed Erickson.

"Maybe. But not necessarily," said Havlicek shrugging his shoulders. "He could have just pulled the hammer back. It would look the same."

"Did you ever get a chance to compare this bullet with one fired from that pistol shown in the photograph?" Erickson asked.

"I examined the pistol that your office gave me one day in Tampa. Mr. Spencer was there." He gestured slightly to indicate Mr. Spencer.

"And?"

"I didn't think there was any need to fire the weapon since I had already seen this bullet."

"And you didn't think the bullet was fired from that particular .45?" Erickson asked.

"I really did not. No, sir."

Erickson looked at his legal pad and ran his finger down the list of points he had prepared for his direct examination. Apparently satisfied that he had covered all the areas he had intended, he closed the pad with an obviously self-satisfied flip of the pages and walked toward G. Markham Hurst. He winked at Pat Caton and enjoyed the confused expression on her face.

"Your witness, Mr. Spencer," Erickson said.

Spencer studied Havlicek as he moved to the rostrum.

"Mr. Havlicek," he began softly. "If I were to tell you that another ballistics expert has examined this bullet and has submitted a report that it is a .45, what would you think?"

"I think he is wrong," said Havlicek confidently. "What is his name?"

"Mr. Havlicek," corrected Judge Haran gently. "Let the lawyers ask the questions. All you have to do is supply whatever answers you can."

"Yes, sir." Havlicek managed a sheepish grin.

Pat Caton leaned toward Erickson and whispered in his ear. "Who is their ballistics expert, Paul?"

"If they had one, they would have listed him as a witness," Erickson whispered back.

"You mean they didn't get that bullet analyzed?" she exclaimed in a hushed voice.

"Yep. They relied only on Leatherman." Erickson grinned and squeezed Pat's hand excitedly.

"No shit," she whispered, genuinely astonished.

"Insurance companies are cheap when it comes to spending money for good investigation," Erickson whispered. G. Markham Hurst turned toward them and gave them a professional frown of disapproval. The unspoken correction was sufficient to redirect their attentions to the cross-examination.

"Mr. Havlicek, could this bullet have been fired from the Colt .45 you see in the photograph?" Spencer stood back, watching his witness. He felt a sudden twinge of near-panic when he realized he had violated one of the cardinal rules of courtroom interrogation: Never ask a question unless you are reasonably sure of the answer you are going to get. His panic continued as Havlicek silently considered his answer, complete with pursed lips, frown, and pained expression in his eyes.

"Maybe. Possibly," said Havlicek after an eternity.

Spencer began to breathe once again. "It could have been fired from that gun?" he repeated.

"Yes, but you would have to shim up the cartridge so that it would fit in the chamber, and even then I'm not sure that the firing pin would hit it right."

"How do you mean, 'shim up the cartridge'?" Spencer was pressing the point for all it was worth and at that instant, the issue was worth plenty.

"Well, sometimes someone will shoot a .32 revolver cartridge from a .38 revolver weapon. But since the cartridge is smaller than the chamber that has to hold it, they will use little pieces of toilet paper or tinfoil to wedge the cartridge into the chamber. That holds it while the firing pin explodes the primer and then fires the bullet. It gives horrible ballistics." Havlicek sat back, contented.

"Why horrible ballistics?" asked Spencer.

"Because the .32 bullet comes wobbling up the .38 barrel and does not strike all the lands and grooves properly."

"Would that have happened in this case if that bullet that you think is a .38 had been fired from the .45 automatic?" Spencer had the feeling that he was in deep water and sinking slowly. He looked quickly at Hervey Higgs but received no help.

"Maybe so. I really don't know about that. I'm only assuming that the .45 Colt would fire this .38. Even then, it would be better if the .38 cartridge was an automatic."

"Was this .38 bullet fired from an automatic?" asked Spencer. He was now covered with sweat.

"I don't think so. It looks mostly like a revolver bullet. But I did not examine it with that question in mind." Havlicek continued to study the lead bullet in his hand. "It's too hard to tell for sure with this particular bullet," he announced.

Spencer walked to the side of his senior counsel and bent to his ear. "What do you think, Hervey? Shall I get rid of him?"

"You'd better do something. He's digging your grave up there."

"What about the cartridge casing at the end of the bed?" Spencer asked. "Should I get into that with him?"

Higgs closed his eyes momentarily for better concentration. "What do we have to lose? The damned thing was there. But why didn't Erickson bring it out?"

"It's not a point to help his side of the case. If it helps anyone, it helps us. I'm going to use it."

Spencer returned to the rostrum.

"Mr. Havlicek, I'd like you to listen carefully to the following hypothetical facts. Suppose that there was a man lying on his back in a closed, locked, motel room. Suppose further that he is armed with a U.S. Army Colt .45 automatic."

Havlicek nodded silently as each fact was presented to him.

"And suppose further that this man holds the gun at his own chest and pulls the trigger. Now, given these facts, Mr. Havlicek, do you have an opinion as to the trajectory of the empty cartridge as it is ejected from that gun?"

"Are you assuming that the butt of the gun is facing his feet or facing his head?" asked Havlicek, half-squinting in concentration.

"The butt of the automatic is facing his feet. He holds the gun with two hands, muzzle on his chest. Like this." Spencer stepped from behind the rostrum and held the imaginary pistol to his own chest.

Havlicek began to nod. "Yes, I can see where that shell is going to go," he said, visualizing the trajectory in his mind.

"Where?" asked Spencer.

"It will fly upward and forward, in that position."

"But where in relation to the body lying on the bed?" insisted Spencer.

"Up above his head," said Havlicek.

"To land on its base on one of the portions of the headboard?" asked Spencer.

"Maybe. The shells do crazy things, sometimes. But usually they fall on their side." Havlicek smiled slightly.

Spencer stared at the expert witness for a long time and wondered if he could score any further than that. At last he decided that he had extracted about all he could from Havlicek and decided to get rid of him. The Hungarian's performance had been damaging enough.

"No further questions. Thank you." Spencer sat down and felt suddenly ten years older.

"Prof. Havlicek," said Erickson from his counsel table. "If you threw a cocked, loaded Colt .45 automatic into the motel room from the opening in the door left by the chain, would the gun go off when it hit the floor?"

Havlicek was already shaking his head. "No. The Colt .45 has a grip safety that has to be depressed along with the trigger before it will fire. I do not believe it would go off if you threw it across the room like that."

"Thank you, sir." Erickson had risen during the answer and now sat down again. "No further questions."

"Mr. Spencer?" asked Judge Haran.

"Nothing more," said Spencer quietly. "Oh yes—one more thing."

Havlicek resumed his seat in the witness box.

"Did you have occasion to discuss this theory of yours about the bullet caliber with any of the other witnesses here today? Namely, Lt. Casper?"

The judge took immediate interest in the question.

"I talked with Lt. Casper when we both were in the little room down the hall," said Havlicek simply. He smiled gently.

"Didn't Mr. Erickson tell you not to discuss the case with anyone?" Judge Haran asked.

"Yes, sir," Havlicek said.

"Your honor," said Erickson, rising to his feet. "At the time Prof. Havlicek and Lt. Casper were together in the witness room, neither of them had testified. So they can hardly be accused of discussing 'testimony.' Both of them at that point were only potential witnesses."

Judge Haran glared at Erickson through squinting eyes that announced he didn't care much for the flavor of the distinction. "Did Mr. Erickson instruct you to discuss this case with Lt. Casper, Mr. Havlicek?" Judge Haran asked.

"No, sir. He told me not to," said Havlicek sheepishly.

The judge continued to examine the facial expressions of Havlicek and Erickson. "I guess that's sufficient to save this case from a mistrial, Mr. Erickson," Judge Haran ruled. "The witness is excused. The court will take a short recess."

32

All stood as the judge left and the jury was herded out by the faithful guardian. Pat unconsciously reached for and found Paul Erickson's hand.

Erickson responded with a reassuring squeeze. "Things will look a little better now, I promise you," he told her quietly. He watched the jury's exit from the courtroom. "I wonder what they would come up with if we could throw the case in their laps right now."

"I think they're on our side at this moment," replied G. Markham.

"But you can never be sure," Erickson commented as the last juror disappeared through the door.

"Here comes the other side," Pat announced.

Erickson turned slightly to see Spencer and Higgs marching across the center stage. Erickson automatically extended his hand and Spencer automatically shook it.

"Hi, Paul," Spencer said. "Mrs. Caton. G. Markham. Do you suppose we could talk?"

"That's all we've done so far in this case, Red," Erickson said.

"Well, after that last round, I think we ought to take a

few moments for some serious considerations of where we all stand at this moment." Spencer twisted his wedding ring unconsciously.

"Red, we are always interested in earnest reconsiderations," said G. Markham, accepting a fraternal handshake from Hervey Higgs. "Especially from the insurance company."

"I haven't got the checkbook out yet," Higgs warned.

"What's on your mind, then?" asked Erickson. His grin had faded from his face but his curiosity now burned brightly.

G. Markham and Hervey Higgs took seats while their younger partners stood facing each other, with folded arms.

"I—er—I was a bit surprised by the testimony of Prof. Havlicek," Spencer began.

"Why? I thought that Lt. Casper had clued you during the last recess." The grin returned to Erickson's face.

"Come on, Paul. I'm not fencing. I'm really confused by the developments."

"So am I," Pat Caton admitted.

G. Markham slid his hand over hers. It appeared as a gesture of comfort and kindness, but the authoritative squeeze told her to shut up.

Hervey Higgs interpreted the movement correctly, even though he didn't watch.

"OK, Red. What's on your mind?" Erickson's tone was more genuine.

Spencer studied him briefly and then sighed. "Well, Paul, when we started out on this case, we felt we had an honest difference of opinion over the death of Mr. Caton." He glanced quickly at Pat Caton but her eyes flashed downward quickly.

"And now?" asked Erickson.

"And now, Havlicek has raised an issue that was not even contained in Dr. Leatherman's autopsy report."

"So? He was your pathologist. You could have hired a ballistics man if you'd wanted to," taunted Erickson.

"Sure, sure. There's a lot we could have done. But

that's not the point now. We're into this and there's no way to back up and change directions," said Spencer. "But that Havlicek and his .38 caliber testimony. Boy! It was like a shot between the eyes!"

"Through the heart," corrected Erickson.

"Yeah. But, Paul," Spencer continued, "what I want to know is what you expect to get out of Lt. Casper and Angela Gaito?"

"Casper and Gaito?" asked Erickson with feigned innocence. "Why nothing, Red. Nothing."

"Bullshit," said Spencer quickly. "Excuse me, Mrs. Caton. But I find that hard to believe."

"You can find that hard to believe if you want, Red, but I'll bet you my eyeteeth that neither one of them is going to add to the testimony in this courtroom." He waited to see if Spencer's expression softened any. It did. "But I'll tell you what I find hard to believe at this point, Red. I find it very hard to believe that either you or Hervey still seriously thinks that you can capture that jury."

"We may have slipped a point or two," Hervey Higgs admitted.

"Point or two, shit! You know damned well that not one of those jurors is still willing to buy a suicide story. You might as well be honest with us. After all, we are standing here wasting each other's time if that's the case, and you know it."

Spencer and Higgs allowed an open, full-faced glance at each other. "All right," said Red Spencer. "Hervey and I have had a few words regarding this case, and I think some sort of a settlement offer is appropriate." He glanced quickly at Pat Caton. Her expression was totally blank. At that very moment she was, incredibly, wondering where Kirby Morris had gone.

"And? And?" urged Paul Erickson.

"And we are authorized to offer a flat settlement of fifty thousand," Red Spencer said rather quickly.

"Fifty thousand?" asked Pat Caton with an audible gulp. From her tone it was impossible to tell whether she was overcome by the magnitude of the offer or crushed by the parsimony.

Paul Erickson did not break the momentum of the occasion by trying to distinguish between these extremes. "Fifty thousand?" he repeated derisively.

"That's a lot of money for the case at this stage in the game," said Hervey Higgs supportively.

"It won't be after you've had a chance to put on your defense witnesses," promised Erickson. "If you think we've done well so far, wait till your own witnesses dig your grave deeper." He chuckled confidently.

"We expect to get some very good testimony from the motel manager, Mr. Peabody and, of course, Dr. Leatherman," said Spencer threateningly.

"That Peabody will be a real gem," Erickson said.

"And who have you got left, other than Lt. Casper and Angela Gaito?" Hervey Higgs probed.

"I told you, we will not get a damned thing from Casper or from Angela Gaito," said Erickson. His smile had mellowed to a smirk.

"And what makes you so sure about the worthlessness of your own damned witness?" asked Spencer.

"Red," said Erickson in a confidential tone. "If you would care to call the Hawaiian Village right now, I'll lay you odds that both of them have checked their asses out and are headed to the airport. If, of course, they haven't already copped a plane for Connecticut."

"Crap," announced Spencer. "Casper is sitting in the witness room like a bullfrog on a lily pad. You might as well get ready to parade him out and let him speak his piece."

"Be my guest," invited Erickson. "Hop right out there and say hello to him." He motioned toward the courtroom doors with a magnanimous sweep of his hand.

Spencer was visibly shaken by Erickson's taunt. He looked at Hervey Higgs for support but found only a mouth gaping wide. "That son of a bitch," Spencer muttered without apology. He turned abruptly and almost ran from the room. As he burst through the double swinging doors, his leather heels slid slightly off balance on the slick, worn, marble tile floor. He went directly to the witness room and loudly threw open the door. Spencer stuck his head into the room and found no one. He turned to see Erickson, Hurst, and Higgs emerging from the courtroom. Pat Caton came along behind them, thoroughly confused.

"Find him, Red?" called Erickson, laughing.

"I don't get it," Spencer called in return. "What got to Casper?"

"He just doesn't seem quite as convinced as he was that Caton's death was an obvious suicide, I guess," suggested Erickson. "Maybe he went off to continue his investigation."

"I'm going to give the Hawaiian Village a call," announced Hervey Higgs decisively.

Erickson quietly offered him a dime. For a moment Higgs stared blankly at the coin and then stalked off toward the telephone without accepting it.

"We can all go along for moral support," Erickson said.

"Hawaiian Village?" Higgs asked when he finished dialing. "Do you still have a registered guest named Casper? Harrison Casper." Higgs tapped his fingers impatiently on the wall. "He what?" Higgs asked demandingly. He placed his hand over the mouthpiece and turned to face the other lawyers. "The desk clerk says that Casper paid his bill but did not check out."

"What do they mean he paid his bill?" G. Markham Hurst asked. "We're covering his expenses."

"Beats me," said Higgs. "That's what the guy said."

"What's he doing now?" asked Red Spencer. He rubbed his chin nervously.

"Ringing the room," said Higgs.

"Any answer?" asked Erickson.

"Nope."

"Ask the clerk about Angela Gaito," said Spencer.

"And Peabody," added Erickson.

Higgs nodded his head. He waited for several more moments as the phone in Casper's room rang.

"Thanks," he said to the desk clerk, who apologized without concern for his inability to complete the call. "Try the room of Angela Gaito. Right. G-A-I-T-O." He placed his hand across the mouthpiece again. "She's still checked in too." Higgs drummed his fingers again and shifted his weight to the other foot. "Miss Gaito?" he asked excitedly. "You're still there?" Higgs looked at Spencer pleadingly. Spencer understood his dilemma in an instant and took the phone.

"Angela? This is Red Spencer. Look. We are a little confused over Lt. Casper's behavior. He stormed out of here while he was waiting to be called as a witness, and now we can't reach him on the phone. Have you seen him or heard from him?" Spencer shook his head to transmit Angela's denial to his colleagues. "He didn't mention leaving or anything like that, did he?" Spencer continued to shake his head. "Well, if you see him, ask him to call either my office or Mr. Erickson's office, will you?" Spencer pointed at Erickson and lifted his eyebrows to inquire silently whether Paul wanted to talk to Angela. Erickson shook his head. "OK, Angela. We'll be in touch with you. Goodbye." He replaced the receiver on the hook and stuffed his hands deep into his trouser pockets.

"What do we do now, Paul?" Pat Caton asked. Silently all four lawyers turned to stare at her. Somehow they had forgotten about the widow Caton, and her question brought her sharply back into focus.

"We go back to trial unless Red and Hervey want to come up with a sensible offer," said Erickson.

"What's your idea of 'sensible'?" Higgs asked.

"Oh, two hundred and fifty to three hundred grand might hold my attention for a minute or two," Erickson said. Pat Caton's eyes opened wide.

"Three hundred grand, my ass," said Red Spencer derisively. "Excuse me, Mrs. Caton."

"For three hundred grand, you do not have to apologize for your ass, Mr. Spencer," said Pat Caton with a smile.

"Be reasonable, Paul," Higgs said. "What would it really take to get us out of here? Remember, we have an insurance company to answer to."

"Talk to me," invited Erickson.

"I think we had better talk to the judge," G. Markham warned. "If we are going to burn up any more time, we had best get an extension of the recess."

"Maybe he would consider quitting for the day," Erickson suggested.

"At four o'clock?" asked Higgs incredulously.

"Tell him something has come up," Spencer said.

"But damn it, Red, you know you can't get a suicide verdict now. Not after the testimony on the bullet," Erickson said.

"But you suddenly haven't got a next witness to call," countered Spencer.

"I don't need him," said Erickson simply.

"Don't need Casper?" asked the astonished Spencer.

"Hell, no. What's he going to do for me at this point?" asked Erickson.

"OK," conceded Spencer. "You can go on without Casper. Who are you going to put on now? Peabody? Angela Gaito?"

"The broad does not take the stand," said Erickson flatly. "I don't think that either of us could trust what she might say." Spencer nodded in agreement.

The toe-to-toe bargaining session was interrupted by the marshal, who announced that Judge Haran had sent him to recall everyone to the courtroom.

"Go back and ask him for a short session in chambers," said Erickson suddenly. "OK, Red?" Spencer shrugged and nodded slowly. "Tell the judge we are interested in expediting this case to a fair settlement and we need to talk it over with him without the jury hearing the whole story."

The marshal turned sharply and returned toward the courtroom.

"What have you got in mind?" asked Hervey Higgs cautiously.

"I'm willing to lay out my theory of the case, as it

stands now, in an honest effort to get you bastards to pry a few bucks out of your wallets. But I'm not going to do it without old Michael F. X. Haran serving as referee. OK?"

Spencer and Higgs exchanged glances, frowns, and then shrugs.

"OK," said Higgs hesitatingly.

"Me too?" asked Pat Caton.

Paul Erickson put his arm around her and pulled her close to him playfully. "If all else fails, you make some suggestive remark to Judge Haran," said Erickson, grinning.

"And we'll all go to Leavenworth," G. Markham said ponderously.

"Oh, I don't know," said Pat Caton. "That old goat might take me up on it."

"And then what?" asked Spencer.

Pat Caton winked at the lawyers, and the group marched off in the direction of the judge's chambers. Erickson and Spencer exchanged glances that said silently, "Maybe she could do it."

33

The heavy wooden door to the judge's chambers bore his name in modest-sized gold letters. G. Markham knocked on it firmly. A gruff voice from within issued a garbled reply which they took as an invitation to enter.

As the door opened, Judge Haran remained seated at his massive mahogany desk. He was no longer wearing his black judicial robe, but sat comfortably in a light-brown cardigan sweater—the kind Pat Caton remembered her grandfather wore when he smoked his pipe.

"Come in, come in," the judge snapped impatiently. He glanced up and saw that Mrs. Caton was among the intruders, and stood up dutifully. "Get Mrs. Caton a chair, gentlemen," he barked a little more cordially. He made generalized gestures to various chairs scattered around the spacious office.

"Your honor," Erickson began. His throat felt a little dry. "I requested this meeting in your office to see if we couldn't come to some agreement."

"Anything you can do to lighten my calendar will be greatly appreciated," said Judge Haran. He allowed a minimal smile and reached for his pipe from a rack on a small table behind him. Pat Caton knew he would.

"Your honor, I promise to be direct and to the point," Erickson said with half-clenched jaws.

"And brief," puffed Michael F. X. Haran.

"And brief," echoed Paul Erickson.

"What do you say, Mr. Spencer?" the judge asked. He shook the match violently and dropped it into the empty metal Government-issue wastepaper can behind his desk.

"I'm agreeable to anything that is fair, Judge," Spencer said easily. He smiled gently to show that he was reasonably comfortable in his role of invitee to the session.

"Mrs. Caton?" The judge looked at her with raised eyebrows. "Are you in agreement to this attempt at a settlement?"

The lawyers watched Pat's every facial twitch.

"Whatever Paul—I mean, Mr. Erickson—says," she blurted nervously.

"I appreciate your confidence in your lawyer, Mrs. Caton, and will admit that in choosing Mr. Hurst you have chosen wisely, but please do not lose sight of the fact that the case is yours. You must make the decisions, based on your lawyer's advice, of course." The judge allowed another minor smile which exposed his yellow teeth and the worn brown edges that identified him as a long-time pipe smoker.

"Thank you, Judge," Pat Caton cooed. "I think I understand most of what Mr. Erickson tries to do for me, and I sure do appreciate it." In fact, Pat understood exactly nothing, making her an average client.

"All right, Mr. Erickson," said Judge Haran.

"As you know, Judge, this has been an involved situation from the very start. Mr. Caton was found in a locked motel room in Connecticut and everyone assumed it was a suicide," Erickson began.

"Including the coroner who signed the death certificate," interrupted Spencer.

"OK, Red, but I notice you haven't made any overtures about putting that particular forensic genius on the stand.

You know what kind of an investigation Doctor Fortunelli turned in." Erickson was warming to the discussion.

"Gentlemen—I'm not going to let you argue this case in chambers while a perfectly capable jury sit twiddling their thumbs in a stuffy waiting room. If you can explain what your points are and come to some agreement, all right. But no bickering, please."

"I'm sorry, your honor," said Red Spencer.

"The insurance company—the defendant in this case—" continued Erickson.

"I know who the defendant is, Mr. Erickson!" Judge Haran threw his eyes heavenward in feigned persecution.

"The insurance company," Erickson began again deliberately, "has refused to pay off the death benefits on the grounds that the death occurred within the statutory period for suicide."

The judge closed his eyes and nodded with mock patience.

"Both sides have hired expert pathologists who collaborated in an autopsy of the exhumed remains. And this is where the plaintiff got her first major breakthrough." Erickson glanced proudly at Spencer, who pretended not to notice.

"As you heard, your honor, the victim in this case was shot, not with a .45 as has been assumed all along, but with a .38! Now that just blows the suicide right out the window, and I don't see any sense in going further with the trial." Erickson sat back triumphantly and folded his arms across his chest.

"Mr. Spencer?" inquired Judge Haran.

"Judge, we will admit that Mr. Havlicek's testimony regarding his opinion of the caliber of the bullet caught us a little by surprise," said Spencer. "But Havlicek's evidence is based only on his opinion, and I think we have a right to bring in our own ballistics man to controvert it."

"Bring in anyone you want, Red," said Erickson openly. "If I thought that Havlicek was wrong, do you think for one minute that I would have put him on? Really, now. You've got your own expert. Put on your Dr.

Leatherman. After all, it was our pathologist who first clued us on that bullet."

"Campbell?" asked Higgs.

"Campbell. He spotted the bullet as being something other than a .45 at the time of the autopsy. When he wrote his report for us he said so. After that, it was only a matter of using a competent ballistics man. Campbell helped us there, too." Erickson grinned.

"But that doesn't exclude the suicide at all, Paul," argued Spencer.

"What did he do, fire the .38 from his .45?" asked Erickson contemptuously.

"Right—and he wadded the space around the cartridge with tinfoil to hold it tight for the firing pin," theorized Spencer.

"And the Middlebrook police just overlooked it?" asked Higgs.

"Sure," Erickson conceded. "For instance, there's nobody in the whole damned case that can testify that the adjoining door was locked when the police arrived."

Spencer and Higgs exchanged quick glances. "We knew that, Paul," said Higgs, "but we really feel that it played a minor role in the facts of the case."

"Really?" asked Erickson with a wide grin. "Do you want to put on Angela Gaito and have her talk about that night?" He glanced at Pat Caton and wished that she weren't a witness to the actual bargaining session.

"She's impeachable and you know it, Paul. She can say anything she wants and both of us will have a field day destroying her testimony. Putting her on would be a complete waste of time." Spencer spoke with quiet confidence.

"OK, I agree. That's why she is not scheduled to go on. I'm keeping her in town as an ace in the hole, but you're absolutely right about her reliability."

"Your honor, the defendant has offered fifty thousand," explained Spencer. "I really think that that is a fair offer in view of the evidence."

"But you won't think so, Red," threatened Erickson.

"There's more, Mr. Erickson?" Judge Haran asked.

"Lots more, sir," promised Erickson. "For instance, let's really think about the night that Myrl died." He used his fingers to itemize the facts. "He was in the room with Angela and Vincent Irafino, right? Then Irafino and he had a fight. Peabody can testify to that. Hell, Irafino even shot the .45 at Caton. Accidentally, of course, but we're building a trend."

"Come on, Paul, lay it on me," Spencer prodded. "There's got to be something else in this fairy tale to make you call us all in here."

"I certainly hope so," sighed Judge Haran.

Erickson adjusted his chair one inch closer to the judge's desk and cleared his throat. "The way I see it," Erickson began, "we've got too damn many people to account for in Caton's motel room." Pat changed her position in her chair but continued to watch Erickson intently. "There's a room which connects and I think we can agree that putting Caton and Angela Gaito together earlier that evening at the bar across the street wouldn't be too hard to do." He looked at each lawyer and found them nodding gently.

"She admits that, Paul," Spencer said.

"Right. But I think the rest of her story is pure bullshit—I mean, fabricated, your honor." He smiled slightly in the general direction of the judge.

"OK, so she lies a little to save face—what the hell, Paul," said Spencer.

"No, more than that, Red. Listen. She brings Caton back to the room and he wants to get friendly." Erickson glanced at Pat Caton and assured himself that she was taking it reasonably well. Spencer nodded and leaned closer.

"But she doesn't shoot him, Paul," said Hervey Higgs. "She didn't leave the motel until the next morning. If she shot him that night, she would have taken off like a goose."

"Sure, she would," agreed Erickson, "if she had been

274

alone." Each of the lawyers looked at each other and then at Judge Haran. His expression remained complacent.

"Alone?" questioned Spencer. "Who's with her besides Caton?"

"At this point, I think you can take your pick between Irafino and Casper," Erickson announced flatly.

"Casper?" asked Higgs, obviously astonished.

"I'll buy Irafino as an interested party," said Spencer, shaking his head, "but Casper—"

"Isn't Casper the police lieutenant?" Judge Haran asked.

"Right, your honor, but more—he's interested in Angela Gaito," said Erickson.

"Crap," said Spencer, dismissing the theory with a wave of his hand.

"Would you rather pay off on Irafino?" asked Erickson. "Either way, it's not a suicide." He allowed himself a modest smirk.

"It's not Irafino either, and you know it, Paul," said Spencer. "The homicide aspects of this case were checked out and dismissed."

"Ah!" said Erickson with delight, "checked out by whom? Dismissed by whose authority?" He held an index finger in the air to keep Spencer on the point.

"By the police department," said Spencer easily.

Erickson continued to hold the finger in the air and began to nod in happy agreement.

"Oh, no, Paul!" said Spencer, grasping Erickson's unspoken conclusion. "You're not going to get me to come up with Casper as the prime suspect."

"OK, Red, point to someone else," Erickson challenged. "How about Peabody?"

"Shit," said Spencer with obvious contempt.

"The maid?" Erickson taunted.

"Come on, Paul, you're going too far. Why would Casper shoot Caton?" asked Higgs.

"Angela," said Erickson simply.

"You got something to hang that on?" Spencer asked.

"Nothing hard, of course," admitted Erickson. "Just some bad thoughts."

"OK, why not Irafino?" asked Spencer. "If you've got to make a murder out of this, why not Irafino?"

"From what Angela Gaito told us at her deposition, Irafino wasn't much of a gun expert," Erickson said. "He damned near shot off his own foot with Caton's .45."

G. Markham stopped holding his chin in his heavily veined hand and joined in the conversation. "Is that why you postulate that Lt. Casper has fled from the Hawaiian Village, Paul?"

"That's certainly why he beat it out of the witness room," conceded Erickson. "And I don't care what the motel desk clerk says, I'll bet he's headed out of town right now."

"But he's a subpoenaed witness," announced Judge Haran officially. Erickson grinned at the judge. "I'll hold him in contempt!" threatened Michael F. X. Haran.

"If you can catch him," said Erickson. "All it took was for Havlicek to let it drop that the bullet they recovered from Caton was a .38 rather than a .45, and Casper began to sweat. As a matter of fact, I'll bet you that he figured the shot had gone all the way through."

"Now let me get this straight, gentlemen," said Judge Haran. "We're in a civil action, brought here because of a diversity of citizenship between the plaintiff widow and the defendant insurance corporation. And now you want to change it into a murder trial? Is that what you plan, Mr. Erickson? Are you going to disprove the suicide allegation by proving a murder?" The judge's mind raced ahead with the legal implications of such an explanation.

"No, sir," said Erickson, smiling. "I do not intend to put on a shred of evidence concerning the homicidal aspects of Myrl Caton's death. For all I know, it might have been an accident—or self-defense. All I want is to have Mr. Spencer and Mr. Higgs admit that, with the evidence brought forth so far, and the theory that I have advanced here this afternoon, their position on the provability of the suicide has been seriously weakened, if not

276

destroyed." Erickson sat back in his chair and folded his arms across his chest confidently.

"Mr. Spencer?" asked Judge Haran, "do you or Mr. Higgs have any further comment?"

"Your honor," said Spencer, "the defendant will admit that the opportunity for proving the suicidal aspects of this case were considerably stronger before we heard the testimony of Mr. Havlicek regarding the caliber of the bullet removed from the body of Myrl Caton by our own pathologist."

Erickson began to shift impatiently in his chair.

"On the other hand," continued Spencer, "I seriously doubt that we would be able to overcome the fact that the bullet was indeed a .38. I'm sure that Mr. Erickson would not have let his case rest on that type of evidence unless he were pretty damned sure of his facts." He looked at Paul Erickson and gave him a tiny, fraternal wink.

"And so?" urged Judge Haran. He looked at his watch, making no attempt to conceal the gesture.

Spencer threw his hands in the air and brought them down sharply on his own thighs. "And so, your honor, having already offered the plaintiff fifty thousand for the case, the defendant is willing to expedite the causes of justice by doubling the offer." Spencer shrugged and closed his eyes.

Hervey Higgs opened his wide and Pat Caton suddenly sat bolt upright.

"You're coming through, Red," said Erickson excitedly. "You are actually beginning to speak in tones that both Mrs. Caton and her counsel can hear."

"But what about the possibility of homicide here, gentlemen?" asked Judge Haran. "It's all right for you people to carve up the proceeds of some involved insurance policy, but what do you think I'm going to do with your evidence, or at least theory, regarding the homicide?"

"You could report it to the Middlebrook police department," Erickson suggested.

"I'll do better than that, Mr. Erickson. I'll present a

copy of our whole transcript to date, along with a letter from my office, to the district attorney for that county and insist on a reply from him."

"But tell him not to expect too much from Casper," warned Erickson.

"Oh, Paul, can it. You've got your offer. Now grab the money and get off this Casper crap," said Spencer.

"You mean you really don't believe my beautiful theory? Can't you see Casper nosing around the Brownstone and then finding out that Angela Gaito has been there too?" Erickson raised his eyebrows and allowed Spencer to savor the incipient scandal.

"What does he care?" asked Spencer.

"Hell, he's been sleeping with Angela too, you know." Erickson glanced apologetically at the judge. "Several others had been too, your honor."

"And then?" asked Higgs.

"And then old Casper comes back later that night, sees Caton's Cadillac still parked in front of the motel.

"Casper cases the joint. Goes around to the other side. You know, just checking everything out. He's a fairly good cop. And sees Angela's car parked in front of the adjoining room."

Spencer looked considerably less skeptical.

"OK, so it's late," continued Erickson. "He knocks on Angela's door—maybe it's unlocked; who knows? Anyway, he gains access to Angela's room and discovers them together."

"And shoots Caton? A jealous lover?" asked Spencer.

"Why not? Why not a fight? Caton's drunk. Casper shoots him accidentally. Maybe to protect Angela. Maybe self-defense?" Erickson threw all these suggestions out rapidly to give Spencer's brain something to work on.

"But I doubt it," Erickson continued.

"Doubt what, Mr. Erickson?" inquired Judge Haran.

"I doubt the accident or the self-defense angles. If he had done that, he would not have faked the investigation. He would simply have reported it."

"And he wouldn't have been so disturbed by Havlicek's conversation with him," added G. Markham Hurst.

"Right," agreed Erickson. "I'm convinced that Casper shot Caton with his own police .38 and then faked the room to look like a suicide."

"He put the chain on the door?" Higgs asked.

"Sure he did. And left by the adjoining door," continued Erickson.

"But the adjoining door was locked," Higgs protested.

"No it wasn't," said Erickson. "Even Casper's own testimony at deposition doesn't lock that door. Only Angela says it was."

"Why didn't Casper lie about it and say it was locked?" Spencer asked.

"Because there were other officers on the scene and he couldn't be sure that one of them wouldn't testify that the adjoining door was unlocked," Erickson explained.

The lawyers looked at each other.

"Do you intend to move to withdraw your suit with prejudice, Mr. Erickson?" Judge Haran asked.

Erickson glanced quickly at Spencer. "I'll tell you what, your honor," Erickson said. "How about dismissing the jury for tonight and letting Mr. Spencer and me have one further shot at coming to some absolutely concrete settlement?"

"Paul, you're pushing me to the wall," Spencer said. "I've already made the offer of a hundred grand. How much more do you expect to squeeze out of us? After all, with this kind of money riding on the outcome of the case, we have to include Kirby Morris as a suspect. And Mrs. Caton too, for that matter."

Pat shot a glance at her lawyer and put a hurt expression on her face.

"Mr. Spencer!" Judge Haran warned. "A little consideration, if you please."

"Well, I'm sorry, your honor, but I just feel like my company is getting the shaft," Spencer moaned.

Erickson looked back at Pat Caton to reassure her. "It's

not a matter of the shaft, Red. I'm only thirsting for justice."

"Justice, my foot!" Spencer said, rising from his chair. "You're bleeding me pale."

"And I also thirst for a martini," Erickson added. "I'll buy for the whole group."

"I'm not going to increase the offer just because I've had a martini," Spencer promised.

"Of course not, Red," Erickson reassured him. "But if you will follow me out to the Hawaiian Village for the martini, I'll show you that Casper—and maybe even Angela Gaito by now—has flown the coop. And that should be worth another twenty-five or fifty grand."

"Why should it?" Hervey Higgs asked, a little bewildered.

"Because if Casper has gone and you guys refuse to be properly impressed by the implication of a police lieutenant's flight to avoid testimony in this case, then I'll move to withdraw the suit from Judge Haran's court and refile it as a triple indemnity in Connecticut."

"And prove the murder?" asked Judge Haran.

"If I can. It's the fear of being unable to prove a murder up there and having to wait behind a criminal case to get back to this civil action that makes me willing even to discuss a settlement with these gentlemen, your honor."

"OK, Paul, it's a bet," said Spencer. "Take us all out to the Hawaiian Village, and if Casper isn't hanging around with diarrhea or some other reasonable excuse as to why he ran from this courthouse, I'll up the ante."

Erickson reached out and eagerly shook Spencer's hand. "You've got yourself a deal."

"Paul?" Pat Caton asked nervously.

Erickson suddenly remembered his client. He had not asked her if she would be willing to go along with the bet.

"Pat, I'm sorry," Erickson said. "What is it, dear?"

"Do I get a martini too?" she asked, smiling.

"Either way, Pat, either way," Erickson promised.

34

The short parade turned left into the Hawaiian Village driveway and looked for parking spaces. G. Markham had won the honor of riding with Pat Caton since he had long ago vowed never again to ride beside Paul Erickson. The squeal of tires and white knuckles were not G. Markham's ideas of Nader-safe transportation.

Pat was out of her Cadillac before G. Markham could make it around the car to play gentleman. His courtly manner did not disappear when he left the courtroom. Paul Erickson had offended the old lawyer one day by announcing that the true test of a gentleman was whether he stepped out of the shower to urinate. G. Markham always did.

Pat Caton waved needlessly to Paul Erickson. They had found spaces several rows apart in the crowded parking lot. Erickson quickly made his way to her side.

"What happened to Spencer and Higgs?" asked G. Markham as Erickson came near.

"They had to pull around behind the first row of rooms and the pool. They'll be back shortly."

"I think I see them now," announced G. Markham, pointing toward the pool area.

"Been for a swim?" Erickson shouted.

"I think it's been a bath," returned Hervey Higgs, carefully titrating his volume to match his approach to the small group.

"Why, Hervey!" Erickson taunted. "I thought you were interested in the causes of justice and the restoration of the injured plaintiff, insofar as the imperfect system is capable, by the payment of equitable sums, and—"

"Can it," said Spencer testily. "Where is this fink's room?"

"Casper's?" asked Erickson with feigned innocence.

"Yeah, yeah, Casper's. Come on, Paul. This may be your hour, but I've had my belly full of your crap, your witnesses, and your cop." Spencer was heating more quickly than Erickson enjoyed.

"Martini first?" Erickson offered. He gestured toward the main building with a generous sweep of his unoccupied arm.

"Afterward," said Hervey Higgs firmly. "That way we'll know who buys."

"Then I suggest that we pay our social call on the lieutenant," said Erickson. "If, of course, we can find him."

"You know where his room is?" Spencer asked.

"Of course, Red," said Erickson. "He's within a cozy distance from Angela Gaito."

"I'll bet it's cozy," purred Pat Caton.

"Angela Gaito," repeated Red Spencer as if the name had just been invented. "Let's check her first."

"Whatever you say, Red," said Erickson amicably. "What do you expect to get from her?"

"I just want to see her expression when I ask her some hard-nosed questions about what went on in that Connecticut motel room that night," said Spencer.

"You going to give her a Georgia Baptist sermon about what happens to women who run around sleeping with traveling tomato salesmen?"

Pat Caton hesitated in her step and took her hand from Erickson's arm. She looked puzzled.

"I'm sorry, Pat," said Erickson, replacing her hand at his elbow, "but this redneck is about to bring on a worthless scene that isn't going to get us a bit closer to your settlement with his damned insurance company."

"I've got plenty to talk to that bitch about," threatened Spencer. His face was flushed and his brow was beaded with the sweat of excitement.

"Spencer the cop!" chided Erickson. "What would you do if she just opened up and spilled the whole story to you? What if she backed off and unloaded the whole plot to get rid of Myrl Caton and steal his business? What if she handed it to you ass end up? Huh? What are you going to do with it, Red? Run back to Judge Haran and crank out some sort of a writ?"

Spencer broke away and stepped back, shaking his head. He paused for a moment, leaning against an unmistakably female mass of volcanic rock.

"Paul, I just don't think it's right that these people should get away with it," Spencer said wearily. "Insurance company be damned."

Hervey Higgs stiffened loyally but remained silent.

"Look," simplified Erickson. He leaned against Spencer's gynecoid rock and placed his hand offensively on the rock's prominent parts. "If there's more to the actual case, we can leave it to Pat to decide what she wants done."

"We were arguing about the proof of suicide, Paul," said Spencer. "We spent months on that angle. Not did he shoot himself or not, but whether or not we can prove it." Erickson nodded in agreement as Spencer continued. "But now you want us to come up with the probability of homicide—"

"Or accident," interrupted Erickson.

"Yeah—or accident," Spencer parroted with contempt, "—and not report it to anyone. It's not right, Paul."

"His argument has merit," said G. Markham Hurst.

Hervey Higgs bobbed his head agreeably.

"Sure it does," said Erickson. He spread his arms wide to demonstrate his attitude of honesty and defenselessness. "I'm not trying to put any of us into some kind of collusion to hide a crime from the police. My position is that we don't need it. You guys have to prove suicide and I have to cast doubt on the suicide. What's under the next unturned rock is really none of our business."

"But it's somehow part of my business," Pat Caton said.

Erickson looked at Pat quickly and saw a widow momentarily. The characterization faded quickly.

"Sure it is, Pat," Erickson said tenderly. He took both of her hands in his own. His manner was so obviously sincere that only he knew it was a complete fraud. "And when we've settled up with the insurance company, I'll be right there to help you do whatever you think is honest and fair to Myrl."

"Including ringing the bell up there in Connecticut?" she asked.

He hesitated for a fraction of a second longer than he wished he had. "Including bringing the whole affair to a grand jury in Connecticut," he announced reassuringly.

Pat Caton smiled happily. Erickson put his arm around Pat's shoulder and drew her close to his side. He aimed her toward the wing which housed Casper's room.

"Let's go see Lt. Casper," Erickson said softly and persuasively.

"Angela Gaito," Spencer bargained flatly.

"Angela Gaito," repeated Erickson in the warm tone that captivated Pat Caton.

The group reassembled like a tiny wedding party and followed Erickson and Pat toward the neo-Polynesian motel wing.

Erickson led them to Angela Gaito's room. They assembled silently in front of the door.

"Nickel side bet she's blown," said Erickson rapping on the motel door.

"You're on," said Spencer softly.

There was a pause between Erickson's first tattoo on

the door and his second series. The second drew a response.

"God damn it, leave me alone," shouted an excited female voice inside.

Erickson knocked again, slightly louder and with more authority.

The brief pause this time was terminated by the door being opened against its latch-chain. A single eye peered out through the crack.

"I ain't dressed," the voice said.

"Angela," said Paul Erickson pleasantly. "We just want to talk to you for a little while."

"All of you?"

"We'll give you a minute to slip into something," Erickson offered.

"To do what?" she asked.

"To put on your clothes," Spencer snapped.

"Well, I ain't exactly naked," Angela blurted as she fumbled with the chain. She threw open the door. She was dressed in a slip, slippers and a terry-cloth bathrobe that went untied and unmanaged. "You might as well come in," she announced passively.

Erickson stepped back to let Pat Caton enter the room first. "Miss Gaito," he said, "this is Mrs. Caton." He paused briefly. "Mrs. Caton, this is Miss Gaito." If he could have managed it, he would have ducked for cover. To his surprise, the two women greeted each other only with icy deference and stiff-armed handshakes.

The bed was mussed, although Erickson recalled that it had been neatly made at lunchtime. Suitcases were opened around the room, and several small heaps of assorted garments lay waiting to be packed.

"Leaving?" Erickson asked.

Angela glanced nervously at the suitcases and clothes. "Not exactly," she fumbled. "You said you wouldn't need me at the trial."

"Uh-huh," he mumbled. He winked at Red Spencer and handed him a nickel.

...la," Spencer began, "we need to talk to you about that night that Myrl Caton died."

Angela glanced quickly from face to face and ended up looking at Pat.

"I already talked with you guys—once up in Connecticut and once I talked with Mr. Erickson down here," she protested.

"We know that, Angela," Spencer said patiently. "Mr. Erickson and I have discussed everything that you said on both of those occasions. Right, Paul?"

Erickson nodded vigorously. Pat Caton wondered just how thoroughly Erickson had disclosed whatever he had learned from Angela Gaito.

"Sit down. Sit down," Angela offered with generous gestures toward the bed and cluttered chairs.

G. Markham Hurst examined the nearest chair as if it had been purchased from a leper colony. Higgs and Pat Caton sat in the available chairs while Spencer took the corner of the bed. Paul Erickson remained standing in the middle of the room. His arms were folded across his chest and his stern, set jaw threatened to dominate every response.

"We have also agreed to make Mrs. Caton a part of the conversation, Angela, so you don't have to be embarrassed to tell us exactly what happened," Erickson said.

"Sure," said Angela softly.

Bullshit, thought Pat and Angela simultaneously.

"Miss Gaito," began Erickson, "I think we can all agree that you knew Mr. Caton on more than a professional plane."

"On what?" she asked.

"You were close friends," suggested Erickson.

"Uh-huh."

There was a noise from the bathroom. The lawyers looked at each other and then at Angela.

"Mice?" asked Spencer.

"You might as well come out," shouted Angela at the closed bathroom door. There was a silent pause as everyone except Angela stared at the door expectantly. The door opened slowly and a sheepish Vincent Irafino emerged.

"Visiting?" Spencer inquired.

"Yeah. Something like that," Irafino shot back hostilely.

"Well, come join us, Mr. Irafino," said Spencer magnanimously.

"Vincent was helping me pack," said Angela weakly.

"I'm sure," said Pat Caton softly. Erickson caught her eye and gave an almost imperceptible shake of his head to tell her not to engage.

"Yeah," said Irafino, joining in Angela's ineffectual excuse. "We figured the trial was getting about over and that we could save some time by packing up."

"You mean Casper came roaring back a little while ago and blew the whistle," challenged Erickson. Spencer arched his eyebrows in anticipation.

"Casper?" said Irafino with mock astonishment.

"Surely you remember good old Lt. Casper?" taunted Erickson. "One of Middlebrook's finest?"

"Yeah, yeah. I seen him," said Irafino. "So what?"

"So what did he have to say?" asked Erickson.

Irafino looked at Angela for help but got none. "He was talking nonsense," said Irafino. He took a cigarette out of his shirt pocket. He lit it nervously and flicked the match onto the motel carpet.

"Like what?" asked Erickson.

"Oh, I don't know," said Irafino, still looking at Angela. "Like his having to get back up north in a big hurry and stuff like that."

"He was pretty excited," offered Angela. "I didn't follow everything he was talking about."

"Me neither," Irafino blurted.

"Did he in fact leave?" inquired Hervey Higgs.

"I don't think so. Hell, he was just here twenty-five minutes ago," said Irafino nervously.

"Check it," Spencer said to Hervey Higgs in an intra-office tone.

Higgs picked up the room phone and dialed the operator. "Has Mr. Casper checked out yet?" he inquired. There was a pause as all waited for the unheard reply. "Thank you," said Higgs shaking his head. He replaced the phone on the stand. "He's still checked in," he announced.

Erickson's smile faded slightly and he offered Pat a small shrug of helplessness.

"You two can be a big help to us in settling this case," said Erickson. "As you both know, we're all caught up in the civil aspects of Caton's death. This is not a criminal case, and none of us is out to get anyone." He paused to give Angela and Irafino a chance to comprehend his cautionary words. "OK?"

Angela and Vincent Irafino nodded in mute unison.

"We talked about some of this before, Angela," said Erickson. "It's OK for you to tell Mr. Spencer everything you know. We just want to settle the insurance part of the case."

"I said all I'm going to about that night," Angela protested. Irafino nodded concurringly.

"But you went out for a drink with Caton the night he was shot," said Erickson. He spread his arms wide and exhibited his palms as a subconscious gesture of open-handedness.

"So what? That ain't no crime, is it?" snapped Angela. "I mean he was over twenty-one and all that."

"Look, Angela," said Erickson patiently. "No one is out to find any crimes. All we want is to know where Casper was that night."

"Casper?" said Angela, half-shocked. "Why Casper?"

"Because our autopsy has shown that Caton was killed with a .38-caliber bullet." Erickson paused momentarily. "And Caton's gun was a .45."

"What the hell does all that mean?" asked Irafino warily.

"We're not sure yet," said Spencer. He watched Irafino carefully; he found nothing but apparently genuine confusion. Somehow, Irafino did not strike Spencer as smart enough to be deceptive and clever.

"You mean someone else shot him?" asked Irafino.

"Maybe," Spencer suggested.

"Like who?" asked Angela.

"Well, cops carry .38-caliber guns," Erickson said testily.

"Cops?" asked Irafino. "What cops? Casper?" His eyes became suddenly wide and dilated.

"You guys think Casper did it?" asked Angela.

"Wasn't he there, Angela?" Erickson said in a matter-of-fact tone.

The Italian woman searched each face momentarily and then looked again at Erickson. "Who?" she asked weakly.

"Harrison Casper," Erickson supplied. "Didn't he come by that night and cause you some trouble?"

"Well, he—" Angela hesitated.

"Casper was there?" Irafino asked in frank disbelief. Angela Gaito nodded silently.

"When did he arrive?" asked Erickson.

"It was like this," said Angela, capitulating. "We got back to the room from Fitzpatrick's and Myrl was pretty drunk." She stole a glance at Irafino, who was more interested than angry. "He could walk, and all that," she continued, "but he was getting real stinko. You know what I mean?"

Pat Caton found herself nodding.

"What happened then?" Erickson urged.

"Myrl made himself and me another drink—God knows he didn't need it—and kinda flopped on the bed." She spoke with a genuine tone that inspired each of the listeners to believe what she was saying.

"Did you stay all night?" asked Erickson. He almost glanced at Pat Caton but caught himself.

"I went to my room," she said.

"Which adjoined Caton's room, right?" asked Erickson. She nodded silently and avoided looking at Pat.

"What happened next?" Erickson pushed.

"Myrl was almost asleep. But when I came in through the door from my room—I had to unlock it from my side—"

"His side wasn't locked?" Spencer interrupted.

"Nope. Just mine. I guess he already unlocked his side," she continued.

"Then what?" asked Erickson.

"Then I just—laid down next to him on the bed and let him talk. We didn't do nothing, if you know what I mean." She held out her hands pleadingly.

"Talked about what?" asked Erickson.

"Lots of stuff. He was drunk. But he wanted to talk about all kinds of things. He was still mad at Vincent from that fight they had—"

"That afternoon?" asked Spencer.

"Yeah. And about me, too."

"What about you?" urged Erickson.

"Well, he was ripped because I was seeing Vincent and I told him that he didn't have no cause to tell me what to do."

"Didn't you say he got sick?" Erickson asked.

"Yeah, he was sick a couple of times. The booze. He always got sick when he drank a lot of booze," she explained.

Pat nodded silently.

"Then what? When did Casper come by?" Erickson asked.

"Oh, a long time afterwards. I guess I left the door to my room unlocked, 'cuz he came into Myrl's room through my side."

"Did he catch you in bed with Caton?" Spencer asked bluntly.

She nodded and glanced at Pat Caton again. Pat watched her through narrowed eyes.

"But Myrl had his clothes on," Angela said. "He was asleep."

"What did Casper do then?" Spencer asked.

"You sure you guys are only interested in the insurance?" Angela was becoming increasingly nervous.

"That's all," Erickson said smoothly.

"Well, Casper started giving me holy hell," she said.

"He should have kicked your ass across the county," Irafino suggested.

"Please don't interrupt, Mr. Irafino," G. Markham Hurst said sternly.

"Casper had seen my car parked in front of my room, I guess. He's always riding around the town at night. He told me he didn't want me to have nothing to do with Caton."

"So what did he do, try to get you out of Caton's room?" Erickson asked.

"He told me to get up and get over to my own room. He said he was going to put Myrl's ass in jail," she said.

"Jail for what?" Erickson asked, professionally.

"For nothing. For being drunk. It didn't matter. Casper can put anybody in jail overnight," she explained. "He's up for captain."

"What'd you do next?" Spencer asked.

"I got up and tried to calm Casper down. He was madder than a wet hen. He said he was going to put handcuffs on Myrl while he was still asleep. I told him Myrl was drunk." Her eyes widened as she warmed to her narration. "Maybe they both was."

"Drunk?" Spencer asked. "Casper?"

"He'd had a few," Angela said, nodding her head for emphasis. "I could smell it."

"Big nose," Irafino said sullenly.

"He went over to Myrl and took his cuffs out. But when he started to hook one of them on Myrl's wrist, Myrl jumped up and grabbed him."

"They had a fight!" Erickson announced triumphantly. He shot a quick glance at Hervey Higgs and almost rubbed his hands together.

"Not exactly," Angela said hesitatingly. "More like a struggle."

"I'd have beat the shit out of him," Irafino said loudly.

"Shut up, Mr. Irafino, please," G. Markham Hurst admonished.

"Myrl reached inside Casper's coat and pulled his gun

291

out before Harry knew what was happening," Angela said. "It was awful." She put the side of her index finger to her mouth and bit gently as she recalled the scene.

"And Casper shot him?" Spencer said cautiously, fearing the answer.

"He didn't mean to," she added quickly. "They was struggling with Harry's gun—it just went off." She looked at Pat Caton apologetically.

"Do you know who was holding the gun when it went off?" Spencer asked.

"They both was," she said simply. "It was in between them."

"You couldn't see the gun or the trigger, could you, Angela," Erickson said smoothly.

"Nuh-uh."

"So what then? You put him back into bed?" Spencer suggested.

"Harry did. I didn't want to see it. I went into my room. I was too scared to say anything."

"Scared of Casper?" Spencer asked.

"Scared of the whole thing. He was scared too," she said. "He's up for promotion, you know."

"Who got Caton's gun out of the car?" Erickson asked.

"Harry did after he seen that Myrl was dead. He said there wasn't no need to cause us a lot of trouble about it. He said he'd take care of it."

"And did he?" Spencer asked.

"I guess so. Least it seemed like he did until he got back from that courthouse today," she said.

"Why?" Spencer asked. "What did he say?"

"He was talking crazy. Wasn't he talking crazy, Vinny? You heard him." She looked at Irafino for support. None came.

"What about you, Irafino?" Erickson asked testily. "What did you have to do with Caton's death?"

"I wasn't nowhere near that damned motel that night!" he shouted. "If I had been there, you would have found more than one dead body." He glared at Angela Gaito.

"Can you establish an alibi for that evening, Irafino?" Spencer asked sharply.

"If I have to, yes," he answered.

"He'll get some broad to lie for him," Angela snapped.

Irafino leaned suddenly toward Angela Gaito and narrowly missed her face with a wide open-handed right hook.

Erickson grabbed his arm and pushed him backward toward the dresser.

"I'll kill that bitch," said Irafino heatedly.

"Do it in Connecticut," said Erickson, struggling with him. Irafino yanked his arms free and tugged at his shirt. He made no further attack on Angela. "She and that cop probably shot the bastard in his sleep," muttered Irafino belligerently.

"Why you no-good son of a bitch. Get him over here, he'll tell you what happened," Angela Gaito shrieked.

"Get who over here?" asked Spencer.

"Casper. He'll set this wop peddler straight in one fat hurry." She nodded vigorously in self-agreement.

"What time did he leave?" asked Erickson.

"About four. I don't know. It was right after he got done in Myrl's room," she said.

"But you never even told us Casper was there when we talked with you before," said Spencer.

"I didn't want to get him in no trouble," she said.

"Trouble? Why trouble?" asked Spencer.

"Oh, you know. Him being a cop and married and all that. And then when Myrl was found the next day and Harry had to investigate the case, I figured that it would be better to keep his name out of the whole mess."

"But you saw him again after that," said Erickson. He was playing the odds.

"Uh-huh." She glanced quickly at Irafino.

"If we call Casper over here, would he back you up on this story?" asked Erickson.

"He damned well better."

"Do you think he'd come over now if you asked him?" urged Erickson.

"Why should he?" Angela asked.

"Because, as you pointed out, Angela, he's a cop and has at least some standing in the community in Middlebrook, and he's now involved—up to his ass—in this death. A death that he called an open-and-shut suicide. That's why. So get on the phone and get him over here right now." Erickson's tone was tough and the accent was Southern. The combination unnerved Angela immediately because it was to her an unknown. She slid across the bed to the phone but kept her eyes riveted on Erickson. She dialed Casper's room number after only a glance at the phone.

"You know his room number by heart, eh?" asked Irafino.

Angela flicked her thumb nail against her upper teeth at Vincent Irafino.

"And tell him," Erickson continued, "that skipping out on a federal subpoena is no light offense."

"Especially for a cop," added Spencer. The lawyers nodded in grave, academic unison.

"Nobody answers," Angela announced after a suitable pause.

"He's gone!" said Erickson almost triumphantly.

"No, he ain't," Angela said. "I was just over there."

"After he left here?" asked Irafino excitedly. She nodded. She was still listening to the phone ring in Casper's room.

"But you said you was going for cigarettes," Irafino protested.

Angela offered a tiny shrug.

"Where do you think he is now?" asked Spencer.

"He's in his room," Angela said. "He's just scared shitless."

"Do you think he'll answer the door?" asked Spencer.

"He'd better," she said with a wink, "I've got his key." She held Casper's room key up in the air like a bowling prize.

"You got his goddamned key?" shouted Irafino. He

moved toward Angela, but Erickson stepped in front of him.

Angela was out the door and down the sidewalk to the nearby room with an athletic step that belied her pudgy physique. The lawyers, Pat Caton, and the still-protesting Irafino followed quickly. She hesitated at the door to Casper's room so that the small group could gather in a new huddle around her. She knocked gently and rhythmically on the door.

"Harry," she said musically. There was no answer. She repeated the name louder several times. There was still no response. Spencer rapped on the door like a hammer. Nothing appeared.

"Shall I try it?" Angela asked nervously.

"Why not?" shrugged Spencer.

She put the key in the lock and turned it sharply. The door yielded and then came up firmly against the door chain. She turned around helplessly and Spencer moved her aside. He put his face to the small opening and peered into the darkened room. The shades were drawn and the bright sunlight outside made it even more difficult to see in.

"Sweet Jesus," said Spencer in a combination statement and low whistle. He slammed his shoulder against the door, breaking the chain. The door swung wide as Spencer half-stumbled into the room.

Erickson and the others quickly followed, with G. Markham and Pat Caton hesitating in the doorway.

"Son of a bitch," said Erickson.

Harrison Casper lay sprawled across his bed, still dressed. A large bloody area surrounded the left chest. Some of the blood had oozed beneath him to partly soil the sheet. His police-issue .38 lay on the floor beside him. The eyes were open and his mouth gaped wide.

"Is he—" asked Higgs.

"God!" exclaimed Pat Caton. She had just managed to view the body from the doorway.

Spencer felt the nearest wrist. There was no pulse. Spencer looked at Erickson and shook his head.

"I guess Angela told the truth, Red," Erickson said with a shrug.

Pat Caton buried her head in G. Markham's well-tailored chest and allowed him to usher her out of the room.

Irafino stood silently at the doorway, apparently in shock. Angela limply held his hand and looked at her shoe.

"What shall we do with him now?" asked Hervey Higgs nervously.

"Call a cop, Hervey, call a cop," Erickson said.

35

The nearby driveways of the Hawaiian Village were filled with Tampa police cruisers parked at odd angles. One of the cars had its bubble-gum light still revolving on the roof. The converted van from the ID section had been brought closest to the room, and a few uniformed officers busied themselves with restraining the small knot of curious guests that had abandoned the bar and pool for the excitement of a crime scene.

Paul Erickson and Red Spencer stood on the sidewalk outside Casper's room. They talked pleasantly with a thick-set, dark-complected man who wore a wrinkled dacron suit and spoke with a Tampa-Spanish accent. Occasionally, a uniformed officer came to him for direction and received a staccato order punctuated with arm-waving and finger gestures.

"We get more of these than you lawyers realize," the man said to Spencer.

"But Sgt. Marcano," said Spencer, "this guy was supposed to be a witness in a trial that Paul and I have going on right now in federal court."

"That don't matter none at all," drawled Sgt. Marcano.

"I done talked to all of you people that found the body and I'm satisfied that we've got an open-and-shut suicide."

Erickson and Spencer looked at each other wearily.

"Just because this out-of-town guest was a cop or was mixed up in one of your insurance trials—that ain't no cause to go and cook up a murder. We got plenty here to support a suicide. Locked door—his gun. What else do I need?" The sergeant inserted a toothpick into the corner of his mouth and attempted to dislodge a fragment of ham left over from his midafternoon sandwich.

"Sgt. Marcano," Paul Erickson began with a sigh, "you'll never believe how involved some of these 'routine' suicide cases can get." He smiled pleasantly and Red Spencer allowed a small throaty chuckle.

A uniformed officer walked up to their group and waited for his opportunity to speak.

"What do you need, Charlie?" Marcano snapped.

"You want me to call the medical examiner?" the policeman asked.

Marcano was already shaking his head. "For what?" Marcano said derisively. "For that guy in there? Hell, even if you could find the medical examiner, we'd just be wasting his time." There were flashbulbs going off inside the room and an ambulance crew stood by to remove Casper's body when it was released by the police.

"You mean no one is going to come out here and check out the body?" Erickson asked incredulously.

"I'm checking out the body," Marcano announced. He thumped on his own chest with an arched thumb. His tone indicated that no further questions on that subject would be welcomed.

"Hey, Sergeant," Spencer remarked brightly, "what about calling up Dr. Campbell out at USF? He's interested in this sort of thing."

"Look," said Marcano firmly, "we don't have to get those university pathologists mixed up in this. The last time they got involved, we had a three-day autopsy and sixty dollars' worth of toxicology. And all that on a simple hit-and-run traffic."

"You catch the driver?" asked Erickson.

"Yeah. We got him," said Marcano. "One of the pathologists pulled a piece of paint out of the scalp and the Bureau in Tallahassee matched it to the car."

"But you don't want the forensic pathologists to look at this shooting?" pestered Erickson.

Marcano gave Erickson a hostile glance and brushed by him to step closer to Casper's room. The police photographer emerged carrying an assortment of Polaroid cameras and flash attachments. He was followed by an identification technician.

"You guys get all your pictures?" Marcano called to the pair.

"Right, Sergeant. I shot one of the body, one of the face for identification, and one of the gun on the floor. And I printed his thumb." The police photographer examined his fingernails as he spoke and picked at one that failed the inspection.

"That's good enough for me," Marcano announced. "Tell the ambulance boys they can cart the body down to the morgue whenever they're ready." He looked at his watch and then at the sun heading toward the Gulf, and decided that there would be no time left for fishing. He stuck his head into the room and took one final look at Casper.

Erickson turned to face Spencer. "He sure thinks he's got an open-and-shut suicide."

"Seems to me I've heard that before somewhere. At least one out of two of these suicides seems real. But what do you think Judge Haran will think of all this?"

"He'll have the state attorney's office chasing their tails for weeks over these two deaths," Erickson offered.

"And in two states," Spencer added.

"At least we've finished our case, Red. I'll tell you what. If you will ease out of here, I'll take you out to the Palma Ceia and let Pat buy you and Higgs that martini." Erickson threw his arm around Spencer's shoulder and turned him toward the parking lot.

"And I suppose I'll have to write Pat Caton that check," Spencer said sadly.

"I sort of had that in mind," Erickson said smiling.

"If I give her the check out there will she buy just a round of martinis or the whole damned country club?"

"If it's big enough, who knows?" Erickson shrugged.

"It's big enough," Spencer sighed, "it's plenty big enough."

THE BIG BESTSELLERS
ARE AVON BOOKS!

☐ **Autopsy** John R. Feegel   22574 $1.75

☐ **Shifting Gears**
    George and Nena O'Neill   23192 $1.95

☐ **Open Marriage**
    George and Nena O'Neill   14084 $1.95

☐ **Working** Studs Terkel   22566 $2.25

☐ **The Loo Sanction** Trevanian   19067 $1.75

☐ **Final Analysis** Lois Gould   22343 $1.75

☐ **The Wanderers** Richard Price   22350 $1.50

☐ **The Eye of the Storm** Patrick White   21527 $1.95

☐ **Jane** Dee Wells   21519 $1.75

☐ **Theophilus North** Thornton Wilder   19059 $1.75

☐ **Daytime Affair** Joshua Lorne   20743 $1.75

☐ **The Secret Life of Plants**
    Peter Tompkins and Christopher Bird   19901 $1.95

☐ **The Wildest Heart** Rosemary Rogers   20529 $1.75

☐ **Come Nineveh, Come Tyre** Allen Drury   19026 $1.75

☐ **World Without End, Amen** Jimmy Breslin   19042 $1.75

☐ **The Oath** Elie Wiesel   19083 $1.75

Available at better bookstores everywhere, or order direct from the publisher.

Readers all over America
found new fulfillment in marriage with
the extraordinary million-copy bestseller

Open Marriage

Now authors *Nena and George O'Neill*
present a new strategy for joy and fulfillment
that will change the rest of your life!

Shifting Gears

THE ONE BOOK YOU NEED
TO SOLVE PERSONAL PROBLEMS
IN OUR RAPIDLY CHANGING WORLD!

OVER 100,000 HARDCOVERS SOLD!

SELECTED BY THE
BOOK-OF-THE-MONTH CLUB!

 Avon
23192/$1.95

AVON ⬣ THE BEST IN BESTSELLING ENTERTAINMENT!

- ☐ **Facing the Lions** Tom Wicker 19307 $1.75
- ☐ **Sweet Savage Love** Rosemary Rogers 17988 $1.75
- ☐ **High Empire** Clyde M. Brundy 18994 $1.75
- ☐ **How You Can Profit from the Coming Devaluation**
  Harry Browne 21972 $1.75
- ☐ **The Eiger Sanction** Trevanian 15404 $1.75
- ☐ **The Flame and the Flower**
  Kathleen E. Woodiwiss 22137 $1.75
- ☐ **Gone With The Wind** Margaret Mitchell 22319 $2.25
- ☐ **Between Parent and Child**
  Dr. Haim G. Ginott 15677 $1.50
- ☐ **How I Found Freedom in an Unfree World**
  Harry Browne 17772 $1.95
- ☐ **Zelda** Nancy Milford 11536 $1.50
- ☐ **The Wolf and the Dove**
  Kathleen E. Woodiwiss 18457 $1.75
- ☐ **Jonathan Livingston Seagull**
  Richard Bach 14316 $1.50
- ☐ **I'm OK—You're OK**
  Thomas A. Harris, M.D. 14662 $1.95

Available at better bookstores everywhere, or order direct from the publisher.